The Way Back to Happiness

Center Point
Large Print

**This Large Print Book carries the
Seal of Approval of N.A.V.H.**

The Way Back to Happiness

Elizabeth Bass

CENTER POINT LARGE PRINT
THORNDIKE, MAINE

This Center Point Large Print edition
is published in the year 2013 by arrangement with
Kensington Publishing Corp.

The text of this Large Print edition is unabridged.
In other aspects, this book may vary
from the original edition.
Printed in the United States of America
on permanent paper.
Set in 16-point Times New Roman type.

ISBN: 978-1-61173-791-2

Library of Congress Cataloging-in-Publication Data

Bass, Elizabeth, 1965–
The way back to happiness / Elizabeth Bass. — Center Point Large Print
edition.
pages cm
ISBN 978-1-61173-791-2 (Library binding : alk. paper)
1. Large type books. I. Title.
PS3602.A84723W39 2013
813′.6—dc23
                                                              2013017086

Acknowledgments

I owe profuse thanks to all my usual suspects for helping me out on this one: Annelise Robey, Meg Ruley, and all the folks at Jane Rotrosen who give me great advice, suggestions, and support. My sister Julia, who seems to know exactly when I need an encouraging nudge. Joe Newman, for winding me up and getting me through each day. And my wonderful editor, John Scognamiglio, and the rest of the talented people at Kensington Publishing who work so hard to make the books possible, and then make them better.

PROLOGUE

June 1985

Alabama stood in the doorway between her closet-sized bedroom and the living room. "Mom, are you okay?"

Diana forced herself to meet her gaze. Her daughter's brow puckered as she looked from Diana to the pill bottle on the coffee table next to her and back again.

Alabama repeated her question, more loudly, over the music. Was she okay?

Diana nodded, even though she was disturbed by a weird delay between Alabama's mouth moving and her own ears hearing sound. Oh boy. What more evidence did she need that the forces of the world were against her—words had to fight their way to her eardrums. David Bowie sounded normal, but now she wondered whether there might be a time delay there, as well. The record was spinning, but who knew how long it took his voice to make it through the speakers and then to her ears?

Ashes to ashes . . .

She reached for a cigarette and lit it, inhaling deeply. Everything became sharper again. Thank God.

" 'Cause I've got to get going soon," Alabama said.

"I'm coming with you."

Her daughter's stance shifted. Tensed. "Are you sure? I can get there on my own."

"You think I'd miss waving you off on your big adventure?"

Alabama mumbled something inaudible and then said, "I can't find a red sock. I'm sure both my red socks were in the bag at the Laundromat."

"Oh . . ." Diana twisted, looking for it. *Red sock. Alabama needs her red sock. I can do this for her, at least.* She tossed pillows and cushions off the couch, unearthing several old tissues, an overdue library book, an empty snack-sized Doritos bag, furry pennies. She pitched them all on the floor. Then she unfurled the crocheted afghan with a snap, unleashing a cloud of dust. But no sock.

"It doesn't matter." Alabama flapped her hands, eager now to drop the search. "I've got enough socks."

Failure lumped in Diana's throat. "I'll find it. I'll mail it to you at camp."

"Camp's only a week, Mom. I'll probably wear sandals most of the time anyway."

That was true. Just a week.

Just forever.

"But if you're coming to the bus with me . . . ?" Alabama left the question dangling, with a hint of urgency.

Diana looked down at herself. She still wore the clothes she'd slept in, even though she'd been up since dawn trying to prepare herself to face this moment. She'd made pancakes and rousted Alabama out of bed at an hour when she was almost too tired to enjoy them. Diana couldn't eat anything herself. She'd been so hopped up she'd had to take a Seconal to rein in her nerves.

"Don't worry," she said. "I'll pull on a skirt and be ready to go. I laid out my clothes last night."

This was one thing she was going to get right. Even if waving her daughter off felt like taking that first step up to the gallows, she was going to grit her teeth and do it.

Weeks ago she'd seen the flyer for the camp—Camp Quapaw—and felt bad that Alabama had never been to one before. Then and there, she'd decided to make it happen. She'd called her mother for the first time since Christmas and begged for money, and Gladys had coughed up the check without the usual accompanying lecture. Diana might have even been able to wheedle more out of her, but she'd felt too proud—too humiliated—to mention getting fired from the department store, or the fact that she didn't know where June's rent was coming from. Besides, this loan was for Alabama. *Because I love her more than life,* she'd thought.

Then, she'd hatched her plan.

You could only kid yourself for so long, although she'd had a phenomenal run: She was the Babe Ruth of self-delusion. For thirty-five years she'd been someone different in her head than she was in real life, despite plenty of people telling her otherwise. She hadn't studied, hadn't applied herself to finding a good job back when she was starting out, hadn't managed to keep even minimum-wage jobs, the ones she considered herself too exceptional for. Daughter in tow, she'd floated across the country looking for something better, something different, some place where she could escape the past, and failure. The men in her life had been disasters—except Tom Jackson, who was the last man in the universe she should have pursued. So that had ended in disaster, too.

No. It had ended in Alabama, who was the one good thing in her life. And now she was going to do this one good thing for her. The best thing.

When you loved someone more than life, you made sacrifices for them.

And yet, as they hurried to the bus stop later that morning, her courage faltered. Maybe there *was* something she could do. Another loan from her mother, another city, another job . . .

A quaking commenced inside her, deep inside, like a tuning fork that had been struck. By the time they reached the community center parking lot, her whole body hummed with doubts.

Kids were lined up to board the Camp Quapaw bus, and Alabama surged forward, her old blue Samsonite bumping against her calf. But halfway there, her feet dragged to a stop. She turned back.

"I don't have to go," she said. "I never wanted to. This was your idea."

Diana could have wept. It was so tempting to agree. *Yes! Don't go. Stay with me.*

But that wasn't the plan.

"Your Gladdie wants you to go." Alabama loved her grandmother and wouldn't want to disappoint her.

"But what about you?" Alabama asked. "What are you going to do without me?"

Diana hooked her arm through her daughter's and escorted her the rest of the way to the bus, praying Alabama couldn't feel her quivering or see the tears building behind her eyes. "I'll have a week to take a good look at myself."

"Mom . . ."

Diana bent down and kissed her on her slightly sweaty temple, breathing in the sharp scent of Irish Spring soap. One last time. She remembered holding Alabama as a tiny baby, and glancing at the little vein in her translucent skin there and being terrified by the vulnerability of that little creature who'd been brought into the world so recklessly. The vein was still there, and Diana turned away from it, shuddering from the pressure building in her heart. *I love you so much.* She hoped the thought carried strongly enough that Alabama could hear it. She wouldn't say the words, because she and Alabama rarely did say them. They just assumed. Knew. If she said them,

11

Alabama might sense something was wrong and not want to go.

Even now, as the bus's engine turned over, Alabama balked at the foot of the small stairwell, dancing from foot to foot, unsure.

Diana gave her a last quick hug and a nudge. "Bye-bye, sweetie."

At last, Alabama rushed up the steps, and Diana stood waving as the old vehicle lumbered away in a plume of diesel exhaust. She was still waving after the bus turned the city block and disappeared from view, and long after the other parents had scattered.

"I love you." In the empty parking lot, it was safe to finally speak the words, and she did, repeatedly, until she noticed a group of teenagers in bathing suits and shorts headed toward the community center stopping to gape at her, a lone woman weeping and waving at air.

She'd never known how fast a week could go by, especially when each individual hour crawled. From the moment she cracked an eye open in the morning, every single empty moment seemed to stall out and hang suspended in time in the hot, increasingly messy, and stuffy apartment. Without Alabama, her life felt untethered, directionless. She had one goal for the week, and she couldn't face it.

Then, suddenly, the week was almost up. Where had it gone? She'd barely dragged herself off the couch since Alabama's send-off. Now she had to act.

One thing was clear: She couldn't go through this sober. She looked above the refrigerator and found an old bottle of gin. It must have been left by some guy, because she couldn't stand the stuff. But what money she'd been able to scrounge from underneath seat cushions and the bottoms of drawers had already been spent on cigarettes and refilling her Seconal prescription.

A note had to be written, and she decided on Bev as the recipient. She was too much of a coward to write to Alabama. And maybe this way Alabama would assume it had all been an accident. She also wanted to write to her mother, to tell her good-bye and apologize for being such a disappointment, but again, she lacked the courage. Her mother was sick now, recovering from pneumonia. Merely thinking the words *Dear Mama* caused her to burst into tears and curl into a ball beneath the afghan.

So Bev it would be, and only Bev.

She gulped down three glasses of gin and wrote the letter out on one of Alabama's old spiral note-books, spilling the words across the page as fast as her hand would move. The apartment's window unit had been on the fritz for a year and a half, and the air felt stifling. She sweated, poured her heart out, and cried.

When she was done, she didn't even read it over. She fished her address book out of a drawer and found the page with all Bev's addresses, which her mother had been dictating to her over the phone all these years in the hopes that someday there would be a reconciliation. Her sister had moved several times, and Diana hadn't been methodical about keeping it all straight. Now fifteen years of information stared at her higgledy-piggledy all over the page, the numbers and street names swimming before her eyes. Her sister lived in a town called New Sparta, she was pretty sure. She swilled another drink and copied the address.

Then she tore the house apart searching for a stamp.

She had no stamps.

In the end, she was forced to walk down the road and buy one at the post office, which thankfully wasn't too far away. The postal clerk there acted snooty toward her—sniffing the air as if Diana reeked of alcohol. "You don't smell like Chanel No. 5 yourself," Diana snapped at her.

And then she thought, *What if this is the last person on earth I ever talk to?* She smiled, adding, "Guess I shouldn't start cocktail hour so early, huh?"

The woman wrinkled her nose but took her grubby coins, and Diana was able to watch the letter land in the bin of outbound mail. Bev bound.

She dragged back to the apartment and laid out the Seconal. Then she sat down for all the last things. Her last record (Joni Mitchell) to be listened to with her last meal (a cheese sandwich). Her last cigarette. A last nasty gin and tonic. Three more last cigarettes.

Finally, she inhaled a ragged breath and picked up the little pill bottle. She flipped the top.

Her thumbnail ripped and she leaped up, cursing. *What the hell?*

She held the bottle up, practically to her nose. It was a new childproof kind, with incoherent instructions communicated via minuscule arrows circling the cap. She shook the bottle, frustrated by the familiar rattle of pills inside that she couldn't get to. She tried again, grumbling under her breath.

If Alabama were here . . .

That thought only upset her more, and she ran to the closet and rooted around until she found a hammer. Then she returned to the coffee table and, clutching the tool two-handed like an ax, she whacked at the bottle repeatedly. Mostly she missed, but finally she scored a glancing hit that sent the bottle flying across the room. It crashed into the wall and fell to the floor, still unopened.

She dropped to her knees, crying. "I can't do this!"

It wasn't just that she was thirty-five and couldn't open a childproof cap. It was that she couldn't do *this*. Her plan. It was all wrong. She hated herself, hated the life she'd squandered, but leaving Alabama this way was wrong.

15

There had to be another way. Her mother would help. Of course she would. True, she only had her pension and Social Security, and now that she lived in the retirement home she didn't have room to take them in. But maybe she could lend them a little to get them by.

Or, if worse came to worst, she could crawl to Bev and beg for help. Yes, she'd even stoop to that.

Realization hit Diana like a cold slap. *Bev!* Her hands rose to her mouth, as if to cover the scream that caught in her throat.

The letter.

Heart somersaulting in her chest, Diana jumped up, reeling for the door. She had to get that letter back.

She streaked out of the apartment and then had to dash back up the stairs to retrieve her purse. She would need ID. Although surely the post office lady would recognize her. *"Remember me? Chanel No. 5? I've made a terrible mistake. . . ."*

Was it even possible to unmail a letter? She might have to lie, might have to say the letter contained explosives, or some kind of poison. Something extremely illegal. They would arrest her, but once the authorities figured out it was only a plain, old, ordinary letter—

She was so focused on her objective, so caught up in this new dilemma, she stepped off the curb without looking.

CHAPTER 1

Silence plucked at Bev's nerves. Mile after mile of silence.

How many times during the school year did she dream impossible dreams of perfect quiet and tranquility? Now here she sat, stuck in a rental van with a mute fourteen-year-old for an entire day, and she yearned for conversation, idle chatter, or even whining. An occasional grunt would have been enough. A wail of grief and pain. Anything.

Without a word, the six hours from St. Louis to Little Rock had stretched like an eternity. Trouble was, there was no peace and quiet inside Bev's head. She couldn't shut off her mind, or stop the memories. Especially the one from two days ago, looking at Diana for the last time at the funeral home, still and serene in death as she'd never been in life. The truck driver, the very last person to see her alive, had said that she'd shot right out in front of him, a human cannonball to her last breath. He hadn't even had time to put his foot to the brake pedal.

It was so wrong. Such a waste. All such a waste.

The road ahead of her blurred, and Bev shook tears out of her eyes. Thank heaven for sunglasses. She sniffed and leaned into the steering wheel.

"Are you sure you wouldn't like to listen to

17

music?" she asked Alabama. The girl had nixed listening to the radio at the beginning of the trip. "I just want to think," she'd said. Thinking had seemed okay hours ago, before Bev had realized that her own thoughts would bubble up from the ooze of regrets and anguish stewing inside her mind.

Hunched against the passenger window, Alabama slowly turned her head and lifted a brow. Bev guessed that meant no radio.

What was going through her head? And how could she possibly stay so dry-eyed? Bev had tried a hundred times in the past week to reach out to Alabama, to offer her a shoulder to cry on, but she evidently wasn't a touchy-feely girl. At least, not with her. She wasn't communicative at all. Every time Bev tried to talk to her, more often than not Alabama would wander off into some corner to listen to her Sony Walkman.

When Bev had picked her up at camp, Alabama's aloofness hadn't surprised her. They were practically strangers, the girl was wounded, and Bev had barely been functioning herself. She still felt shaky. They needed time to get used to each other. By "time," she'd presumed a few days. But the more days that passed in St. Louis, the more Alabama shut her out. Bev was starting to wonder if it was personal . . . but how could it be? She was here to help, ready to open her heart and home. Anyway, disliking someone required knowing them, and Alabama didn't know her at all.

She's frightened. Devastated. It's not about me.

But when someone sat like a lump in the passenger seat for six hours, unresponsive, it was hard not to take it personally.

"I'd like to listen to something." Bracing her left arm against the steering wheel to keep the van steady, Bev reached over and fiddled with the radio knobs. Finding a station acceptable to both of them posed a challenge. One tidbit Alabama had divulged over the past week was that she detested country music, which ruled out half of what blared from the dashboard speakers as Bev roamed across the dial. She finally found a soft rock station doing a two-for-Tuesday afternoon, which seemed perfect until the DJ followed "Feelin' Groovy" with "Bridge Over Troubled Water." Even at the best of times, that song reduced Bev to a puddle. And this was not the best of times.

One chorus in, she was rooting in her pocket for a tissue. A truck stop loomed ahead and she peeled off at the exit.

At the change in direction, Alabama straightened and braced herself as if for a crash. "What are you doing?"

Words, at last.

"We need to stop."

"You filled up an hour ago."

"My eyes are tired." Bev sniffled. She doubted she was fooling anyone. "I need to rest, maybe drink some coffee. Driving in this sun is no picnic."

"We have to get to Dallas today," Alabama insisted, refusing to move even after they were parked and Bev was halfway out the driver's-side door.

"We'll get there, but I need a break." When Alabama didn't move, she added, "You can't stay in the van—you'll broil. Come in and have a cold drink."

On a sigh, Alabama climbed out and assumed a posture of rigid forbearance. Once inside, however, her demeanor relaxed and she cruised an aisle, managing to scoop up gum, packets of Skittles, a large bag of chips, and a can of cream soda in the time it took Bev to pour a cup of coffee. Bev paid for it all and gestured with her head to an unoccupied Formica-topped table by the window.

Alabama dug in her heels again. "We need to get going."

"Just a few minutes to stretch our legs."

"How can we stretch our legs sitting at a table?"

"It's bound to be more comfortable than sitting in the van."

It wasn't, actually. The slippery bench seat was as uncomfortable as the cargo van, which they could see from their vantage point by the window.

The remains of Diana's entire life were squeezed into that small vehicle. The idea of packing up her little sister's apartment had been daunting—but on arriving in St. Louis last week, Bev discovered that Diana had acquired very little in her life that was worth keeping. Despite the heat beaming through the plateglass window, Bev shuddered, remembering her sister's apartment, with its peeling plaster and kitchen walls sporting grease like a topcoat of paint. She'd found mouse droppings in a closet. Diana hadn't even bothered to buy frames for the beds—simply left the mattresses and box springs on the floors. No doubt she thought it was bohemian. Bev called it primitive.

Poor Alabama. She was probably one step away from being one of those feral children you hear about who are rescued from basements of abusive parents. Kids chained to radiators and such like. Small wonder she didn't want to talk.

I'll make it up to her. I'll spoil her.

Across the table, her niece ripped the end off her Skittles package and upended it into the maw of her upturned mouth.

I'll teach her table manners.

Taking care of a fourteen-year-old was nothing she'd planned for. It would be a pinch. The logistics of the two of them living in her little house were going to require some working out, and there hadn't been any time to prepare. The spare bedroom was her craft room and was crammed with supplies. Alabama would have to sleep on the couch the first few nights, which wasn't exactly an ideal way to welcome her. It might get them off on the wrong foot.

Maybe *she* could sleep on the couch, and Alabama could take her room. That would be better.

Except that she was so tired. All week, she'd longed for her little house—a grease-and-mouse-dropping-free sanctuary. On Diana's mattress, which was saggy from age and had the scent of a tart, chemical perfume clinging to it, Bev had spent nights alternately tossing and weeping. Having the mattress on the floor messed with her center of gravity, made her feel disoriented, pressed down, disturbed at being in Diana's world again. Diana's screwed-up world, which Bev had known nothing about and in her ignorance had sometimes actually envied Diana for.

Oh, she'd envied Diana for a lot of things, all their lives. Envied, and sometimes even thought she hated her for. Thinking back on it, the ugliness of her own character made her ashamed. And now there was no one to apologize to.

All she could do was try to pick up the pieces. That included Alabama, who was all alone in a way that Bev could barely fathom. If she herself felt grief, and regret, and fear for the future, that was nothing compared to the devastation Alabama must be suffering. That had to explain her unresponsiveness. She was still in shock, numb.

The immensity of all that sorrow, that gaping loss, frightened her.

She took a deep, reassuring breath. She could do this. Alabama belonged with her.

"You'll like New Sparta," Bev said. "We have an excellent school system—though of course, I'm biased." She chuckled, then stopped when Alabama didn't react. "Also a library, a movie house, a public pool . . ." What else was there? The roller rink had recently burned down, but most New Spartans agreed that was just as well. It had always attracted a bad element on weekends. Unfortunately, there wasn't much else to mention. Alabama didn't strike her as the type to be over the moon about the new and improved Food-Save.

"Is there anything in particular you like to do?" Bev asked.

Alabama shrugged, busy with the enormous wad of Skittles in her mouth. Did she know anything about the food groups and proper nutrition? She'd hardly eaten a thing since Bev had arrived in St. Louis—apart from bowls of cold cereal and a little of the pizza Bev had bought one night.

"New Sparta has several restaurants," she continued. "And a new Walmart . . ."

Alabama laboriously gulped down what was left

23

of the wad of candy. She pushed out of the booth and stood. "I'll be right back."

"Where are you going?"

"To make a phone call."

"You're calling someone?"

"That's the idea," Alabama deadpanned. She slouched toward the pay phone across the store, near the restrooms.

Who was she calling? Could she possibly have a friend on the outskirts of Little Rock, Arkansas? Diana had moved around a lot, but Bev couldn't remember if Arkansas had been one of the places she and Alabama had lived.

She hoped Alabama wasn't phoning a boy. She hadn't even considered the possibility of a boyfriend. Until a week ago, she'd still been thinking of Alabama as the four-year-old she'd been the last time she'd seen her, not as a young woman. Post-puberty, anything could happen. By Alabama's age or thereabouts, Diana had already been sneaking out her bedroom window at night. Maybe that was why Alabama was being so quiet about everything. Maybe, aside from grief, she was stunned at being pulled away from some Romeo—some pimply Jason or Randy. Sudden separations were hard for young people to endure.

Visions of being plunged into an *Endless Love*–type scenario gave her pause.

No. I'm ready for this. I can handle it. Everything will be fine.

On the other hand . . . Screaming fights. Adolescent anguish. House on fire.

She jumped up, grabbed her purse, and headed back to the pay phone. As she barreled down an aisle flanked by motor oil on one side and Dolly Madison Zingers on the other, she nearly crashed into Alabama coming from the opposite direction.

"What are you doing?" Alabama asked her, going on tiptoe to peer over the shelves at their table. "Did you leave all my stuff sitting there?"

"Were you calling a boy?"

"What?" Alabama snorted out a confused laugh. "No! I called Gladdie. She wants to talk to you."

Bev's brain scrambled to catch up. "You called Mama?"

"Uh-huh. You'd better hurry. She's waiting on the line, and it's a collect call."

Bev dashed to the phone, the receiver of which was still swinging from its metal cord. "Mama?"

"For Pete's sake, Bev," her mother said by way of greeting, using her Gladys-Putterman-at-the-end-of-patience voice. She tended to be more clipped on the phone than in person anyway, due to her dread of long-distance charges. "Do you have to be so inflexible?"

Inflexible? Bev went rigid. Who was the one who'd hopped on the first plane and spent a week on a smelly mattress on a floor, arranging a funeral and Goodwill pickups and a rental van?

Exhaustion made her defensive, until the sane part of her brain—growing ever tinier—piped up, *Of course I did those things. What else could I have done?*

"What are you talking about?" she asked her mother.

"Alabama doesn't want to go to New Sparta," Gladys said.

"Does she have anywhere else to go?"

"Here."

Bev took a moment to try to process this. Her mother lived in a retirement home. The Villas was nice—she had her own one-bedroom apartment with a kitchenette, and her situation still gave her the option of taking her meals in a communal dining room and participating in group activities with the other residents. Plus, there was a nursing facility attached to The Villas, which was one of the features that had drawn them to the place when Gladys was looking to relocate after her knee replacement. That health center had proved a godsend weeks ago, when Gladys came down with pneumonia. After getting out of the hospital, she'd been transferred to the health center. That's where she'd been when the call about Diana had come.

"Mama, Alabama cannot live in an"—she almost called the place an old folks' home—"at The Villas. It's impossible."

"Why?"

"Because she's fourteen. I don't remember all the papers you signed when you moved in, but I'm pretty sure they have regulations about guests. And probably age restrictions, too."

"Fiddle-faddle. She's not a guest, she's my granddaughter."

"I know, but—"

"It's what she wants."

"But she has to go to school."

"It's still summer."

"And come the end of August, then what?"

"There are schools in Dallas."

"But it's crazy!" Bev blurted out.

Silence crackled over the line before her mother declared, "You're as intractable as Alabama said."

Bev's hand squeezed the plastic of the receiver so hard her birthstone ring bit into her finger. "How could Alabama say I'm anything? She doesn't talk to me. She didn't utter a word for three hundred miles!"

"I'm beginning to see why."

Bev flushed, opened her mouth to defend herself, and then shut it.

Fine. Let Alabama be Gladys's problem.

Why should she care about any of this? She'd done her duty, why take on more? Fostering a fourteen-year-old was going to disrupt her life, and maybe destroy one or several of the dreams she still clung to. Even if her dream job didn't pan out, she could imagine what Derek would say

27

when she told him she was now the guardian of her crazy sister's teenager. The man was already skittish about settling down.

So why was she digging in her heels at *not* taking care of Alabama? Why was a demented voice in the back of her mind howling that this was all wrong? That Alabama belonged with her.

The reason was there, reaching out to her, but her conscious mind bobbed and weaved away from it.

"Just leave her with me," her mother said.

Bev made one last appeal to reason. "Mama, how can you take care of a teenager? You're recovering from pneumonia."

"I'm fine," Gladys insisted.

Not fine enough to attend your favorite daughter's funeral, Bev thought, but said nothing. Part of her wondered if Gladys would have made it to the funeral even if she'd been in tip-top shape. With one glaring exception, she'd always recoiled from moments of high emotion, which had made her particularly ill-equipped to deal with two squabbling daughters.

"What if the management won't let her stay?" Bev asked.

"Leave that to me."

The past week, grisly and sorrowful, pressed down on Bev. There had been so many sad, mundane details of life and death to tend to during the day. Funeral home, insurance company, van rentals, police reports with blood-alcohol levels . . . And each night thoughts of Diana, worries about Alabama, and contemplating how her life was about to be upended, had drained all of her leftover energy. Having someone snatch the reins from her hands for a little while felt . . . good. A niggling voice in the back of her mind tried to get her attention, but Bev knew she couldn't fight her mother now. Better to give in. Chances were, she would simply be dropping Alabama off in Dallas for a week, or two at the most. Doing so would allow her some time to get her house ready. It might actually work out well, in the long run.

See? I'm not inflexible.

"Bev?" Gladys prompted.

"All right," she agreed. "We'll see you in about five or six hours, Mama."

After she hung up, she took a deep breath and tried to focus herself as she did during the hectic school year. *One day at a time. One foot in front of the other. Think about the next thing, not the last thing.* Maybe a breather for a week or two would enable her to get Diana and all that messy stuff out of her head. She hadn't really spoken to her sister in fifteen years, but these past few days, with her sister and the past clinging so ferociously to her thoughts, it was hard to remember that Diana hadn't been her whole life.

It was still impossible to accept Diana's life really was over. Gone in a flash. And suddenly,

29

out of the blue, Bev remembered not the Diana of high school and beyond, but little Diana decked out in a yellow dress that matched Bev's, with a crinoline that itched like mad, squealing with glee because she'd found more Easter eggs than her big sister.

Another crying jag threatened, and she wobbled back to the table where Alabama was gulping down her cold drink. Bev gasped in a breath. Sitting there with the sun on her, she looked so much like—

No.

The next thing, not the last thing.

She mustered a cheery voice. "Are you ready to hit the road? It'll be late when we get to Dallas, but at least we'll miss the worst of the traffic. Once I drop you off, I'll take the van back to New Sparta and unload everything so I can return it in the morning."

Alabama lifted her head. "I'm staying with Gladdie, then?"

"That's what Mama wants."

"Then I'll need all my stuff. My mom's stuff, too. You can't just take it. It doesn't belong to you."

"But—" Bev stopped herself and tried to tamp down the instinct to point out again the wrong-headedness of Gladys and Alabama's scheme. They were both grieving, not thinking straight. Gladys would see things differently when the reality of a teenager and a van's worth of moving boxes hit her apartment, and then she'd talk sense into Alabama.

"Okay." Bev's brain felt limp. "We'll unload it at Mama's."

Back at the van, the inside of which now gave off heat like a furnace on wheels, Bev gritted her teeth as she slid onto the scorching vinyl seat. She tried to pick up as if they were resuming a normal road trip.

"You feel like listening to music now?" she asked.

Alabama tilted her head, considering the question, and then nodded. "Yeah. I do."

Finally. She actually seemed willing to entertain the idea of being sociable. Maybe the second leg of the trip wouldn't be as excruciating as the first.

"Find something you like," Bev told her.

As she backed out of the parking lot and maneuvered toward the interstate, she heard Alabama rooting around her backpack, stashing away her chips, candy, and gum. Maybe they were making progress. Sharing music was often a tentative first step in making a connection with someone.

But when Bev next looked over at Alabama, the girl was pulling out her Sony Walkman and clamping the orange foam headphones over her ears. Then she slumped against the passenger window and closed her eyes. A faint, tinny, rhythmic thumping—all the music Alabama was going to share that trip—filtered through the headphones into the cab of the van.

Chapter 2

According to her grandmother, Alabama wasn't the youngest soul at the retirement home. That honor belonged to a balding old guy in bright golf pants named Wink Williams, who lived upstairs from her grandmother and loved jokes. Hokey, harmless practical jokes, usually—but as the director of The Villas was reported to have said after one ill-considered prank, a whoopee cushion on a wheelchair was no laughing matter.

Alabama liked Wink. In those first awful weeks, having someone joking with her was better than the long faces she was growing used to—better than the inexpressibly sad expression she glimpsed when Gladdie thought she wasn't looking, and a million times better than Aunt Bev's sorrowful lip nibbling, constant nervous chatter, and eyes red-rimmed from crying.

Wink was also the first person who'd ever asked Alabama to marry him. Repeatedly.

"What do you say we elope today?" he'd ask in the mornings over scrambled Egg Beaters and reduced-sodium toast.

Too bad he was seventy-nine, or she might have taken him up on it. Then again, she felt as if she were fourteen going on eighty. The old ladies around her, stooped and slow-moving, a few shrouded in permanent gloom and lonely dejection, didn't seem alien to her. In her heart, she was one of them.

Some days she woke up and couldn't believe she had to function for another fifteen hours, talking to people and eating and brushing her teeth. *Mommy,* she would think as her eyes blinked open. Mommy, a name she hadn't used since the days of nap time and *Romper Room*. Her mother had been Mom since Alabama started first grade. But if she could have her mom back, squeeze her thin body one last time, she knew what word she would cry out. *Mommy.*

How sad could a person feel before the heart just stopped? She faced every day feeling weak, wrung out, wondering why she was here. Why she was anywhere. Some days Wink's stupid joshing seemed the only good thing in the whole wide world.

His one-sided banter with her was met with laughter by all the other residents, except her grandmother. From time to time Gladdie would give him a brusque smackdown, especially if she worried he was embarrassing Alabama. "Once she found out those pearly whites of yours were removable," Gladdie would say to him after his usual proposal, "the honeymoon would be over."

Gladdie always seemed lukewarm toward Wink. "There's an operator if I ever saw one," she would say, eyeing his loud clothes and louder smile with suspicion. Everybody else, even the whoopee-cushion victim, adored him as if he were the resident mascot or pet. They could usually work up a chuckle or two for even his worst joke, and the time he'd brought his ukulele to the lounge and belted out "Paddlin' Madelin' Home," you'd have thought he was Mick Jagger. He'd had every lady there in thrall. And everybody—including, she bet, Gladdie—knew his attention to Alabama was his way of trying to cheer her up.

Alabama thought she fit right in at The Villas. Unfortunately, the place had a one-week guest policy. After Alabama had overstayed that limit by a week, Brenda Boyer, the director of the complex, made the trip up to Gladdie's apartment to serve them notice that Alabama would have to leave. Soon.

Her words panicked Alabama, but Gladdie stayed cool, responding in an icy, polite tone that clipped the soft edges off her Texas drawl. "We'll see about that."

Brenda always wore a shell-shocked expression, as if she were stunned to find herself stuck in midlife in a constant tug-of-war between "the management" and a building full of dentured malcontents. Her trouble was, she had a heart. During this particular conversation, she took in Alabama, the boxed piles of Alabama's belongings stacked nearly ceiling high in a corner of the living room, and then Gladdie's implacable expression. "I'm so sorry," she said, already backing out the

35

door in retreat. "Naturally, we understand that sorting out these situations takes time. . . ."

During their next conversation, a few days later, Brenda suggested that perhaps she should speak to Miss Putterman about the issue. Meaning Aunt Bev. Evidently, even people who had never suffered through one of her home economics or freshman health classes addressed her as Ms. Putterman. Aunt Bev's unflattering homemade clothes and never-fashionable hair screamed old maid as plainly as if the sexual revolution, the seventies, and *Cosmopolitan* magazine had never happened.

Alabama loathed Aunt Bev. Always had, always would. She'd grown up hearing stories about her from her mom—about how Bev narked on Diana for sneaking out past midnight. About Bev being the A student to Diana's C's and D's, even though anyone could tell Bev wasn't all that smart. ("She studied all the time, was all," was how Alabama's mom dismissed the disparity in their academic performances.) Bev was the diligent, worthy ant to Diana's grasshopper. Even at the age of seven, Aunt Bev had saved all her Halloween loot, portioning it out so it lasted till Christmas, while Diana had immediately scarfed down every popcorn ball, Baby Ruth, and Tootsie Roll until she was ready to burst.

When her mom and Aunt Bev were older, something really bad had happened, a final bust-up that Diana never wanted to talk about. The few times Alabama tried to find out about it, her mom had ended up stopping before she could explain, as if the incident still upset her so much it shorted out her brain. Even though it had taken place before Alabama was born, The Really Bad Thing was always there in the way her mom's voice tightened and quavered when she spoke of her sister. Whatever it was, it framed her and her mother's life, separating them from Gladdie, who lived in Dallas.

"I can't live in the same state with *her*," Diana would answer, meaning Bev, when Alabama questioned why they'd never lived in Texas. God knows they'd moved everywhere else. Alabama always liked staying with Gladdie, who doted on her the few times Alabama had visited her. Well, as much as Gladdie doted on anybody.

Even Gladdie wouldn't enlighten Alabama about The Really Bad Thing. Whenever the subject of the rift between her daughters came up, she would start talking about how maybe she'd been too old to start a family when she did. Her husband had died when Diana and Bev were in elementary school, and while Gladdie had been scrambling at a bank to make a living, she'd "lost control of the girls." Alabama assumed she meant that she'd lost control of Diana. It was impossible to imagine Aunt Bev out of control, and it was no secret that Diana had been a wild teenager—she'd been temperamental all her life. And reckless. Nobody knew that better than Alabama.

But no matter what had happened, it was easy to see how Bev had jumped on Diana's nerves.

Alabama had experienced her fill of Aunt Bev back in St. Louis, during those days following the worst day of her life—the day she'd been called away from a last swim in the pool and arrived dripping in a towel at Camp Quapaw's main office, where Gladdie was on the other end of the phone line, waiting to break the awful news about the accident. The police had traced Gladdie through their apartment's superintendent—she was the reference Diana had given on the rental application. Gladdie also informed Alabama that Bev was on her way to fetch her from camp and would be there in a matter of hours.

For about two seconds Alabama was almost glad to see her aunt, until she realized what her being there meant. After Gladdie's call, she'd retreated in a funk to her upper bunk in the rustic cabin, where all her cabin mates were filtering out to catch buses or be picked up by parents. Packing up her things, Alabama convinced herself there had been some mistake, or that she'd dreamed the conversation with Gladdie. Her mother couldn't have died while she was here, horseback riding, canoeing, and swimming. She couldn't have died, period.

But Bev's arriving to pick her up confirmed that the worst had happened, and the following days were a nightmare. Aunt Bev was so bossy, so judgmental of how she and her mom had lived. Back in the apartment in St. Louis—which, granted, seemed a lot messier than when Alabama had left it—her aunt's face puckered in distaste every time she looked around. Worse, she kept bursting into tears, and when she wasn't weeping outright, she was nattering on about how brave Alabama was, and how she must have been very strong to endure Diana's moods, Diana's troubles.

Alabama finally exploded at her. "We were *happy!*"

Which, obviously, wasn't the whole truth. But they had been a little happy a lot of the time.

And a lot happy some of the time.

And then Bev had started going on as if it was a given that Alabama was going to move to New Sparta with her. *As if.*

The woman was delusional. There was no way that arrangement would work, and what's more, Alabama couldn't figure out why Aunt Bev would want to live with her. Alabama never made the tiniest effort to pretend she liked her. Bev's own mother knew that the two of them together would be a domestic train wreck, and Gladdie couldn't have been happy about having moving boxes stacked ceiling high in her living room and Brenda Boyer breathing down her neck.

The next time Brenda broached the subject of "talking to Miss Putterman," Gladdie declared, "Alabama is not moving in with my daughter Bev," with a finality that Alabama found comforting, even if Brenda didn't.

What changed everything was the tapioca incident. One night in the dining room of The Villas, Alabama made the fatal error of taking the last tapioca cup. She grabbed it from the dessert buffet, sat down, and then, three spoonfuls in, she caught sight of an old woman named Penny making her torturous route toward the buffet. Penny had suffered a stroke a few years back, and now she moved in slow, tiny steps that always made Alabama think of Tim Conway in a Carol Burnett skit. Having painstakingly locomoted her way to the dessert table, Penny stopped, collapsing against her walker when she saw that the only thing left was orange Jell-O.

Disappointed, the old lady turned back. That's when her gaze locked onto Alabama's tapioca.

Now, as a guest at The Villas, Alabama—or Gladdie—paid seven dollars for the evening meal. Highway robbery, Gladdie called it. The sum was more than what the normal residents paid, and probably ten times what the food was actually worth. Occasionally Alabama didn't even bother going down for dinner, preferring peanut butter crackers in front of *Jeopardy!* to noodles

Stroganoff and diverticulitis discussions. But never mind that she was paying through the nose. At that moment, Penny Beauchamp glared as if Alabama was a freeloader. A tapioca thief.

The next day, a hesitant tap at Gladdie's door announced Brenda again. "I'm sorry to bother you, Gladys." She edged into the room. "We've had complaints."

Gladdie's guard went up instantly. "Who complained?"

"I'm afraid I'm not at liberty to divulge that information, but—"

Gladdie cut her off. "You don't have to. Everyone with working eyeballs still in their heads saw the look Penny sent Alabama last night."

Brenda's gaze skittered toward Alabama. She hitched her throat. "Yes, well, the fact is, Gladys, we *do* have the one-week guest policy."

"Tough tiddlywinks," Gladys parried. "We also have a no dogs policy, yet there's Bonnie Tucker on the second floor with her ridiculous poodle. Who I like, by the way. I like the dog better than Bonnie, to tell you the truth. I'm *happy* an exception was made for Noodles."

"Yes, but . . ." Brenda clearly hadn't anticipated Gladdie's drawing a comparison between her granddaughter's situation and a poodle's. "People . . . that is, many residents . . . are beginning to ask how long this can go on. It's against policy,"

41

she insisted. "I need to be able to tell them something. . . ."

"A foolish consistency is the hobgoblin of little minds," Gladdie said. "You might tell them *that*."

When Brenda was gone, Gladdie aimed a scowl at the living room rug. Anxiety about her future shook Alabama. If she couldn't stay with Gladdie, what would happen to her?

"Do they still have orphanages?" Alabama asked.

"Don't be ridiculous," Gladdie said. "You're not an orphan."

Maybe she meant that Alabama still had relatives. But so did Anne of Green Gables, Heidi, that girl in *The Secret Garden*, Dorothy in *The Wizard of Oz* . . . All those characters had a grandparent or an uncle or something, but it was the no-mother-and-no-father thing that made them orphans. Alabama's father had died before she was born, and now she was motherless. She couldn't have been any more an orphan if she'd clapped a red wig on her head and started belting out "Tomorrow."

"Well, technically, maybe you are," Gladdie allowed. "Ever since Diana . . ." Unable to finish the thought, she tottered toward her cabinet of solace and pulled out her crutch reserved for moments of high tension—her jar of candied orange slices. Those and her ever-present rolls of Tums were all she ever snacked on.

She tore open an orange slice with her razor-sharp nails and bit off half. The gumdrop consistency of the candy caused her jaw to pop as she chewed, and Alabama sensed that the effort of keeping all her dental work in place helped hold Gladdie's tears at bay.

"If only Diana had said something to me about how bad things were . . . maybe I could have done more."

"You know how Mom was," Alabama said, automatically wanting to comfort her, even though she didn't like the implication that her mother's accident was caused by their financial situation. She'd walked in front of a truck. What did that have to do with money?

"I thought I *was* doing more," Gladdie continued. "When she called me and asked for money to send you to that camp, it sounded like a good thing— get you out of the city for a week, and let Diana have some time by herself to unwind."

Alabama had relived that week a thousand times. Her mom alternating between overblown excitement about the camp and catatonic depression. The ever-present prescription bottle on the coffee table. Her own fear, mixed with irritation. At times she wanted to scrap the whole idea of going. She was too old for camp, wasn't she? But in the next moment the desire to get away, to breathe fresh air, and to not worry about anything for once in her life would overwhelm her.

She couldn't believe now that she'd ever *wanted* to leave her mom. Even for a second.

"If I'd only known how things really were," Gladdie said, "she might not have—"

Alabama jumped up. "She didn't *do* anything! It was an accident."

Gladdie's eyes widened, and after a moment, she nodded. A tear slipped out of the corner of her eye.

Despite Gladdie's assurances, after the tapioca incident Alabama became more nervous than ever that she would be packed off to New Sparta. That couldn't be allowed to happen. She had to do something.

"If I can't live here at The Villas," she told Gladdie later that afternoon, "then I wish I could rent a place of my own nearby."

Gladdie hooted at that suggestion. "You're fourteen."

"I can take care of an apartment. I took care of Mom and me."

This was true. Alabama often had to remind her mom to pay the rent and bills every month. She was the one who'd dealt with the super when the bathtub drain backed up with black sludge, or soothed the neighbors when Diana spent two days listening to Janis Joplin at wall-shaking volume. They might have been evicted several times, if not for Alabama's intervention.

"I'm sure you're capable," Gladdie said. "But

I don't think a fourteen-year-old is allowed to sign a lease."

"I don't want to live with Aunt Bev."

"I know, but—"

"And if I were here, nearby, I could take care of you."

Since her arrival, she'd done all the stuff for Gladdie that she'd managed for Mom—reminded her to take her pills, tidied the apartment, played cards with her at night. Her grandmother was getting over pneumonia and wasn't as strong as she'd been the few times Alabama had visited before.

"I don't see why you even live at this place," she told Gladdie that evening. "You're not as old as most of the people here."

"I'm seventy-seven."

"So? Some of the people here are in their sixties, but they seem a lot older than you. You don't really belong here."

This was what she'd decided: The easiest solution would be for Gladdie to move out of The Villas. This would be best for Gladdie, who didn't seem all that happy in the old folks' home. If they left together, she could continue to look after Gladdie, and Gladdie would be her Bev buffer. It would be best for both of them.

At first she didn't think Gladdie was listening. But then she noticed her grandmother zoning out while they were watching *Falcon Crest*, which was Gladdie's favorite show. She loved Jane Wyman.

"I saw Arnelle asleep in the lobby today," Gladdie said during a commercial. "She was sitting there with her chin collapsed on her chest. The receptionist had to go over and poke her to see that she was still alive. I hope I never reach that point."

"Please!" Alabama rolled her eyes. "You're not even close to that yet."

"Neither was Arnelle, when she first moved to this place." Her voice was sharpish. "That wasn't so long ago, either. A year and a half."

After that, Alabama thought her grandmother was paying attention to the show. During the next commercial, though, Gladdie mused, "I do miss having a little garden. Growing my own tomatoes. Those grainy things they serve downstairs are pitiful."

Alabama sighed shamelessly. "I've never even had a garden."

Naturally, there was a stumbling block. Named Bev.

"Move out? No—the whole idea is ludicrous. You only moved in here two years ago!"

"Maybe that was two years too soon," Gladdie said.

"But where would you move to?"

Aunt Bev had seemed agitated since she'd walked in the door. It wasn't hard to guess that

Brenda Boyer had given her an earful on her way in, but Alabama also sensed something else upsetting her. Her radar for gauging unhappiness had been fine-tuned over the years.

"We'll have to find a place," Gladdie said.

That *we* brought Bev's focus to Alabama, and her irritation was clear. "The easiest solution for everyone would be for Alabama to come live in New Sparta. Soon, before the school year begins. And before this place ends up kicking both of you out."

Gladdie rapped her hand against the arm of her chair. "They won't have time to evict me. I'm leaving here on my own steam. I never belonged here in the first place—*you* were the one who was telling me I couldn't cope on my own."

Red flooded into Bev's cheeks and Alabama thought she was going to witness some real fireworks. Then her aunt took a deep breath. "What are you going to do about money? You barely have enough to cover the bills here."

"Because this place is costing me a fortune. As far as I'm concerned, that's another good reason to leave." Gladdie must have been worrying about finances a lot. The orange slice jar was practically empty. "We might have to rent an apartment. A small one, right at first. Or who knows? We could decide to stay there permanently."

"I like apartments," Alabama said.

Bev leveled a glare at her. "Excuse me, young

lady, but you're fourteen. You should not be deciding this matter."

"Why not?" Gladdie's voice sounded as hot as Alabama's face felt. *Young lady?* "She's going to live wherever it is we end up. And we can't stay here."

Bev's temper boiled over. "But you *can,* Mama. I know your pride's hurt now because they're giving you a hard time, but you've got to see this situation from their point of view. If they make an exception for Alabama, they'll have to make exceptions for everybody."

"You've been talking to that mousy Boyer woman." Gladdie sniffed at the thought of Brenda. "She can't even stand up to a few petty biddies."

"You signed an agreement when you moved in here. You have to live by the rules."

"Not if I move out, I don't."

Bev jumped out of her chair. "How will you and Alabama manage on your own? She's fourteen and you're . . . well, it's been a while since you've taken care of a place."

Alabama liked the stubborn tilt of Gladdie's chin. She wasn't going to change her mind. Thank God. "Alabama's a real helper. See how nice this apartment looks?" She conveniently gestured away from the leaning tower of boxes in the corner. "Look what she did yesterday—got the tea stain out of your rug."

She always called the rug in the middle of the living room "Bev's rug." Alabama wouldn't have claimed it, either. Obviously one of Bev's craft projects, it featured a giant orange-and-yellow daffodil against an olive-green background.

The moment Gladdie mentioned the stain was gone, Bev forgot all about the argument they'd been having and sank to her knees, inspecting the part of the petal where the old mark was now barely a shadow. She rubbed her hand over the hooked nubs and then glanced at Alabama in surprise, as if she hadn't thought her capable of doing anything useful. "I tried and tried to get that out. What did you put on it? Vinegar?"

She shook her head. "Scrubbing Bubbles foaming bathroom cleanser."

Bev bit her lip and leaned back on her heels. Her face crumpled, as if she were about to finally burst into tears. Alabama had never seen anyone so demoralized by her own stain removal failure.

"For pity's sake, what's wrong with you today?" Gladdie asked her.

Bev swallowed, trying to compose herself. "I got rejected this week."

Alabama had heard Gladdie muttering about some guy named Glen, who was Bev's boyfriend, or lover, or something. Imagining Aunt Bev's sex life was enough to gag a maggot, so she tried hard not to think about it.

But when Bev said she was rejected, Alabama

assumed she was talking about this boyfriend. She took vicious pleasure in asking her, in complete innocence, "Who rejected you?"

"NASA," Bev said.

Not the answer Alabama had been expecting.

For a second, she could only gape at her aunt. "Huh?"

"I got the letter on Tuesday telling me that they'd turned down my application." Several tears spilled down Bev's cheeks. "I mean, I knew they probably would. What were the chances? But it's been in the back of my mind—you know, that hope. That hope that something exciting and wonderful might happen to me."

Alabama still had no idea what she was babbling about. She turned to Gladdie, who arched her brows in return. "Bev applied to be the first teacher in space."

A laugh burbled out before Alabama could stop it. Then she looked again at those tears and realized that Bev was genuinely crushed. She struggled for something to say, but all she could manage was, "But you're a home ec teacher!"

Bev's eyes flashed. "I think it would be neato for the first teacher in space to be a home economics instructor. It could help give the subject a little of the respect it deserves." She sniffed. "And I teach health, too, you know."

Wow.

Alabama had to admit she was impressed.

50

Looking at Bev, with her wraparound skirts and floral blouses, no one would guess the woman harbored dreams of being an astronaut. *Astronaut* reminded her of *The Right Stuff*, what's-his-name the senator, and Sigourney Weaver in *Alien*. Was that how Bev saw herself? Sigourney Weaver floating around in zero gravity, beaming down meal planning and hygiene lessons?

She struggled to think of something more to say to her aunt. "Better luck next time" didn't seem to fit the occasion. For one thing, Bev was thirty-eight. At some point, a person was too ancient to dream of becoming an astronaut, or being anything besides whatever boring thing they actually were.

"I guess I wasn't born a lucky person." Bev allowed herself one last moment of public moping. Then she squared her shoulders and became irritating again. "But that's just too darn bad, right? A person has to persevere and create her own luck."

Gladdie mumbled skeptically, but Alabama was too appalled by her own thoughts to agree or disagree. *My God. For a moment there I almost liked her.*

That night at dinnertime Alabama settled in to watch television and eat peanut butter and crackers, but Gladdie tapped her on the shoulder. "You come to dinner with me."

After the tapioca incident, the prospect of going down to the dining room made Alabama anxious. "But—"

"No buts. We're not going to hide you away up here like a criminal."

She didn't feel like a criminal. She just wanted to watch *Love Connection*.

At her grandmother's insistence, however, Alabama got up—although she made a solemn vow to leave the dessert buffet alone. Even if it was chocolate chip cookie night.

The first person they saw when they got off the elevator was Wink. He sat next to Alabama at the table and did tricks with his food, making a cucumber disk disappear (she could see it in his other hand) and tossing cherry tomatoes in the air and catching them in his mouth. His success rate hovered around 30 percent, but each time he caught one, he winked at her in triumph. It was a little like sitting next to a seven-year-old. Across the table, two ladies spoke in hushed tones about Rock Hudson, who had AIDS, and on Alabama's right, Gladdie and another woman were discussing a plane crash that had happened off the coast of Ireland. Alabama turned when she heard them mention a number over three hundred.

Three hundred victims. The number knocked the wind out of her. All those people . . . even people she didn't know . . . lost. Three hundred people— but a lot more than three hundred people left behind, wondering what had happened. Maybe kids all on their own now. They were lost, too.

The sound of a fist striking the table made Alabama jump, and she twisted back. Wink was staring straight ahead, his face a reddish purple.

"He's choking!" Gladdie cried out. "Somebody run for help!"

The only one in the room capable of running, Alabama hopped up and sprinted toward the front office, shouting Brenda's name until she saw that the office was closed for the weekend. She grabbed the reception phone and punched the button for The Villas' health center, bleating out a cry for help. Then she raced back to the dining room, where a woman was pounding weakly on Wink's back.

"Here." Alabama nudged her aside. She'd studied the Heimlich maneuver in school once, and had practiced it on a friend in a goofing-around sort of way. She wrapped her arms around Wink's middle. "Can you stand up?" she asked him.

He didn't answer, but with her half hauling him, he lurched to a bent-kneed stance. She squeezed hard, but nothing came out of him—not even a wheeze. She tried again, harder this time, trying to picture what the teacher had taught them, with fists at the base of the diaphragm. But she must not have done it right. Or whatever it was in his windpipe—one of those cherry tomatoes, she guessed—was wedged tighter than a boulder in a drinking straw.

Beneath her hands, Alabama could feel the life draining out of him. People were talking at her—voices intent on instruction and nervous encouragement. She didn't hear them. She was whipped back in time, back to the cool, carpeted room in the funeral home where her mother was. So still, so cold. Not really her mother at all. Her mother without life, without emotions, without the ability to sing off-key at the top of her voice . . . her mother without those things was nothing.

She'd stood over her, running through those last moments they'd had. *Why didn't I get off the bus?* That morning, preparing to go to camp, nothing had seemed right. Her mother had been so confused, so out of it and sad looking. As the bus had pulled away, Alabama had to bite her lip to keep from calling out to the bus driver to stop, from crashing to the front of the bus and running back across the parking lot to her mom. Why hadn't she? She might have prevented everything, kept her alive. . . .

At the funeral home, she'd bent down and kissed her mom, crying into her mouth as their lips touched. If only it had been a fairy tale, like one of the stories her mother had read to her over and over when she was little, the one where a kiss restored life. It happened in the movies, too. You'd think someone was gone, and then eyelids fluttered open, music swelled, and miraculous reunions happened.

But not in real life. Not in hers, anyway. Not then.

Not now, either.

Wink sank back against her, and they staggered in an awkward dance. The health center nursing crew burst into the dining room, and one of the guys wedged behind Alabama, sandwiching her between him and Wink. She slipped out and watched as Wink, maybe the only man who'd ever want to marry her, sagged lifelessly against the male nurse.

CHAPTER 3

"I've taken steps to find a place for Alabama and me," Gladys announced.

Bev was only beginning to come to terms with those words when her mother added, "I don't belong here with all these old people, any more than Wink did."

"Who's Wink?" Bev asked.

"He choked on a tomato," Alabama said, curled up in a wingback chair. "He might not be dead. We don't know."

Gladys fidgeted with the clasp of her purse. "We know that he was full of life, and energy, and this place choked the life out of him."

"It sounds like it was the tomato's fault," Bev said. "A person can choke to death anywhere. You can't blame The Villas for that."

"He was still breathing when they took him away," Alabama insisted. "They stuck a tube in his throat. He might still be alive."

"They'd have told us if he was." Dressed in her best blue suit and square-toed navy pumps, Gladys paced across the living room, popping Tums from the half-unraveled roll in her fist.

Why was she so dressed up? Bev wondered.

"That's how they operate here," her mother continued. "When one goes, they don't say anything about it—just hope the senile old folks don't notice that the herd's been thinned."

"Mama! I'm sure that's not the case."

"Yes it is. Of course, you can hardly blame them for not making a fuss. If the management stopped to acknowledge every passing, this place would take on the feel of a nonstop wake." She paused, shaking her head. "But even so, Wink was special."

So special that she'd never mentioned him before. Bev still couldn't place him. Unless . . . "Was he that man in the colored pants?"

Alabama nodded.

Bev had seen him around and ridden on the elevator with him once—he'd whistled "Mairzy Doats" for three floors, then told her a corny joke as she was trying to get off. She remembered him clamping a liver-spotted hand against the elevator's door to keep it from sliding shut on his punch line.

He'd reminded her of an old supper club comedian. Certainly not the kind of personality Gladys usually admired. She wondered if her mother's mind was transferring her grief from Diana's death to Wink's.

"He was an essential part of the community here," Gladys said. "Full of vitality. And now he's"—shaky fingers freed another chalky tablet—"gone."

"Mama, just because an elderly gentleman died

here doesn't mean that you should move out."

"Maybe not the way you see it, but from my perspective, that's exactly what it means. And this time I'm not going to let myself be railroaded by you, which is what landed me here in the first place."

Railroaded! When, in the old days, Gladys had called her several times a week, sometimes several times per day, upset and complaining that she couldn't take care of a house and yard anymore? When she had barely been able to hobble up her own front stairs? When she'd phoned The Villas to request a tour of it herself? "That's revisionist history if I've ever heard it," Bev said.

Gladys, still pacing, didn't seem to be listening. "I was easily persuaded then. I'd had that knee replacement, and besides, I didn't know any better. This time I've taken steps. Now I see that these places are like those roach motels you see on television, you check in but—"

Bev didn't let her finish. "What steps? What are you talking about?"

"I've called Woodrow. He said he could take Alabama and me house hunting this afternoon."

House hunting? *This afternoon?* What time is he coming?"

"Around noon. He's taking Alabama and me out to look at some properties."

Bev waited for her to say "You can come, too," but she didn't. Being left out stung, but she tried not to show it. "Mama, I drove up here today to see if we could get some things settled with Brenda. She called me yesterday and—"

"They will be settled. Alabama and I are moving."

Bev glanced over at Alabama, who was smiling complacently at the ceiling. She wore a pair of red shorts and a T-shirt with shoulder pads, which Bev supposed was her version of dressing up. She was all ready for her day of house touring with Woodrow, an old family friend Bev hadn't seen in decades.

"Woodrow must be eighty by now," Bev said.

Her mother eyed her sharply. "He still has his realtor's licence. *He* hasn't been put out to pasture yet. And he says he's looking forward to meeting my granddaughter."

Gladys and Alabama exchanged a smile.

A spike of something unfamiliar, or long buried, rose in her chest. A sharp, hurtful stab like a thorn in her heart. Back in the day, Diana had always managed to charm their mother despite being irresponsible and troublesome. Bev might have been the daughter who stayed closer, but she had never been her mother's favorite.

She tried to shake off the feeling. Alabama was not Diana. Grandchildren were different from children.

"But if you want to make yourself useful while you're here," her mother said, "then you can run me out to the drugstore. I'm almost out of Tums. We've got about enough time to get there and back before Woodrow arrives."

"All right," Bev agreed. "Maybe we should take my car, though. It's right out front." She hated navigating the crazy Dallas traffic in her mother's land yacht.

They left Alabama at the apartment in case Woodrow showed up early. Alabama was not the best candidate for a greeter—she barely spoke and she didn't know Woodrow. But the opportunity to be alone with her mother for a few moments stopped Bev from voicing these doubts. They hadn't talked in private since Alabama's arrival.

As they drove to the drugstore, though, every time Bev tried to bring up the subject of the move and how ill-advised it would be, Gladys cut her off or changed the subject. She spent precious time fiddling with the air-conditioning knobs in Bev's car and scolding her for not buying American. "You should get yourself a Buick instead of this tuna can. The Japanese aren't up to the job of cooling off cars in a Texas summer."

"Mama—"

"Now don't say that's racist," her mother argued, before Bev could say anything at all. "I ask you, does the mercury ever top a hundred degrees in Tokyo?"

Bev frowned. "I don't know." *Did it?* "I'm sure their engineers make allowances . . ."

As her thoughts scurried down the mental maze her mother had laid for her, she stopped herself and took a deep breath.

"Have you told The Villas that you intend to move out?" Bev asked, directing them back on track. "Please say no."

"Why should you want me to say no? Why shouldn't I leave that place? Life is short—look at what happened to Diana. Unless . . ." Gladys frowned. "It *was* an accident, don't you think?"

They hadn't had a chance to really talk about Diana's death until now. It wasn't something they wanted to discuss in front of Alabama. For weeks, Bev had been itching to unburden her doubts on the matter to someone. But now, seeing the sadness and the worry in her mother's eyes, the doubts wouldn't form on her lips. "The coroner said she'd had a lot to drink. And you know Diana. There was a whole bottle of Seconal in the apartment, unopened. If she'd wanted to kill herself, she wouldn't have needed to jump in front of a truck."

For some reason, the words seemed to give her mother comfort. "And there was no note," Gladys pointed out.

Bev nodded. "She probably just wasn't paying attention."

"Poor Alabama. It would be terrible for her if . . ."

Gladys shook her head. "Well, as you say, it was an accident. Had to be."

If they hadn't been in bucket seats, Bev would have hugged her. Losing Diana so suddenly had devastated her mother. She never laughed now, rarely even smiled. Diana might have stayed far away, but her mother had always tried to keep track of her, and Bev knew that she'd been draining her savings to keep Diana afloat all these years. Gladys loved Diana, her baby, so much, she would have given her anything.

Small wonder she wanted to cling to Alabama now.

For a moment, Bev thought her mother was going to cry, but instead she twisted in her seat as they approached the pharmacy's parking lot. "Careful to turn in correctly, Bev—the spaces are slanty. Last time you went in the wrong way and we ended up parked all woppy-jawed."

Inside the drugstore, Gladys debated what size container of antacids to get, finally deciding on the economy-sized tub.

"If you need a vat of antacids to get through the day, there's something wrong," Bev pointed out. "We should get you a doctor's appointment."

"I'm fine. I have a sour stomach, is all. Besides, pill for pill, this size is cheaper. No sense tossing money away."

Bev lugged the container up to the counter for her. When it was their turn at the register, she reached into her purse to grab some money to pay and dug around, searching for the ten-dollar bill she was certain she'd put there this morning. "I can't find the change I got from the gas station." She snapped open her coin purse in hopes that she'd stuck it there.

Where had it gone?

Gladys produced a bill from her own pocket-book. "You don't have to pay for my things. I'm not a child." She paid and marched out of the store, purse clutched under one arm, opaque plastic jar under the other.

Bev remained so distracted by the loss of the ten dollars that she almost forgot why she'd wanted to talk to her mother alone until they were almost home.

"I wish you would rethink this moving business, Mama. In fact, I wish you would rethink the whole idea of keeping Alabama with you. You don't know what a handful teenagers are."

"I don't?" Gladys crowed. "And how many children have *you* raised?"

"I meant teenagers nowadays," she amended quickly. "I do know something on that subject."

"You might think that I'm too old to deal with a teenager, that I won't have the energy to pay attention. But my life is settled, while you've got your job and a house to deal with, and some man friend to claim your attention."

Derek claimed less of her attention than she

would have liked, actually—although she wasn't sure she should tell her mother that. Her mother always looked askance at Bev's relationships, sure they would never amount to anything. But part of the reason Bev suspected Derek hadn't popped the question yet was because they were both older and settled in their ways. Maybe he needed a little help envisioning them as a family.

They traveled a few blocks in silence. "I see what you're trying to do," Gladys said. "You want to seize this opportunity to rewrite history."

Bev gripped the steering wheel tighter. "That is *so wrong*."

"Is it? All these years, I've watched how that business with Diana affected you."

"How?"

"Like last year, when you tossed away a perfectly good boyfriend . . . what was his name?"

"Glen? Glen wasn't 'perfectly good.' He had his faults."

"Who hasn't, for Pete's sake? But he wasn't exactly like Tom, was he? And now, with Alabama. You still want what Diana had."

"Have you forgotten, Mama?" It was hard to keep from shouting. "What Diana had was mine!"

Her mother turned her head, staring out at the passing road.

Bev gulped in several breaths to calm herself. "I'm offering to take Alabama in because I feel terrible for what's happened, and because it's the only thing that makes sense. For all of us."

"I don't agree. She's my grandchild, and you . . ." Gladys hesitated. "You're too conflicted."

The car's interior felt so blistering hot Bev could hardly stand it. Maybe her mother had a point about Toyotas and air-conditioning. But she was way off base when it came to her own family. "You think I'm so unhinged about my little sister that I'm going to take it out on Alabama?"

Gladys squinted at her. "A girl going through what Alabama's going through now needs time, and love."

"You think I can't show love?" Bev asked.

"I didn't say that. It's just you can be forceful . . . and, it has to be said, a tad judgmental. Children need understanding."

Bev mashed the brake pedal to keep from running the red light at the entrance to The Villas. When Bev and Diana had been growing up, Gladys had been overworked and short on patience, and she'd run their house with all the understanding and love of an office manager. Now she was acting as if she were Dr. Spock, Judy Blume, and Captain Kangaroo all rolled into one cuddly, grandma-shaped package.

Gladys twisted toward the center of the seat to grab her antacid jug. She struggled with the top. "Why oh why do they make everything so darn hard to open now?"

That was so like her mother. Lob an incendiary comment in one breath and change the subject in the next. *You're demented when it comes to your sister and incapable of love. Where are my Tums?* Bev's arms shook against the steering wheel. She felt . . .

Demented.

"Oh good," Gladys said as they sailed up the drive to The Villas. "That's Woodrow's car pulling in now. Just drop me off, Bev. No need for you to come in."

The first thing Bev did after her drive home from Dallas was head for the kitchen, where she poured herself a Crystal Light lemonade from the ice-cold pitcher. After a long gulp, she considered her options, reached into the cabinet above the fridge, hauled down the vodka bottle, and upended a few glugs into her glass.

Better.

Usually when she came back from visiting her mother it was evening already, but today she'd driven up and basically turned right back around and come home. The entire return trip, all the things she could have said—should have said—tumbled through her mind. Too late. It was so frustrating. She couldn't believe she'd sat there and listened to her mother talk about her as if she lacked sympathy and understanding. Why, she was so understanding it was practically a handicap.

She was helping kids all the time at school, the ones who came to her with problems during her conference time. Of course, she wasn't always able to *do* much for these kids. Time remained the surest remedy for most afflictions of adolescence. But she was there for them. She listened, she understood.

And when *she'd* been young, troubled, and brokenhearted, who had she been able to turn to? Not her mother, that was for darn sure. Gladys had always been able to shed a tear or two over the gentle wisdom of Marcus Welby, but when it came to the drama in her own house, she'd remained aloof. Even when Bev's life had been ruined— permanently, irretrievably shattered to bits— Gladys had said she had to remain impartial. Impartial meant taking Diana's side. As usual.

Old resentments filled her chest until she felt overinflated, breathless. She exhaled and forced herself to turn her thoughts in a different direction. *Forward, not backward.*

There was so much she had to do. For one thing, she'd emptied out her craft room in anticipation of Alabama's moving in, and now its contents sprawled through the rest of the house—wood and tools heaped in corners, bolts of cloth and yarn spilling across the dining room table. The sewing machine stood in a hallway, forcing her to walk sideways to squeeze past it every time she made a trip to the bathroom.

She'd intended to organize the garage to absorb the overflow, and had even gone so far as to contact Keith Mitchell about building shelves, but now Alabama wasn't coming. The spare room could be the craft room again. Maybe that's where Keith should build the shelves. But what should she do with the furniture in Alabama's bedroom? The dresser might come in handy for storage, but the painted iron daybed she bought at a flea market would never be used enough to justify the space it took up.

The truth was, she hadn't only been excited about the room, but also about the prospect of having someone else in the house. She hadn't had a roommate since college—not that Alabama would have been a roommate, exactly, but she would have been company. Not very pleasant company all the time, if the past few weeks were any indication, but even a hostile Alabama would have been someone to share life with. Lately the years were spinning by faster and faster, and sometimes she felt so alone. Friends from high school had met their soul mates, married, had kids, pulled away from her. They had all moved away or were still in Dallas, busy with their lives, and she was busy, too, her own life consumed by school, hobbies, after-school Future Homemakers of America meetings and parent-teacher nights, and driving once a week to see her mother and run the same errands again and again.

Each time she stole out to visit old friends, it seemed they had less in common. These women griped almost boastfully about their busy days tending to children, and the trouble their sprawling suburban homes caused them, and the tribulations of school as seen from the other side. And vacations! Everyone had always just come back from or was about to jet off to somewhere exotic. When they asked about Bev's life at all, the questions highlighted its deficits. *When are you going to get married? Do you see kids on the horizon?* They were waiting for her life to begin so she'd have something to talk about that interested them. She was waiting for that, too.

Of course, she had Derek.

Then again, she *didn't* have Derek. He was independent, and both of them had been living alone for so long. Half the time she felt she'd die if he didn't pop the question, but occasionally after he got into his truck and drove away, she'd collapse in relief to be alone again. Was a life as Mrs. Derek Matthews really her destiny? Was he really what she wanted?

Of course he was. Why else would she have broken it off with Glen? She had *pursued* Derek, who was more of her ideal. She wasn't shallow, but everyone knew you couldn't build a relationship if the physical part wasn't right. Derek reminded her a little of Tom—unpredictable. Although other than that they were night and day.

Her breathing stilled as her mother's words echoed in her head. *You still want what Diana had.*

Why had her mother flung those words at her? Diana had been the covetous one. Diana was the one who'd taken what she'd wanted, consequences be damned.

The impulse to dig out her old photograph album spurred Bev to the hallway. She looked up at the square in the ceiling, the entry to the attic. All she had to do was reach up and draw down the ladder. Yet she resisted. So many nights had been lost that way—staring at photos of Tom, wallowing in memories until she was messy drunk on them. She'd finally stowed the pictures out of easy reach.

Of course, her memory didn't require a visual prompt. Her mind could spin her back through the decades all on its own, but she'd done a fairly good job of training it to avoid the more maudlin pathways. Or she thought she had . . . until she'd looked into Alabama's eyes. They were Tom's eyes—brown, not Diana's blue-green. Alabama didn't have Diana's auburn hair, either, but a dull blond closer to Bev's own. Looking at her, she could almost imagine how it would have been if . . .

No.

Familiar footsteps tromped up the front stairs, and Bev hurried to the front door to meet Cleta, the mailwoman. *Letter carrier,* she corrected herself. During the school year, Bev was rarely at home when the mail arrived, but in summer Cleta was sometimes the only person she talked to all day long.

"Hey there," Cleta said, surprised when Bev opened the door. "I didn't expect to find you here today. Thought you were going to Big D."

"I got back early."

"Good for you. Gives you time to enjoy your Saturday instead of battling Dallas traffic."

She handed Bev a bundle of mail and tapped the envelope on the top of the stack. "Sorry about that one. Got misdirected—address was wrong, I guess. By the looks of it you'd think it'd been to China and back." She laughed. "Maybe it has. Anyhow, the envelope got ripped somewhere and somebody taped it back up, but I doubt it was actually tampered with."

Distracted, Bev didn't even look at the letter. "I'd rather you apologized for the junk. All these catalogs! Do so many people actually order things by phone?"

Cleta's gaze rolled toward the sky-blue painted porch ceiling. "Whoo-ee! They certainly do. Mark my words, the day's coming when folks won't leave their La-Z-Boys even to buy groceries. Everything'll come mail order. If that sounds like science fiction, believe you me, it's not. Yesterday I delivered a frozen pot roast packed in dry ice to somebody."

Bev shook her head in amazement and commiseration, and then Cleta hitched her mailbag and marched off down the street.

Bev retreated into the house, going straight for the trash can to deposit the catalogs and junk mail. Then she noticed the letter Cleta had been talking about, and stopped in her tracks. Scotch tape formed a jagged scar on the top of the envelope, but even more notable were the cross-outs and scrawled corrections across the front in different colors of ink, in several hands. *Not at this address. Returned. Redirected.* And at the center, the heart of all the chaos, a familiar loopy handwriting chilled Bev's blood.

Diana's handwriting.

She hadn't seen it in years, except on the occasional letter lying around Gladys's.

Why would Diana have written her? *How* could she have written her?

She squinted at the postmark. It was from early June. The tenth.

The day Diana died?

Spooked panic gripped her as she stared at this missive from beyond. How . . . ?

A breathless moment passed before realistic possibilities occurred to her.

Probably, by the time the letter was sent on its way, Bev was already in St. Louis, and Diana had been gone for twenty-four hours.

She lurched for the kitchen table and sat down,

unable to pull her gaze from the envelope. No zip code, of course. No return address. And Diana had gotten her address all wrong, putting down a street name and number that Bev had lived at when she'd taught, briefly, in San Angelo. 202 Oak Street. The number was scratched out, and the street name. Evidently, the person at 202 Oak Street, New Sparta, had started to open it before realizing the error. Bev had done that once, and had foolishly worried that the postal police would come after her. Maybe this envelope had sat in a drawer before the person taped up the damage and sent it back.

Someone at the post office, someone who knew Bev, must have finally gotten hold of it, because the correct street address appeared in red ink in another hand.

Light-headed and feeling compelled to move, Bev stood, paced to the living room, then pushed aside a bag of buttons and other notions so she could lower herself into a chair at the dining room table. She tapped the letter against the tabletop. Diana had never written her in all these years. What was this—a parting shot? A final dig?

She ripped open the envelope and pulled out a piece of spiral notebook paper with fringe still clinging to the left side. One corner bore a jagged tear from when the sheet had been ripped out. Typical Diana not to bother with stationery. Or neatness. Although this penmanship was beyond bad. It was frightening. Blue ink dipped down the page and up again, heedless of lines, a weaving car of text. Bev frowned and flipped the page. The erratic childish scrawl covered both sides. And then her gaze snagged on the last line.

I'm at the end of my rope, Bevvie.

She turned the paper back over and slapped it down on the table. Vodka and lemonade churned in her stomach.

Could this be the missing suicide note?

No. Diana's death had been an accident. Had to have been—for all the reasons she and her mom had discussed.

But why after all these years would Diana decide to write her, out of the blue, right before her fatal accident? Wasn't that too much of a coincidence?

From the beginning, Bev had suspected suicide. But then she'd met Alabama at the camp, and she doubted. No matter what Diana had done wrong in life, she'd always kept her daughter close. Alabama had been her life. She wouldn't have abandoned her like that.

Or would she?

She wasn't sure she wanted to know. Cold dread filled her. Dread and cowardice. Maybe it would have been better if the letter had stayed lost. But now that the thing was in her possession, what choice did she have but to read it?

It was hard to keep her hand steady as she picked up the page again. Her heart jackhammered, and her eyes strained to focus on the words.

Dear Bev,

You'll probably think I'm crazy, writing to you after all these years. Swear to God, I'm not. You won't believe that.

Maybe you won't even open this letter. You'll see it's from me and toss it. Please don't do that.

Knowing you, you've been wanting an apology from me all these years. Well, here it is. I'm sorry. Really, really sorry. There. But it feels so small, not nearly enough. Do you believe it? Would you believe it if I told you that I've felt that way for a long time? How long I don't know. Longer than you'd think. Since around the time I realized I had screwed up my life pretty much for good and all. I tried to do my best after that, to make up for all the things I messed up earlier, but I guess I didn't go about it the right way. I thought I could keep going forward without bothering to fix things, fix us, and repair all the damage I left behind.

Because how could I have done that? Tom died and you hated me and I understood all that. I'm sure you still do hate me. Why shouldn't you?

If it makes you feel better, I don't like me, either.

Well, I still can't fix the past. I can't fix anything. Everything I touch, I ruin. That's the truth. You knew it all along, but it's taken me a whole lot longer to figure myself out. I can't get things right. I lost my job last month and I can't find another that's not minimum wage. Alabama and I can't live on that, and I can't ask Mama for money again, I just can't. I've already bled her dry. The one thing I'm good at— sucking the life out of people. You know that as well as anyone.

There's only one positive thing that's come out of my life. Alabama. She's all that's left. But she deserves more than this, doesn't she? More than me, I mean. I was a better mom than I was a sister, but I guess you know how little that adds up to. When I look at her I sometimes wonder, how long till she's as messed up as me?

And this is the really hard part, the part I haven't wanted to face until now. That maybe all my problems are a result of me doing such a terrible thing. I mean, she should have been yours, shouldn't she? I started to write this so I could ask you to take care of Alabama. But maybe that's not right. Maybe I should ask you to take her back. Take back what I stole from you. Will you do that?

I wish I had the nerve to ask you over the phone. Or in person. But I can't do that. On top of everything else, I'm a coward. You'll understand when you read this.

Will you tell Alabama I did my best? Even if my best wasn't all that great? Will you tell her I love her when I can't?

Or better yet, just make her feel loved. And safe. And happy. I think I managed to do that sometimes. But not anymore. I can't seem to manage anything anymore.

I worry she won't understand. That she'll hate me. Do you think she'll hate me? I don't know what else to do. I'm at the end of my rope, Bevvie.

Bev read the letter over and over until a strange sound made her tilt her head. It was only then she realized that the sound was the keening cry coming from her own throat.

Diana had sat in her apartment, her disgusting apartment, writing this. When? Maybe it was the last thing she had done. Twelve hours later, Bev had arrived. By then, Diana had been taken away, but the glass and bottle she'd been drinking from were still on her coffee table. She'd drunk that gin, written that letter, and then staggered out to a mailbox. And then she'd done it.

I wish I had the nerve to ask you over the phone.

If only she had found the nerve! If she'd called Bev—or called Mama, or *someone*—maybe they could have talked her out of it. Of course, Bev would have been the last person she'd reach out to. . . .

The thought stopped her cold. Diana *had* reached out to her. This letter probably represented not only her sister's last will and testament, but also her last words, maybe her last thoughts. And they'd been of Alabama, the daughter she was leaving behind. Purposefully.

How could Diana have done that? How could she have been so selfish, so . . .

She rose on wobbling legs and staggered as far as the couch, where she curled up in a heap. How could this have happened? How had they traveled from those button-cute girls in matching scratchy Easter dresses to this? *I was her big sister, I should have taken care of her. Watched over her.*

Forgiven her.

Too late now.

Now there was only Alabama. What had Diana said? *She's all that's left.* For weeks, Bev had felt a growing frustration that Gladys wouldn't give up on the idea of taking care of Alabama herself.

She hadn't been able to figure out why this bothered her, much less put the uncomfortable feeling into words. She'd simply felt that it should have been her responsibility. Now she wondered if it hadn't been her sister haunting her conscience.

The *brrrrrringggg* of the telephone whiplashed her upright. Her hand groped for the princess phone on the table, which she answered with a dazed "Hello?"

The snuffling over the line confused her at first. She'd been expecting Derek to call. They usually got together on the weekend.

"Who is this?" Bev asked.

"It's me," a familiar voice answered.

For a moment, Bev's heart stopped.

Diana?

"Alabama." The name came out more like a croak, as if Alabama was on the verge of crying. And there were noises in the background. People talking in loud, urgent voices.

Bev's nerves jumped in alarm. "What's wrong?"

"It's Gladdie. They're going to take her to the hospital. She—" Alabama broke off and silence stretched over the line.

"Alabama?" The handset shook in her trembling hand. "Hello?"

"Gladdie's . . ." Alabama's voice cracked again. "She . . . she's having some kind of attack."

79

CHAPTER 4

Alabama rode in the back of the ambulance, perched on a narrow seat as an EMS guy hovered next to Gladdie, taking her vital signs. Now that she was strapped to a gurney, Gladdie questioned the seriousness of her condition. "I probably just have indigestion," she said, before closing her eyes and shuddering as if a bulldozer of pain were rolling over her.

"Mm-hm," the EMS guy said, unconvinced.

The driver hadn't turned on the ambulance's siren, but the vehicle made rattling noises Alabama didn't understand until the emergency guy turned to her.

"Are you okay?"

She gulped. "Me?"

The rattling stopped momentarily and she realized where the sound had originated—from her own teeth clacking together like dice in a Yahtzee cup.

The rest of the way, she focused on maintaining an outward calm. Or at least not shaking visibly or audibly. It took a lot of effort, because her insides had jellied. Even holding herself upright required effort.

Mom. Wink. And now Gladdie.

She was the angel of death.

An unspoken prayer tapped through her head

like Morse code, over and over. *Please don't let her die, please don't let her die, please don't let her die. I'll do anything.*

At the hospital, they rolled Gladdie away almost immediately. Vomiting in the emergency room got results, evidently. After that, a woman behind the admitting desk peppered Alabama with questions about Gladdie. *Address?* Alabama didn't even know the street address of The Villas. *High blood pressure? Medications? Family doctor? Supplemental insurance?* The woman asked the information in a rushed manner, not paying attention to the fact that the person she was talking to was only fourteen.

"I don't know anything," Alabama finally said. "You'll have to wait for my aunt. She's on her way. She lives in a place called New Sparta? She'll know."

The thought of Aunt Bev's arrival bumped her anxiety level up a notch, and yet she was impatient for her to get there because she felt so useless. So helpless.

The woman said they had taken Gladdie in for diagnostics and Alabama would have to wait, so Alabama hovered in a hall near the emergency admitting area. Worrying. Dreading.

This was all her fault. The whole moving scheme had been her brainchild. House hunting in the heat of the afternoon, which had obviously worn out Gladdie? Alabama's idea had instigated

81

it all. Then Woodrow, her grandmother's ancient friend, had taken them out to a late lunch— Italian food, Alabama's favorite—and Gladdie had appeared exhausted but had insisted they live it up and even have cheesecake for dessert, as a treat for Alabama.

I should have said I wanted to go back. What if Gladdie died because of her?

Standing there in the emergency wing's main hallway, white fluorescent tedium punctuated with tragedy, she lost track of time. She couldn't say if it had been minutes or hours when she looked down the corridor and saw Aunt Bev bearing down on her. All other activity blurred— the nurses bustling past in scrubs, the people sitting in various postures of impatience or pain in the waiting room, the man attached to an IV shuffling down the hallway. Her vision zeroed in on Aunt Bev's clench-jawed, mottled-red face . . . and also her outfit. Mostly the outfit. A white skirt and a belted oversized blue jean shirt with a big red ladybug appliqué on it. As the bug barreled closer, Alabama tried to speak . . . but nothing came out. Her mouth was sand. She braced herself for the blistering accusations she knew were coming. Bev had been against her and Gladdie's plans from the beginning, and now look.

Her aunt steamed within a few feet of her without seeming to slow down. Did she intend to run her over, to crush her with anger?

Before impact, Alabama closed her eyes, and in the next second she was choking in a cloud of Youth Dew. Her aunt grabbed her by the shoulders, pulled her noodly body into hers, and squeezed. A moment passed before Alabama realized that this was a sympathy hug, not a punishment.

"You poor thing!" Bev sobbed. "I'm so sorry! I'm so sorry!"

In Bev's boa constrictor embrace, it took effort to breathe, never mind figure out what Bev had to be sorry for. Alabama tried to back up a step, but the wall was right behind her. She was trapped. "The doctors are still trying to figure out what's wrong," she squeaked. "They're running tests."

Bev released her finally and dug through her big denim purse for a Kleenex. "You poor thing," she repeated, honking into her tissue. "I feel so terrible. I should have been here for you. . . ."

Why? Alabama wondered. *I'm not the one who's sick.*

Bev blew her nose again and stuffed the tissue into her skirt pocket as a doctor in a white lab coat approached them. He knew right away that Bev was the person to talk to.

"Mrs. Putterman is . . . ?"

"My mother," Bev said.

"We're taking your mother in for surgery now. She's had a gallbladder attack. Rather severe—the sonogram shows stones and acute inflammation. After the surgery, we'll keep her here for several days, but there will be a significant recovery period, even if all goes well."

Bev's face pinched in worry. "Oh dear. Well, perhaps I can take her home with me."

The doctor was already edging away from them. "I'll give you an update after the surgery."

They trudged back to the waiting area and kept up a vigil there for hours, Bev drinking vending machine coffee and Alabama munching listlessly through a package of Bugles.

"Do people die from gallbladders?" Alabama asked.

Bev reacted as if she'd been poked in the back. "Die? Mama's not going to die. She's having surgery so she won't die, or get sick again. She . . ." Her gaze met Alabama's and all of a sudden she reached over and seized her. Bugles went flying and Bev clasped Alabama to her bosom so that Alabama found herself nose to nose with the ladybug. "Don't worry," she cooed tearfully. "Your Gladdie will be fine."

Alabama wrestled herself free. "I was just asking."

Bev sat back and watched her with an uncertain look.

"Really," Alabama assured her. "*I'm* okay."

Bev, on the other hand, looked like she was going to fall apart.

After that, the wait seemed even longer. Alabama took care to get up, stretch, and sit back down two seats away from Bev. The next time her aunt became overemotional and wanted to hug, she'd have to hurdle over a man with an oozing head wound to get to her.

Before midnight, a different doctor in green scrubs came out to tell them that the surgery had been a success. They were allowed to see Gladdie in the recovery area, but she was groggy and a nurse shooed them away after a few minutes.

They drove back to The Villas. Even though Alabama had lived there for weeks, without Gladdie there she felt like an intruder.

"You poor baby!" Bev said as Alabama dug through her suitcase to get the tee she used as a nightshirt. "What a day you've had—and tomorrow will be another long one."

She enunciated those last words with such maudlin relish, they shot through Alabama like sonic doom.

"Why?"

"We need to get up early to start packing the car," Bev explained. "So you'll be ready to come back to New Sparta with me."

This was her aunt's plan: Alabama would go immediately to live with Bev in New Sparta, with Gladdie to follow as soon as the doctors released her from the hospital. Then, after she recovered, Gladdie would return to Dallas while Alabama remained. She would enroll in school there.

Probably Bev hoped she would get stuck there and become her latest craft project.

Alabama had other ideas, but she had to be realistic. Staying in Dallas while Gladdie was hospitalized was a battle she couldn't win. Maybe this was part of the bargain she'd made in the ER. *I'll do anything,* she'd prayed. Welcome to anything.

But surely she could come back once Gladdie was released?

She hadn't predicted how awful Gladdie would appear when they visited her. She was flat on her back in a bed that had bars like a stainless steel crib, with only a curtain between her and someone wheezing on the other side of it. An IV tube dripped into her arm—an arm that looked more slack and veiny than Alabama had noticed before. Her face was paler than it had seemed the previous night, even.

My fault.

Gladdie's reddish-blue eyelids fluttered uncertainly before she stared up at them leaning over her.

"How are you feeling?" Bev asked in a loud voice.

"They took out my gallbladder, not my eardrums."

A geyser of nervous chuckles spewed out of Bev. "That's the way, Mama—laughter is the best medicine."

Gladdie's lips tensed in a grim line. As her eyes met Alabama's, her gaze conveyed so much—exhaustion, irritation, resignation. Her grandmother's thin hand covered hers, giving it a feeble squeeze, and Alabama felt guilty for the depression and anger she'd been prey to all morning. Being taken away to New Sparta sucked, but Gladdie was way worse off.

"Done in by a cheesecake," Gladdie said.

"We'll get you out of here."

" 'Course we will," Bev said. "In a week or so, you'll be home with us."

Weak Gladdie might have been, but Bev's words seemed to clear the fog of morphine and give her a jolt of strength. "I'll be returning to The Villas in a week or so."

"But you'll need someone to take care of you," Bev argued.

"I can stay at the health center."

Following her bout of pneumonia, the health center at The Villas was the place Gladdie had dreaded most. And now she was going there again willingly rather than stay with Bev.

New Sparta must be quite a town.

"You said you hated the health center," Bev said. "Let me look after you this time."

"I'm not ready to live the rest of my life on a rocking chair on your front porch, Bev." Before Bev could lodge her protest, she added, "Besides, that house of yours isn't big enough for all three of us." Gladdie looked at Alabama. "I'm sorry. Our plans will have to be . . . postponed."

Alabama nodded quickly. "That's okay." *Postponed.* That word gave her hope, even if it was contradicted by the dull resignation in Gladdie's eyes.

"When the wind's not in our favor, we adjust our sails," Bev said, a determined smile on her lips.

After that, the visit seemed to drag. No one really knew what more to say.

"Can we get you anything, Mama?" Bev asked as they were about to leave for lunch.

Gladdie swallowed and blinked. "No thank you."

"Would you like us to turn on the television?"

"Good Lord, no." From her tone, Alabama would have guessed she never watched TV. Television would have been better than listening to the wheezer, in her opinion.

"You can't just lie there," Bev argued.

"I can if I want," Gladdie said petulantly.

Her aunt backed down. "Well . . . we're heading out to The Villas to load up Alabama's things. We'll come back this afternoon on our way out of town."

"You should go straight home," Gladdie said. "You don't want to get stuck in traffic."

"It's Sunday," Bev reminded her. "We'll be back."

At The Villas they loaded up Bev's tiny car with

as much of Alabama's stuff as possible. When Bev wasn't paying attention, Alabama slipped down to the garage, to Gladdie's rarely used Buick, and retrieved the shoe box containing her grandmother's cassettes from the front seat.

She was on the way back up in the elevator when it stopped on the ground floor to let in a ghost.

At least, Wink startled her as much as a ghost would have. A ghost in light green pants and a pink plaid shirt. "Well, if it's not my little lifesaver!" he said, beaming.

Not a ghost, then. Confusion flustered her. "I-I didn't save you. The health center guys did." There was a small bandage on his throat to testify to that fact.

But he was alive! She'd thought she would never see him again. Maybe she wasn't the angel of death after all. She wanted to hug him, but that would have been too weird, so she smiled.

"They told me you called health center," Wink said.

"Well, yeah . . . any moron could have done that."

"But not just any moron did, did they?" Wink laughed and pressed the button for his floor, which was one above Gladdie's. "How's Gladys?"

She shrugged. "She had gallbladder surgery. I guess she'll be all right."

"Sure she will! That's one of those things

nobody really needs—tonsils, appendix, gall-bladders. Better off without 'em."

"But she's stuck in the hospital, and my aunt's taking me away to New Sparta. . . ." Her voice broke, leaving her feeling like an idiot.

Wink grabbed her shoulders and squeezed them. For once, the look in his eye was dead serious. "Don't you worry. I'll go visit your grandmother every day—every day, do you hear me?—and try to keep her spirits up. I'll even bring my ukulele."

Gladdie'll love that.

"Starting tomorrow," he promised. "And tell her to phone me if there's anything she needs, you hear?"

The doors opened on Gladdie's floor.

"Okay," she said. "I'll tell her."

Warn her.

He grinned, and she hurried away so quickly that she stumbled on the hallway carpet.

"See you next trip!" Wink called after her.

When Alabama and Bev stopped back at the hospital on the way out of town, Gladdie looked even more glum than she had that morning. To cheer her up, Alabama blurted out, "Guess what? Wink's not dead."

Her grandmother lifted slightly in surprise, then winced. "He's not?"

"I met him in the elevator at The Villas. He looked the same as always."

"There now," Bev said. "You see? Another medical miracle!"

"He said he's going to come visit you."

Gladdie's forehead wrinkled with apprehension. "What would he do that for?"

Alabama shrugged. "He also said to call if you needed anything."

"Why would I need anything?" Gladdie looked perturbed. "And if he's going to pop up at any time with that ukulele of his . . . well, that's going to be a lot of botheration."

Alabama hadn't even mentioned the ukulele.

"I think it's nice," Bev said. "And don't dismiss music as therapy. It can do a world of good."

"You've never heard him play that thing," Gladdie grumbled.

The talk about music made Alabama remember the shoe box. She took out the paper grocery sack she'd brought with her that contained her Walkman and the box, picked out *The Sound of Music* sound track, and inserted it into the player. Of Gladdie's music, it was Alabama's favorite. It always reminded her of when they'd show the movie on television when she was a kid. It was usually Sunday night, and her mom would make a big event of it—they'd get a pizza delivered and change into their pajamas, and half the time Alabama would be stuffed and asleep on the couch by the end. She'd been eleven before she'd seen for herself that the von Trapps made it to Switzerland.

But Gladdie didn't know what was in the Walkman, and her gaze darted suspiciously at the device, even as Alabama explained, "I'm leaving you my antisocial doodah," which was what Gladdie had dubbed it. She placed the metal headband over Gladdie's permanent wave, attached the orange foam headphones to her ears, and turned it on.

In a few seconds, Gladdie's eyes widened and she said too loudly, "Now I see what these contraptions are good for!"

Alabama smiled. Then she put the rest of her cassettes and a bag of orange slices on Gladdie's side table, bent down, and kissed her good-bye.

For weeks Alabama had been numb, but during that first drive from Dallas to New Sparta, she was practically having an out-of-body experience. Her head kept going all Shirley MacLaine-y, imagining she was floating outside the car, watching herself slumped in the shotgun seat, wishing herself anywhere else.

All that time at Gladdie's, a part of her had felt as if what was happening was a bad dream. That at any moment her mom would waltz through the door. Okay, she knew that wouldn't actually happen. She'd seen her mother in the funeral home, endured the funeral, and had been at the graveside. But the true finality of it hadn't really sunk in until now, when she was yet another step removed from her mom. She'd never see her again. Never meant forever.

Aunt Bev didn't seem to notice that her passenger was astral projecting. She was all positive thoughts and big plans—voiced in that grating first-day-of-kindergarten tone she had.

"You'll have plenty of time to get settled and registered for school before it starts." Alabama's lack of enthusiasm didn't have any visible effect on her aunt's sidewise smile. "What are your favorite subjects?"

Alabama shrugged.

"Come on now, *everybody* has a favorite subject. I bet you're smart enough to make honor roll." She cast a few expectant glances her way, but Alabama didn't give her any satisfaction. "Or are you the athletic type?"

Alabama was the opposite of athletic—she was a PE hypochondriac. Any ploy to get her to the bleachers would do. When the cramps excuse had worn thin, she'd moved on to headaches, stomachaches, back spasms, and shooting pains in her legs. She'd perfected a wincing limp that had fooled more than one gym teacher.

"Don't like sports, either?" Poor Aunt Bev. She was performing a monologue. "Do you sing? I direct the school choir."

Alabama's mouth twitched into a smirk.

But then she remembered her mom, who said she'd always wanted to be a dancer. Diana had taken classes in school, and she'd taught Alabama a few steps. She'd even sent Alabama to a tap class one summer—a big splurge. Her mom always said Alabama was more graceful than she looked. At the time, the comment had bumped Alabama's bs meter off the charts, since *looking* graceful seemed sort of the whole point of *being* graceful. Now she embraced the possibility that she was more than she seemed. More like her mom . . . or at least what her mom dreamed of being.

"I want to be a dancer," she announced, trying out the sound of it.

Bev did a double take, doubt all over her face. "Really."

Alabama eyed her steadily, daring her to voice her skepticism.

"I mean . . . that's fine, of course. So healthy! But it reminds me of . . ."

Alabama narrowed her eyes.

Bev swallowed. "That's terrific."

Mom still makes her uncomfortable. From guilt, obviously. Whatever Bev did that had caused Diana to flee her home was still eating at her conscience.

It was a good thing New Sparta was only an hour's drive from Dallas, because it looked like the kind of place you'd want a quick escape route from. Bev pointed excitedly to the city limits sign—POPULATION 8,482, not a number that raised Alabama's drooping spirits—and gave her a guided tour of the pathetic outskirts, where a housing development, a couple of second-tier fast food joints, and the Walmart were located. To Alabama's relief, Bev confessed she didn't actually live in the "good" part, but had one of the older houses closer to downtown. Unfortunately, downtown turned out to be a joke—a courthouse, abandoned storefronts, a doomed dime store, and a Western Auto. Even the movie theater just had one screen. She and her mom had always lived in big cities. Now she felt like a hamster being demoted from a Habitrail to a shoe box.

Before they got to the house, Bev circled the school: a network of older brick edifices, portable structures, and a modern one-story building. "The stadium behind the school is where the Fightin' Jackrabbits play."

"Wow," Alabama said. "You guys have a scoreboard and everything."

"Of course." A beat late, Bev laughed. "Oh—I get it. Sarcasm." She reached over and squeezed her knee. "I know who you got *that* from!"

Alabama sucked in a breath, wishing for nothing more than to reach the house so she could flee the car. Then, a few minutes later, they were pulling up in front of a tidy wood-frame home, and she wished Bev would turn the car around and drive somewhere else. This place was *so* not her. Butter-yellow paint. A porch festooned with potted begonias and impatiens, with a smiling sun cut-out hanging on the blue front door. Precious. She stepped out into the steamy late-afternoon air and marched up the petunia-lined walkway like a prisoner on the way to a *Good Housekeeping*–approved death house.

Aunt Bev didn't get it. She was too busy playing tour guide, showing off what little there was to see. The house was a box—living room and kitchen on one side, two bedrooms separated by a bathroom on the other. The bedroom designated for her was as plain and bare as a cell. Four white walls and a twin bed—a daybed covered with a cheery yellow spread—and a painted yellow dresser.

She made a mental note to despise the color yellow, starting now.

"I know about teenagers and their rooms," Bev explained. "You'll have a million ideas for how you'll want it to look. It's your space, so don't worry that I'll interfere."

"Is there a lock on the door?"

Bev blinked at her. "No." Alabama shrugged, and was ready to collapse on the bed when her aunt asked, "Why don't we peek at the rest of the house? Get your bearings."

Alabama trudged after her, taking in the living room—a nightmare of elaborate slipcovers and upholstery experiments, needlework pillows and shadowboxes full of cutesy garage sale finds. A seashell mobile hung in one corner. The really surprising thing was the mess—Bev had been so snooty about the apartment in St. Louis, but here there was loads of clutter and crafty crap strewn everywhere. Bolts of cloth propped in corners. Unpainted wood stacked in the living room. Boxes on the dining room table marked BUTTONS, RIBBONS, and MISC. Lots of MISC.

In front of the double doors leading to the backyard, wedged next to the dining room table, stood an old dressmaker's dummy, looking like a headless torso that had been impaled on a hat rack.

Bev saw her staring at it and laughter trilled out of her. "Let me introduce Rhoda." She put her hand on the wooden knob that was the thing's neck stump. "I named her after Rhoda Morgenstern on *The Mary Tyler Moore Show*. Isn't she fun? I wish I could have dressed her up for you."

It would have been better if she had draped something over that pinky-beige torso. An old spill had stained one of the bumps that were supposed to be breasts, and a Frankenstein scar cut across the abdomen where the material had been torn and resewn.

Bev dropped her hand abruptly. "Well. I guess we should fix some dinner."

"I'm not hungry," Alabama said, but that didn't stop Bev from marching toward the kitchen.

Cabinets opened and closed as her aunt half hummed, half sang "Billie Jean."

Slouching against the door frame, Alabama took in the kitchen. It was done in sandy peach and pale earthy greens, attempting more or less to replicate a Southwestern look, judging from all the stenciling on the cabinets and walls.

"You have to eat," Bev told her. "At least a little bit. And then I'll fix a dessert. Derek's probably coming over."

"Who's Derek?"

Puddles of red leaped to Bev's cheeks as she stood back from the open fridge door. "He's my friend. My *very good friend,* if you know what I mean."

Alabama frowned. "I thought his name was . . ." She couldn't remember. "Not Derek. Glen, maybe?"

"Glen!" Bev's eyes widened. "Who told you *that?*"

Who did she think? "Gladdie."

"Well." Bev shook her head. "Mama wouldn't know a thing about it."

The Secret Life of Bev Putterman.

Ick.

Bev rushed over to her. "I really want you to like Derek. And for him to like you, too, of course."

Alabama didn't know what to say to that. She couldn't exactly promise to like someone she hadn't met yet, could she?

Bev turned back to the counter. "I bet you'll go crazy for my spaghetti and meatballs. It's one of my specialties. And for dessert I've got peach cobbler. I bought scads of peaches at a stand the other day and made a few things. I preserve and freeze a lot during the summer. Makes meal preparation during the school year a snap-a-rooni."

She was so nervous, it was painful to watch.

"I'm really not hungry," Alabama repeated.

"You will be when you smell that scrumdiliumcious peach cobbler bubbling in the oven. And we've got Bluebell ice cream to go on top."

Her stomach was actually rumbling, but what Alabama really wanted was to grab the tub of ice cream and a spoon and run off and be by herself.

"I'll go empty out the car," she said.

"Oh!" Bev swiveled on her heel. "I'll help you."

Alabama cut her off. "No—I can get it. Stay with your meatballs. I'll have to try those."

That managed to repulse her aunt's advance. Thank God.

Alabama emptied the car of all the boxes and then hid in her room until Bev flushed her out at dinnertime.

Derek was late, but he called and told them to start without him. The meal was served at the cramped table in the corner of the kitchen. The dining room table was reserved for events, Bev explained, as Alabama picked over spaghetti and grayish meatballs dandruffed with parmesan from a green shaker container.

"Tomorrow we can go shopping and buy you all the things you like," she said, noting that Alabama wasn't making a dent in the plate of food.

"I'm not a big eater." At least, not of *Ladies' Home Journal* food.

"You need to watch that. You don't want to end up like . . ." Bev broke off, her expression stricken.

"Karen Carpenter?" Alabama finished for her.

Her aunt shook her head and took a long sip of iced tea. "I *loved* her. Well—I might as well say I *love* her, because I still do. That's the point of art, isn't it? It lives on, even when . . ." Her eyes glistened with tears. "Such a waste! Last semester I spent a day on Karen in health class. I played 'Rainy Days and Mondays' during the anorexia discussion. Some girls cried."

Alabama was beginning to think she should just eat the meatball.

On the wall, the cat clock's tail swished back and forth extra-slowly. How could it not even be seven yet? She wouldn't be able to go to bed for hours.

Then she remembered Gladdie. This day probably had seemed a hundred times longer to her. She sent up a prayer for Gladdie's speedy recovery. Maybe this move to New Sparta wouldn't be permanent. If Gladdie got better, there was no reason why they couldn't go ahead and look for an apartment in Dallas, like they'd planned.

The doorbell rang, and Bev hopped up. "That'll be Derek. Come on out and meet him."

Before dinner Bev had changed into a fresh skirt and button-down blouse and spritzed herself with perfume, which added a sticky sweet odor to the scents of tomato sauce and baking peaches. Now she fluttered to the door and opened it, admitting a stocky guy with dark blond hair and a bushy mustache. The mustache ran all the way across his upper lip and spilled over the corners of his mouth onto his cheeks, so that he appeared to be frowning even as he smiled.

There was no mistaking the wary, slightly dazed expression in his eyes. Not a fan of kids, Alabama guessed. "You're older than I expected," he said.

"I'm fourteen."

"She's going to be starting high school this year," Bev said with an anxious grin.

One of his bushy eyebrows darted up, and he dug his hands into his Levis. "Everything all right, then?"

Alabama didn't know how to answer, so Bev darted in. "Oh yes!" Then, on second thought, she frowned. "I mean, no. Mama's in the hospital. The doctors are saying that recovery might take a while. I want to bring her home with us, but she's determined to stay in Dallas."

"Probably a good thing," Derek said.

Bev's smile reappeared. "But Alabama's here to stay."

"Temporarily," Alabama said.

Derek swung back to her. "Alabama's an unusual name. Unless you're a state." He laughed.

Ha ha. No one had ever thought of *that* before. "I was named after 'Moon of Alabama.' That's a song."

His shoulders hunched. "Don't know it."

"It's Jim Morrison," she said.

He snorted. "That's why I don't know it." Tired of the conversation, or Alabama, he headed for the kitchen, specifically the fridge. He found a bottle of Dos Equis, opened it, and sat down. Bev placed a plate of spaghetti in front of him, and he dived right in, not even waiting for them to join him.

When they did, he seemed uncomfortable. "No point in us sitting here staring at each other all night. Y'all want to watch *Knight Rider*?"

Bev sprang to her feet again and snatched up his plate to carry it to the living room. "I forgot all about that. There's been so much drama this past day, I'm surprised my head's still screwed on." She was almost into the living room when she turned back. "Get yourself some cobbler, Alabama. I don't mind eating in front of the television, if it's a special occasion."

Alabama tried to think what the occasion was.

Knight Rider? Or her arrival, or Derek's being there?

She grabbed a bowl and picked the chair farthest from the television. Derek and Bev were on the couch, with Bev on the middle cushion, creating a lopsided effect.

"Isn't this nice?" Bev asked. "It's like we're a little family."

Alabama stabbed a piece of cobbler but couldn't force herself to eat it. Even when her mom had boyfriends, she'd never said they were part of the family. Family meant the two of them, Alabama and her mom, and Gladdie far away. Now she was by herself, and Gladdie was still far away, and her mom . . .

Will I ever step onto an elevator and find Mom there?

She watched David Hasselhoff through a blur.

She didn't belong here.

She'd been prepared to feel out of place, and sad. She'd been sad for weeks, so that was nothing new. What surprised her was the anger.

Rage welled in her. Frustration at being fourteen and not in control of her own life. Anger at Bev and her smothering personality. She even felt hacked off at gallbladders, and Gladdie.

But those things paled in comparison to the fury that boiled in her veins, all of a sudden, over her mom. What was the one thing a mother was supposed to get right? *Protecting her child.* And yet Alabama was at the mercy of the person Diana had hated most. Her archenemy. And she felt helpless. All these people around her—Gladdie, and Bev, and even somebody like Derek—they all had their impenetrable adult crusts protecting them, goofy or grouchy personality armor as tough as that stupid car's on the TV screen. Alabama always considered herself smart and able to take care of things. Mature. But next to these people who now held her life in their hands, she was like a newly formed Play-Doh person, barely solid and likely to get smooshed.

This was her mom's fault. She'd been so care-less . . . careless with drinking, careless crossing the street, careless with her life. Half the time while growing up, Alabama had felt as if she was taking care of her mom. Of both of them. Why? Why should she have had to do that?

Unexpectedly, the rage doubled back on herself. *Why did I have to go to that stupid camp? I should have been with Mom, at home. Maybe then she might not have . . .*

She bit her lip so hard she tasted blood.

What was she going to do for the rest of her life without her mom?

How was she going to survive this? She had no one.

She jumped off the couch, hurried to the kitchen, and dumped what was left of her cobbler into the trash. Before she could turn around from the garbage can, Bev was hovering near, her face pinched and anxious. "Is everything all right?" her aunt asked.

"I'm tired. And I don't like that show."

"Would you rather watch *Murder, She Wrote*?"

"I just want to go to my room."

"That's completely okay," Bev said. "Of course you can be excused."

Excused?

Resentment spiked in Alabama's chest. "Am I supposed to ask permission every time I want to get up? Do I need a hall pass?"

In a flash, she realized she'd made everything more tense. What's more, she didn't care. She was glad.

Bev's eyes became saucers, wounded and defensive. "No, of course not. I was only trying to say I don't mind . . ."

If her aunt had been someone she liked, Alabama might have apologized, or at least backed off. Instead, she remembered her mom and felt a surge of satisfaction to be striking a blow for the home team. "I'd like to be excused now, Miss Putterman."

Lip curled, she scuttled out. In her room, she tossed herself facedown on the bed, her breaths coming in ragged gulps as she inhaled the scent of the unfamiliar laundry detergent in the bedding. Everything was foreign here. She didn't have a home anymore—only a place she was being parked till she was an adult. Which she couldn't wait to be. She wanted to be old.

Low voices filtered through the closed door, the words indistinct. Derek's gruff rumble rose in spiky inflection, and Alabama imagined him asking "What the hell's wrong with her?" A little while later, the volume dropped, until she couldn't distinguish anything over the sounds of the television.

Maybe they'd gone out to the kitchen or even outside to discuss her.

Or maybe they weren't talking about her at all.

Maybe she didn't matter to anyone anymore. Maybe she really was all alone in the world.

CHAPTER 5

"Alabama, it's time to go."

Grumbles sounded from inside the bedroom. Except for those moments when Alabama would jerk it open and quickly slam it shut again, the door always remained closed. The girl might claim to dread attention, but when she wasn't semi-comatose, she tended toward oversized gestures, like a character in a French farce.

This wasn't how she'd behaved in Dallas. Gladys had said she was so helpful, so mature. Ha.

Bev despaired. Not just for today—although she hated getting a late start on Dallas days—but for their future. It had been two weeks since Alabama moved in, and their relationship had stalled out at a tense standoff. The source of the friction remained a mystery. Bev had tried, Lord knows. She didn't complain when everything from Jim Morrison to Prince thumped from the phonograph player in Alabama's room at house-quaking volumes. (She missed the Walkman.) Her lip remained firmly buttoned when Alabama didn't help her around the house, and even sat sulking while Bev did everything. Her helpful rug-cleaning days ended when she'd left The Villas, apparently. She had even sat through *The Breakfast Club* twice at the local movie theater, even though she found the film crude and a woefully one-sided depiction of high school. She did things like that for Alabama, but Alabama rebuffed her attempts to establish camaraderie between them.

Alabama hurled herself out of her room, landing on the couch with a thump to stuff her feet into a pair of ancient sneakers. "I don't know why we have to leave so early."

"We'll have more time to spend with Gladdie."

"More time to run dumb errands, you mean." Alabama sighed. "Craft stores. Fabric stores."

In the past weeks, it had become apparent that she and Alabama weren't interested in the same things. Unfortunately, Bev couldn't quite discern exactly what Alabama was interested in.

In the car, after they were buckled in, Bev announced that they needed to gas up. Alabama sank down in the passenger seat. "You couldn't have done that while I was getting ready?"

"Certainly—if I had known it would take you so long to put on a T-shirt and shorts that I could travel to the gas station and back at least eight times."

Alabama turned slowly, aiming that cold stare Bev's way, and for a moment Bev's words echoed around the car's interior, making her blush at the snippy sound of them. That was another thing about Alabama. She made her feel so old, so nerdy and naggy, so uncool. She rolled her eyes at expressions Bev used, and her hooded gaze seemed to hold Bev's clothes and activities in constant contempt. As a single, modern woman, Bev had never questioned her up-to-dateness. And she *was* cool—more so than a lot of adults, at least. A person couldn't spend a lifetime in a high school without absorbing teen lingo and mannerisms and being pretty darn hip to youth culture.

Maybe things would get better when school started. Much as she cherished her summers, fall's approach always hailed a new beginning, a time for optimism.

She turned into the gas station and was dismayed when a familiar vehicle pulled into the pump directly behind her. Bev jumped out as Glen Hill got out of his car. He smiled at her, and she felt an all-too-familiar tightness squeezing her chest, along with a blush creeping up her neck. Why did she have to run into him like this? Hazards of small town living, she supposed. But the encounters always proved awkward.

"Hi," he called over to her.

She smiled and stuffed the gas pump nozzle into her car. For a moment she breathed in the fumes and was glad for the distraction of watching the dollar total roll slowly higher. This gas station was ancient, but she liked giving her business to the local folks more than to the newer places on the interstate.

Alabama got out of the car. "I'm going to get a

soda," she said. "You want me to pay for the gas?"

"Sure—grab my purse and tell Jimmy I'm getting twelve dollars' worth. And take money for your pop, too. And could you get me a Diet Dr Pepper?"

"Okay." From Alabama's hint of a smile, Bev had the uneasy feeling she'd fallen into a trap.

When Alabama had disappeared, Glen spoke again. "Is that your niece?"

"That's Alabama."

"I'd heard she was staying with you."

New Sparta might be a pokey, dying town, but its grapevine flourished.

She couldn't help casting a furtive glance at him. He looked good—lean and tanned. He'd been out in the sun this summer. *Doing what?* They used to go to his parents' lake house during vacations. She wondered if there was someone else he'd been taking there this year. She'd been so preoccupied with family problems she hadn't been paying attention to local gossip.

His gas pump finished before hers and he strolled over. "I was sorry to hear about your sister. That must have been so difficult for you."

"Thank you."

"I know you two weren't close, but still."

Yes. *But still* . . . Diana's loss hurt more than she could have ever dreamed. She thought about the letter locked away in the bottom of her file cabinet, which she hadn't been able to face reading again. She hadn't told Alabama about it, of course—she couldn't—and she hesitated to show it to her mother until she was feeling 100 percent again. Given how disturbed Gladys had seemed when they'd discussed the possibility of Diana's having taken her own life, she wondered if telling her would ever be a good idea.

I'm at the end of my rope, Bevvie . . .

Why pass those haunting last words to another person? Why burden anyone else with that pain?

She'd even considered burning the letter and holding its sorrows to herself forever.

But strangely, she found herself wanting to open up to Glen. He would know how traumatic it had been for her. He felt things deeply, sometimes a little too deeply. After she'd broken up with him last fall, for instance, he had spent the rest of the school year acting like the walking wounded whenever their paths crossed. Which, in the fishbowl that was New Sparta High, meant constantly.

He didn't look broken up now. Just concerned. He crossed his arms and leaned against her car. "Did she . . . ?"

Bev nodded, and when his big hand clamped around her upper arm, squeezing it in comfort, she bit her lip to hold back tears.

In the next moment, he was clearing his throat and smiling at someone coming toward them. Bev twisted and saw Alabama, her arms loaded down with enough junk food for a road trip to California. She tilted her head cautiously at Glen.

He pushed away from the car and offered her his hand. "Hi, Alabama." The ensuing handshake nearly resulted in an avalanche of snack cakes, soda cans, and candy bars. "I'm Glen. I teach school with your aunt."

"Hi." Alabama's curious gaze studied them both.

A click beneath her hand alerted Bev that the pump was done. She glanced at the total and clucked at her absentmindedness. $14.32. She'd been so distracted, she'd gone over.

"Run and give Jimmy another $2.32, will you?" she asked Alabama.

Alabama paled and shifted legs. "I used all your cash."

All of it? Bev thought there had been more money in her purse than what the gas and even the pile of junk food would have cost. Her money seemed to be disappearing a lot lately. Of course, she didn't want to make accusations without proof. And she certainly didn't want to get into it now, in front of Glen.

"I'll have to write Jimmy a check," she said.

Glen stopped her before she'd taken two steps. "Never mind. I'll give Jimmy the difference when I pay for mine."

"Oh, but—"

He laughed away her objection before she could

even voice it. "Allow me my Galahad moment. They don't usually come as cheap as $2.32."

She relented. "Thank you. I guess I'll see you at school soon anyway. I'll pay you back then."

A cloud crossed his face. "You heard that Lon Kirby got married, didn't you?" Lon was the principal. "His wife, Leah, is a teacher . . . and choir director."

Bev frowned. "In another district."

"Lon hired her for New Sparta this year." He hitched his throat. "I think she might be taking over the choir."

She swallowed. "Oh."

"I'm not positive," he added quickly. "But I got that impression."

How on earth did a person *get the impression* that a person was going to usurp her spot as choir director without it being said flat-out? "When did you hear this?"

"A few weeks ago, at the picnic for Lon's birthday."

She looked away. A picnic she hadn't been invited to.

"I was sorry you couldn't make it," Glen said. Then, after a moment's hesitation, he confessed, "Jackie invited me."

The words jolted Bev. Jackie Kirby was Lon's sister and erstwhile housekeeper, and served as the school's secretary and guidance counselor. Now, with Leah working at the school, too, the three would form a regular Kirby cabal at New Sparta High. Did Glen count himself as part of the inner circle . . . or was he just interested in Jackie? She was pretty, and no doubt at domestic loose ends now that her brother was a newlywed.

She forced a smile. "Alabama and I had better shake a tail feather if we're going to have any kind of day in Dallas. Thank you again for the loan, Glen. I promise to pay it back."

"Forget it," he said. "A friend in need is a friend indeed."

Back in the car, her mind raced. So Jackie was trying to get her claws into Glen. And Lon's new wife was going to take over the choir. *Her* choir. Bev had already spent a few days this summer picking out songs and special numbers they could do.

Lon, a hometown boy made good, had only boomeranged back two years earlier to take the job as principal. The New Sparta equivalent of coming home in a blaze of glory. Unfortunately, he'd disliked Bev from the start. He was one of those newfangled principals who'd spent more time studying theory than actually standing in front of a class teaching—all diploma and no chalk dust, some of the teachers grumbled. His concerns were for grading systems and standardized test scores. And winning things. He'd been withering about the choir's failure to garner any prizes last year, even though several people had told Bev that their showpiece—"Where Did Robinson Crusoe Go With Friday on Saturday Night?"—was one of the cutest things they'd ever heard. Lon had made a joke about Lawrence Welk . . . as if there was anything wrong with a fun, old-fashioned song.

For that matter, what was wrong with Lawrence Welk? The man was a national treasure.

"So there really is a Glen," Alabama said, breaking into her thoughts.

"Did I ever say there wasn't?" Bev asked.

Alabama aimed her gaze out the passenger window, to the last swelling hills before the flat blackland prairie took over the landscape. The car devoured several miles of highway, and then Alabama spoke again. "Was he the guy before Derek?"

Bev shifted uncomfortably. "This is a personal matter."

Alabama let out a snort. "Oh, right. Excuuuuse me." She opened a Twinkie packet and stuffed one in her mouth.

"Is that your breakfast? It's nothing but chemicals."

Alabama smacked her lips. "Yummy chemicals!"

She's trying to get a rise out of me. Exactly the way Diana used to. But Bev wouldn't let her. She gritted her teeth through the popping open of a soda can and the slurping that followed. When Alabama broke into a bag of M&M's, however, Bev could no longer hold her tongue.

115

"I made oatmeal this morning."

In reply, Alabama crunched down on a piece of candy.

"You have to eat *something* nutritious," Bev said.

"I am." Alabama held a green M&M up for inspection. "That's why I got the ones with peanuts."

"They're candy."

"If Glen likes you," Alabama said, backtracking, "why do you have the thing with Derek?"

"Why do you think Glen likes me?"

Alabama shrugged. "I could just tell. He's a lot nicer than Derek."

"You only spoke to him for a minute."

"That's about as much as I've ever spoken to Derek," Alabama said. "Even though he's been to the house three times."

The two had not hit it off. Of course, Derek was naturally a little prickly around strangers, and maybe he wasn't used to being around teenagers. And Alabama hadn't done much more than mope while he was around.

"You have to admit that Derek is better looking."

Alabama's lips scrunched. "He looks like that actor . . ."

"Tom Selleck," Bev said. "I always thought so, too."

"No . . ." She chewed another M&M, thinking. "That other actor—the sleazebag guy."

Sleazebag!

"What's his name?" Alabama frowned in concentration. "The guy who makes the action pictures?"

"Mel Gibson?" Bev guessed.

"Charles Bronson!"

Surprise caused Bev to swerve the car, hitting the shoulder. She opened her mouth to tell her how wrong she was, but Alabama smiled and offered her candy.

"M&M?"

Distracted, Bev held out her hand and Alabama shook a few into her palm. Bev took one and crunched busily for a few moments. Maybe Derek wasn't quite Magnum, p.i., but on the Selleck-Bronson continuum, he definitely fell more toward Selleck.

Not that it matters.

She didn't care about looks. The essence of a person was the important thing. Derek was solid, yet exciting. He'd swept her off her feet. No one like him had ever looked twice at her before. Of course, she couldn't go into sex appeal with a fourteen-year-old. Anyway, Alabama was probably saying she liked Glen better just to be contrary. She didn't know the first thing about him.

Charles Bronson! Derek looked nothing like him. Nothing.

Except for the mustache. And maybe a little around the eyes.

What had Glen been up to back there at the gas station, anyway? Was he trying to panic her? That stuff about the choir might not be official. *She* hadn't heard anything. All Lon would have to do was pick up the phone and call her to let her know. Of course, that's all he would have had to do to invite her to his birthday picnic, and he hadn't done that, either.

"*Death Wish* was an okay movie, though," Alabama said. "I watched that with Mom."

Irritation growing, Bev tightened her grip on the steering wheel. She didn't want to discuss Derek, so she switched topics. "When we get home tonight, you and I need to have a little talk about money."

"Why?"

"I know you've been sneaking money out of my purse." Before Alabama's protest could reach full throttle, she added, "And back there at the gas station, you should have asked me first before buying all that junk in the store."

"It's food. I have to eat."

"Not that, you don't."

Alabama looked like she was going to put up an argument, then stopped and twisted her lip. "So why wait?"

Bev tilted her head. "Wait for what?"

"Why wait till tonight to talk about it? We're sitting here in a car with nothing to do. Do you think by waiting till we get home I'll have had hours to become trembly and sorry for stealing your money? Or do you need more time to think of something to say?"

Bev's jaw dropped in astonishment. Sass like that would have earned her a swat or even a sharp slap when she was young—but she didn't believe in raising her hand to other human beings. Also, she was staggered by the sheer crust of Alabama's retort. She'd admitted to stealing, then added the distracting flourish of an insult at the end.

"I realize that you've been getting by without an allowance," Bev said, pressing forward reasonably. "We should have addressed this earlier. I was thinking I could give you five dollars a week."

Alabama practically crowed. "Wow! Five dollars. Thanks, Auntie Bev! I might be able to go to a movie every once in a while on that."

The sarcasm riled Bev. "I'm not going to give you more money so you can throw it all away. And you have all your food and clothing paid for."

"I do?"

"I was going to make you a few things next month," Bev told her.

Alabama groaned.

Bev stiffened. "Acting ugly is not the way to get what you want."

"You have no idea what I want!"

The outburst blew Bev back a little in her seat. "How could I? You never tell me." Her glance shifted from the road in front of her to her niece's face contorting in incoherent rage.

Finally, Alabama bit out, "I don't want anything. I didn't ask to be here. I'm only staying with you until Gladdie gets better. So you can keep your money—and your dorky clothes. I'm not starting high school wearing insect appliqués and Peter Pan collars. If I need anything, I'll ask Gladdie."

Bev supposed that was supposed to hurt her feelings. Well, an insult only hurt if you let it. She wouldn't let it.

Anyway, she'd already decided she was tired of that ladybug shirt.

In Dallas, she stopped at the fabric store.

"What are we doing here?" Alabama's voice brimmed with exasperation.

"I need batting. I thought I would make you a quilt."

"I have a quilt."

Bev held back a shudder. The "quilt" was some horrid thing Diana had slapped together. Not that she liked to speak ill of the dead—even when it came to their woeful crafting skills—but the thing was atrocious. Diana had taken old clothes and sewn them randomly onto a blanket—old pants and shirts, pajamas, and even one of Alabama's little coats from when she was a toddler. Not *scraps* of the clothes, mind you, but the garments themselves—buttons, zippers, and all. The result was a lumpy mess, and when Alabama threw it over her mattress, it looked as if someone had upended a dirty clothes hamper on the bed.

"I mean a real quilt," Bev said.

"I like mine."

"Well, fine. I have some other things to pick up, too. Meantime, you should look through the pattern books and see if there's anything you'd like." When Alabama opened her mouth to protest, Bev stopped her with, "You may not want anything now, but you'll be whistling a different tune once school starts. You can't wear shorts to school."

Alabama got out of the car and started to trudge toward a convenience store. "I'd rather play Space Invaders."

"I thought you didn't have any money."

"I might have a quarter left."

Bev smiled tightly and held out her hand. "Then you owe it to me."

Alabama blinked. "Seriously?"

"You took the money from my purse. Anyway, you said you didn't want my money."

"You've got to be kidding."

But Bev's unmoving stance forced her to believe. Alabama finally shook her head, dug her hand into her shorts, and slapped the change she came up with into Bev's palm.

It was a small victory, but it felt sweet.

After she'd finished at the fabric store, Bev

drove to a florist to buy a little something to spruce up her mother's room at the health center. Flowers would brighten Gladys's mood, and also give them something pleasant to talk about, if only for a minute or two.

As she and Alabama headed down the hall to Gladys's room, the health center nurse stopped them. "Mrs. Putterman is back in her room."

Bev experienced a moment of confusion. "That's where we're heading now."

The nurse shook her head. "I meant, she's back in her apartment. She said she didn't want to stay in the health center anymore."

"But she needs help," Bev said.

"She said she *has* help." The nurse added apologetically, "It was her decision."

As they made their way back to the main building from the health center, Alabama grinned. "Gladdie escaped!"

Bev couldn't share her glee. "Why didn't she tell me when she called to talk last night? I told her we were coming, and she didn't mention a thing."

"Maybe because she knew you'd react like this."

"Like what?"

"Like a wet blanket."

She could read Alabama's thoughts. If her grandmother was well enough to leave the health center, maybe she was feeling peppery enough to want to move out of The Villas altogether. She would start up that stupid scheme again, and bring Alabama back to Dallas.

Bev frowned. She was so tired. Why should she care anymore? Alabama obviously hated her—hated her even when she was offering her a home and an allowance. Living together had been a disaster. Alabama was no company, and Bev suspected Derek was staying away now because of all the friction. The school year was about to start up again, and if Glen's hints were any indication, that wasn't going to be a picnic, either. She should just let Alabama go. It would be one fewer thing to worry about.

But then those words repeated in her head. *I'm giving her back to you.* Diana's last wish. *I'm at the end of my rope, Bevvie . . .*

At Gladys's apartment, she knocked and settled in to wait for Gladys to make the journey from the bedroom to the door. The last time she'd visited, her mother was getting around slowly with a walker.

But the door was yanked open immediately—by Wink, wearing a light plaid sports jacket, kelly-green pants, and white shoes. He beamed an outsized smile at them. "Well, hi! C'mon in!" he turned and called back, "Hey, Glad-Rags—come have a look! Greeks bearing gifts. Should I let them in or not?"

"Oh, why not?" she called back.

He laughed and ushered them in as if they didn't know the way.

Wink had been a visitor at the hospital and the health center, but for some reason, Bev was surprised to see him in the apartment. Among her mother's things—the sea-foam green velvet furniture, the china cabinet, and shelves of bric-a-brac—he seemed too large, too brash.

"Can I get you young ladies anything?" he asked, playing host.

"I'd like a root beer," Alabama said.

Wink grinned. "Comin' right up."

Frowning, Bev headed back to Gladys's bedroom, and met her coming out of it. "Mama," she whispered, "what are you doing?"

"What do you mean? I'm back home. I'd have thought you'd be glad." She eyed the flowers Bev had brought. "Oh, thank you. You can put those on the table next to Wink's."

Bev eyed the arrangement of bright summer flowers topped with Mylar balloons with cartoon birds on them. Oversized and in questionable taste, just like Wink, Bev thought as she set her modest little spray next to them.

"Mama, how are you going to manage on your own?" she asked in a low voice. "We'll have to hire a private nurse."

"Wink is helping me. He's quite the housekeeper."

"But—" Bev listened to Wink and Alabama

124

talking in the kitchen and lowered her voice to a whisper. "What about helping you with . . . private things?"

Her mother leveled a cold stare on her. "I can go to the toilet on my own. Although he did run a bath for me the other night."

Oh God. He was helping her in the bathroom? "But—"

"Don't be such a prude, Bev. I can manage."

"It's just—"

At that moment, Wink came in with a tray of Gladys's crystal stemware—which Bev had always assumed was merely ornamental, since she'd never seen it used. The toasting flutes were all topped off with root beer. He passed them around. "I thought everybody could use a libation," he said. "Come on, Bev. Take one."

Bev did, and before she knew what she was doing, she'd slugged it back.

Wink laughed. "That's it—down the hatch!"

Gladys settled into her favorite chair, and Alabama sat down on the ottoman next to her. Gladys patted her hand. "Is everything all right with you? How are you getting along?"

"Okay, I guess," Alabama said. "But what about you—don't you need me back here, to take care of you?"

"Oh, I'm managing all right."

"But if you should be in the health center, maybe you need someone like me around."

Gladys leaned toward her. "Between you and me, I wasn't getting much value for my money over there. They charge a twenty-dollar surcharge per day, you know. And that's not counting all the extra costs I've had since the operation."

Alabama frowned, obviously doing calculations. "I guess I cost money when I was staying here, too."

Gladys squeezed her hand. "Worth every penny."

"This is temporary, though, right?" Alabama asked. "I mean, I'm still coming back to Dallas when you're better."

Gladys didn't seem to know how to respond. Bev knew her well enough to know that she'd already made up her mind about something and didn't want to say. Her plain-speaking mother could be as craven as the next person when she dreaded disappointing someone.

"Mama's still recuperating," Bev said, unable to stand the tension. "Nothing's certain. And soon school will start up and you'll be making friends in New Sparta. You might never want to leave."

Alabama slumped a little.

"Let's leave it like this for now," Gladys said.

"Okay," Alabama agreed.

Bev could tell she was still clinging to hope, which broke her heart.

On the other hand, that hope wasn't very flattering to herself.

"Hey!" Wink's exclamation broke the tension in

the air. "How about some canasta? Glad-Rags and I made fudge last night in honor of your visit."

As he bustled around, bringing out the card table from the closet and arranging everything, Bev felt as if they'd fallen into the hands of a very ebullient cruise director. And that her mother had fallen under the spell of either a very nice man or a consummate manipulator. When Wink pulled his chair closer to her mother's than necessary—or desirable in a competitive card came—and Gladys didn't object, Bev and Alabama exchanged glances.

Of course, maybe Gladys was just using him. She'd wanted back in her apartment, and it was handy to have a person nearby to help out. He was someone to talk to, and eager to lend a hand, and tall enough to change lightbulbs. . . .

As these thoughts circled her head, she made bad decisions and lost a hand. Wink burst into a thirties crooner version of "With Plenty of Money and You," and Gladys, bobbing her head joyfully, joined in.

CHAPTER 6

"You have an appointment to see Dr. Land tomorrow," Bev said, darting her head into Alabama's room. "Ten thirty."

Alabama, lying across her bed, frowned. Her one meeting with Dr. Herbert Land, psychologist—better known to her brain as Dr. Bland—had been underwhelming. The man did nothing but sit in a chair behind a desk and ask her boring questions. *How are you feeling? What do you miss about St. Louis?* Cleta the mail lady was more interesting to talk to, and more understanding. Plus Cleta didn't have a distracting Gene Shalit mustache.

Dr. Bland seemed as bored by her as she was by him. When he listened to her, his face barely moved—not even the occasional twitch of the 'stache. After thirty minutes in his puffy suede armchair she knew her future objective would be Bland avoidance. So she'd declared herself fine, perfectly fine, and had walked out hoping never to be sent back.

Where had she gone wrong?

"I didn't make an appointment," she told Bev.

"I did."

"Why?"

"You need someone to talk to."

"Yeah, right. Which is another reason not to go back to Dr. Bland. He doesn't say anything."

"He's a respected doctor—"

"He's a quack."

"—and it's not easy to get an appointment. He's only in New Sparta once a week."

"What's the matter with this place? There aren't enough lunatics to support a full-time shrink?"

Wrong thing to say. Bev rushed forward, her face all concern as she sat down on the bed. Then she winced and shifted off a toggle clasp of Alabama's first-grade coat. "No one thinks you're a lunatic, sweetie."

Alabama rolled her eyes. "I know that."

"I'm just concerned. You've been through so much, and you don't seem to want to share your feelings with me. . . ."

"Where is Dr. Bland usually?" Alabama asked. Anything to veer Bev off the topic of feeling sharing.

"Dallas, I think."

"See? Dallas is probably full of shrinks. When I live with Gladdie, I'll have no trouble getting appointments with quacks."

At the mention of Dallas, anxiety clouded her aunt's expression, and Alabama was pretty sure why.

"You're worried about Gladdie, aren't you?" she asked. "Because you don't like Wink." During their last visit, Wink had been there the entire time.

Bev shrugged, perplexed. "I don't know him. It's . . . odd . . . that they're so friendly all of a sudden. And I guess I'm a little jealous, too. She seems so . . ."

"Happy?" As far as Alabama was concerned, if Bev disliked Wink, he was doing something right. Besides, he'd always been a friend to her. "So what don't you like about him?"

Bev frowned. "It's like my mother's life has been taken over by Rodney Dangerfield. They're so different! And she's vulnerable right now."

"But she needed someone, and he promised to help," Alabama pointed out. "Maybe that's all it is. You should be relieved. She's happier now than before she went in the hospital."

Happier than when I was with her, Alabama grudgingly admitted to herself.

"True," Bev said. "I guess I need to work on my attitude of gratitude."

Alabama studied the room, the posters on the wall—her mom's old concert posters. Most everything was Diana's stuff that she'd saved from the apartment. The things in Alabama's old room in St. Louis hadn't seemed worth the trouble of boxing up, but she couldn't imagine leaving behind her mother's belongings, which she'd been looking at since she was tiny. Her mother had always emphasized the worth of it all—the quality of her turntable, left behind when an old boyfriend had been sent to jail; the fact that her Janis Joplin poster would be worth a fortune someday; the incredible value of a metal lamp that had been a lucky find at Goodwill.

Securing places for all these things had been Alabama's first order of business after moving to New Sparta. They were like voodoo tokens to keep the evil Bevnicity from seeping into her space.

Bev stood up. "I'll drop you off at Dr. Bla—Dr. Land's in the morning on my way to school, but you'll have to make your own way back home. It's not far to walk."

"So why can't I walk *to* the appointment?"

"I want to make sure you get there."

"You mean you don't trust me."

"I simply think it's super-important that you have someone to talk to. Don't you want to talk to somebody?"

No doubt she harbored some hope of Alabama having a big breakthrough with her shrink, like Timothy Hutton in *Ordinary People.* Bev probably envisioned a few sessions with Dr. Bland would get rid of all Alabama's unpleasantness and transform her into a normal teen who wanted to be a cheerleader and do easy-sew projects on weekends.

Alabama crossed her arms. "I'm not going to turn into a zombie teen for your benefit."

"A what?"

"Some kind of personality-less Stepford kid."

Her aunt lifted her shoulders in frustration. "Who said I wanted to take your personality away?"

"Why else would you send me to Dr. Bland?"

"Because you're unhappy."

"Of course I'm unhappy! Mom died. *Mom*."

Bev flinched, but her voice stayed maddeningly steady. "I'm not saying you shouldn't be unhappy, but you shouldn't have to feel you're alone."

"I didn't, until I came here," Alabama muttered.

Bev's arms were rigid at her sides. "There's no excuse for acting ugly."

"I'm only telling the truth. *You* dragged me here. I didn't want to come. And now that I'm miserable you're acting as if it's all my fault or something."

"I didn't say it was all your fault. I just think Dr. Land will be able to help you."

"Maybe *you* should see him, then. You're the one who's been living with a headless dummy and dating a creepy guy." She couldn't help an additional dig. "And now you're jealous of your mother's boyfriend—that's totally screwed up."

Bev's mouth opened and closed, like a guppy's. Then she turned and stalked away, calling out, "The appointment is at ten-thirty" over her shoulder.

Alabama sank down onto her back again with the vague sense of disappointment she always felt after a tussle with her aunt. No matter how rattled

Bev became, it never quite felt to Alabama that she'd scored a true victory.

The next morning, she was ready—on time—to go to the doctor's. Bev, who was beginning her in-service week at school before all the students started, bustled around nervously, and repeated three times that she was going to be late on her first day because of Alabama's appointment. Alabama reminded her that she'd volunteered to walk, and that in fact she hadn't wanted to go to the doctor at all.

Not that it mattered. Bev was in her own world of worry. "Lon has already been giving me the cold shoulder all summer. I hope this doesn't start me off on the wrong foot for the school year."

It was bizarre to see school from behind the scenes, from a teacher's perspective. Before, Alabama had barely thought of teachers at all. Once, when she was in elementary school, she'd run into her teacher at the grocery store and felt stunned at the idea that teachers bought things like normal people. To see the angst, preparation, and politics involved with school was eye-opening. It was even strange to hear these people referred to by first names—Lon, Cindy, Glen—when she knew that in a few weeks they'd all be Mr. and Ms. to her.

They drove up to the squat building on the edge of town where Dr. Bland's office was. Alabama climbed out of the car and wished her aunt luck for her first day back. Bev seemed surprised, then suspicious. Alabama headed up the walkway to the front door of the office, waved, then stood there with her hand on the knob until she heard her aunt drive off.

She watched the Toyota disappear around a corner, and then she did an about-face and headed back toward downtown. New Sparta still didn't impress her. The courthouse was about the best-looking building in town, and was the hub of all the action . . . such as it was. A block away from the courthouse stood the movie theater, which was showing *Witness*—a movie Alabama had seen with her mom ages ago, back in April. Back in another lifetime. That was the last movie she and her mom had gone to together. The last ever, and they hadn't known it.

Preoccupied, she passed a lawyer's office, a diner, the Western Auto, and a bank. Then she walked a block farther, hoping to hit a convenience store. Her weekly five dollars was burning a hole in her pocket. The bulk of it she intended to use to dye her hair. Red. Two days earlier, Cleta had told her that she had hair *exactly* like her aunt's, and that in fact she was practically the spitting image of Bev. Obviously, this needed to change.

She'd also saved up quarters to play a couple of rounds of Pac-Man, if they had that here. Surely they did. The town might be a backwater, but it still existed in the twentieth century.

If New Sparta did have a convenience store, however, it was a very inconvenient one. She didn't find it. Finally, she passed a newer, one-story sandy brick building that housed the New Sparta Public Library. It was already broiling hot out, and the idea of sitting in the air-conditioning lured her inside. She took a moment to adjust to the blast of cool air after dragging around in the heat, and then made use of the water fountain and scoped out a spot to sit down. It was early, so she was surprised to see a group of teenagers crowded around one table, talking in voices that were low enough to keep the librarian from swooping down on them. A few of them gawked at Alabama openly, as if she were a pelican at the zoo.

To avoid them, she veered back to a quieter section, near the magazine shelves along one wall. She heard the teenagers laugh, then get shushed by someone. Had she caused their outburst? She couldn't think why. She was wearing a favorite crocheted vest of her mom's over her tank top and shorts, but it didn't look *that* weird.

Then, she realized what it was—she was a stranger. The new kid. She'd walked this gauntlet of curiosity and hostility in one form or another every time she changed schools, yet it always took her by surprise.

Only one week until school starts. She dreaded it. How could she possibly go back to school now? She could barely think about anything. All she'd wanted to do since her mom died was sleep, listen to music, and watch TV. Those were practically the only things she was capable of. Now the world expected her to study and make friends and act like everything was fine. But it wasn't fine and never would be.

Tears threatened, and she focused on the magazines. *People* caught her eye because of the cover story about Rock Hudson. She sprawled in a chair and started reading about Rock's secret life . . . which, according to the people in the article, wasn't all that secret except to television viewers. Her mom had been a faithful watcher of *McMillan & Wife*; she would have been wrecked to see how AIDS had reduced the commissioner to a bony shell, so sunken-eyed and vulnerable. Alabama was glad to read that Doris Day and Angie Dickinson were standing by him.

Not everyone was, apparently. The lady seated next to her, an elderly woman with a startling blue-green tint to her tight curls, squinted her eyes at the cover of the magazine and shook her head.

Alabama turned to her. "What?"

"You never know about people—that's all I have to say," the woman declared in a library whisper.

"He's *dying*."

"Of course he is." She clamped her lips together.

Whacking the woman over the head with the magazine would have felt so good—that's probably what her mother would have done. But

Alabama's nerve failed her. Instead, she got up, went to the desk, filled out an application for a library card, and hated herself for being a coward. She needed to be bolder. More like her mom.

The librarian informed her that she could check out books, but not magazines. Alabama put *People* back on the rack and was walking out when she noticed a boy about her age with curly brown hair passing by the noisy teen table. One of the guys stuck his leg out and sent the boy—and his armload of library loot—sprawling.

The curly-haired boy stayed splayed on the ground. Alabama couldn't tell if he was hurt, assessing the damage, or gathering courage for a fight.

"Oh—I'm sooooo sorry." The guy who'd tripped him didn't even bother to move his leg back to hide the fact that he was the culprit.

Finally, the boy who'd fallen unfolded himself, stood, and methodically began to gather his stuff. When most of the books were wedged in his arms again, another of the clowns behind him aimed a sharp karate chop at the spines and sent them flying out of the crook of the boy's elbow.

He spun, glaring at the guy who'd done it. Karate Boy grinned. "Do you really wanna hurt me, Stu-loo?"

The table exploded in laughter, and someone started singing the Boy George song, which brought the librarian over in a big hurry.

"You all are too old to behave like this in the library!" she scolded them. "Quiet down right now or you'll have to leave." She glared at the pile on the floor. "Stuart, library materials do not belong on the ground. If you can't take better care of them, you won't be permitted to check them out."

"Pick 'em up, Stu-loo," one of the boys drawled.

The curly-haired kid—Stuart—sighed and began gathering them up again.

On impulse, Alabama joined him. The books were large hardcovers, mostly—collections of plays, biographies, and one giant book about movies. The record was an original Broadway cast album—*Evita.* She picked it up and stepped back a safe distance away from the mean kids. Stuart's big brown eyes—they had the thickest black lashes, like Bambi's—blinked at her curiously, as if he didn't understand why she was helping him.

"Do you need to check these out?" Alabama whispered.

"I already did," he said.

She gestured toward the door and started walking. He followed.

Once they were outside again, she took a deep breath. Even given the hot, humid air, it felt better out here than inside.

"Is this Bad Person Day at the public library, or are all the kids around here like that?" she asked.

"Nah," he said. "Not *all* of them."

Not exactly a ringing endorsement of New Sparta youth. Alabama tossed an irritated glance through the double glass doors. "You shouldn't let them push you around."

"That's what my brother says. I try to ignore stuff like that, usually."

"It's hard to ignore being tripped."

"Those kids are just idiots with nothing to do. No interests. I feel sorry for them."

Sorry for them? Okay, maybe the "loo" in Stu-loo stood for lunatic.

God, it was hot. She supposed she should find a pharmacy and get started on her hair project. It would be hours before Bev got back, and she could savor the time while the dye set by playing records loud and watching soaps and game shows. Or she could snoop around Bev's stuff. The last time she'd been home alone she'd done a quick sweep of the house, but the only thing interesting she'd found was a cache of romance novels.

A heat vapor rose from the parking lot, making her wonder if the asphalt might actually be turning squishy under the sun.

"Anyways . . ." Stuart's leg jiggled nervously. "Thanks for helping me."

"My name's Alabama," she said.

He squinted at her. "Seriously?"

She lifted her chin. "I was named after a Jim Morrison song. 'Moon of Alabama.'"

He looked incredulous. "You mean 'The Whiskey

Song'?" He hummed a bar of the haunting melody, which dumbfounded her. He was the first kid who'd ever known what she was talking about. "Your parents named you after *that?*" he asked.

"Yeah."

"Wow—that's grim. I mean, it's a song about alcoholics, right?"

She guessed it was, maybe. "My mom liked it."

"And you do know that Jim Morrison didn't write it, right?" he said. "It's Brecht."

"Who?"

"Bertolt Brecht. He wrote for musical theater. *The Threepenny Opera?* You must have heard of that."

She was beginning to understand why this kid got picked on. Still, it was embarrassing not to know where her name really came from. Or to have thought she knew and be wrong.

Why hadn't her mother told her it was an old song?

"Anyways . . . I'm Stuart." He snorted a laugh that made her like him again. "No one ever wrote a song about *that.*"

She smiled, wishing she could think of something to say as a reassuring comeback.

"Guess I'll see you around," he said.

And then, without warning, he tore off— walking fast like other kids she'd known who'd been the targets of bullies. The smaller you were, the quicker you scooted. As he disappeared around the corner of the block, Alabama regretted not keeping him talking. She could have asked if there was a pharmacy nearby, or where to play Pac-Man. Anything to keep a conversation going. This kid—Stuart or Stu or Stu-loo—was the first person her age she'd talked to since Camp Quapaw.

She looked back through the glass of the library door, at that table of kids. She'd switched schools five times in ten years. She'd never worried about getting along—mostly because she never took the problems at school too seriously. She'd had problems galore at home. But she might have trouble here. And the wiry, curly-haired boy who'd fled the library might be her best hope of making a friend in this weird place.

The next second, she was running across the parking lot, the heat of the asphalt shooting up through the thin soles of her sandals. The boy had probably disappeared already. Why was she running?

But then she rounded the hedge and saw his mop of curls up ahead.

"Stuart!" she hollered after him, breath heaving. That was one drawback to sitting on the bleachers during PE.

He turned, instinctively wary. But then when he saw who it was, he smiled—as if he'd been

141

hoping she'd follow. As if they'd been friends forever.

Alabama hurried to catch up. He might not have any degrees like Dr. Bland, but she'd finally found someone she wanted to talk to.

CHAPTER 7

At teacher orientation—which Bev scooted into, late, after dropping off Alabama—Lon introduced his stunning new wife, Leah. She really was beautiful, with perfect blond hair showing off the right amount of shine, curl, and bounce, like a shampoo ad. She also had a great figure and a Christie Brinkley smile. At least half the student body was sure to love her. When she was introduced as a new English teacher *and* choir director, people applauded, although Bev caught a few puzzled or embarrassed glances aimed her way.

Lon noticed them, too. "And let's also give a round of applause to Bev Putterman, who did such a terrific job filling in as choir director after Dory Whitlow left us."

As everyone applauded again, a flush crept up Bev's neck. True, she had stepped in after Dory's tragic stroke, but she never considered herself to be *filling in.* She had taken the choir seriously—taken pride in the work she'd done—and now she felt like a mother having her baby yanked from her arms so it could be given to another woman. No one had even discussed this with her!

Except Glen. She should have taken his warning more seriously, once she found out he was part of the Kirby inner circle.

She shot a glare at the top of his head. Of course he was sitting near the front. Traitor.

After that, the assembly got down to the nitty-gritty. Big changes were coming to New Sparta High School. A whole day of orientation was going to be allotted to the new Scantron scanning system of preparing and giving multiple-choice tests. Another day was going to be devoted to something called computer literacy, to encourage teachers to start preparing lessons on computers. Bev couldn't see much use in that.

But the computers were practically all Lon could talk about. As a result of the lobbying efforts of Lon and some of the school board members, including Lon's old buddy Mayor Keith Kerrigan, a tech company in Dallas had donated four machines to New Sparta High School, which was now the first AA school in East Texas—practically the whole state—with a computer lab. Lon was even more puffed with pride over the computers than he was over his new bride.

For Bev, the biggest blow came when the class schedules were handed out. Bev received her sheet and was flabbergasted to find that she was only to teach one home economics class. One. She flipped the paper over, thinking perhaps that the time for the advanced class would be on the other side. But no. The second side was blank. The first side showed that she was to teach one section of home economics, two sections of health, study hall sixth period, and something simply designated *Monitor*.

Within seconds, hands shot up—especially those of the veteran teachers. "What is 'monitor'?" Lois Carlson asked.

Lon explained that, as an experiment to deal with delinquency, class skippers, and vandalism, they were starting a pilot program of faculty hall monitors. All teachers except those carrying the heaviest schedules of classes would be expected to patrol the school corridors during certain free periods. "You'll be our cop on the beat," Lon said. "We're hoping this will have the dual effect of reducing incidents of mischief *and* making the students feel safer."

Frank Atkins, who taught algebra and was the oldest faculty member, went red in the face. "You mean you're getting rid of Gerald?"

Gerald Owens was the school security guard, and perhaps the only person at the school older than Frank.

"No," Lon said. "Gerald will still be here—but Gerald can't be everywhere at once."

So teachers were now going to be backup security guards. As this realization rippled through the assembly, the temperature in the room plummeted several degrees. Bev, still dealing with the blow of having her favorite class shaved off the curriculum, bristled at the prospect of being a hallway policeman. And it wasn't all teachers who had this additional duty, only the ones whose course loads had been pared down. What message did that send to kids—and other members of the faculty—except that some teachers were worth less than others?

She'd bet dollars to donuts that Leah Kirby wasn't going to be walking a beat.

After the assembly, she plucked up her courage and hurried after Lon, catching up with him in the hallway. "I need to speak to you," she said.

Lon stopped, as did Leah, at his side. The woman aimed a benevolent-queen smile at Bev, but Lon bristled with impatience. "There will be time for discussions in the coming week, Bev."

"Yes, but—"

"If it's about the choir, I realize you're dis-appointed."

To heck with the choir, she almost said. "What's happened to advanced home economics?"

He sputtered a little indignantly at the question, as if *she* was being childish for wondering how an entire subject level could disappear. "A year should be enough to teach kids how to boil an egg, shouldn't it?"

Only the utmost restraint kept her head from exploding. "That is a very dismissive way to speak about a time-honored school subject."

"Last semester advanced home ec only had twelve students."

"So? How many students make it all the way

to Spanish 4? Not twelve, I guarantee you."

"Spanish is an *academic* subject," Lon argued. "We need to be forward-looking. Face it. A decade ago, every girl in school wanted to take home-making. Now you have to compete more with electives like photography and journalism. And computers—we want our girls to be interested in all subjects." He brushed her off with a glib smile. "Women's lib, Bev. Aren't you for it?"

He took his wife's arm and strolled off.

Women's lib! Who was he kidding? The man was a Cro-Magnon masquerading as a progressive. All he cared about were objective performance results and school ratings. If there were home economics tournaments, he would be *adding* classes. But no. Sewing projects couldn't be evaluated by multiple choice. Graciousness, deportment, and real-life skills weren't things that could be ballyhooed in school assemblies and cheered about in pep rallies. No one yelled "rah" for balanced household budgets or planning a week of nutritious meals. But those things were every bit as important to a teenager's future happiness as algebra or calculus. More important, probably.

The day went from bad to disastrous when she eyed her schedule more closely and discovered she was being evicted from the home economics portable building. Her home away from home had been requisitioned for the new computer lab.

It was now official. She hated computers. The mania for those stupid things couldn't die out soon enough for her taste.

Her new site was the old cavernous science room—one of the few remaining structures from the original school building, which had been built in the 1940s. It was Oren Sewell's lair, where he taught biology. Bev had used the space for health class, but never home ec. It wasn't appropriate for home ec. Plants, petrie dishes, and ancient jars of fetal pigs and other nauseating things lined the granite-topped counters. A skeleton resided in one corner, and a lop-eared rabbit—Bugs, who was the Fighting Jackrabbits' unofficial mascot—lived in a wire cage in the corner of the room.

She and Oren would be teaching so many classes here, neither could have much prep time in the room. They'd have to do their prep and paper grading in the faculty lounge. Already, she noticed Oren shooting her nasty looks, as if she was an intruder.

How was this going to work? The space itself was also a problem. It didn't have enough cabinets for supplies. Cooking sections had always taken place in the cafeteria kitchen, but what about her sewing machine? It would have to be squeezed in the back of the room somewhere. Of course, all the big sewing projects had taken place in advanced home ec, which no longer existed. . . .

At lunch, she flopped down next to her friend Cindy Greggs, the typing teacher. The morning must have been especially difficult for Cindy. After Lon had first come back to New Sparta to take the principal job, he and Cindy had been an item for a while.

"They cut advanced typing and shorthand, too," Cindy commiserated. "I'm not even full-time anymore. I'm on contract."

"Oh no." Bev's appetite disappeared . . . although staring at fetal pigs all morning probably had as much to do with that as Cindy's bad news. "Why?"

"Lon thinks the students should focus on computer skills, not typing."

"But computers are just glorified typewriters, aren't they? What else are they really good for?"

Cindy's blank look reflected exactly what was running through Bev's mind. How would they know? Neither of them had sat in front of a computer. They were dinosaurs . . . and like dinosaurs, soon they would be extinct.

"Well, at least you've got your health classes," Cindy said. "They can't get rid of those."

Bev grunted. "I heard Larry had asked about getting more hours. He taught science once at the junior high, so he could step in and teach health." And Larry Oaks, the junior varsity basketball coach, was Lon's uncle. "They gave him a bus route, but what if that doesn't work out?"

"You're right. He has a bad hip, too. Those buses aren't easy to shift."

Gloom hung over them as they picked at their salads.

As the afternoon dragged on, Bev tried to come to terms with the new reality and spent a few hours arranging her corner of the biology lab, attempting to make it welcoming. She and Oren circled each other, grumbling, until they finally decided on a strict schedule of who would be in the room when—O time and B time.

By the end of the day, she tried to talk herself into believing that the change was perfectly appropriate. What was she teaching children if not science? The science of making a life for themselves. There were formulas and . . .

Oh, who was she kidding? She was being winnowed out.

Dispirited, she went to the office and called Derek. Maybe they could all go out for a pizza tonight, when this was all over. She couldn't wait for the day to end.

But when she tracked him down, after ringing three numbers and then waiting while a gum-smacking woman at the end of the line hunted for him, he was brusque. "Sorry, babe, no can do. I'm in Wichita Falls till the weekend. I'll call you Saturday for Sunday."

"Why not for Saturday?"

"Because I'll be dead tired from working all

week and driving home, that's why. I'll see you Sunday."

"Of course," she said quickly. "I'm sorry. I've had a bad day at work today . . . a few disappointments."

"Join the club."

They hung up. Of course she was probably overdramatizing her problems. It was just everything snowballing on her. It seemed there was nowhere, no one, to turn to with her problems anymore. Her mother was being romanced by some shady old guy. . . . God knows what was going on there. And then with Alabama always so ornery and sullen at home. This wasn't how she'd envisioned her life.

At the end of the day, she braced herself for another bleak evening ahead. She would float the idea of pizza, but she fully expected Alabama to turn it down. Nothing that Bev thought up was ever a good idea, in Alabama's opinion. So she'd spend another evening alone listening to Jim Morrison blaring on the other side of Alabama's bedroom door.

When she pushed open the door, however, a strange smell greeted her. Chocolate and butter. Happy smells . . . and something else, too. Chemicals.

The B-52's thumped through the house. The music sounded almost . . . cheery.

What was going on?

"Aunt Bev?"

Alabama zipped in front of her. Her hair was covered in some kind of crazy hippie-scarf-turban, and she was grinning. *Grinning.* "Hey! I invited a friend over—hope you don't mind." She held her hand out and then pulled a boy over. A curly-headed boy with big brown eyes and a shy smile. "This is Stuart Looney."

At first she was nervous to think of a boy being over while they were unchaperoned—but Stuart didn't strike her as the type of boy who might burn down the house one day.

"Hi, Ms. Putterman," he said. "I'm hoping to take your home economics class this year. I'm going to be a freshman, too."

"That's terrific," she said. Boys rarely volunteered for home ec. The few who landed in it were usually there because they needed hours and no other elective fit.

"Stuart made *the best* chocolate chip cookies," Alabama said. "Also, he helped me with my hair. He's very artistic."

"The house smells great. I wasn't expecting . . ." Bev eyed the turban with increased wariness. "You did something to your hair?"

The two of them nearly fell over laughing, which ramped up her anxiety a notch.

"Shut up!" Alabama said to Stuart. "I *like* it."

Stuart looked at Bev, shaking his head. "It didn't

come out quite the way I wanted. I mean, I didn't quite envision it looking like—"

"It does not!" Alabama punched his arm, which he reacted to as if she'd knocked him over.

For a moment, they were incoherent with laughter.

Bev stared at them, speechless. She'd never seen Alabama like this.

"What did you do?" she asked, when they were winding down.

"Is it time for the unveiling?" Stuart asked Alabama.

"It is," she said.

Before Bev's panic could fully register, Stuart whipped the scarf off Alabama's head like a magician pulling a cloth from a table.

"Ta-da!" Alabama said, striking a pose.

Bev gaped. Her niece's sandy-blond hair was now striped with bright red. It was as if a circus big top had landed on her head.

But it wasn't the dye job that left Bev slack-jawed. The hair was stunning, but even more amazing was the sight, and sound, of Alabama laughing.

CHAPTER 8

The morning of the first day of high school seemed to last a decade at least. The whole time, people stared at her as if she were an insect. First they gaped at her because of her hair—and okay, maybe there was a good reason for that—but then they also sniggered because of the name Alabama. The friendliest or most curious asked if she was related to the home ec teacher. It felt as if any attempt to make a new start was doomed. No matter what she did, or how different she tried to be, her identity was sealed as Miss Putterman's niece, which was the one thing she didn't want to be in the first place.

At lunch she braved the cafeteria, keeping an eye out for Stuart as she pushed her tray through the line. He hadn't been in any of her classes since second-period algebra. He wasn't in the cafeteria, either, so she surveyed her options. The popular table announced itself by the Dentyne-fresh appearance of the kids gathered there. Two girls wore cheerleader uniforms, and she veered away from them by instinct. Nearest to her was the nerd table—and sympathetic though Alabama was to geeks, she wasn't ready to throw in her lot with the protractor set yet. Finally, in one corner she spotted a table that appeared more mixed—black and white, jocks and normal kids—and she headed in that direction.

"Okay if I sit here?"

All conversation stopped and they looked her up and down—mostly up. Her hair was an eyeball magnet.

Nobody indicated not to so she sank into a plastic chair and started gulping down mashed potatoes.

The girl across from her nodded at her hair. "Did you do that yourself?"

"Sort of," Alabama admitted. "But I had help."

"Not enough help," the girl said, sniggering.

The other girls nearby cracked up. Alabama smiled along, but for lack of anything to say, she kept bolting her salty, starchy, slightly nauseating food. She felt nervous and disheartened, and a lump of dread sat in her stomach, such as a prisoner facing a life sentence might have on his first day in the slammer.

Thirty seconds later she'd almost finished her food when Stuart sped over to the table, set down his *Return of the Jedi* lunch box, and began unloading a little feast, including a sandwich, broccoli florets with a container of ranch-dressing dip, a cored and sliced apple in a Ziploc baggie, a Capri Sun juice pouch, and a Little Debbie Star Crunch for dessert. He said hello to the other kids, most of whom ignored him. He didn't really seem to care. Stuart might be new to high school, but he'd been around these people all his life.

He noticed her staring at his lunch. "What's the matter?"

"I haven't seen anyone use a lunch box since . . ." Since fifth grade, actually, but she didn't want to insult him. "The last one I got had the Muppets on it."

"This one's from last year, but it's still good. The thermos got kind of stinky over the summer, though." He was too distracted by other things to keep his mind on lunch boxes. "I was signing up for play auditions. *Alice in Wonderland.* You should try out."

"Why?"

"I thought you were interested in theater."

Stuart was obsessed with this subject, and was so over the moon to be able to take theater as an elective that you'd think his whole life had just been a prelude to the moment when he could sign up for Drama and Speech 1. He probably thought that since she listened to him talk about his enthusiasm, she shared it.

"I've never been in a play."

"I was a Cratchit kid in *A Christmas Carol* one year. It was great."

It must have been. On the basis of this one experience, he'd woven an entire life plan. He wanted to be an actor of stage and screen, like Meryl Streep. He loved Meryl and owned videocassettes of several of her movies, which he watched all the time. He even did a very plausible dramatic imitation of her as *The French Lieutenant's Woman*.

Even so, imagining movie audiences flocking to see Stuart Looney in anything was difficult.

"You should let Mr. Hill know that you're a dancer," he told her, dipping a floret in dressing. "He probably could use people who are good at dance in the production."

She squirmed a little. When Stuart had been going on about his ambitions, she hadn't wanted to lie to him, exactly, but she'd have felt weird confessing she had no interests of her own. Or that her interest had always been survival, and making sure her mother kept it together from day to day. So she'd said she was a dancer . . . and maybe she had overstated her experience.

Which—big reality check—was exactly one three-month tap class and a dance recital at Lil' Steppers Dance Studio in Cleveland, Ohio.

"Mr. Hill says the costumes are going to be amazing."

She frowned. "Mr. Hill . . . is that Glen?"

His jaw dropped. "You *know* him?" It was as if she'd revealed she was on a first-name basis with Martin Scorsese.

"My aunt does."

"That is so cool. I was just talking to him, and he was saying that there's going to be a talent

157

show, too. On Halloween. I've got to think of what I'm going to do for that."

"You're going to enter a talent show?"

"Of course—it'll be like *Star Search*, only more . . ." He frowned. ". . . rinky-dink."

She remembered the kids making fun of him in the library. "Did you sing a Boy George song once at a talent show?"

Stuart looked amazed, and pleased. "You heard about that?"

"Sort of."

His reaction, including a modest shrug, showed he believed there was no bad publicity. "It was only a lip-sync, but I put together a great costume, with makeup and everything. I even plucked my eyebrows. Ouch! Man, that hurt. But this year I want to do something *really* memorable."

As if an eighth grader dressed as Boy George in New Sparta, Texas, wouldn't stick in people's minds.

"I'm going to make a costume in home ec. I hope."

She felt like hitting her head against the cafeteria table. "I still can't believe you want to be locked in a classroom with my aunt every day. I went out of my way to fix my schedule so I *wouldn't* have to take home ec. I had to sign up for choir, and I can't sing a note."

It was that or PE, so she'd decided on the one that offered fewest possibilities for sweating. This meant she'd have to take PE next semester, but by then she'd at least know the people undressing next to her in the locker room.

"I wanted to take choir." Stuart shook his head in frustration. "There's not enough time for everything. I wish there was a way to go to school and take nothing but electives. Wouldn't that be great?"

"Yeah, but I don't think it would count as school."

He laughed. "Right. Then it would be fun."

The weird thing was, even in algebra, Stuart had appeared to be enjoying himself—or enjoying not enjoying himself. He had a knack for finding entertainment even in life's unpleasant bits.

Looking over to see that the others were involved in conversation, he hesitated a moment and then said, "When Ms. Michaelson called out your name in homeroom today, she said Alabama Putterman."

"That's my name."

He looked confused. "So . . . Ms. Putterman is your father's sister?"

She took a long drink of chocolate milk. "My mom's."

"Then how come your name's Putterman, too? Wouldn't your mom have had a different name from your aunt?"

She bit her lip. "My dad died before I was born. He was in Vietnam. He and Mom never got married."

"Oh."

It was faint, but she could sense that tiny catch of judgment in his tone.

"They were going to." She wanted to kick herself for making excuses, but she couldn't seem to help herself. "Except he got killed."

"That's really sad. So maybe that's why your mom—" He broke off.

"Why my mom . . . what?"

Two red splotches appeared in his pale cheeks. "I don't know. I guess I assumed . . ."

"My mother died accidentally."

"I'm really sorry." From the distressed look on his face, he meant it. "I shouldn't have said anything. Especially not in the cafeteria. I've never known anybody without parents before."

Much as she wanted to stay mad at him for bringing up the subject, she couldn't. "Me neither, actually."

She'd known lots of kids with one parent. She'd met kids who lived with grandparents because their parents were screwed up, or in jail. She'd known kids who'd been adopted. But her situation was completely new to her. She lacked a road map to deal with it.

"You should come over this afternoon after school," he said. "I found the *Sunday in the Park with George* Broadway cast album at the library yesterday. We can listen to it after we circle by the tennis courts on the way home."

"Why would we want to do that?"

"Because it's Stephen Sondheim!" He frowned. "Don't tell me that New Sparta's already turned you into a Top 40 zombie, country music freak, or worse"—he shuddered—"one of those Amy Grant girls."

"I meant why would we want to go to the tennis courts? It's eight hundred degrees outside."

"To ogle the tennis players," he said, as if this should be obvious. "Have you ever seen Kevin Kerrigan in shorts? He's a hunk."

The first time she realized she and Stuart lusted after the same guys, it had taken her by surprise. He was the only boy she'd known who admitted—to her, at least—preferring other boys to girls. But it really didn't make any difference to her. In fact, when she thought about the dumb or catty way girls acted sometimes, it amazed her that more boys weren't gay. Although maybe it didn't work that way, like choosing sides. Stuart said the only girl he'd ever had a crush on was Tracy, David Cassidy's youngest sister on *The Partridge Family*, but he now suspected that had been intense envy more than love.

Anyway, being on the same page boys-wise simplified things, and gave them something else in common.

"Okay," she said. "But afterwards, at your place, won't your parents be sick of me? I'm over there a lot."

He looked surprised, then laughed. "They're sick of me, maybe."

Not likely. The strangest thing about Stuart's family, the most amazing thing, was how normal they all were, and how kind. His dad owned a car dealership—"Looney Deals!" was the slogan of all the ads—and his mom stayed at home and kept house. His big brother, Justin, was a jock. Medals and trophies from the endless sports activities Justin excelled at crammed a cabinet in the family room.

When she'd first set eyes on the cabinet and realized that it was basically a shrine to Justin, she'd muttered something about how lopsided the parental attention seemed to be in the Looney house. Like with her mother and Aunt Bev—Bev, the oldest, the A student, had gotten all the praise, all the attention.

Stuart had been puzzled by her reaction. "Justin's really good at sports. They don't give out trophies for the things I like," he explained. "But when I win my Oscar, it'll go here." He patted the cabinet proudly, as if it was a mere matter of time before the gold statuette would be residing next to the tiny track trophies and faded blue ribbons.

She'd never been around optimists before. Not genuine ones, like the Looneys. People who really felt happy, and weren't just manic to appear that way so they wouldn't swirl down into a depression if they let their guards down.

Actually, it was a nice change. Her one fear was that the Looneys would worry about her corrupting their sunny-natured son, but they always welcomed her with open arms.

"Okay," she said. "Thanks. It beats going home."

Somehow she managed to survive choir, which had a surprising number of boys in it, and then she went to English. Her teacher, Mr. Ferrell, seemed really nice. He didn't make any snarky comments about her hair. No other teacher had been able to resist a sarcastic remark or two.

At the end of class, he handed out paperback copies of *Great Expectations* by Charles Dickens. It wasn't the longest book she'd ever read. The copy of *Love's Savage Fury* she'd stolen from Bev gave Dickens a run for his money in the page-count department, and she'd polished that novel off in a few days. But this looked a lot harder, and Mr. Ferrell instructed them to read carefully, find definitions for unfamiliar words, and keep an eye out for imagery.

Last period, she had study hall, and she sat in a classroom reading the assigned pages of *Great Expectations* for the next day. The book was told in first person by an orphan living with his mean older sister and her kind husband. The text wasn't actually that hard, and she became so lost in Pip's story that she forgot to look up words she didn't understand, or to hunt for imagery. She read several chapters beyond the first chapter Mr.

Ferrell had asked them to and almost resented it when the final bell rang.

Waiting for Stuart at the bench in front of the school, she opened the book again and was so absorbed that she only grudgingly closed it again when he showed up.

When she and Stuart walked into his house, a pan of iced brownies awaited them on the kitchen table, warm from the oven and filling the house with *Leave It to Beaver* goodness. His mom even set out glasses of milk for them.

"Thanks, Mom," Stuart said.

Mrs. Looney, a tall woman with short, naturally curly dark hair, looked like Stuart, only more athletic. Stuart said she was as good at sports as Justin was. "How was school?"

"Great. I'm going to try out for the school play, and there are a million parts, so I might actually get one."

"Way to go," Mrs. Looney said.

Once they had consumed brownies, they went to Stuart's room. Geeked up from sugar and first-day excitement, Stuart alternated between *Sunday in the Park with George*—Alabama had to learn all about who George was—and reading from monologues he was considering for the talent show.

Her own head was still filled with the book. "Have you read *Great Expectations*?" she asked.

"How could I? We just got it today."

"I started it in study hall. It's really good—it's about an orphan, and a crazy rich old lady starts taking an interest in him. She becomes his secret benefactress. That's what I need."

"What about your grandmother? You told me that you hoped you would end up living with her."

"Yeah, I know. . . ."

But the last few visits to Dallas had made her wonder if that would ever happen. For one thing, she kept hearing murmurs about money. While Gladdie seemed rich next to how Alabama and her mother had been, she couldn't spend a lot because she was on something called a fixed income. She'd overheard Gladdie and Bev talking about medical expenses, and the horror of dipping into the principle—whatever that meant. It all sounded dire.

And then there was Wink, and how Gladdie seemed around him. Happy. After one visit, Alabama tried to remember if she'd ever heard her grandmother laugh before. She certainly hadn't while Alabama had been staying with her.

Gladdie deserved to have laughter. She deserved to be with Wink if she wanted to be, without having a teenager around to worry about.

"I think I'm going to need a benefactor who's not distracted," Alabama said.

Stuart sank down onto the floor next to the bed. Sometimes it was so easy to read his face, he could have been walking through life with a cartoon think balloon over his head. Right now his forehead scrunched as he put all his brainpower behind solving this conundrum. "It's like trying to win a scholarship for your life, but who gives those out?"

She slipped down next to him, hugging her arms around her knees. "Crazy old ladies in books."

"What about your other grandparents? Are they still alive?"

"I guess so. But I've never met them."

"Oh." He blew out a breath. "That makes it harder."

But not impossible. *My other grandparents.* Once the thought took up residence in her head, it refused to be dislodged. Before, whenever she'd imagined her father, he'd been a soulful-eyed soldier in uniform she'd stumbled across in a picture buried in her mother's bureau drawer. Her mind had tried to construct, without much success, the brief whirlwind romance between her parents—a girl with long hippie hair and corduroy bell-bottoms, and a soldier with a buzz cut. She'd always felt vital details were missing—details her mother was always too shaky to provide when the subject came up.

As a result, her father had never seemed quite real, and she hadn't considered much beyond him. But now it dawned on her that there was a whole family out there that had helped produce him. Parents. Maybe siblings. Alabama knew her mom had revealed her existence to this other family, the Jacksons, and that they hadn't been thrilled. Diana had always referred to them as the Jackasses, but she had been prone to make snap judgments of people—clerks she thought too snooty, cranky neighbors. She'd even hated Alabama's third-grade teacher because she'd sent a note home complaining that Alabama was sleeping in class. *"Of course you're sleeping"* her mother had fumed. *"Kids need sleep! The woman's just a slave driver."*

But Miss Hodges had always seemed really nice to Alabama. She'd even slipped Alabama milk money when Alabama "forgot" it. If Diana had been wrong about Miss Hodges, maybe her mother hadn't been right about her father's family, either.

Did the Jacksons ever wonder about her? Did they ever spare a thought for the grandchild they'd never laid eyes on?

She had nothing to lose by finding out.

That night after Bev was asleep, Alabama dragged the phone as far from her aunt's room as the cord would reach, and dialed information.

"I need a number in Houston," she told the operator.

"I'm sorry, miss. You'll have to speak up."

Trying not to wake Bev, she raised her voice as far above a whisper as she dared. "I need a number in Houston."

"Name?"

"Jackson."

"First name?"

"I'm not sure."

"There are many Jacksons in the directory."

Alabama frowned. "Could you read a few out?"

"You don't have a name?"

"I do—but he's dead."

A pause ensued before the operator said, "Miss, you do realize it's against the law to make prank calls?"

"This isn't a prank. I'm looking for the family of a man named Tom Jackson."

"When did Mr. Jackson die?"

Alabama did some rapid calculating. "Nineteen seventy?"

The woman's huff of exasperation reached her ear as a roar of static. "I'm sorry. You'll need to find more information."

"Well, duh. That's why I called you."

The operator disconnected.

Alabama laid the receiver on the cradle and stretched out on the hard floor. Overhead, there was a rectangle cut out of the hallway's ceiling. A crawl space, or an attic. Bev probably had more junk crammed up there. The whole place was a warehouse of crafty crap.

She tried to think of a plan. She needed to talk to someone who'd known her dad. Gladdie probably knew something about him—although she'd never mentioned him. But how could she start asking questions about this other family without hurting Gladdie's feelings? *"Do I have grandparents who could take care of me?"* That didn't sound very nice. Upsetting Gladdie was the last thing she wanted.

Bev might also know something about Tom Jackson, but Alabama wouldn't stoop to asking her. Not that she'd mind offending Bev, but how reliable would she be? Bev had hated Diana. What were the chances that she'd liked Diana's choice of a fiancé? Plus, Bev would act all patronizing about her search for more family—as if it were reaching out for love or a cry for help. She might even want to send her to the shrink again.

Alabama didn't need a shrink. She needed a private detective.

She got up and stowed the phone, then crept back to her room. It was too hot still for the blanket, but she crawled under it anyway, breathing in the lingering smell of cone incense that clung to it. In a few months that scent would be gone, and it would reek of Murphy Oil Soap and vinegar like everything else in Bev's house.

A crater of longing cracked open inside her. She'd thought it had been shored up, that she was doing better, but she missed her mom so much. Missed even the little things, like the way they felt comfortable watching TV together at night, sharing the afghan on the couch. She missed having a home she felt she belonged in.

Think, Alabama.

What did she know about Tom Jackson? She sat up, reached toward her desk for her algebra spiral, and flipped it to the back.

First, his name. She wrote it out. *Thomas Thelmer Jackson.*

It was hard to imagine her mom married to a guy named Thelmer. That was one thing she had in common with her dad, she realized—a weird name. She wondered if he ever got teased.

Focus.

He was in the army. A private first class. She wasn't sure what that meant.

He was twenty-three when he died.

His family lived in Houston, and he went to college at the University of North Texas in Denton, Texas. Her mother hadn't gone to college at all, so how they met always seemed a little sketchy. Diana had said she was a waitress when she met Tom. Alabama always imagined their gazes locking as he ordered a club sandwich. But would her mom have gone to Denton just to wait tables?

Alabama's fingers cramped around the pen. Why hadn't she asked all this stuff when her mom was alive? It was dumb to be trying to piece it together now, when there was no one to speak to except Gladdie, who would get upset when she mentioned Diana. Or Bev, who Alabama didn't want to talk about private things with.

One thing her mom had said was that Tom's family had plenty of money, and that she'd never stoop to asking them for any. Apparently, they hadn't been at all happy about their son marrying a waitress.

Snobby rich people might be bad in-laws, but those traits made them perfect benefactor material. The only trouble was finding them. Obviously, telephone operators weren't going to help. And the Jacksons might not still live in Houston. Look at the number of times she and her mother had moved.

From now on, she'd have to be her own detective.

That weekend, she and Bev paid their usual visit to Gladdie. Before they got there, Alabama turned to her aunt. "Can I go to the library while you guys run errands?"

"The library?" Bev's brows gathered in suspicion. "What would you do there?"

"Read."

"But you don't have a library card for Dallas—you can't get one because you don't live here."

She had to rub that in.

"I don't want to check anything out. I just want to read."

"You can read in the car."

171

"I want to read something that's *in* the library."

Their gazes locked.

I'm not going to tell you, Alabama telegraphed with a stony stare.

Later, when she found herself with a few minutes alone with Gladdie, she asked, with careful casualness, "Why did my mom live in Denton?"

Gladdie stopped sifting through coupons and eyed her across the top of her bifocals. "She never did."

The words sounded measured, almost wary.

Alabama twisted her lips, thinking. "But Mom always said my dad went to college in Denton, and she must have met him around that time, just before he went into the army. And his folks lived in Houston. So where else would she have met him?"

Gladdie's gaze remained riveted on a Rice-A-Roni coupon. "Here, I suppose. In Dallas."

"But how could a waitress in Dallas meet a boy from Houston who was going to school in Denton?"

"From Denton to here isn't far."

"Yeah, but what was he *doing* here?"

The old clock sitting atop her grandmother's china cabinet ticked loudly.

"My memory is that they had a mutual friend," Gladdie said.

"Oh." That made sense.

But it didn't help her much.

"What did they do?"

"Who?"

"My dad's family? The Jacksons."

Gladdie studied a coupon for canned peaches very intently. "I think they ran a lumber business."

Lumber. There—that sounded like something that would stay in the same place, and make loads of money. Rich people were different from poor people. They owned big houses, and businesses. Alabama felt confident that the Jacksons were still in Houston.

When Bev dropped her off at the library, Alabama headed straight for the reference section and asked the librarian if there was a Houston phone book. The woman escorted her to a remote stack and pulled out a chunky, floppy White Pages. Alabama lugged it to a table and thumbed as fast as she could to the page where the Jacksons started. As the operator had warned, the Jacksons went on and on. There were Thomases, Toms, Ts, and just plain Jacksons. Scanning the names even for half a minute made her eyes ache. And then she saw it: *Jackson, Thomas Thelmer.*

That was them! It had to be. How many Thelmer Jacksons could there be in the world?

She shivered as she scrawled the number and the street number written next to it. She had found her other grandparents. They really existed.

That night, she waited till Bev was in bed again

and dialed the number. A woman answered. "Hello?"

Tongue-tied, Alabama failed to produce a response. What was she supposed to say? *"Is that you, Grandma?"* The lady would probably hang up on her.

"Hello?" the voice repeated impatiently.

"I-I'm searching for Thomas Thelmer Jackson," Alabama said.

A pause ensued, followed by the voice again. "Who is this?"

Alabama countered with, "Do I have the right number?"

"Thomas Jackson was my husband. He passed away last year."

Alabama felt a strange stab in her chest. Died. Last year. She was one year too late to have a grandfather. "I'm sorry. I really am. So . . . I guess you knew Thomas Thelmer Jackson Jr.?"

"He was my son. He is also deceased," the woman said with no emotion other than rising irritation in her voice. "Will you please state your business?"

"I . . . I just wanted information."

"Then I suggest you contact my late husband's company."

"What's its name?"

"If you don't know that, young lady, then I wonder what business you could have calling here in the first place, especially after ten at night.

Now, I'm going to hang up. You shouldn't be calling at this hour, pestering people. It's bad manners."

"But—"

The line went dead.

Alabama kept the receiver in her hand until the recorded voice reminded her that the call had been terminated and the dial tone returned.

She had been terminated.

Her grandfather was dead, and apparently the only person left on that side of the family was a cranky old lady who already didn't like her.

Then again, no one ever said finding a benefactress would be easy.

CHAPTER 9

"I don't think you need to go to all this trouble," Stuart said. "My family will adopt you."

"If only."

"They would. They really like you."

She suspected this was true, which surprised her. Alabama couldn't imagine being in a family as normal as the Looneys. Her whole life had been so the opposite. Not that she would have traded the life she'd had with her mom for his white-picket-fence existence.

She tried to focus on the letter she was composing. It needed to be perfect.

"Do you think I should call her something besides Mrs. Jackson?" she asked Stuart.

"What's her name?"

"I don't know."

"Then what else could you call her?"

Alabama considered. "Grandmother?" That sounded so formal, though. "Granny? Grandma?"

"I'd stick with Mrs. Jackson. Getting a letter from somebody calling me grandma would freak me out. Besides, you can't go wrong being too formal and polite."

Right. This was why it was a good idea to run the letter past Stuart. He knew all about things like manners. Without his help, she probably would have written *Dear Granny Jackson* and blown the whole relationship before she could actually put any plan in motion.

"What do you think about the rest of it?"

He draped himself over the back of the sofa and read over her shoulder. He was so lean, he was almost feline—a curly-haired cat with grape Hubba Bubba breath.

Dear Mrs. Jackson,

I'm very sorry for bothering you on the phone last night. That was me calling, by the way. My name is Alabama Putterman. My mother was Diana Putterman, who I think you met? She spoke to me about you, for sure. My father was your son, Thomas Thelmer Jackson, although he passed away before I was born. (As you know.)

I am writing you now because Mom recently died in a tragic accident, and in my newly orphaned state I have become curious about my Jackson heritage. I would like to find out about my father, beyond the fact that he died so heroically. Where did he grow up? What were his interests and hobbies? What was his family like? Any information along these lines would be gratefully appreciated by me. I don't know who else to ask but you.

I hope you will write me back. You can reach me here in New Sparta, Texas, where I am currently living with my aunt Bev until a better, permanent situation can be found. You can probably guess that me being here has put my aunt in a difficult position, since she has low income, a small house, and very little experience raising children. Not that I am difficult. Actually, I make decent grades and am pretty responsible and independent for my age.

Thank you for reading this letter. It's my biggest dream to meet my Jackson relatives someday soon, and get to know you better.

Yours truly,

Alabama Putterman

"It's a pretty good letter," Stuart said. "But you probably don't need to remind her that you woke her up the other night."

He was right. Why begin on a negative? The woman might never put two and two together. Alabama crossed out those lines.

Over her shoulder, he added, "Your handwriting isn't very tidy. You need to copy it over on nice stationery."

"I don't have any."

"My mom does. I'll ask to borrow some of hers and bring it to school tomorrow." He sighed as he looked around. "I don't know why you'd want to leave your aunt, though. She's got such cool stuff."

Stuart was crazy about Bev's place, which is why lately they'd been ending up at her house after school, even though the best snacks and the large-screen TV with VCR and MTV were over at his house. The Looneys' living room was like a little movie theater, but Stuart took all that for granted. *He* wanted to sift through Bev's crafty crap, and he was obsessed with the dummy, Rhoda Morgenstern. He was always sticking scarves and hats on it, or the wig they'd found while they were "exploring," which he'd wanted to leave on for Bev to see, as a joke, until Alabama had pointed out that the wig would be a dead giveaway that they'd been snooping in Bev's closet.

He lay down on the carpet and frowned. "I don't know why you want to live in Houston anyway." He lifted his legs toward the ceiling. He was always doing some stretchy thing or vocal exercise that he swore was essential to being a great actor. In the middle of a conversation, she'd be startled by him making clicking sounds with his tongue, or practicing arching his eyebrows one at a time. "Although they have the Alley Theatre. I wouldn't mind going there."

"Even if my grandmother does like me, she might not want me to live with her. A lot of benefactors just send their wards off to boarding school." *In books,* she added silently to herself. What were the chances that she would get so lucky in real life?

She stared at her paragraphs again, impatience coursing through her. Did she really need to wait for nice paper? She wanted the letter to be on its way, now. "I think I'll just write it over again on notebook paper. It's the feeling behind the words that counts, right?"

Stuart grunted his doubts, then crossed his arms behind his head. "What if living with your grandmother is worse than being here with your aunt? Have you ever thought of that?"

Worse than Bev? "How could it be worse?"

"You said she didn't sound very nice on the phone. When you think about it, it's like *Let's Make a Deal.* Right now, you've got the Broyhill sofa and the year's supply of bacon—which is okay, but not spectacular—and you're about to chuck it all for what's behind Door Number Three. And what's there might be a Zonk car, or a donkey."

"Or the jackpot."

He frowned at the ceiling. "Speaking of doors . . . what's *that?*"

A rectangular section of wood was in the hallway's ceiling, attached by a hinge at one end. Eggshell-white paint, the same color as the Sheetrock around it, served as camouflage.

"Maybe the entry to the crawl space up there?" she guessed.

"Or an attic." Stuart was already on his feet, scanning the room for a chair to stand on. He dragged one over from the dining table.

Alabama shuddered at the thought of what might actually be up there. If the house she'd once lived in with her mom was anything to go by, they could expect wasp nests and rodent droppings. "I'm not sticking my head through that hole."

At the prospect of hidden treasure, Stuart was fearless. He stretched his hand up to the corner of the ceiling opening and got a handle on it. When he pulled down, the squealing hinge of the trap-door caused Alabama to wince. While she hung back, expecting critters to fly out, he unfolded the ladder attached to the back of the closure and scrambled up it.

"Oh my God!"

She hovered at the bottom of the ladder, eye level with his skinny, hairy calves. "If something's dead, I don't want to see it."

"This is amazing! It's like a whole room."

"Really?" Curiosity getting the better of her, she slanted a glance upward. "What's in it?"

"Come see." His sneakered feet disappeared through the hole.

Tentatively, she crawled up to join him. By the time she hoisted herself onto the dusty cedar plank floor, Stuart had already located the bare bulb at the center of the ceiling and pulled the chain to turn it on. The bright light made her squint. There was really only enough headroom to stand at the very center, where the peak of the roof was at its highest. The rectangle of finished floorboards was rimmed all around by pink insulation, giving her the feeling of being on a cedar plank island.

Stuart inspected the boxes stacked in piles along one side of the space, and lifted one lid. "Christmas decorations. She has them very well organized."

She grunted, unsurprised. "Don't expect me to open anything. There'll probably be some of those Texas-sized cockroaches crawling around." She shuddered at the memory of seeing one scuttling across her floor toward her bed one night. She was an old hand at dealing with buggy places, but this creature had been like something out of a science fiction movie. Killing it had taken all of her courage and skill.

"How big are non-Texan cockroaches?" Stuart asked.

"You know . . . insect-sized. Bigger than a flea, but smaller than a squirrel."

He laughed. "Well, I don't think there will be many up here. Look how tidy it is."

Alabama detected no cobwebs on the rafter beams, and not much dust anywhere, even on the floor. Bev obviously took good care of this space, but she'd never said anything about it, even when they'd been trying to figure out what to do with all the craft stuff. She'd had the shop teacher from school build storage shelves in the garage.

Strange.

Stuart continued his inventory in growing disappointment. "More holiday stuff . . . old aquarium . . . curtains—" His voice cut out abruptly.

The silence made her turn.

"Wow," he said.

He'd pulled out an oversized clothes box, like a coat might have come in. But what he lifted out of the box—almost reverently—was an ivory-white dress with long chiffon sleeves and an elaborate embroidered panel in the front, sprinkled with seed pearls. The oddest thing about it was the length—it was short, like dresses people had worn in the sixties. The neckline of the dress didn't dip very low, but that length made it look a little risqué.

"What is it?" he asked.

"I don't know . . . Bev's old prom dress?"

Stuart unearthed a box within a box, and from folds of tissue pulled out a short wedding veil attached to a satiny headband.

"This is so cool!" he exclaimed. "It's like a wedding dress Julie Christie might have worn."

She frowned. She wasn't sure who Julie Christie was, and for some reason she resisted the idea that this was a dress meant for a bride. "Are you sure it's a wedding dress?"

He settled the veil on her head and fluffed it in admiration. "What else? Have you ever heard of anyone wearing a veil to a prom?"

She frowned at him through the tulle scrim. "Maybe the veil was from . . . I don't know . . . Gladdie? And it just happened to get packed with the prom dress. . . ."

"Which just happens to be a modest bridal white, decorated with pearls, and looks like it's only been worn once, tops?"

He was right. But who had been the bride?

Not Bev. Bev had never been married. Neither had her mom. "The last wedding in my family would have been my grandmom, but that was back forever ago. During World War Two. Did war brides wear dresses like that?"

"I don't think so. This is mod. I wonder if your aunt wore go-go boots with it!"

She yanked the veil off her head. It wasn't her aunt's dress. "My aunt's never been married. I'm sure of it. Her name's still Putterman."

Bev would have changed her name like a shot. And if she'd married young and had been widowed, you could bet she'd have the guy's picture all over the place and still be wearing her wedding ring.

"You should try the dress on," Stuart said. "Looks like it's your size."

She recoiled at the idea. Something about that dress made her uncomfortable. "No thanks."

"Then let's model it on Rhoda Morgenstern. It's so cool."

"I'm not sure . . ." Alabama wasn't joining him

184

in the rush toward the ladder. "It's like the wig thing all over again. Aunt Bev'll know we were going through her stuff."

"But this isn't her bedroom—it's an attic. People are supposed to go through stuff in an attic. If you want to hide something, you put it under your bed or in a locked closet."

And we'd find it there, too.

"I don't know." She didn't want to be a killjoy, but . . . "I'm not sure I should drag stuff that doesn't belong to me out of here."

"The entrance to the attic wasn't locked," he pointed out. "And did she tell you not to look around up here?"

No, she hadn't. Alabama let out a breath. "Well, okay."

Stopping Stuart might have been impossible anyway. He was excited about the dress, even more so because of the mystery behind it. Back downstairs, he carefully dusted off the dummy in preparation for dressing her.

Alabama watched him but her thoughts scrambled to make sense of the dress, which seemed even smaller and more stylish when Stuart slipped it over the figure. And then the answer came to her.

Stuart had said it looked like her size . . . so it couldn't be Bev's. Bev was at least three sizes bigger.

"I bet it was Mom's."

"You said your mom never got married, either," he reminded her.

"But she was engaged to my dad. Or practically engaged, I think. Maybe she got Bev to make her a dress for when my dad got leave, but then he was killed."

Stuart placed the veil on the wooden knob that stood in for Rhoda's head. There was no way to keep the veil from going slightly askew, and something about that crookedness and the way the silhouette of the dress stood out in the fading afternoon light seemed sad.

Had it ever been worn, ever been the centerpiece of a happy day? So much care had gone into the design. Its sparseness had an elegance to it. Compared to the Princess Diana fairy-tale concoctions brides swathed themselves in nowadays, this dress seemed spare, stylish.

And hopelessly out of date.

Trying to shake off the glum feeling, she got up and put on her new Talking Heads album that she'd just received in her big shipment from Columbia House Record Club. *Little Creatures.* Which was maybe their best album ever. She left her door open so that "And She Was" could blare through the house. The thumpy backbeat lifted her mood. In fact, an idea occurred to her that made her feel better about everything.

"Maybe the dress wasn't for anybody in the family. Aunt Bev could have made it for a friend, somebody who ended up not using it."

"I bet the bride was going to do her hair up in a beehive," Stuart said over the music. "Wouldn't that have been cool?"

They grabbed iced tea out of the fridge and Alabama unearthed a package of cigarettes Derek had left behind. She lit one and the two of them hopped around dancing and laughing until Rhoda in her dress began to seem like a guest at the party. Stuart even took one of the long gossamer sleeves in his hands and did a spin into her.

Alabama laughed, but the sound died when Stuart stopped, his face so pale it was almost green. "Is it the smoke?" she asked.

He shook his head as his eyes remained fixed over her shoulder. "Hello, Ms. Putterman."

Laughter bubbled to her lips. He was pulling her leg. Then she turned.

Her aunt stood next to Derek, gaping at the dress. Her face was nearly as pale as Stuart's. "What do you think you're doing! Where did you find that dress?"

"It was in the attic," Alabama said, as reasonably as she could manage.

"I never said you could go up there."

"You never said I couldn't."

"Is that a wedding dress?" Derek asked.

"Yes." The word snapped out of Bev in answer to Derek's question, but she was staring daggers at Alabama.

"Did you sew it, Ms. Putterman?" Stuart asked feebly. "It's really cool. I was telling Alabama that it's—"

Bev cut him off. "I'm disappointed in you, Stuart Looney. Snooping? *Smoking?* You know how bad that is for you. It's a disgusting, filthy, lowlife habit."

Derek scowled at her. "Thanks."

"Of course it's different for adults," Bev said.

"What age does it become not filthy and disgusting?" Derek asked. "Sixteen? Eighteen? Twenty-one?"

For once, Alabama wanted to high-five Derek, but from the deepening color of Bev's face, she could tell his questions were making everything worse.

"Stuart had nothing to do with it," Alabama explained. "He thinks smoking's disgusting, too."

"It just makes me sort of vomit," he piped up quickly.

"I'm going to have to call your parents," Bev said.

"I understand." Stuart was backing toward the door. "In fact, I'll go tell them myself right now. I'm sorry to have disappointed you, Ms. Putterman."

He turned and fled—a rat leaving a sinking ship. Alabama wished she could escape with him. When the door closed behind Stuart, Bev laid into her again.

"You should be ashamed of yourself!"

Even Derek flinched. "Jesus Pete, Bev, it was one lousy cigarette. They said they were sorry."

"*They* didn't. Stuart did. Alabama's not sorry."

"Yes I am." Suddenly, frustration and tension got the best of her. "Sorry for everything. Sorry for being stuck here. Sorry for being alive!"

Bev started crying.

"Oh Christ." Derek sighed. "I should go."

"No, don't," Alabama said. "I'll go to my room." She stomped off, but she could still hear Derek trying to get away.

"I really couldn't stay anyway," he told Bev. "I've got that job in Waxahachie. I won't be around much for the next couple of weeks."

A minute later, his truck's engine revved and then she heard the tires peeling off down the street.

If only I had somewhere to peel off to.

She kept to her room. Even with her headphones on, she could hear Bev stomping around the house, overhead in the attic, and then back down in the kitchen. Then came the sounds of dinner being made, resentfully. Cabinets and drawers smacked shut . . . pots clashed against burners . . . silverware clattered on Formica.

She couldn't concentrate on *Great Expectations*, which she was almost done with, way ahead of the class. Tension clouded her thoughts. What she wouldn't have given to be able to beam herself out of this house, like they did on *Star Trek*. Just transport herself back in time, to last year.

What had she been up to? Beginning eighth grade. Not in a new school, so there was less stress than usual. And her mom had started her job at the department store, and was going out with a musician—a saxophone player named Charlie. Whenever he stayed the night after a gig, the case of his baritone saxophone had taken up half their living room. But in December he'd up and gone to Chicago and hadn't come back. Her mom had wanted to move, too, but then she'd called Charlie's place one night and a woman had answered. That had made for a rough Christmas. And things had limped along afterward, until late in the spring, when her mother was fired from the store. And then she'd announced that Gladdie had offered to send Alabama to camp. . . .

Alabama buried her head in her pillow. Even fantasy didn't provide a good escape. Teleporting back would just mean that she would have to live through it all over again.

Hiding from her aunt wasn't doing any good, either. Maybe if she went out and faced her, Bev would vent all her anger and get it over with.

But when she entered the kitchen, slipping into a chair at the table as quietly as possible, her aunt seemed to be doubling down in her effort to keep a lid on her emotions. Usually during dinner preparations Peter Jennings would read them the news, or Bev would play an album from her folk rock collection and hum along. Not tonight. Now the silence was broken only by the angry squidge of her Naturalizers against linoleum.

"Do you want me to put on a record?" Alabama asked, as a peace offering. "*Best of Bread*? Jim Croce?" Bev often cleaned house to Croce, boogying around to "Bad, Bad Leroy Brown."

"No." Bev plopped a plate in front of Alabama. Tuna croquettes, string beans with pimentos, a wedge of lettuce, and a roll. Even raging mad, her aunt could produce a dinner that looked like an ad in *Family Circle*.

They ate in rigid silence, the kind of silence where crunching a lettuce leaf sounded like an ax chopping wood.

Ten minutes of it was all Alabama could endure. "It was one little cigarette."

Irritation flared in Bev's eyes. "It wasn't the smoking."

"Then what?"

"You went through my things."

"We were just up in the attic, loafing around. We thought it was a cool dress. Did you make it?"

"Yes." The word came out a staccato.

"Whose is it?"

"It's in my house, obviously, so it belongs to me."

"Oh—so it's just your house now." Alabama

grunted a sarcastic laugh. "So much for making myself at home."

Bev tossed her napkin onto the table. "You've never opened up to me or confided in me. You've barely been civil—and that's fine. But excuse me if, in return, I don't feel like divulging matters that are none of your concern."

She stood and marched out of the room. For the first time in their short history of housekeeping, Bev was the one who went into her bedroom and slammed the door behind her.

CHAPTER 10

Bev lay in bed, sleepless, eyes closed. Just when she thought she'd finally regained control of her emotions, she'd remember walking in the door and seeing that beautiful dress, and Alabama and Stuart goofing around with it. And her anger would surge all over again.

They had no right to that little bit of her past, that scrap of personal history she kept to herself and held sacred. The reminder of that last moment of innocence in her life. Maybe they'd found the pictures, too. She should probably bring all those things in the attic back down. She could get a lock for the closet door. Or better yet, rent one of those storage lockers.

She let out a breath. Renting storage for old memories was probably the first step on the road to Cuckooland.

Seeing that dress on Rhoda Morgenstern had thrown her off balance. How long had it been since she had taken it out and looked at it? In some recess of her mind, she'd been patting herself on the back for her restraint. Not obsessing over the old days anymore felt like a sign that she was progressing. Of course she didn't want to forget completely. But she didn't want to go back to the time when the mere touch of the silk of that dress could send her into a weeklong funk.

But it was always worse when other people violated her privacy. Like Diana had done the day Tom had come to visit. That horrible date that was scratched into her psyche forever: May 1, 1970. Friday afternoon. The day everything went kerblooey.

That afternoon, during the bus ride home from the school where she was student teaching, she'd felt woozy and tired. She'd distracted herself by thinking about her dress lying nearly finished in the bottom drawer of her bureau. She'd been working on it forever—she'd bought the pattern while she was in college, and squirreled materials away as she found them. Finally, this spring, she'd broken down and made it—all except the finishing touches. This was going to be her masterpiece. An heirloom.

The only thing that made her slightly nervous was the fact that Tom hadn't proposed yet. Was putting a wedding dress together before there was an engagement ring jinxing her hopes?

She'd never fretted about these things before. All during college, where she and Tom had met, they'd taken it slow. No pressure. Bev had assumed things would happen in due time. And of course Tom was a gentleman—a real gentleman— and she appreciated that trait in him. She did. And yet, the yearning they felt when they were together sometimes felt hopelessly old-fashioned, when half the other students around them were going at it like rabbits.

Then again, the other girls she saw didn't seem any happier than she was. Giving themselves so freely seemed to go hand in hand with heartbreak.

Besides, in college Bev had focused on her own goals. Her degree. Teaching. And she never worried about Tom, or was jealous of other girls. If anything, she was jealous of his family. He had bucked his father, once a colonel and now the head of the family's lumber business, by going to a regular college instead of a military school. Then he'd majored in liberal arts instead of engineering, when engineering was his father's choice. Tom prided himself on being a black sheep, marching to his own drummer, yet he never seemed to be able to shake the fact that he was marching along in the shadow of his family's disappointment. Parental pressure lived in his head like an ever-present, messy roommate.

As school had drawn to a close and it came time to find a job, Tom was at sea, and the I-told-you-so's from his parents wounded him. Bev had tried to explain that starting out could be the hardest moment of any career. She suggested he apply for teacher training, too. The long months after graduation he'd flailed, finally taking a job at the family business.

In letters and phone conversations, he'd seemed increasingly depressed. They so rarely got together that he might have been on the moon, not a four-hour drive away. Then, in February, he'd stunned her by calling her to announce that he'd joined the army. He was on the way to Fort Sill, Oklahoma, for basic training, and he wanted to stop in Dallas to see her.

The news had thrown her for a loop. The idea of gentle, bookish Tom being sent off to a jungle filled her with horror. Several boys from her high school class had become casualties of the war. And Tom was such a sweet, goofy soul. He loved Edmund Spenser and Chaucer, Simon & Garfunkel, and romantic movies. His idea of fun was trying to carry on a conversation in Old English. He was obsessive, yet absentminded. In school, he would burn the midnight oil to finish a reading assignment, only to realize the next day that he'd picked the wrong book off his shelf. He was always forgetting to bring pen and paper to class.

And now . . . *the army?* How could this end well? She imagined him going out on patrol and forgetting his rifle. Setting off to face wily guerillas armed only with a head full of *The Faerie Queene.*

After Tom arrived in Dallas, she wasn't surprised or shocked when he asked her to stay the night with him. It didn't cross her mind to refuse. Here he was, about to risk making the ultimate sacrifice for his country. How could she begrudge him physical closeness and love before he left her? There was a chance she would never see him again.

He rented a hotel room near Love Field airport, and there they'd spent a night dispensing with her virginity. Tom seemed to enjoy it. Bev had been mortified, not to mention confused. How could something accompanied in movies by stirring string orchestral arrangements and fireworks turn out to be so painful and sticky?

But then there was Tom, cuddling her, clinging (she couldn't quite banish the sticky nature of it all from her thoughts, even in the good moments). Every time she closed her eyes, their relationship would unspool in her mind, from the first moment she'd spotted him in the student center, looking sweet and gangly like Jimmy Stewart, right through to the present and even forward, to an unimaginable tragic end. The war that awaited him. The fear that their time together might be ticking down to final minutes panicked her, and she would tilt toward him again, offering herself.

In the early morning, their eyes gritty from lack of sleep, Tom had taken her home, bid her good-bye in Old English, and driven off down the street. That morning, he'd mentioned writing to her, loving her, but not marriage. But that was okay. Later, in his letters from camp, he revealed that he kept her picture by his bed and wrote often, albeit vaguely, about their future.

A wedding would come, she was sure. Tom was an honorable boy—an honorable man—and their relationship had lasted three years. Marriage was the next logical step. So she'd worked on the wedding dress and waited.

In the past week, however, setting a date had come to seem imperative. She'd often felt dizzy, feverish, and she'd missed a period. After basic training, Tom had gone directly to his parents' house, but he'd promised to spend time with her before returning to Fort Sill for officer training.

The day of his scheduled visit was a long one—the Friday after a long week teaching during the day and trying to get the house in spic-and-span order at night—and she felt tired and weak.

Even more than seeing Tom, she wanted to curl up and go to bed. She headed straight to her room and got out the dress to add a few more beads. Her vision seemed unfocused, however, and she had to put her needle and the dress aside. *I'm just keyed up,* she assured herself. Tonight, Tom would be here, staying with her family for the first time ever. Aside from the time she'd spent a long—very long—weekend with his family, they'd always met on neutral ground. So his insistence that he wanted to meet her family and stay the weekend was a huge step.

There was still so much to do. She needed to give the kitchen and bathrooms another pass before he got here. But she couldn't seem to pull herself off the bed.

The scratch of Diana's stereo came through the wall separating their rooms—The Beatles singing

"Across the Universe," which might have been a good song but was really beginning to grate on her nerves. Bev flopped back against the chenille bedspread. Diana overplayed records until the grooves were etched on the brains of everyone in the house.

The volume increased suddenly and Bev heard Diana's Dr. Scholl's clopping toward her down the hallway. Without knocking, her sister poked her head into her bedroom.

"You look shitty," Diana said.

The vulgarity made Bev sit up. "I hope you're not going to use language like that while Tom's here."

Diana leaned a bony, shorts-clad hip against the door frame and laughed. "Right—wouldn't want to shock him. No one cusses in the army." As always, she looked great, even with her hair just parted in the center and hanging lank. *Why couldn't I have inherited red hair instead of dishwater blond?* Diana's long, slim legs were tanned, too, and it was only April. How had she managed that?

Of course, Diana worked nights at a restaurant, so she was free to laze about in a lounge chair in the backyard during the day, soaking in sun. It was hard to look at that tanned, lithe body without feeling a pang of envy. Especially when she felt like a sore, puffy blob. Bev shivered, fighting back another wave of exhaustion.

"What's Tom like?" Diana asked.

"Why do you want to know?"

"Well, if we're going to be entertaining him this weekend . . ."

"*We?* Aren't you going to be busy, as usual?"

"Nope—I quit my job. The boss was a groper." Diana grinned. "I was thinking I need to look for something better anyway. And maybe Mama will stake me to some dance classes this summer."

"Dance classes?" Was she twelve?

"Well, why not? You went to college."

Bev sputtered. Where to begin? And now there would be this family drama playing out during the weekend, with Tom here.

Diana inched farther into the room.

"So is he all starch and snap, your guy? Gets a woody during John Wayne movies?"

"You are revolting. And you don't know what you're talking about."

"Whose fault is that? You've been dating the guy forever and kept him hidden from us the whole time. Like you think he's too good for us."

She did think that. He was.

Why had she thought it would be a good idea for Tom to spend time with her family?

Diana's eyes focused on the bed. "What's this?" Coming closer, she grabbed the dress before Bev could snatch it away. Her pointy jaw went slack. "Has Tom popped the question already?"

Her sister was the last person in the universe she

wanted to confide in. "It's just something I've been working on."

"It is not. It's a wedding dress." Diana lifted up the dress and held it at arm's length for inspection. "Hello, 1966! How we've missed you."

"Put it down," Bev said.

Her sister did, dropping it into a small heap on the coverlet. "Wow, what a vision you're going to be, Bevvie. I'll bet on your big day you'll have as much sex appeal as Pat Nixon. Maybe more, even, if Dora at the Chat-n-Curl does a really bang-up job with your perm and set. Snappy Tom won't be able to keep his hands off you on the wedding night."

She was so irritating. Like the persistent *buzz buzz buzz* of a gnat in her ear. Bev wanted to slap her away.

"That'll be a gruesome crash course in the birds and bees," Diana drawled.

In this one key area of life—sex—Diana had always been years ahead of Bev. Bev had resented it, especially since Diana's staying out past curfew, or sneaking out and not coming back till morning, had caused so much friction during their high school years. She'd run with a bad crowd—and the boys she'd picked up! Every fuzzy-wuzzy scuzzball who'd come down the pike. Diana's teachers, the principal, their pastor, and their old family doctor had all predicted a dire end for a girl who didn't take school seriously, drank and smoked, and was boy-crazy so young.

Yet somehow, Diana had managed to graduate from high school—heaven only knows by what miracle—and worked steadily, even though she changed waitressing jobs so often Bev often had a hard time remembering what restaurant to avoid. All these years of screwing up, and somehow Diana always landed on her feet. True, her life wasn't anything to crow about, but she hadn't crashed and burned as predicted. Booze, drugs, late nights, bad boys—nothing seemed to affect her.

And yet, after one measly night at a hotel with the boy who was practically her fiancé, Bev was the one who was *in trouble.* Life was so unfair.

"Marriage is a trap invented by barbarians," Diana said. "But I guess it will be fine for you and your soldier. These G.I. Joe types always want a wifey and a brood of kids, don't they?"

The idea of Tom as a G.I. Joe type was almost too laughable, but the crack about the brood of kids hit the epicenter of her frayed nerves. "You don't know Tom."

Diana lifted her brows. "So . . . he *doesn't* want to marry you? What's the dress for, then? You're stampeding him to the altar?"

Bev growled in frustration. "I'm not doing anything!" She collapsed against her pillows. "I'm trying to take a nap."

Diana stepped closer, eyes narrowed. "What's the matter with you?"

"I think I might be getting sick."

"Do you want some water or something?"

Bev nodded and Diana darted out. A minute later she came back, a glass of water in her shaky hand. Bev took a sip, but swallowing required effort.

"What am I going to do?" The plaintive question crossed Bev's lips before she could think. Obviously, Diana was the last person to ask for practical advice.

But Diana shocked her by coming up with a reasonable idea. "I could call Dr. Gary."

Dr. Gary. The man who had been called since they were babies, who kept lollipops in his medical bag for rewards after shots. She couldn't bear the thought of having to confess her condition to him.

"No," she told Diana.

"What about Mama?"

"She's at work. Anyway, there's nothing she could do."

Diana sank onto the bed in exasperation. "Well, I can't let you die, can I? Mama would *love* that."

"I'm not going to die." She was about 60 percent certain.

"Really? Because if it were me, and I looked in the mirror and saw my face all puffy like that, and

I knew my boyfriend was showing up tonight, I'd probably want to die."

Bev groaned. "Is it really bad?"

Diana leaned in for a closer inspection. "It looks like you've got a goiter."

Bev lifted a hand to her neck, which felt tender. She didn't understand. She'd never heard pregnant women complain of puffy necks. What was going on there?

Unless . . . oh God. Three empty chairs in a classroom flashed through her mind. All out sick.

But it couldn't be.

But what if it was?

"I think you'd better call Dr. Gary."

An hour and a half later, the doctor was there, confirming her fears. The mumps. Several children in her classroom had come down with it, but she'd never dreamed she could be at risk. The avalanche of problems this would bring down on her crowded her mind.

And then, embarrassing though it was, she confessed to Dr. Gary that she thought she was pregnant.

He responded with an avuncular chuckle. "You've got the mumps. Pregnancy causes swelling in other places."

A comedian. "But I've missed my period. And I . . ." She lowered her voice. Really, his lack of shock was stupefying. Didn't he realize how much this confession was costing her? ". . . I had relations."

"Do you have a young man?"

What did he think? That she'd done this to herself?

"My fiancé." Honesty forced her to add, "Practically. He's visiting here. He arrives tonight."

"Has he had the mumps?"

"I . . . I don't know. Don't they vaccinate them in the army?"

"Could be. The vaccination's relatively recent, and not one hundred percent effective. He'd be well advised to stay away from you anyway. No close contact. No"—that chuckle again—"relations." He pulled out a needle attached to a tube. "I'll draw some blood for a rabbit test."

While he poked her, she took deep breaths to calm herself.

"Young man have prospects?" he asked, finishing.

"He's about to begin officer's training."

"Ah—a wartime romance! Well, I've seen a lot of those in my day."

"How do they usually turn out?"

"Fine—except for the ones that don't." He rooted around in his bag, placing the vial there. Then he pulled out a lollipop and handed it to her. "You always liked green, didn't you?"

Soon after Dr. Gary left, her mother came home from the bank and rushed into Bev's room still in the gabardine dress, short jacket, and matching shoes that was her workaday uniform. "I ran into Dr. Gary in the driveway," she said, clearly distressed. "I've never heard of an adult getting mumps. How did you manage it?"

"I didn't mean to." Had he told her about the other thing? Obviously not, or her mother would have shut the door to give her a real talking to.

"And Dr. Gary said he'd be calling back early next week about tests." Gladys's brow furrowed. "Why would he be testing if he'd already diagnosed you as having the mumps? Does he think it could be something more serious?"

Diana appeared in the doorway and cleared her throat as if she was trying to rescue Bev from an awkward moment. How much had she heard when the doctor was here? "You want me to go to the store and get some groceries?" she asked. Diana loved to go on grocery runs. Gladys always let her keep the change.

"Soup and juices, the doctor said." Gladys dug through her handbag and handed over a five.

"What about food for the honored guest?"

Their mother looked confused for a moment. "Is he still coming?"

"I should call and tell him not to," Bev said.

"You sure you want to do that?" Diana asked. "Given the circumstances?"

Bev eyed her sharply. She must have overheard her talking to Dr. Gary. And if she had, she knew Bev's secret.

Gladys looked from one to the other. "What circumstances?"

Diana smiled. "The boy's about to go off to training camp, then to war."

Gladys frowned. "Oh, yes. I forgot."

"I'll try to call him," Bev said, "but he might already be on his way." She frowned. What a mess. "But he probably won't want to stay anyway."

"That's right." Her mother looked relieved. "Of course he won't want to stay. Why would he?"

But she was wrong. Tom *had* stayed, and in retrospect, the reason was obvious.

CHAPTER 11

Every day on her way to lunch, when she passed the auditorium, Alabama's gaze was drawn to the sign-up for the talent show posted on the school bulletin board. Stuart's name was easiest to read, because it was first, written in big block letters, and he'd decorated his name with shooting stars inked in with a yellow highlighter. He was super-excited about the talent show, especially since he'd failed to get a part in the fall school play. For a while, his was the only name on the list, but as the weeks went by, other names appeared.

Seeing his name there always made her throat tighten. Stuart might have parade float self-confidence, but she was nervous for him. He changed his mind about what he was going to perform every week. One moment he was going to recite Shakespeare, the next he would be planning a lip-synching routine or a tap dance.

"You don't know tap," Alabama pointed out.

"You do," he said. "You could teach me."

And here she suffered even more, because she risked being unmasked as a liar. All her tap-dancing knowledge was what she'd learned in a kiddie class—waltz clog, grapevine, time step. Her mother had combined these into a routine set to "Rock Lobster"—basically a series of time steps connected by grapevines. This didn't qualify her to choreograph the Ben Vereen-Gene Kelly-Baryshnikov-style Broadway extravaganza number that Stuart envisioned. He didn't seem to understand pesky things like learning curves, and limits. And he hadn't figured out that she was way out of her depth.

But before she'd been forced to confess, he had already switched to the idea of lip-synching a Madonna song. That made Alabama uncomfortable, too. Stuart seemed oblivious to what he was setting himself up for. She imagined herself squirming in her auditorium seat among the hooting throngs of students, watching her only friend in the school make himself into a walking target for teasing.

As she passed the list today, she stopped in her tracks. A new name had appeared: hers. It was number twelve on the list, and it also had stars trailing after it that had been inked in with a yellow highlighter.

Quickly, she thrust her hand into her purse and fumbled for a pen or pencil, or an eraser. Anything. She had to get her name off of there. In her panic, her books slid out of her arms and crashed to the ground.

Kevin Kerrigan happened to be walking by and knelt down to help her gather her stuff. For a moment, Alabama wondered if she was hallucinating. Kevin was the boy both she and Stuart worshipped from afar and speculated about.

Never in a realistic way, of course. Kevin was an upperclassman god, the son of the mayor, and had a car. A date with Kevin Kerrigan for either of them seemed about as likely as a date with Harrison Ford.

He picked her stuff up and handed the pile back to her, grinning. His skin was bronzed from his afternoons of playing tennis, and the contrast between his deep tan and his Pepsodent-white teeth dazzled her.

"Gotta watch those books," he said. "They're always trying to make a run for it."

"I'm such a klutz," she moaned, flustered.

He laughed, and then the list caught his eye, and her name on it. "You signed up. Brave girl!"

Wait. "You know my name?" As soon as she said it, she realized how dorky she sounded.

"I make it a point to find out the names of all the new girls." He leaned closer. "And you're sort of hard to miss."

As soon as that statement lifted her spirits, they crashed right back down. He meant that she stood out because of her hair.

She looked back at the list. How could she confess to self-confident sun god Kevin that she'd been about to chicken out? *Stuart and his stupid highlighter.*

"What are you going to do?" he asked.

He started walking and she tripped after him. "I-I haven't decided yet. Maybe . . . dance?"

"Of course—you're the graceful type."

He was kidding her, but she didn't detect malice in it, so she didn't mind.

They went into the cafeteria together. Kevin, of course, didn't pick up a tray. He probably ate off campus, since he had a car, but she'd seen him hanging out here before with his friends. The moment they crossed the threshold, he veered toward the table of boys he usually sat with. Alabama snatched a carton of milk and two pieces of bread from the end of the line. She could almost feel her aunt's disapproval of her poor nutritional choices beaming in waves at her from the faculty table.

She made a beeline to where Stuart was sitting.

He gawped at her. "Did you just walk in here with Kevin Kerrigan?"

She flopped down as if it were no big deal, even though she still felt a glow from being in the presence of so much upperclassman hotness.

"Did he say anything to you?"

Her lips tightened. "He said it was cool that I signed up for the talent show. Which is weird, because I didn't even remember putting my name up there."

She'd expected an apology or at least a shame-faced expression, but Stuart lit up at the reminder. "What do you think?"

"That it would have been nice to be consulted?"

"I've got the perfect idea for you. Here's how I

see it." He put down his sandwich and suddenly was all showbiz and jazz hands. "A dance. We incorporate the beehive look of the B-52's, Miss Havisham from *Great Expectations*, and your expert tap moves, and *voilà*! Magic!"

Her stomach knotted. "I wouldn't call my moves expert."

"People around here won't be able to tell. Besides, what's important is how you sell it. We'll need the dress."

"What dress?" she asked.

"The one from your aunt's attic."

"I can't use that dress," Alabama argued. "Aunt Bev seemed kind of funny about it, in case you didn't notice."

"She was just mad because she thought we'd been snooping. And the cigarette didn't help matters. I told you smoking was hazardous to your health. Mine too."

True to her word, Bev had called Stuart's parents and told them about the incident. But while Alabama had sacrificed two weeks' allowance, the only punishment Stuart had received was a stern talking-to. Which was fair, since he really hadn't done anything. Still, he took his "punishment" harder than she did.

"I'm sorry, Stuart."

He shrugged. "To tell the truth, I think my parents feel relieved when I get into normal teenager trouble."

She frowned in confusion.

He leaned toward her. "You know—the same reason they're happy when they see us together. They think it makes me more normal."

She thought about the over-the-top reception she always received at the Looney house. The big smiles, the brownies. Anything she and Stuart wanted to do together was always okay, even if it meant Stuart's missing a lovingly prepared meal, or required picking them up late from the movies. Never mind that they went to the movies to ogle the same heartthrobs.

They exchanged glances and laughed.

"So . . . what do you think of my idea for your number?" Stuart asked.

She looked over at the teachers' table, where Bev was. "I still might have trouble using the dress." *Or getting on a stage.*

"Your aunt won't care, I know she won't. She promised to help me work on my costume in home ec."

"During class?"

"We're doing sewing basics, but I already picked up most of that stuff from my mom."

"So you're going to do Madonna?"

"No—I think I want to try something more serious, after all. Maybe *Hamlet.* Every actor needs to tackle it sometime."

From his book bag, he produced an old over-sized library book with black-and-white photos.

One plate he pointed to showed Laurence Olivier wearing a white shirt with flowing sleeves, a vest, and tights. "What do you think?"

"Madonna might be safer."

"No kidding." He shook his head. "Getting those sleeves right will be murder."

No, standing up in a vest-and-tights getup in front of an auditorium full of teenagers would be murder . . . but that fear didn't register with Stuart. His crazy enthusiasm humbled her.

Even better, it distracted her. For the first time in months she was focused on something that wasn't depressing. Something besides her mom. At the thought, guilt shivered through her. *How could not thinking about Mom be a good thing?* But despite her mixed emotions and her many doubts, she found herself seduced by Stuart's mad visions of talent-show glory.

CHAPTER 12

Bev picked at her salad and cottage cheese and pretended not to watch Alabama and Stuart. They looked as though they were plotting something.

Her attention was jerked away suddenly by what felt like an insect dive-bombing her. She slapped the back of her neck and thought she felt a bug back there, but her hand came up empty. She returned it to her lap, uneasy. Her spastic movements drew a few curious glances from the other end of the faculty table, including a concerned look from Glen. He was seated at the center of a group that included Leah Kirby, Jackie Kirby, and Sonya Hendricks, the Spanish teacher. Bev was alone at her end. This was her day to be cafeteria monitor, so she would be stuck here for the full forty-five minutes, watching the others come and go until the last student had shoved the last filthy tray onto the discard counter.

Underneath the normal cafeteria noise—trays, plates, and cutlery clattering over the hum of conversation, punctuated by shouts or shrieks of laughter—Bev heard snickers behind her. She tensed, waiting. A second missile hit her hair. She looked down as a sunflower seed dropped to the floor. Evidence.

She shot to her feet and turned.

Marvin Nickerson slumped in his chair and

regarded her with a practiced blank stare. He was seated with a crowd of older boys, including Kevin Kerrigan, who often were involved in shenanigans of some kind.

Bev held out her hand. "Give it to me."

Marvin's eyes widened. "What?"

"The straw, or pea shooter, or whatever it is you're using."

There were titters around the table, but Marvin had the sangfroid of a seasoned troublemaker. His innocent expression didn't break. "I didn't do anything."

Bev rolled her eyes. "I know you did. You were tossing seeds."

"What seeds?" Marvin said.

She pointed to the ground. "There."

The table glanced down, and now the faculty table was taking notice of the argument, too. "That sunflower seed," she said.

The boy shrugged. "That could have dropped off your salad."

"Or anyone's," his friend Kevin said.

"Yeah, that's right. I didn't do anything," Marvin insisted.

"All fibbing will gain you is a detention," she said. "Do you want me to send you to the principal's office?"

To her relief, Lon Kirby appeared at her side. "It might save time if we clear the matter up right now. What's going on?"

"These boys have been tossing food," Bev said. "Sunflower seeds."

Lon shook his head, but there was no mistaking the smirk on his lips. "Is this true, gentlemen?"

"I don't know what she's talking about," Marvin said.

The others around the table agreed. "We didn't do anything."

"She found a seed on the floor and freaked out, blaming us."

"It hit me," Bev insisted.

"And you saw who did it?" Lon asked.

Bev was suddenly aware of the quiet around her. Conversation had died at the surrounding tables, and both faculty and students were focused on her.

"No," she confessed. "But I know it came from this table."

Lon chuckled. "Well, I'd say that's insufficient evidence, Miss Putterman. I'm not sure that I'd be up for punishing six students over one sunflower seed anyway. Let's just give the young men a caution, shall we?"

A caution? "For hurling things at a teacher?"

Lon leaned into her. "It was a seed, Bev," he whispered. "Get over it."

He strolled out of the cafeteria, leaving Bev standing there like a fool. She turned and sank back into her chair.

The other teachers—even Glen—cut their glances away from her. *"We're all on the same team,"* Lon had told them at the last faculty meeting. But evidently some of the team members were varsity, while others were bench warmers and water carriers. Some could be harassed by students without any repercussions.

Heat crept into her face. No one was on her side. And what was more, the other faculty members seemed influenced—cowed, even—by the fact that she was now a persona non grata in the eyes of Lon Kirby. Even after Lon was no longer there, no one commiserated with her. But of course he'd left his B team—Leah and Jackie, his second eyes and ears. Seeing the way Glen was smiling at the two women, sucking up, made Bev nauseated.

In high school, it was sometimes hard to tell who the real adolescents were.

She couldn't imagine that in years past one of her colleagues wouldn't have piped up on her behalf. Letting hooligan students bully teachers? Was this New York City?

Alabama and Stuart got up and left together, but before they disappeared, Alabama flashed a scornful look Bev's way.

Had she truly overreacted to the sunflower seed incident? Maybe—and yet, sometimes the small crimes were the hardest to deal with. But let them slide and what did you have? Chaos. It didn't take many Marvins to create a blackboard jungle.

Bev focused on her plate again as the other teachers at the table filtered away.

When lunch hour finally ended, she had an hour as study hall proctor before she could get back to her classroom, which was being used for biology. O time.

She wished she could be in her old classroom. For years before, the portable building had been her own kingdom. Of course, even more than the loss of her building, she mourned the cancellation of advanced home ec. Important lesson blocks from her second-year class lesson plans—such as sewing projects, smart consumerism, and presentation and professional poise—now needed to be wedged in to the two short semesters. And students who took Home Economics 1 last year would never receive important information—that was the tragedy. Thanks to the stats-crunching standards of Principal Kirby, an entire batch of students would be launched into the world underprepared for the most important subject of all: living.

But of course they would be standardized tested within an inch of their lives.

When study hall ended, she was finally free to get back to the room. Walking in the door, inhaling that initial whiff of formaldehyde and rabbit urine, she noticed immediately that one of her unit one posters had fallen since that morning and lay curled against the wall near the rabbit. As she leaned over to pick it up, she looked at Bugs. She wasn't normally fond of rodents, but her heart went out to this one. He seemed so lonely. And were rabbits supposed to be this tubby and lethargic? Sometimes the only sign of life from him was the frantic twitching of his little nose. Often when she had her free period in the classroom—her B time—or when she stayed after school, she would let Bugs out of his cage to hop around the classroom. It was hardly a frolic in a field, but at least it allowed him some freedom.

She let him out now and set her egg timer for twenty minutes so she wouldn't forget to put him back before the students came in for eighth-period health.

Meanwhile, she had to get the poster back up. First she hunted down the fallen tacks. She really needed a stepladder, but she decided to make do with a chair.

Her poster series—*Get Ready! Get Set! Sew!*—was one she'd made the previous year, and the blame for its falling rested squarely on her shoulders. The *Get Ready!* poster in particular featured "The right tools for your task" and had all sorts of items glued to it—an old measuring tape, spools of thread, and a pair of scissors she'd painstakingly cut from cardboard and painted to look almost real. She liked the collage effect, but the thing was so heavy it wouldn't stay up. Of course, she'd had the poster last year and it hadn't fallen from the old portable building's Sheetrock walls. These old plaster walls, on the other hand, crumbled like chalk.

Just as she was wobbling up on the chair, leaning to push the first thumbtack in, the classroom door opened and shut quickly. Glen hurried over and stood at the foot of her chair. "What are you doing?"

In spite of herself, her pulse sped up a notch. Whether to put that down to anger from the scene at lunch or some residual feeling for Glen, she wasn't sure.

He nodded to the message beneath her fingers. "The right tools? In this case, wouldn't that mean a ladder?"

"I didn't have time to hunt down maintenance," she said. "I have so little prep time with the classroom to myself."

He seemed to understand. "Well, at least let me spot you."

She was glad to, even if she felt a little self-conscious about his being so close to her, his eyes at buttock level. She made quick work of the remaining pushpins, hopped down, and dusted off her hands. "Thank you. That should hold it for another hour or so. Now . . . what can I do for you?"

He returned the chair to the correct spot at the long table and pushed it in carefully. "I came to apologize for lunch today. It was awful." He followed her to the oak teacher's desk at the front of the room. "I should have told Lon that I saw Marvin toss that sunflower seed."

She jerked her chin up. "Did you?"

"No . . . but I'm sure it happened like you said."

"I wouldn't want you to lie for my sake. Two wrongs don't make a right."

"But the way Lon treated you!" He pressed a fist into his palm.

His vehemence surprised her. "You didn't seem to mind at lunch. Or was that because you were sitting next to Jackie?"

"I know it probably looked like I didn't mind," he said. "I'm not an acting teacher for nothing, I guess. This whole year, I've been pretending that I don't care about what's happened between us, that I barely notice you anymore. But it's not true, and I never should have left you out on a limb like I did today."

"It's okay." Gratifying as the apology was, she didn't want to return to how things were last year, when Glen was the walking wounded. They were both moving on, which was for the best.

"I still don't understand what happened last year," he said, "but I respect your choices. And I hope that I never act so ungallant as I did today again."

Gallant. The word made her smile. It was hard to picture Glen as a knight in shining armor. That's why she had held back before.

What had her mother said? *You tossed away a perfectly good boyfriend . . .*

But what could she say? The spark with Glen had died out. Was it wrong to want a little sizzle in her life?

Glen's eyes narrowed. "What's that ticking sound?"

She gestured to the egg timer. "I have it set to let me know when Bugs's time is up."

His eyes grew wide as he looked at the open cage door and then searched around the room. Clearly, he expected to find the bunny in a pot over a Bunsen burner.

"I mean when it's time to put him back in his cage." She laughed. "Did you think I was cooking the school mascot?"

"No, I just . . ." He laughed, too.

"You looked like you were ready to call the ASPCA."

Their shared laughter was a relief after the stresses of the day. It was good to have a normal moment with Glen again.

Normal didn't last long. Something in his expression shifted, and the next thing she knew, he was staring at her intently.

"Are you still seeing that man?" he asked.

"Yes." She began to fiddle with her class notes. *Seeing* at this point was theoretical. She hadn't even heard from Derek since the day Alabama had found the wedding dress.

"I saw you and Alabama at the pizza parlor last weekend."

"I spotted you there, too," she said. "You didn't come by and say hello."

"I was picking up takeout. I wasn't sure you were by yourselves, so I didn't want to butt in."

"Derek's got an out-of-town job. He doesn't come back here often."

"Where's the job?"

"Waxahachie."

"That's not so far," Glen said. "He doesn't come back to see you on weekends?"

She bristled, even though she had been thinking the same thing. But a break was probably good for her and Derek. Their relationship had definitely been more strained since Alabama had arrived. She couldn't believe now how naive she'd been, thinking that she'd bring her niece home and they'd all settle down like a happy family. Crazy. *Happiness—just add water and stir.* Nothing was ever that simple.

"Derek and I are busy with our own work, but we're still an item," she assured Glen.

"Marriage plans?"

She eyed him with steady impatience. "No."

He crossed his arms. "What do you see in him? What do you have in common?"

"What does anyone have in common with anyone else?" she asked. "Reading the same books, liking the same movies? That doesn't always guarantee success."

Look at us, she wanted to say.

"It's something, though."

"Variety is the spice of life," she said.

His lips tightened and curved down. "And that's what you want—spice."

"Yes. Also, Derek speaks his mind. I know how he feels."

"*You* know?" He laughed bitterly. "In the year and a half we were together, I was the one who never knew where I stood with you. You always kept me at arm's length."

"I did?" Her voice rose in surprise.

"NASA?" he reminded her. "How could I feel sure about you when you were hatching hare-brained schemes like that?"

"It wasn't harebrained," she said. "They picked a woman, even. It could have been me."

"The point is, I couldn't even tell if you wanted to be with me in a year's time, or up in orbit. You certainly didn't want to make a commitment."

"Well, NASA didn't pan out, obviously." Nothing had.

"I'm sorry," he said.

She shrugged. "Like you said, it was a long shot. Maybe I was using the application as an escapist tactic."

"There—you said it. You wanted to escape." He frowned. "Though I would have preferred your escaping into outer space than throwing me over for Derek."

"He's not so bad."

He didn't say anything for a long time. He didn't move at all. "That's not exactly a glowing recommendation."

She blushed. "I was just . . . well, I spoke without thinking."

When he just studied her without saying anything more, she cleared her throat. "Glen? I don't mean to be rude, but I need to get some handouts prepared."

He crossed the distance between them in three strides and pulled her into his arms. She was so stunned she didn't have time to gird herself. She collided with his chest at the same moment his mouth descended on hers.

Glen had always been a good kisser—something she'd almost forgotten. Derek was more perfunctory about anything that smacked of foreplay. For a few moments, her and Glen's mouths remained firmly locked, lips and tongues hastily and clandestinely reacquainting.

It was wrong on so many levels. She shouldn't be enjoying kissing Glen when she was dating someone else—someone she'd left Glen for. She wasn't a cheater.

Yet here she was. Cheating.

And at school! Anyone could walk in. Students. The principal.

Jackie Kirby.

A bell went off, and the unexpected noise caused them to jump apart. They both cast horrified gazes toward the classroom door. But it was closed.

They looked back at each other, and in that second, Bev realized the sound was the egg timer. She groaned and grappled for it, tossing it in the desk drawer.

"I shouldn't have done that," Glen said.

"No, you shouldn't have. And I shouldn't—"

Before she could argue more, he held his hand out, traffic-warden style. "No need to explain."

But she couldn't remain silent. "I hope it was nothing I said."

"No, it's what you didn't say," Glen said. "You didn't say you love him. Or that he loves you."

She spluttered. "But that's . . . of course I . . ." But no matter how much she felt was riding on choking out *I love him* for Glen to hear and believe, the words lodged stubbornly in her throat.

Glen watched her struggle for a moment. "I get it. I behaved like a lunatic just now—like a barbarian. Don't worry. I won't lunge at you again. There's no reason we can't continue on as before. Civilized. Professional. Right?"

She nodded. That was exactly what she wanted. So why did she feel so disappointed?

Glen spun on his heel and marched out the door, and she collapsed like a wet noodle into the chair behind the teacher's desk. She looked at Bugs, whose little nose was twitching with curiosity. She imagined her own heart was beating as fast as his.

CHAPTER 13

Every day after school Alabama raced home, either alone or with Stuart, to check the mail. She needed to get to the box ahead of Bev, for two reasons. First, the Columbia House Record Club was sending her demands for payment that she couldn't make until her allowance started up again. Also, she was expecting a letter from Granny Jackson.

The demands came like clockwork. The other letter never arrived.

Because Bev had so many afterschool activities to oversee, or work to finish up, she was rarely with Alabama to witness the disappointment over her grandmother's failure to write back. She wouldn't have understood her letdown anyway. Granny Jackson was still Alabama's secret, but she wanted to keep it that way until the day she could announce to Bev that she had found a benefactress.

Just when she was beginning to lose hope of that day ever arriving, a creamy envelope appeared in the mailbox, addressed to Miss Alabama Putterman in an elegant cursive hand. She ran to her room and shut the door for privacy even though Bev wasn't there. Tossing herself on her quilt, and then wriggling around so that the zipper of an old dress didn't poke her back, she opened the envelope and pulled out two sheets of matching cream stationery, covered front and back with that small, perfectly slanted handwriting.

Dear Alabama,

You might imagine my surprise upon receiving your letter. It's not every day someone offers herself to me as a granddaughter.

I was very sorry to hear about your mother. In your letter you seem like a curious, somewhat practical girl, and I sincerely regret that you're experiencing such terrible sorrows so young. Of course, anyone with a brain in their head could have predicted that Diana Putterman would not come to a good end, but that is certainly no fault of yours.

It's not clear how much your mother told you about your beginnings, and I doubt I'm the proper person to shed more light on that subject. Indeed, I know very little . . . and that is the crux of the dilemma. Suffice it to say, you were born (reputedly) after the death of my son, Tom. Tom and your mother were never married, and in truth, we were never entirely convinced of the seriousness of their relationship, or the verity of your mother's condition. It seemed a confusing business to us, one might almost say slapdash. Tom rarely mentioned Diana Putterman in his letters home from the war, which made us skeptical of your mother's later claim that he had fathered her child—a claim that seemed both questionable and, considering the fact that our son had recently died in Vietnam and could not confirm it, bordering on bad taste. A claim, I remind you, that Diana never pursued beyond a single phone call, during which we strongly suspected she was inebriated.

As anyone will tell you, I am not a woman of strong prejudices. In fact, I detest people who make snap judgments. Yet I must confess that after my one experience in person with your mother, we were not on cordial terms and probably never could have been. It's not my way to speak ill of the departed, but when Diana Putterman was here she seemed a brash, extremely disagreeable person, and showed not even a passing acquaintance with good manners or reason.

Whoever's child you are, Alabama, I hope you will try to develop good sense. It's in short supply nowadays. My son, who you call your father, was a kind, sensitive soul, an emotional young man who loved literature above all things—

traits that did him no good whatsoever. Beware of fiction, Alabama. It rarely does people any good and more often than not makes them dreamy, peculiar, and weak-willed. On the other hand, if you are my son's daughter (mind you, <u>I am not saying you are</u>) it can only be hoped that a little of Tom's mild personality will counteract the unpleasant Putterman temperament. You'll need to watch out for that.

Now, what are we to do with you? Before his recent passing, I relied on the good judgment of my husband, Thomas (Sr.), in serious matters. This business sounds like a job for lawyers, so I intend to show your letter and a copy of this one to my daughter, Dot, who is a federal magistrate and has always shown good sense.

In the meantime, you should consider yourself lucky to have found a home with your aunt. For a Putterman, she's probably about the best that can be hoped for. Yet I can certainly sympathize with your desire to better your situation. I will be in touch with you after I've consulted with my daughter. Please let Bev know that she should be expecting a call from us.

Sincerely yours,

Dorothy Mabry Jackson

P.S. I have pieced together that you were the girl who telephoned me late one evening. Not confessing to that shows a lack of character, but I will try not to hold the lapse against you, as you are young, and were raised by Diana Putterman, and this is a singularly unusual circumstance.

When Alabama finished the letter, her heart was thumping so hard in her ears it drowned out her thoughts. The insinuations and insults swam before her eyes. And then those final words: *Please let Bev know that she should be expecting a call from us*. No! This was not what she wanted!

She had to read it over again to try to make more sense of it. The second time through, her cheeks puffed with anger at the passages about her mother and the way some things were phrased. *Whoever's child you are . . . who you call your father?* Did Dorothy Jackson think she was making this up?

Next, she went to the dictionary and checked the word *inebriated.*

Unfortunately, it meant exactly what she suspected it did. Drunk. She could imagine that phone call—her mother slurry and loud on one end, and the sensible, not-opinionated-but-very-opinionated Jacksons on the other.

What had her mother said to those people to

make them hate not just her but Puttermans in general? The lady acted as if she knew the whole family.

Consider yourself lucky . . .

Lucky! That showed how clueless Granny Jackson was.

She put the letter aside and stewed for a while. So much for finding acceptance from a new family. Then, taking it up again, she tried to ignore the anti-Putterman attitude. Maybe Dorothy Jackson viewed this as a legal, financial issue. Which is kind of what she herself had been doing when she started on this benefactor quest. But she'd also wanted a place to escape to—a new home. Even if it was only during vacations between semesters at boarding school.

The mention of lawyers disturbed her more than her grandmother's skepticism. Lawyers were serious, and they didn't deal with fourteen-year-olds. Scariest of all was the prospect of Dorothy Mabry Jackson's sensible daughter calling Bev. This letter was mailed days ago, so that call could happen at any moment!

What was she going to do? There was no way she could hide what she was up to if they were going to call her aunt. She would have to fess up and face the wrath of Bev.

She spent the next hour setting the stage. Using what she could find in the fridge, she started making a meal. Hamburgers were safe. She could do that. Bev had forgotten to buy buns, which wasn't like her, but they could manage with sliced bread. While she worked, she put on an album of her mom's—Jim Morrison—and cranked up the volume till breaking on through to the other side of something felt like an achievable goal.

It's not clear how much your mother told you about your beginnings, and I doubt I'm the proper person to shed more light on that subject. . . .

What had Dorothy Jackson meant by that? Who would be the right person?

She was tossing a salad when—unheard—Bev appeared at her elbow. Alabama screamed, which made Bev shriek. Salad ended up tossed on the floor, and Alabama streaked out to the living room to turn down the volume.

"Sorry," she said.

Bev was surveying the goings-on in the kitchen, arms akimbo. "What are you making?"

"Cheeseburgers."

Her aunt sucked in her breath. "Did you use all the ground chuck? I was going to fix meatloaf."

That would explain the no-bun situation. Oops. "I didn't know."

Her aunt sighed and dropped her purse on the table. "Oh well, it's no biggie. I've had a rough day, and tomorrow we have to drive to Dallas. It'll be nice not to have to cook."

A rough day was a bad sign. But maybe she could shake her out of it—before the day got rougher. "Good—you just sit there. I'm doing everything. Would you like a glass of tea? Crystal Light?"

Bev lowered herself into a chair, her expression guarded. "Why are you doing everything?"

Alabama shrugged. "Because I felt like it."

"You felt like cooking?"

"I used to cook for my mom and me sometimes. I thought you'd be pleased."

"I am . . ." Her head remained tilted at a suspicious angle. ". . . I guess."

"Here—I'll put on Judy Collins." "Both Sides Now" could usually be counted on to soothe the savage Bev.

Not today, however. When she ran back to the kitchen, her aunt's eyes burned into her as if she could see right through to her conniving little heart.

"What's going on?" Bev asked.

"Nothing," Alabama insisted. "I'm just trying to do something nice for you. Jeez."

"I could almost believe that you would make dinner to be nice, especially since you like hamburgers anyway. But you've never voluntarily put on one of my records. So you might as well tell me what's going on. Did you break something?"

"No."

"Do you need money? Because I told you, going without your allowance is part of the punishment."

"I know that. It's not about money."

"So there is something."

"Well . . ." She'd hoped to butter Bev up before confession time. She hadn't expected the buttering up part to backfire on her. "Okay, here's the deal. I got a letter today from my grand-mother."

"From Mama?"

"My other grandmother. Dorothy Jackson."

Her aunt's face went white, which threw Alabama. Bev wasn't supposed to wig out until the subject of lawyers came up.

"She wrote to you? Why? I didn't even know those people acknowledged your existence."

"They didn't . . . until I wrote to them."

Bev let the words sink in. "You wrote to the Jacksons."

"There's just one now," Alabama explained. "Mr. Jackson died."

Bev absorbed this with a slow nod. "And what did you say to them?"

"I said that I wanted to get to know my father's family."

"Why?"

Alabama blinked. "Why what?"

"Why do you want to know them if they never acknowledged you before?"

"Why shouldn't I?" Alabama couldn't keep the defensiveness out of her voice. "He was my father, and I know nothing about them."

"That's right. You know nothing about those people. And now, out of the blue, you decide to look them up. Why?"

It dawned on her that Bev was getting mad. Really mad. "Because . . . because I wanted to see if they had any interest in . . . you know."

"Taking you in?"

Alabama nodded.

Bev tossed her napkin on the table. "I see. Because you're so mistreated here. One little punishment—no allowance for two weeks—and you're ready to move out."

"No—I'd already written her by then."

"You started this that long ago? Behind my back?"

Alabama felt like a worm squirming on the hook. Why should she have to apologize? "She's my grandmother. Why shouldn't I want to get to know her?"

Bev looked as though she was about to argue some more, then she hiccupped a breath. "And so she wrote back to you. What did she say?"

"Well . . ." Alabama exhaled. "I might as well show you." She got up and retrieved the letter from her room.

As Bev scanned the note, she issued clucks and grunts with increasing volume as she slapped the pages over. When she finished, she exclaimed, "*A claim! Reputedly!* She's writing as though you're trying to finesse your way into riches, like that Anastasia woman, the tsar's daughter. Who I've always believed, by the way."

Alabama's discomfort increased. In a way, she *was* trying to finesse her way in. Not that she wanted riches. . . .

Although Columbia House wouldn't wait forever.

"Let them call," Bev said. "I'll give Dorothy Jackson, or her daughter-minion, Dot, a piece of my mind."

Alabama shot to her feet. Bev was going to ruin everything. "Don't do that, please," she said. "They might think I told you to."

Bev blinked at her in disbelief. "You mean you still want to meet this person?"

"She's my grandmother, isn't she?"

"Yes, but read what she says. I don't mean to hurt your feelings, Alabama, but you don't even have to read between the lines here. She thinks that Diana was lying and that you're angling for something." Bev huffed. "I'd like to strangle her skinny neck."

Alabama leaned against the counter and watched her aunt go over the letter again. The trouble was, she understood where her grandmother was coming from. In her own letter she'd sent to Mrs. Jackson, she hadn't wanted to gush or plead. Maybe she hadn't made herself seem personable enough, either. If she'd included a picture, maybe the woman would have seen her differently, would have reacted with more emotion. "She doesn't know me."

"Whose fault is that?"

Alabama wasn't sure. Maybe it was the fault of the Jacksons, for whatever had happened all those years ago. But her mother obviously hadn't helped. "What do you think Mom said to those people to make them so mad? It's like Dorothy Jackson's got a grudge against our whole family."

Bev shoved the letter away from her, and suddenly her expression shuttered. "I was never quite sure."

"But you knew about them?"

"A little."

"I wish someone had told me more about the Jacksons," Alabama said. "Mom never wanted to talk about them, except to call them names. I asked Gladdie, and all she said was they owned a lumber business. She didn't seem to like me mentioning them, even. Why would she care?"

Bev aimed a sharp gaze at her. "Mama stood by Diana all those years when those people wouldn't have anything to do with her . . . or you."

"Of course. Mom was Gladdie's daughter. Gladdie knew she was honest."

Bev lurched to her feet. "Alabama, I'm so sorry. I'll handle it however you want when they call. If they call. If you really want to be involved with those people, I can't stop you."

"Those people?" Alabama repeated, at a higher volume. "They're my family. Aren't they?"

Bev raised her hands to her temples. "I'm not feeling well. I'm just not up to thinking about all of this, okay? In fact, I'm going to take a nap. You can wrap my hamburger patty in foil and put it in the freezer. But wait till it cools. And make sure the seal on the foil is tight. Otherwise the meat will get frosty."

Her aunt drifted out of the room, spewing food freezing tips until her bedroom door snicked closed and Alabama couldn't hear her anymore.

Left alone in the kitchen, she felt as though she'd wandered into the middle of a mystery movie and was missing vital information. She approached the letter on the table. She didn't read it over again—she'd already pored over the pages so often she had it memorized—but she did marvel at it. The power of it. Something in those words had seriously disturbed Bev.

CHAPTER 14

Gladys hadn't said why she wanted them in Dallas on a Friday. "I have an appointment," she'd said. "Wear a dress, and make sure Alabama looks nice, too."

"What kind of appointment?"

"An important appointment. You need to be here at ten o'clock on the nose."

Probably it had to do with her lawyer, which would explain the mystery. Gladys had been raised in the days of party lines and still didn't trust phones for talking about anything financial or legal. The instructions to be nicely dressed also seemed peculiar, but Gladys believed any errand that involved "going downtown" required a dress, dress shoes, and substantial foundation garments. She wore a girdle to get her teeth cleaned.

The secrecy of her mother's plans aggrieved Bev, especially since she was having to skip an in-service day. Sneaky was the fashion, evidently, like Alabama and her Jackson correspondence. No one was behaving how she wanted them to, Bev thought as they were on the road to Dallas. Her mother was being mysterious. Derek wasn't calling. Glen wasn't fading into the background. Alabama wasn't settling in . . . and obviously had no plans to.

That horrid letter from Dorothy Jackson! The

mere threat of talking to that daughter of hers had required two BC Powders and an evening in bed. But nothing had banished that family from her thoughts. Hard to believe she and Dot Jackson had once thought they would be sisters someday, or that they had spent a weekend sharing a room.

The spring that she and Tom had graduated—spring of '69—when Bev had visited Houston to meet his family in their large house in River Oaks, she'd been surprised to be put up in Tom's sister's room. The family had told her they were redecorating the guest rooms . . . but Bev always suspected the reason she'd spent three nights in the twin bed next to Dot's was so Dot could keep tabs on her and report back. As if Bev had anything to hide! Tom wasn't the kind to engage in hanky-panky in his parents' house—and of course, neither was she.

During the visit, his parents, Dorothy and Thomas Sr., had been cordial but frosty. Their manners brought to mind noblesse oblige—and Bev was the peasant they were obliged to put up with. She felt like a shopgirl who had bumbled into the House of Windsor. It didn't help that on her first night there, she'd busted a Lalique figurine in the library.

Oh, they extended a chilly hand of hospitality, although Bev guessed from the stiff curl of Dorothy's lip, and the way the maids quietly removed all the valuable breakables in sight, that the woman believed her son could have found someone better. Or at least someone less destructive.

It was a stressful visit. Even in the privacy of Dot's tastefully decorated bedroom, which resembled a bed-and-breakfast more than any teenager's room Bev had ever seen, relaxation proved impossible. At the end of an evening listening to Dorothy Jackson holding forth on anything and everything, Bev just wanted to collapse and turn her brain off. But that's when Dot went into Grand Inquisitor mode, peppering her with questions as they prepared for bed.

"Are you and Tom getting married soon?" she'd asked the first night, as soon as the door closed.

The subject was one Tom's parents had shied away from. Heck, it was a subject *she* shied away from, and Tom did, too.

But not Dot.

"Tom and I are just good friends," Bev told her.

Dot impatiently tapped her slipper. "That's what girls always say about boys they're interested in hooking. But y'all have been dating for several years. I saw one of your letters to him last summer. Its tone was more than friendly, I'd say."

"You read Tom's mail?"

"He left it right out in the open on the dining table. That's a communal area."

She said it as though some hard-and-fast rule excused her behavior.

"Well, yes," Bev admitted. "We've dated for . . . a while."

"I see." Dot bobbed her head sagely. "He hasn't asked. That's so typical of Tom. We were all curious, see, because he's never brought a girl home with him before. Not to stay over. Of course, he probably mostly wants you here as a buffer."

"A buffer?"

"Because he has no future plans. I guess he thinks if you're here Mother and Daddy won't pester him about what he's going to do with his life, after college. He hasn't planned on a profession."

"He'll make his way," Bev said. "He's very bright."

Dot's eyes widened. "*Tom?* He can't be that smart—his grades weren't good enough to get him into an Ivy League school. And he refused to even think about West Point, like Daddy wanted. I'm probably going to Stanford or Radcliffe myself. And then law school. I've known that for ages."

"Well, Tom's different."

"That's why Mother and Daddy are so worried. They wanted him to be more goal oriented. Like me."

"Not everyone can be like you," Bev said. Thank God.

"Which is a good thing, I suppose. If people like

Tom went to prestigious colleges, they wouldn't be prestigious anymore, would they?"

Bev didn't have an answer for that—not a polite one, anyway.

But Dot was already moving on to a new topic. "You're training to be a teacher, aren't you? What do you want to teach?"

"Home economics."

"My school doesn't offer home ec. It's a private school, so homemaking's not our scene, although I guess some skills like that are important to know—sewing and cooking and things like that. Especially if you don't have much money. You make your own clothes, don't you?"

"Most of them."

"I guessed that."

Seventeen. People said all kinds of thoughtless, pretentious things at seventeen that they would never dream of saying once they became a sentient adult. Trouble was, it was hard to tell whether Dot was being thoughtless and pretentious because she was seventeen, or because that's who she really was.

The only good thing to say about Dot was that she was a lot less intimidating than her parents. Or, rather, her mother. Thomas Sr. seemed as though he could have a nice side, although he was hard to get to know because of his wife. Dorothy Jackson might be a Southern lady who wore gloves to the supermarket and would remain planted in the car until the person she was with came around to open her door, but she was no wilting violet. She talked right over her husband—over everyone—making puzzling pronouncements in such an unswerving tone that they would sometimes stop the conversation cold.

"Your mother is a widow?" she asked Bev one night at dinner.

Bev was happy to turn her attention away from the seafood aspic on her plate. All those little shrimps and bits of crab and scallop looked like salmonella suspended in Jell-O. "Yes, ma'am, she is."

"A war widow?"

"No, my younger sister and I were both born after the war. My father died quite a few years after he got back from overseas, from appendicitis."

Dorothy put her fork down to take this in. "He had an appendicitis attack when he had two little children?"

Bev shifted uncomfortably and looked over at Tom, but his aspic had apparently mesmerized him into a blue funk. "I'm sure he didn't mean to die."

"Well, naturally not. But if he had died in the war, that would have seemed more excusable," Dorothy proclaimed.

Bev glanced at the others. No one else appeared to think it odd that a person would intimate that a man would need permission to have his appendix rupture. Or if they did, no one challenged Dorothy on it.

During the day, Dot tagged along with Bev and Tom and would inject herself into their conversations. A professional Nikon camera—"I'm on the school paper"—always hung around her neck, and Bev never knew when that telephoto lens would zoom in on her—sometimes when she was with Tom, sometimes when she was merely wandering around the house, looking at things. It was hard to tell if Dot was capturing memories or gathering evidence.

The nights unfolded in a relentless pattern. Around midnight, Tom would peck Bev on the lips in the dark hallway outside Dot's room, and Bev would go inside and be harangued by Dot, and slowly curl into a defensive fetal ball until she dozed off into a fevered sleep of insecurity.

The worst was the final night when the interrogation turned to sex. As Bev was brushing her teeth, Dot, sitting on the bed and staring through the bathroom door, asked her, "Have you and Tom been intimate yet?"

Bev narrowed her eyes at the mirror, fixing on the relentlessly inquisitive face over her shoulder. *I will not answer that question.* But with a mouthful of foam, all she could manage was a shake of her head.

"That's what I guessed." Dot scrunched her

knees to her chest and hugged her arms around them in satisfaction. "I just couldn't see it."

This was too much. Bev spat into the sink. "You're not supposed to see it. It's not your business."

Dot was either deaf to the anger in her tone or delighted by it. "You're not at all like Tom's other girlfriends. The flakes he used to gravitate toward! You're so sensible. It's the best thing about you. We're all grateful for that, at least."

Dot was fond of using the Jackson royal we, which meant Tom Sr., Dorothy, and herself. The entire weekend, Bev never saw them talking in private—in fact, most of the time the parents seemed as coolly formal toward their own children as they were toward Bev—yet Dot always seemed to have her pulse on Mother's and Daddy's thoughts on every subject. It was eerie. As far as Bev could tell, the three of them communicated via mind vibes.

"Although we figured you would have more of a steadying influence on Tom than you've actually had," Dot went on. "Maybe he needs an outlet . . . if you know what I mean."

Bev huffed toward her bed. She'd never thought she'd be glad to go home. She'd always imagined Tom's home as a paradise—big house, two parents, plenty of everything, a smart little sister instead of crazy, unpredictable Diana. Now she understood where his insecurity stemmed from.

"I'm not an outlet." She tossed the covers over herself.

"I didn't mean that you should serve the function of a prostitute. Believe me, Houston's got plenty of those, if that's all he needed. But I think Tom needs it all—sexual and emotional stimulation."

Given that this was his little sister talking, the conversation veered too close to gothic creepiness for Bev's comfort. She flipped off the light. "Frankly, you shouldn't be thinking about your brother's needs. Or his career plans, or anything else, except maybe his happiness."

"I was only trying to make you feel better," Dot said. "If you're trying to trap Tom into marriage, I don't think Mother and Daddy would be totally opposed. You're not their ideal daughter-in-law. I'm sure they dreamed of his marrying a debutante or something like that, but Tom's always acted like he's above all that social register stuff. They'll bear up eventually."

Every sentence out of the girl's mouth seemed to be designed to needle her rawest insecurities. As she blotted out Dot's voice and squeezed her eyes shut, all her fears bubbled to the surface. A popular girl had broken Tom's heart freshman year, sending him into a tailspin. Then he'd met Bev. Of course she wasn't like his other girl-friends—she was his tailspin rebound girlfriend. Tom hadn't strayed . . . as far as she knew . . . but there always seemed to be something missing. That spark. He never seemed as excited about their relationship as he was about Dante, for example. Surely that wasn't a good sign.

She tried not to care what the Jacksons thought of her, but being the acceptable alternative to Tom's dippy former girlfriends was unsettling.

"I'm not trying to trap anyone," she declared.

After the visit, it took her two weeks at home again to get the sour Jackson taste out of her mouth and remember that she loved Tom. And that he seemed to love her. Their relationship had nothing to do with tailspins, good sense, his snobby family, or her practical homemade clothes. It had stood the test of three years.

In retrospect, what galled Bev was how quickly Dot had sussed the situation, how psychologically astute she had been, even at seventeen. And, as horrible as it was for Bev to admit it now, maybe the next spring she *had* been trying to trap Tom—with the wedding dress, and then the baby . . . and her desperate hopes. And then her bitterness. That had been the biggest trap of all.

"You aren't planning to tell Gladdie about me and the Jacksons, are you?" Alabama asked.

Bev sucked in her breath. She'd been so lost in thought, in history, she'd nearly forgotten that anyone else was in the car.

"I don't want to upset Gladdie," Alabama said.

Bev had to switch gears from the distant past to the current conflict.

"But it would be odd not to say anything until you were packing your bags to move to Houston." They'd have to mention something. A courtesy warning, say, along the lines of *FYI, your grand-daughter is going over to the side of Satan.*

"I'm not moving," Alabama said. "Mrs. Jackson doesn't even believe me."

"She will."

"Why do you think so?"

"Because it's the truth." She couldn't help glancing over. "You're her flesh and blood."

Alabama's eyes widened, and Bev focused her full attention on the road again.

"How do you know? I mean, *really* know?" Alabama asked.

"Because . . ." Bev swallowed. "I believed Diana."

Alabama let out a puzzled sniff. "Mom wouldn't have taken *your* word on anything. She didn't trust you."

"You're wrong about that. Diana—"

Diana even trusted me with you.

Luckily, she stopped her words, but she couldn't stop the hysterical emotion sneaking up on her. Poor Diana. Poor all of them. The back of her throat gummed up, and her arms shook on the steering wheel. Bev recognized the symptoms as the warning signs of a grief meltdown. Blurry vision would be next, in four . . . three . . . two . . .

"You two didn't even like each other," Alabama said.

To the right, a weigh station appeared, and Bev wrenched the wheel so they could make the turn in time. The Toyota donuted into the exit with a squeal.

Alabama assumed the pre-crash position, feet pressing an invisible brake, arms bracing the dashboard for impact. "What are you doing?" she yelled.

Bev kept driving, sandwiched first between two honking eighteen-wheelers, and then darting over to the shoulder. Mashing the brake sent both of them crashing forward against their shoulder belts.

Alabama glanced frantically out all the windows. "I don't think we're supposed to be in this place."

Bev dug a tissue out of her purse and blew her nose.

"Is this about Mom?" Alabama's tone intersected at the corner of understanding and impatience. "You're so crazy. You weren't even that close."

"We lived together half our lives," Bev said.

"And hated each other! You weren't friends."

"We didn't have to be—we were sisters. I'm sorry you don't know what that means. And I guess maybe Diana didn't always say the nicest things about me. But even when times were at their worst, I know she still considered me her big sister."

She ended the speech with a hiccuping sob and mashed her fist against her forehead to regain control.

"Ooo-kay . . ." Alabama said. "So you two had some weird psychic bond. Funny she never mentioned that to me."

"You don't understand. You don't—"

Knuckles rapped against the window next to her left ear, and Bev jumped in her seat. She cranked the window down a crack. But only a crack.

A craggy face smiled tentatively at her beneath a *Where's the Beef?* gimme cap. "Y'all doing okay?"

Bev's lips automatically stretched into a big smile, which, combined with the tear-streaked makeup she glimpsed in the rearview mirror, probably made her seem even more like a madwoman. "We're fine!" she singsonged back. "Just felt a little under the weather . . . you know. . . ."

"Uh-huh." The man tilted his head and inspected her face, and then he darted a meaningful glance over at Alabama, no doubt trying to match it to his memories of recent milk cartons. "How are you doing today, little lady?"

"Fine," Alabama said.

"School day, isn't it?"

Torn between outrage at the interrogation and relief that there were still Good Samaritan truckers on the road, Bev opted for full disclosure. "I'm her aunt, and a teacher. We're on our way to Dallas to see my mother." She added. "Who has an appointment at ten."

The trucker tapped the roof of the car and smiled again. "Just wanted to check that you weren't lost or having car trouble."

"No, everything's fine."

" 'Cause you seemed . . . distressed."

"Everything's fine," she repeated, and then rolled the window back up. When the man gave up and ambled back to his rig, she blew out a breath.

She tried to remember what had brought them to this point, and to think of some way to get them past it. "I'll just let Mama know first contact has been made between you and the Jacksons," she told Alabama. "I have to do that much. There's always a chance that the Jacksons will try to get in touch with her, too."

"Why would they do that?" Alabama asked. "They probably don't even know I've got another grandmother."

Oh, they knew.

"Can you at least not talk about it in front of Wink?" Alabama pleaded.

That would be difficult. Nothing of moment happened at Gladys's anymore without Wink's presence.

"Wink might think my contacting the Jacksons was sort of . . . disloyal," Alabama said.

"I don't know why it should matter to him."

"Because he wouldn't want Gladdie's feelings hurt."

So Alabama worried about Gladdie's feelings, and even Wink's. But she didn't seem to lose much sleep over how Bev might feel. Bev tried not to take it personally, and yet . . .

What had she done wrong? She'd thought she'd been so welcoming. But from the very start, something hadn't clicked. Maybe she just wasn't cool enough. Alabama was always talking about the stuff the Looneys had at their house. Big-screen television, MTV, something called Nintendo, and a videocassette player. How could she compete with all that?

Since Gladys had specified ten o'clock, once in Dallas they went straight to The Villas, foregoing the usual trip to Bev's favorite craft store. Whizzing past it caused a twitch. Buying teaching supplies had been her rationale for skipping the ten o'clock faculty meeting and coming to Dallas.

Well, they could stop on the drive back, even if it was on the wrong side of the road and would require more treacherous left-hand turns. She needed pipe cleaners for the upcoming Thanksgiving project.

Alabama must have sensed her longing. "Why do you always need to go to that place?"

Bev had to laugh. "Oh, I know. It's a sickness. Like an addiction."

"You've got *so much* crud already. You could practically open your own store with the junk lying around the house."

"Wouldn't that be a kick?" Bev asked. "Owning a craft store . . . being around all that fun stuff all day long, seeing what other people are up to, and holding crafting classes on weekends?" It sounded like a dream.

Alabama didn't appear convinced. "Better than being a teacher, maybe." She shook her head. "But not by much."

Gladys met them at the door wearing her royal-blue dress decorated with an orchid corsage. The outfit was also accessorized with the biggest smile Bev could ever remember seeing from her mother. For a moment, she looked like an entirely different person.

"Wink! The bridesmaids are here!"

Bev froze. *Bridesmaids?*

In the next instant, she was swept into the apartment, where elderly ladies swarmed, dressed in their Sunday best. Somewhere, Benny Goodman played. When had her mother picked up a stereo? Confused, Bev spun, surveying the room. A woman was mixing champagne-and-orange-juice cocktails in the kitchenette, and someone from a nearby clump of guests offered one of these mimosas to Bev in a Dixie cup.

Her gaze snagged on an unfamiliar bookcase against the wall. It wasn't only the people making the room feel crowded. The room was stuffed with new furniture, little of which matched her mother's.

Bev grabbed her mother's elbow. "What's going on?"

"I thought it was obvious. Wink and I are getting married."

From over her shoulder, she heard Wink laugh. "She probably wasn't sure who you were marrying—me or some other fellow. Is there someone you haven't told me about, Glad-Rags?"

Gladys laughed, too—she was as close to a state of bubbliness as Bev had ever witnessed. "The activity van is going to take us all to City Hall. You don't mind if it's not a religious ceremony, do you, Bev? I know you're a traditionalist."

Bev managed to steer her mother into the bedroom without attracting too much notice. The guests probably thought they were tending to last-minute details.

"I don't care what kind of ceremony you have," Bev said, "but why all the rush?"

"Wink and I aren't getting any younger."

"And why keep it a secret from me?"

"I thought you'd enjoy the surprise." But when Bev continued to pin her with a stare, she admitted, "And I thought you might not be very enthusiastic. It appears I was right."

"I'm not trying to be a wet blanket, but it seems so . . . odd. All these years, you never once spoke of remarrying. And now, after a few months of knowing this person—"

"We've lived in the same building for eight months."

"And for six of those months you disliked the man."

"There you go." Gladys picked at her corsage. "Inflexible."

"No, I'm not. But it hasn't been that long since you two started . . ." Bev searched for the corrected word. *Hanging out* didn't sound right for senior citizens. *Going together* reminded her of her students.

"Courting?" her mother said. "It *hasn't* been long, but Wink's so enthusiastic. He wants us to move in together—to save money, for one thing—but I couldn't live in sin. I don't mind for myself so much, but it would set a bad example for Alabama, I think."

It was all Bev could do not to laugh. "She grew up with Diana, and you're worried about bad influences?"

A withering frown of reproof chilled her. "I won't have any of your talk against Diana this morning. I want today to be pleasant."

"I don't understand why things couldn't go on as before," Bev said.

"Because we think we'll be happier this way.

Also, two people can live as cheaply as one. At least we won't be paying for two apartments. I want to have some money to leave to you and Alabama when I'm gone."

"Don't worry about that." Maybe now was the moment to bring up the Jacksons . . . although on second thought, that also would fall into the category of unpleasantness.

While she ruminated, Gladys thrust a small bouquet into her hands. "This is for you. You're maid of honor."

"Thank you, Mama."

"Wink claimed Alabama for best man."

Bev bent and sniffed the scentless posy of carnations and baby's breath. "I really do hope you'll be happy."

"I know you do, Bevvie. You're too . . . well, too much like me, I guess." Gladys laughed. "That could explain why this family hasn't seen a wedding for fifty years."

Bev smiled, but then, as the words sank in, a stricken expression crossed her mother's features—an expression she was certain mirrored her own.

"I'd better get back to my guests." Gladys turned and hurried out of the bedroom.

Throughout the morning, Bev attempted to throw herself into the proceedings. When not everyone could fit into the van, she piled more into the Toyota's backseat. Luckily, she hadn't partaken of too many of those Dixie cup mimosas. In the judge's chambers, she stood up tall and tried to feel enthusiastic as her mother swore to love, honor, and cherish a man in a multicolored check jacket and pink-and-green striped tie. Her head told her it was a hopeless mismatch, but her heart couldn't help rising to the joy of the occasion. She clapped as excitedly as anyone when, after the exchanging of rings, Wink took out his ukulele and sang "I Found a Million Dollar Baby."

Back at The Villas, she handed out beverages and finger sandwiches, and chuckled like everyone else that Clara, who had glaucoma, had chosen a sheet cake with a homecoming theme by mistake. It was seasonal and festive, everyone agreed, and the little marzipan footballs tasted delicious.

For the honeymoon, Wink was going to whisk Gladys away to a night at a fancy hotel that had a swing band on weekends. He'd even ordered a limo to take them. It was hard to imagine Gladys Putterman dancing the night away and then luxuriating in the honeymoon suite at the Mansion at Turtle Creek. In fact, Bev tried very hard *not* to imagine it.

She fretted that she wouldn't have a chance to say a word to her mom before they left, but at the last minute, Gladys pulled her aside.

"I'm so glad you were here, Bev. It meant so much to have you and Alabama with me."

"It was a lovely day, Mama. I wish you had warned me, though, so I could have done something special."

"We wanted to do it our way," Gladys said. "Frankly, a bigger event wouldn't have seemed right. Not this year, with Diana . . ."

And there it was again, the broody uneasiness that had been right below the surface.

"I had something to tell you about Alabama," Bev said.

A frown creased Gladys's brow. "What's the matter?"

"She's written to the Jacksons."

Gladys went ashen. "What does she want with those people?"

"She wants to be part of their family."

"Good Lord in heaven. She asked me about them weeks ago, but I never dreamed . . ."

"Mrs. Jackson's consulting her lawyers. Dot Jackson's on the case, too."

Her mother poked Bev sharply in the breastbone. "Don't you let them get our girl in their clutches."

"You don't understand. I don't think the Jacksons want to have anything to do with Alabama. They never have."

"Horrible people." Gladys tilted her head. "Did you tell Alabama about . . . everything?"

"Not exactly."

To Bev's surprise, her mother nodded her

approval. "Good. Poor girl. First to lose Diana, then to bump heads with that pack of hyenas down in Houston."

Wink darted his head in. "Limo's here. Ready, Twinkle-toes?"

Gladys laughed and gave Bev a bracing pat on the shoulder. "We'll talk more about this later. We probably haven't heard the last from those people."

"No," Bev said. "I'm sure we haven't."

They were both right. That very evening, while Alabama was at Stuart's—thank goodness—Dot Jackson called. It was the call Bev had been dreading, yet it caught her completely unawares.

Although she should have known. Even the ring of the phone sounded more pesky than usual before she picked it up.

"Bev? This is Dot Jackson," the caller greeted her matter-of-factly. "I don't imagine you've forgotten me."

"Oh no," Bev said. "I haven't."

They exchanged formal, halfhearted how-are-yous before Dot got right down to the crux of the matter. "I don't need to tell you how disturbed Mother's been after receiving the girl's letter."

Bev pursed her lips. "Mm. I can guess." *A guilty conscience will do that.*

"We're weighing the situation very carefully. Of course, we have no way of knowing . . ."

"Yes, you do."

Dot snorted. "Let's not mince words, Bev. I'm sorry about your sister, but Diana was no saint, and not exactly the most dependable person on the planet. And as you'll recall, the last time our parents heard from your people, there was talk of another grandbaby . . ."

"You can drop that subject right now," Bev said. "And if it's *ever* mentioned to Alabama . . ."

"I have no intention of telling Alabama anything," Dot said, cutting her off. "I only wanted to call to let you know that we're taking these allegations *very* seriously."

"Allegations?" Bev clenched her hand on the receiver. "She's not an allegation—she's a teenager."

"But whose?"

"Tom's. Your brother's."

"There's a lot at stake with this, Bev," Dot said. "Maybe Alabama doesn't understand that, but I'm sure you do. In fact, I'm not convinced that you aren't the guiding force behind all this."

Anger made her hand shake so hard that it was all she could do not to slam the phone down. "I knew nothing about that letter. And believe me, I wasn't particularly happy about it. But Alabama's just lost her mother, and she's reaching out for family."

"And Mother's just lost her husband last year, and she's feeling vulnerable. I guess *that* didn't occur to you."

"I didn't know until Alabama told me," Bev said. "And I was sorry to hear about your father. But, again, the first I heard about the correspondence was when I read your mother's reply. Which didn't exactly fill me with warm fuzzies for reconnecting with the Jacksons, by the way."

"We're still weighing what to do next," Dot said. "I only wanted to warn you not to get your hopes up . . . or the girl's. And please—no more letters."

"I don't control *the girl's* outgoing mail. Alabama's fourteen. But I don't think your mother's reply struck her as being eager to hear from her again. She's not a fool."

"So she doesn't take after Tom or Diana . . ." Dot let the statement dangle, and Bev could have sworn she actually heard the woman smirk. "Maybe she takes after you?"

CHAPTER 15

Stuart read through Dorothy Mabry Jackson's letter again. "This is the woman you want to be your long-lost grandmother?"

"She *is* my grandmother, whether I want her to be or not. Why shouldn't I get to know my dad's family?"

"She sounds snobby. And she really didn't like your mother."

That bothered Alabama, too, but she wasn't willing to give up yet. "She just didn't think my mother was telling the truth about me. She says she only met her once. Maybe my mom was having a really bad day." Her mom had had a lot of those.

He squinted at the words, studying them like a gypsy reading tea leaves. "Well, if you do want to meet her, you should definitely send her a picture. You've got to make her see you as a person, not just a Putterman."

Alabama nodded and spread the photographs she'd picked as possibilities out on the bed. "This is probably my best one." She pointed to the snapshot that had been taken last year, by Charlie the sax player, after they'd been to a concert in the park. She was standing behind her mom with her arms draped around her, smiling like she could barely remember smiling in her life. A sitcom smile of perfect happiness. Her mom was beaming.

On second thought, she picked up the picture and tucked it back into the envelope it had come from. "It's my favorite picture of my mom. I can't send it."

"We could make a copy."

"That would take too long."

He nodded. "Plus your mom's in it. No offense, but she doesn't seem to be a good selling point with Granny Jackson."

"Right. I think I should send her one of this year's school pictures." She gestured to the photo of her against a boring slate-gray backdrop. She wasn't smiling, but it seemed a pretty accurate representation of herself at this moment. Her potential benefactress might as well realize what she'd be taking on—weird hair, unhappiness, and all. Plus, her forlorn expression might make Granny Jackson more inclined to rescue her. She looked like a CARE kid who'd gotten into dye trouble.

"Yeah, that would probably be best." Stuart leaned back and sighed. "I don't know why you want to leave beautiful, bustling New Sparta."

She laughed, but he didn't.

"I don't know why you want to leave me," he said.

"I'm not leaving *you*." She nudged him. "Besides, you'd abandon me quick enough if

Kevin Kerrigan came along and swept you off your feet."

"Of course. But I'd still be here to wave at you occasionally across the cafeteria."

She tossed her second-grade picture at him.

"Okay," he said. "Stick your photo in an envelope so we can get on with important matters. Talent show. Have you been thinking about it?"

"Yeah. I've thought a lot about scratching my name off the list."

He rolled his eyes. "Don't be a coward. It would be so cool if I won first prize and you won second."

"What do we win?"

"A ribbon."

"I'm supposed to humiliate myself for a ribbon?"

"You're not going to humiliate yourself."

"Dressing up weird and tap dancing to 'Rock Lobster'?"

"It'll be cute."

"No, it was cute when I did it in elementary school. Now it's going to seem weird."

"That's what's so great about it. It's, like, surreal. Like a Thomas Dolby music video."

"Only I won't be on MTV, I'll be in the New Sparta High School auditorium, humiliated."

"You need to learn to take risks," he said. "Besides, maybe you can use the Miss Havisham costume to earn extra credit in English."

Though a long shot, that outcome was a compelling carrot to dangle in front of her. Her grades needed a boost. Concentrating on schoolwork was tough this year. During classes, even ones she liked okay, her attention would veer off. The scratch paper on her algebra test would fill up with doodles, not numbers. The sight of the janitor mowing outside the window would distract her from a biology lecture. Though she craved dreams, when she could be with her mom again for precious flashes of time, she could only sleep fitfully at night. Yet sit her at a desk in the middle of the school day and she was instantly narcoleptic.

Her teachers probably thought she was really stupid.

"Where is the dress?" Stuart asked.

"Back up in the attic, I guess."

His eyes brightened. "Can we go look at it again? I'm thinking of stuff we could put on it."

"I'm not sure Bev would like that."

"Nothing permanent—we'd just pin stuff to it. How could she object to that? In class she's always telling us to do more with less, by accessorizing what we have and using things for two purposes. That's part of home economy. Well, we're finding a dual purpose for a dress."

Alabama still hesitated. "I think this is what they call peer pressure."

He smiled. "Is it working?"

Minutes later, they were rummaging through the attic again. Alabama found the dress in its box and pulled it out. Never satisfied, Stuart kept excavating. "Do you think she had some gloves—long ones?"

"I don't know."

Alabama held the dress up to herself. *Whose was it?* That's what still puzzled her. It was her size, too small for Bev. The dress had to have been her mom's.

Maybe that's what had upset Bev when she'd seen the dress on the dummy. She was obviously prone to coming unhinged when it came to her sister.

"Oh boy—more pictures." Stuart unearthed an old photograph album and sat back against a trunk to leaf through it. "Maybe we'll find a better snap to send to Granny Jackson."

Alabama frowned and lowered herself down next to him. "There won't be any of me in there. I'd barely met Bev before this June."

"Yeah, these are all ancient." Stuart flipped through the thick board pages. "I love old pictures. People used to look so much better."

To Alabama, people in old photos usually seemed stiff and overdressed.

"This must be your grandmother," Stuart said.

"Yeah, that's Gladdie." In the black-and-white photo, Gladdie was standing next to a tall man on a porch. She was so young! Alabama felt a buzz of excitement to find a whole new set of photos of the family. Most of the ones she'd seen were the few her mom had had, or the framed ones Gladdie kept in her apartment. "That's my grandfather. I've only seen a couple of pictures of him before." Now she drank in his features—the straight, thin mouth and sober, light-colored eyes. He and Gladdie gazed seriously at the camera, as if they knew he wasn't going to live long enough to take many more pictures.

What if they'd had a crystal ball to tell them Gladdie would end up married to Wink Williams? Maybe that would have made them laugh.

"Is *this* your mom?" It was hard to miss the disappointment in Stuart's voice as he stared at the picture of Diana, leaning against a tree and grinning, with hair that reached almost down to the low hips of her jeans. "She wasn't a beehive girl. She was a hippie."

"Wasn't she pretty?" Alabama couldn't take her eyes off her, even when they began to cloud with tears. She wanted to crawl into that picture.

Stuart moved on. "And this must be Ms. Putterman."

On the facing page was Bev, in a black-and-white shot different from the rest of the pictures in the album. The glossy photo looked almost professionally done, even though it was just a candid shot of Bev staring at a grandfather clock.

"She looks so cool," Stuart said.

"Aunt Bev? *Cool?*" Alabama inspected the picture more closely, but all she saw was Bev. It irked her that Stuart preferred a photo of Bev to the one of her mother. But of course he knew Bev.

"She's wearing a cool dress—like Audrey Hepburn in *Breakfast at Tiffany's*. And who's this mystery man?" he asked.

The face smiling up at her was one she'd only seen in the faded color snapshot her mother had kept in her drawer. Tom Jackson. Here he was in a wrinkled suit jacket and tie, arms folded, grinning puppyishly.

"That's my dad." She reached out to touch the edge of his head, as if he would be flesh and blood. Her chest felt tight.

"He was cute," Stuart said. "I thought you said he was in the army."

"Not always, obviously."

"Yeah, but I expected somebody more serious."

Actually, so had she. Of course, her mother had said that her dad was a bookworm, but she hadn't mentioned that he had a goofy, sweet smile that tugged at your heart.

These photographs confused her. Who had taken the picture of her dad? It seemed to come from the same batch as the picture of Bev and the grandfather clock. Maybe her mom? Alabama squinted, searching for clues. The background didn't resemble Gladdie's old house.

"Are there any more pictures of your mom?" Stuart asked.

There weren't. She found a few more of Tom, though. Some were cheap yellowed color snapshots that looked as if they'd been taken at college. The last pages of the album remained empty, leaving her with the uneasy feeling of something that had been interrupted. "This is weird. I wonder if this was my mom's photo album. She might've abandoned it when she left home."

"Why would your aunt have it, then?"

Good question. Alabama supposed Bev could have purposefully salvaged it from Gladdie's house when Gladdie moved to the apartment. Maybe that's how her aunt ended up with a lot of this old stuff, including the wedding dress.

"Or maybe your aunt had a crush on your dad."

Alabama recoiled. "Yuck! Why would you say that?"

He nodded toward the album. "Because she kept his pictures."

She was tempted to swipe several of the pictures, if not the whole album, but she remembered her aunt blowing her stack about her snooping in the attic the last time. The pictures going missing would be a dead giveaway. But if this was Bev's photo album and she cared about it so much, why was it stowed away in the attic, out of sight?

Alabama had thought her aunt was really mad about her getting in touch with Granny Jackson, but over the next week, Bev acted as though it had never happened. Instead, she'd decided that as a big treat, they should invest in a videocassette recorder. "That way we can have movie nights here. Derek loves movies, and you can invite Stuart over, too."

Bev put more thought into buying the VCR than most people gave to choosing a new car. She read everything she could find about the topic, and then they spent an entire weekend shopping. "Derek is coming back next week," she explained to Alabama during the trip to Tyler to make the final purchase. "This will give us plenty of time to get the machine all set up for Saturday night."

On Saturday, the shiny black VCR was out of its box, the instruction manual had been read by Bev cover to cover, and their first rental tapes waited on the coffee table, but Bev nearly ended up having a nervous breakdown trying to set it up. "I can't make heads or tails of this." An increasingly angry series of phooeys and gosh-darnits emanated from behind the television, and when Bev came up for air, her face was as red and sweaty as if she'd been running a marathon.

She puffed out a breath. "I don't know. Maybe it's broken. I'll have to take it back."

Moments later, Stuart arrived, pinpointed the

problem, and connected the machine in about two seconds.

"It's perfect," he said, admiring the machine effusively enough to smooth Bev's ruffled feathers. He was also excited about the movies they'd rented. He picked up one with Bette Davis. "I've always wanted to see *The Old Maid*."

Alabama knew that, which is why she lobbied for it extra-hard at the video rental place—which, in New Sparta, was also a bait shop. Bev had thought *The Old Maid* sounded depressing, so she'd insisted on renting two films.

"Tonight we're going to watch *Any Which Way You Can*," Bev told Stuart. "Derek loves Clint Eastwood movies."

Stuart's enthusiasm was effectively doused. "Really? Even the monkey ones?"

"I loved Clyde!" Bev said.

Derek hadn't been around for nearly a month, and now it was as if royalty was coming. Ten minutes before his estimated time of arrival, a can of his favorite beer was put in the freezer so it would be at optimal chill when it reached his hand. The oven was already preheated so a frozen pizza could be popped in if Derek showed the slightest impatience to eat. Bev's air popper and a jar of Orville Redenbacher stood at the ready.

But Derek didn't show up. Six o'clock—magic hour—passed, then seven. The telephone, the focus of all Bev's interest, crouched silent on the end table. Finally, at seven thirty, they decided to go ahead and make popcorn and at least start the Bette Davis movie. No harm in that, Bev said.

No harm, except that Alabama had never sat down and watched an entire movie with Bev in the living room. They both had regular series they followed, with tastes that intersected at *Moonlighting* and *Newhart*, but usually Alabama tried to avoid getting stuck in the living room for anything longer than an hour-long series. True, they'd been to movies. But in the New Sparta movie theater, a single-screen operation where the owner patrolled the aisle looking for propped feet and smuggled-in snacks, Bev was always courteously silent.

Now, at home, she provided a running commentary, as if she were standing at the back of a classroom during an educational film. "This is set during the Civil War. I love those kinds of stories, don't you?" When no one answered, she remained silent until the observations could be held back no more. "Bette Davis was so beautiful back then, wasn't she? She had such distinctive eyes."

"You could write a song about them," Stuart said.

Bev laughed. "Oh, I know—unoriginal, right? But just look at her. And she seems so old and cuckoo now when she's on *Johnny Carson*." After a minute of film flickered by, she said, "Her sister's fiancé is so handsome. What's that actor's name?"

"George Brent." Stuart sounded less annoyed by the intrusion than Alabama was.

In the film's opening scenes, Bette spent the night out with George, which caused Bev to shake her head. "You know what that meant back then, don't you? No birth control in those days." And when Bette turned up pregnant, Bev was right there to say I told you so. "We saw that coming, didn't we? Now what'll she do?"

Alabama was pretty sure if Bette could have done anything at that moment, she would have stepped out of the television and strangled Bev. She was almost glad when the lights from Derek's truck swept across the windows. Better to have color commentary ruin a Clint Eastwood movie than one she really wanted to watch.

Bev jumped up and practically jogged to the front door. Alabama winced at her overeagerness. Couldn't she show a little pride?

Derek murmured something at the door, then came in and parked himself on the couch. He looked annoyed, and as a result the room bloomed with tension. Where Bev's face had been full of anticipation all evening, along with a little anxiety, it now appeared a frozen mask of nerves.

"Maybe we should stop the film," she said. "I was going to heat up a pizza."

"What the hell is this?" Derek leaned forward

and picked the plastic cassette case off the coffee table. "You rented this? They show this stuff on television for free every night of the week."

"We've got Clint Eastwood, too," Bev called from the kitchen.

Alabama reached for the remote control, her fingers fumbling over the unfamiliar tiny keypad.

"It's okay," Derek said, his voice gruff. "Might as well leave it on, since you've already started."

He pushed himself off the couch. The whole house rattled when he walked around in it. Or maybe Alabama's nerves were rattling. Bev's mood had worn off on her. Whenever Derek was around, her aunt's anxiety to please ramped up to Edith Bunker intensity.

She tried to concentrate on the movie, but she couldn't help picking up snatches of words from the kitchen. First, she heard Derek's gruff "already ate" followed by a disappointed response from Bev. The voices lowered, and all she could pick up were "don't have time . . . stupid movie . . . kids . . ." The intensity of the whispers rose then, and Bev's plaintive, "What *have* you been doing for an entire month?" came through loud and clear.

Alabama stood up. "Maybe we should go outside for a minute."

"Okay." Stuart's rapid response tipped her off that he had been distracted by the kitchen drama, too.

Outside, they sat down on the iron lawn furniture Bev had so carefully painted red, white, and blue, and pretended not to listen as the argument in the house escalated.

It was impossible. "My parents never fight like that," Stuart said.

"They aren't my parents." Thank God.

She was so embarrassed. *The one time I have a friend over for an evening to do something fun, and this happens.* Poor Stuart. His family was so perfect, he probably wasn't used to raised voices, even.

"I really hope Granny Jackson writes me back soon," she said under her breath.

Inside the house, glass shattered.

"Should we call the police?" Stuart asked.

Alabama hadn't even thought of that. But her mother had always said that the police were the last people you wanted at your house. "No—let's wait."

Luckily, it wasn't long before the front door slammed and they heard Derek's truck roar down the street.

"At least that's the end of the monkey movie threat," Stuart muttered.

They ventured back inside. All was quiet. The silence should have felt soothing, meaning as it did the absence of Derek, but Alabama's stomach clenched and she rushed to Bev's door. "Aunt Bev?"

A moment passed before Bev answered. "I'll be right out. Keep watching your movie."

Turning, Alabama nearly stepped on Stuart, who was right behind her. After a puzzled exchange of glances, they shuffled back to the living room. With the couch free now, they settled on opposite ends and had a minor foot fight as each tried to stretch out. Laughing, they turned the movie back on.

A few scenes later, Bev emerged from the bedroom and hurried to the kitchen. "Y'all want pizza?" she called out brightly.

"Sure." Alabama's stomach was rumbly. All they'd had so far was a little popcorn.

Bev wasn't big on eating in front of the television except if Derek was there, but she brought plates out, along with soft drinks and coasters. Once they were all served, she took a chair farther away from the television.

"Did Bette have her baby?" she asked. "What happened to George Brent?"

"He died in battle, and Bette had the baby in secret and gave it to her sister, Miriam Hopkins, to raise," Stuart said, filling her in. They all pretended the movie was the only drama that had happened in the house that evening. "Now the girl thinks Bette's her maiden aunt, and doesn't like her."

"That's terrible," Bev said.

It all seemed hokey to Alabama, but the end

reduced Bev to a puddle of tears. In fact, she was weeping so hard, she had to retreat to her room again before the credits finished and they turned on the lights.

Alabama and Stuart cleared their plates, stacked them in the kitchen sink, and then went to her room. Alabama put on a record and flopped onto her bed. "What was *that* all about?" she wondered aloud.

Stuart remained quiet, which was unusual for him.

Great. The evening had probably scarred him for life. "You won't tell your parents about this, will you? They might not let you talk to me again if they knew what a lunatic my aunt is."

He tilted his head thoughtfully, hesitating another moment before asking, "What if she wasn't your aunt?"

Alabama snorted. "I'd throw myself a party."

Stuart didn't join in her laughter. "I mean . . . what if she's your *mother?*"

She propped herself up on her elbows. He had to be putting her on. "That's not even funny."

"But think about it."

"I don't have to. I *have* a mother." Had.

"I know it sounds weird at first, but look at all the odd stuff that's happened. First there was the mysterious wedding dress."

"That could have been anybody's. Bev probably sewed it for someone. Maybe even my mom."

"But you said your aunt got bent out of shape about it. So much that you didn't want to use it in the talent show at first."

She still didn't, but that was a separate issue. "Bev never told me that the dress was hers," she pointed out. "Just that it belonged to her now, because this is her house."

"Then there were those pictures of your dad that we found," Stuart continued. "In your *aunt's* attic."

"I told you—there are all sorts of reasons why they could be up there."

"Okay, but how do you explain that letter from your Granny Jackson? She seemed to know Bev, and maybe even like her better than your mom."

"She only mentioned Bev in passing because I had told her I was living with her. That doesn't mean she knew her. Maybe she'd heard Mom talk about her. Even as a teenager, Bev was Little Miss Perfect."

"You think."

Alabama bristled. "I *know*. My mother told me."

"The woman you thought was your mother told you. You might be just like the girl in *The Old Maid*."

"Wait. Are you saying that my life is following the plot of a Bette Davis movie?" She laughed. "You've got to be kidding!"

Stuart didn't back down. "The movie is what got me thinking. Did you notice how your aunt, your so-called aunt, reacted to it? She was weeping."

"So? Bev weeps at anything. I've seen her cry during deodorant commercials."

"And you said yourself that she really resisted renting the movie to begin with."

"Because it was called *The Old Maid*. Which probably seemed like a turnoff to her because *she's* an old maid," Alabama pointed out. "My old maid aunt. Not my mother. It's ridiculous."

For a moment he shut up. Then, quietly, he pointed out, "You look like her."

She puffed out a breath. "We're related."

"But you look more like her than your mom— the woman you call your mom."

"Would you *stop?*" Alabama said, anger rising. "You don't know what you're talking about! My mother was my mother. She went through hell bringing me up all by herself. It wasn't easy for her. We never had enough of anything, and yet she never gave me up, ever. I'm sure it would have been easier to come live near Gladdie, but Mom never wanted to do that because she hated Bev so much and didn't want me around her. . . ."

Her words trailed off. What seemed like an argument for her case turned into something else when she spoke the words aloud.

"Why would she have struggled all those years to take care of me if I wasn't really hers?" she finished.

Stuart didn't have an answer for that. Of course

he didn't. His whole theory was idiotic. She wanted to laugh at him but she was too furious.

Bruce Springsteen sang on while they both sat frowning in silence. Finally, Stuart stood. "I should go."

She got up, too. "I'll get Bev."

He shook his head. "That's okay. Don't bother her. It's only a fifteen-minute walk."

"But it's dark."

"This is New Sparta, not New York City."

"Well . . ." Even though she'd been angry at him thirty seconds ago, she didn't want him to leave. "I'll walk with you."

"Then my parents would insist on driving *you* home."

She sagged. "Yeah, you're probably right."

When he was gone, Alabama returned to the dark living room and flopped onto the couch. She picked up the movie again and stared at the cover that had been cut out and slipped into the movie's plastic rental case. An uncomfortable doubt scratched at the back of her mind. Why *did* Bev have so many pictures of Tom Jackson?

Bev's door opened and Alabama shoved the case back onto the coffee table, almost guiltily.

"Where's Stuart?" Bev asked.

"He went home."

"What? When?" When Alabama told her, Bev lurched toward the phone. "What is the Looneys' number?"

Alabama reeled it off and turned onto her stomach while Bev dialed and then issued a heart-felt apology to Mrs. Looney for allowing Stuart to walk home after dark. "I had no idea. He left so quickly. . . ."

Mrs. Looney's laughter came through the receiver, followed by tinny words Alabama couldn't make out.

"No," Bev said, "I know this isn't New York City, but . . . Well, as you say, all's well that ends well. . . . Stuart is such a good guest. And such a good worker in class, too," she added for good measure.

Bev hung up and sagged into her chair with a sigh. "I owe you an apology for tonight, too," she said. "I'm sure that was unpleasant."

Alabama had been so focused on Stuart's cockamamie theory, she'd almost forgotten about anything else. *You look like her,* Stuart had said. She sat up, reached to turn on the lamp on the end table, and gazed into her aunt's face, hoping not to see a resemblance.

Her breath caught. Bev's nose was swollen. In fact, the whole side of her face appeared mis-shapen.

"Oh my God! What happened to your nose?"

But even as she said it, she knew. Derek had done this while she and Stuart were outside.

"It's all right," Bev said. "I ran into a door."

The words sounded surreal coming from her

aunt. That was the kind of thing women said on soap operas. "You should have said something. How could you just let us watch a movie and eat pizza?" Worse, Bev had served them the pizza and they hadn't even noticed her. She felt ashamed. "Derek should be arrested!"

Bev raised her hand and gulped in a breath. "No—I don't want that. It was an accident."

"No, it wasn't."

"We were arguing, and he slammed the kitchen door. He simply forgot it was a swinging door—and it swung on me."

Alabama bit her lip. Maybe that was the truth . . . or maybe it was the truth Bev could live with.

"At any rate," Bev said, "he's gone and he won't be back. Don't worry about that. But if I get involved in some sort of scandal, it could hurt me at school. The principal already hates me. I don't want the police involved. It would be all over town tomorrow."

"But your nose looks really bad. It might be broken, even. Don't you need to go to a hospital?"

"No—I've been putting ice on it in my room. And even while we were watching the movie." She glanced at Alabama. "I don't think Stuart noticed anything, do you?"

Alabama shook her head. *He was too busy imagining us all living in a Bette Davis melodrama. . . .*

"Why was Derek so angry?" Alabama asked

her. "Was it because of Stuart and me being here?"

Bev's eyes widened in alarm. One of them. The other looked as if it was swollen half shut. "No—heavens, no. He . . ." She gulped. "I think he's found someone else."

It was weird enough that one person wanted to date Derek. Two at once? "Who?"

"I don't know. It doesn't matter. Someone he likes better than me." Bev shook her head and blew her nose, which caused her to cringe in pain. "Story of my life."

Alabama frowned. What *was* the story of Bev's life?

And how do I fit into it?

CHAPTER 16

The trouble with noses was they sat right there in the middle of your face. If something went wrong with a nose, it was impossible to hide. Even with a messed-up eye, you could always creatively arrange bangs to mask the damage at least partially. Or you could heap on copious amounts of blue eye shadow, add fake eyelashes, and pretend it was your new televangelist look. There were disguises for eyes—patches that could be explained away as medically necessary, or dark glasses.

The bridge of Bev's nose was so swollen, no glasses would stay propped there. Not to mention, the injury already kept up a steady throb that radiated from the top of her forehead to her teeth. Glasses would just make matters more ouchy.

Her nose was barely functioning as a breathing apparatus. But to her shame, she focused less on the consequences for her respiratory system than on the cosmetic angle. What did it matter if oxygen reached her lungs if she showed up at school looking like Rocky in the twelfth round? All day Sunday she kept running to the bathroom to check the damage. Each time she flipped on the light, it seemed to have progressed to a different color. What had started out an angry pink overnight had morphed into a blue, and then by evening a bluish green. In any color, it was hideous—as if a decomposing gourd had taken up residence on her face.

At some point, she even stopped thinking of it as hers. It became simply *the nose*. That the thing between her eyes and lips was actually part of her body didn't seem possible. She couldn't breathe through it, so she was forced to become a mouth breather.

Alabama was an angel that Sunday. She made the meals and brought Bev plastic bags of frozen peas and corn to ice the nose. She suggested they watch the Clint Eastwood movie, but after fifteen minutes Bev shut the player off. It felt shockingly wasteful—like walking out of a movie they'd paid good money for—but she didn't care. "I didn't really like those monkey movies all that much, I guess."

The strange thing was, she felt the same way about Derek today as she felt about the orangutan in the movie. What had been the attraction?

And why did she still feel like crying now that it was all over?

Well, she knew the answer to the last question, at least. She was thirty-eight years old, had never been married, and probably never would be. She would never have children to call her own—she'd just be the maiden aunt of a girl who didn't like her very much. Her newlywed seventy-seven-year-old mother had more romance in her life.

Meanwhile, her own second attempt at a grand passion in this lifetime had resulted in the tragedy of the nose.

Alabama peered at her as they sat in front of the dark television screen. "Have you ever noticed how much my nose looks like yours? I mean when it's not . . . you know."

"Pulverized?" Bev snorted, then shuddered in pain. She needed to remember not to find anything amusing. Which shouldn't be difficult, actually. "You don't think this would be a good look for you?"

Alabama remained serious. "I look a lot like you did when you were my age, don't I?"

She nodded. "I think we take after Mama's mother. Same coloring."

"But it seems odd that we look alike enough that even Stuart would notice, don't you think?"

"Stuart's very bright," Bev said. "And perceptive. That's the sort of thing I would imagine he'd be good about picking up on."

For some reason, Alabama didn't seem pleased by her answer. Maybe she didn't want her appearance compared to anyone whose nose looked as if it should be hanging on a meat hook. Who could blame her?

Monday morning, Alabama was eating toast in the kitchen when Bev came out dressed for school. Her niece drew back in horror. "Oh God!"

The nose was yellow-green, with an angry

purplish welt across the most bulbous section—where the door must have scraped. Bev had thought it was an improvement, but apparently not.

"Well, it's not *quite* as bad as yesterday," Alabama allowed diplomatically, once she'd gotten her initial revulsion under control.

But Bev scuttled back to the bathroom mirror, stared at it some more, and decided a panicky *oh God!* was the more honest reaction. What was she going to do? "It's hideous."

"Maybe if you put on another layer of base. . . ."

"Then it looks like I'm trying to cover up something even worse."

"What could be worse?" So much for diplomacy. As soon as she blurted out the words, Alabama paled. "I mean—well, this is what cover-up is for, right?"

Bev dabbed more on, and then groaned at the result. The discoloration defied cosmetic concealment. The nose would not be denied. "It's so obvious," she wailed in despair. "I'm going to be fired."

"They can't fire you for having a nose injury," Alabama said, outraged. "Can they?"

"Oh, Lon Kirby is looking for any excuse."

"Why? You're a good teacher. At least, Stuart says you are."

Bev shook her head. "I don't fit Lon's ideal. I'm too old-fashioned, too . . ." *Too me.*

"But somebody's got to teach health, and home ec," Alabama argued. "You said yourself that your home ec class is packed."

"Well . . ."

But now there was one fewer section than there had been last year. And though the home ec class had been full initially, several of her students had dropped out since the first day. To add insult to injury, most had rearranged their schedules to switch to choir. Lots of boys were taking choir this year—no doubt Leah Kirby and her tight dresses had something to do with that. So now girls who could barely warble a note were wild to don the blue robes of the New Sparta Songsters. The size of the choir had doubled since she'd been the director. Lon and Leah probably crowed about that over their Wheaties.

"Why don't you call in sick?" Alabama asked.

"That's probably what Lon's waiting for. He grumbled enough when I took off the in-service day."

Besides, calling in sick might just be putting off the inevitable. Who could say that tomorrow she would be any better? She couldn't hide away for a week. At the last minute, she decided on a more clinical approach to concealment. She pulled down the first aid kit and covered the unsightly appendage with gauze and surgical tape.

"If anyone asks, we were in a car accident in Dallas yesterday."

"Lie, you mean?" Alabama asked.

"No one would believe the truth anyway."

Alabama bobbed her head. "That your thug boyfriend slammed a door on your face? Yeah, that's a stretch."

"I meant they wouldn't believe that it was an accident."

"No, probably not."

At school, the reaction to the bandages was so overwhelmingly sympathetic that Bev felt vindicated in her decision to fib. Lon nearly dropped his coffee mug when she stopped by the office. "You poor thing." He rushed toward her. "What happened to you?"

After her quick explanation, he admonished, "You should be at home today."

She merely shrugged as she retrieved her mail from her cubby. "I'll be fine." She couldn't help making a dig, though. "We've got so much ground to cover in class, now that two years have been consolidated into one. I'd rather not waste a single second."

His expression, for once, was almost admiring. "That's dedication, Bev. Let me know if you need help today."

The only hiccup came when she passed the auditorium where Glen was rearranging a bulletin board. Stuart was with him. When he caught sight of her, Glen's eyes bulged.

"Good grief! What happened?"

"Car accident in Dallas." She kept walking. For some reason, lying to Glen was more difficult than lying to everyone else. "Sorry—can't stop now. I have to prep for first period."

She quickened her pace, half expecting him to follow. He didn't.

But later in the morning, he tracked her down while she was doing hall monitor duty. Finding her wasn't hard. There were places Lon designated as hotspots of likely misconduct—all the isolated bits of corridor, and of course the restrooms—and during a shift the hall monitor was expected to visit them all, like the stations of the cross.

She was in a small stairwell inspecting a discarded cigarette, trying to see if she could determine whether it had originated with a student, one of the cleaning staff, or Gerald the security guy.

"I'm worried about you," Glen said.

"So am I. I thought I was a teacher, but now I'm examining cigarette butts for clues."

He folded his arms. "I mean I'm worried about what happened this weekend."

"Why? It was only a fender bender, but if you hit your nose the wrong way—"

"Bev." He shook his head. "You weren't in Dallas yesterday. Your car was outside your house the two times I drove by."

She tossed the butt in the garbage. "You're spying on me now?"

"No, but I still notice when I drive by your house. Is that a crime? This is a small town." He ducked his head and admitted, "I did consider knocking on your door yesterday."

Thank heavens he hadn't. Seeing him before she'd put her story together—even an obviously false story—would have unraveled her last thread of composure.

When she didn't respond to his visit-that-wasn't, he continued. "Another reason I don't buy your trip to Dallas yesterday is that Stuart also said he thought you'd been at home."

She'd thought Stuart was eyeing her curiously during class this morning, and wondered if Alabama had filled Stuart in on some of the details he'd missed Saturday night. Then again, *everyone* was eyeing her curiously.

"What else did Stuart say?" she asked.

"Nothing."

Bev was doubtful.

Glen's gaze narrowed. "What could he have said?"

"Absolutely nothing," she said quickly.

"He did seem worried about you."

"I never thought you were the kind of teacher who would gossip with students about another teacher."

He squared his shoulders. "And I never thought you'd make excuses for a jerk like that guy you're seeing."

This was her cue to admit that she and Derek were kaput. But to confess that, she would practically be admitting that his suspicions about her supposed car accident were true. He could tell Jackie, who might tell Lon. And then the jig would be up concerning the charade of the nose.

"Derek had nothing to do with the accident in Dallas," she insisted.

Glen's gaze pierced her so steadily that she almost shrank back against the wall. "No." His voice held a hint of disgust that made her ashamed and sad. "I'm sure he didn't."

Her mood deteriorated over the course of the afternoon. Her nose throbbed, as did her conscience. She couldn't do anything about the latter now, but she did buy a Diet Dr Pepper to hold against her face during study hall.

Toby Beggs, a born smart aleck, called her out. "You said no beverages in study hall, Miss Putterman."

"This one's not open," she said.

"So you're trying to absorb it, like through osmosis or something? That's totally awesome!"

The class laughed and it took another minute to threaten them back into silence again.

At home, she got into a fracas with Alabama.

"I guess it was too much to ask that you not tell your little friend about what happened Friday," she sniped at Alabama, without intending to.

"What are you talking about?" Alabama asked.

"Stuart. He seemed to know why my nose was swollen."

"He probably guessed. He's not an idiot. But I didn't tell him anything."

Bev wasn't sure. The two were thick as thieves. "Well, I'll thank you to keep family business private from now on."

Alabama dropped her books on the dining room table with a crash. "Fine. Why not? It'll be good practice for my lifetime as a Putterman. Keeping secrets is what we do best!"

She ran to her room and slammed the door.

Bev sighed. Why had she said anything? Alabama had been so kind to her this weekend.

She should start dinner now, but instead she took an aspirin and succumbed to the lure of a nap in her darkened bedroom.

Her head ached—not only from the nose, but from the stress of the day. The stress of the lie.

She should have stayed home, but she hated taking time off to be sick. She hated to be sick, period. Staying home while the rest of the world went on without her made her nervous. It always reminded her of those days when she'd had the mumps, when everything had gone on without her. By the time she was no longer bedridden, the world had turned on its head.

On that night back in 1970, Tom had arrived to find Bev quarantined. Neither he nor Diana had ever had the mumps, so Tom was only allowed to wave at her once from the doorway, which was probably just as well. Much closer, Bev feared she would have been a fright.

She expected Tom to turn around and drive straight back to Houston. To her surprise—not to mention her mother's—he stayed. The first night, her soup tray came with flowers and a note from him.

Hey, Miss Sicko! What a disappointment. Your mother has kindly agreed to let me stick around until you're back on your feet again. Anything beats Houston right now. I can't seem to please the old folks at home no matter what I do. I guess I'll spend a day or two all by my lonesome seeing the sights of Big D. Get yourself well, and don't worry about me.
Feel groovy soon.
Love,
T

P.S.: Your sister has offered to entertain me this evening. From what you've told me about her, this could be an education!

The thought of Tom spending a night on the town with Diana sent panic through her. She sat up and started sloughing off bedcovers until her mother put out her hand and pressed her back against the pillow.

"You stay right where you are. For heaven's sake—do you think we're so uncultured that we can't be trusted to socialize with Tom for a few hours?"

"It's not you who worries me."

"Diana's not completely uncivilized. I'm sure she's read a book at some point in her life."

Bev scoffed. "The last book I saw in her hands was *Make Way for Ducklings*." Poor Tom. She could imagine him being dragged into one of Diana's beads-and-weed dens. "She'll scare him off."

Gladys laughed. "If contagious disease didn't send him running, I'm sure he'll weather Diana."

"But I won't be able to see him alone this weekend," Bev lamented. How would she be able to tell him about the baby with everyone around? Of course, she suspected Diana had overheard her talking to Dr. Gary, so she would be lucky if her sister didn't spill the secret first. She considered writing Tom a note back. *Have fun—and by the way, you're going to be a father!*

Her head throbbed, and her throat felt as if it was on fire. She dropped into sleep, sleep that fell across her like a lead blanket, smothering her so that even while she was out she struggled to wake again. Her dreams were fitful, disturbing. She would fight to consciousness to flee them, only to find herself in a hellish state of aches and soreness that made her wish she'd never woken up. Rinse, repeat.

Saturday morning's breakfast tray brought Cream of Wheat and no new note from Tom.

"He's still asleep on the foldout couch in the living room." Her mother was already dressed for work. The bank was open half days Saturdays. "He and Diana went to see a movie last night."

"Which one?"

"I don't know. *Airport* was what they mentioned wanting to see."

"Didn't you ask what they did when they came in?"

"I didn't hear them—it was too late." Gladys plucked at the scarf at her neck. "I'm going to the bank, but I'll try to take off early today. You go to sleep and I'll have some hot soup for you when you wake up."

"I feel ridiculous. Of all the times to be sick. Tom has so little time . . ."

"Just rest," her mother said. "The doctor didn't prescribe worrying."

True to her word, her mother presented herself at Bev's bedside around midday with a bowl of chicken and rice soup. Again, there was no note.

"What is Tom up to?" Bev asked. "I thought I heard Jim Morrison earlier, while I was dozing. I hope Diana didn't wake him up."

"They're not here. They must have decided to go out to lunch, or shopping."

That afternoon Bev stayed awake, waiting to hear them return, but the only person who came into the house was Dr. Gary, who declared Bev's illness was progressing nicely. Recovery was just around the corner. Then, he lowered his voice a little. "How are you doing with . . . the other?"

The other. Nice way to think of a baby. "Fine."

"I should have conclusive results on Monday. There's been no change? No pains, anything like that?"

"No." She frowned. "Should there be?"

"Just take it easy, young lady. Told your mom yet?"

"No. I thought I'd wait until I'm sure." Or at least until she had told Tom. "Can't I get up tonight and watch TV? My boyfriend's visiting—he only has a few days before he has to report for officer's training."

"And do you want him to contract mumps and miss it? Do you want to expose him to the same risks you're running? What if he developed meningitis and died? Would having watched a little television make you feel better then?"

She shrank back, gripped by hypothetical guilt. But a part of her did think it would be wonderful if some life-threatening but not quite fatal illness rescued him from his duties. He wouldn't have to go . . . and it wouldn't be his fault. Neither the US

Army nor his family could blame him. She could encourage him to leave Houston and live here. They'd get married, rent an apartment. She would teach, and Tom . . . could find a job somewhere. Or go to graduate school. That's where he belonged.

Sunday morning, Gladys brought more Cream of Wheat and disturbing news. "They didn't come back last night."

Bev sat up. "Didn't come back from where?"

"I don't know. Yesterday evening they returned briefly to eat and change and told me they were going for a drive."

"Where could they have driven to?"

"In fourteen hours? Where *couldn't* they have driven to?"

The nightmare of the following days would stay with her always. By Sunday night, it was clear that Tom and Diana's disappearance had nothing to do with losing track of time. All sorts of crazy thoughts occurred to Bev. Had they picked up a hitchhiker and been kidnapped? Had they fallen prey to some psychotic killer, like Charles Manson?

By Monday afternoon, Bev was more exhausted from worry than illness. Calls to the police, hospitals, and all of Diana's friends revealed nothing. A terrible reality was beginning to settle in. Tom and Diana had run off together. As her mother grew more agitated, Bev's worry seemed to settle into a painful ache in the core of her being. Her mother didn't know that her fears were almost all self-centered. *What am I going to do? How am I going to manage?*

Finally, after strenuous arguments from Bev, Gladys called Tom's family.

From the sound of things, Dorothy Jackson answered the phone. Her mother kept her gaze trained on Bev even as she spoke over the line. "We were wondering if you'd seen Tom, Mrs. Jackson," she said after introducing herself. "Yes, he *was* here, but now he's gone, and he's taken my daughter with him. I was wondering if he had gone to Houston. . . ."

Even as her mother said it, Bev realized again how ridiculous the idea was. Tom wouldn't have gone to Houston—it was the last place he wanted to be. Her mother hadn't understood that.

"He's not with *Bev,* he's with Diana." Her mother's face reddened as she listened. "I know you haven't been introduced to Diana—that's not the point. She's my younger daughter and she's disappeared with your son. The essential question is, where are they?" She sank down in a chair, hand clenched around the receiver. "Diana did not *take* him anywhere. Nineteen-year-old girls do not generally kidnap soldiers. . . .Yes, I said *kidnap.* . . ."

Her mother listened a moment longer and then put the receiver against her chest. "She's putting her daughter on the line. Now what good is that going to do?"

Bev pried the receiver out of her mother's hands. "Dot, this is Bev."

"Mother says your mother is accusing Tom of kidnapping your sister," Dot said.

"Have you seen them? Have you heard from Tom at all?"

"No, of course not. Mother's very upset. The word *kidnap* has legal implications, I believe."

"All right—they've run off together."

"But why would they have done that?" Dot asked. "He went down to visit *you,* didn't he?"

"I have the mumps."

There was a pause. "Are you serious? Isn't that a childhood disease?"

"Not exclusively, obviously."

"The mumps!" Dot practically brayed the word. "Maybe Tom was right to take off. The last thing he needs is to start catching diseases from you people."

Bev pulled the telephone cord taut. "If you hear from them, let us know. Please?"

"Okay, but I think it would be best if you didn't disturb Mother anymore. She's very upset."

"What kind of people are they?" Gladys asked after Bev had hung up. "Every time I said something, she would counter it. She answered 'Where is my daughter?' with an attack on my daughter's pedigree."

"That's the kind of people they are," Bev answered.

"Do you think Tom joined the army to get away from them?"

"That could be. His father was in the military, but Tom doesn't support this war. Maybe he thought that by enlisting he'd get away from them and finally earn a tiny drop of their respect. I think he's confused."

All Bev knew for sure was that the doctor had been wrong. Mumps hadn't been the danger to Tom. If she'd roped Tom into watching television, everything might have ended happily. Instead, she'd followed the doctor's orders and he'd fallen prey to Diana. He might have survived a bout of mumps, or even meningitis. But he'd had no antibodies against freewheeling Diana.

As she stood, her hand still on the phone, a knitting pain inside that she'd been too pre-occupied to think about escalated into a cramp too strong to ignore. She gripped her middle, nearly doubling over.

Gladys jumped to her feet. "What's wrong?"

"It's . . . I feel sick."

It was worse than sick. It was pain so sharp she thought she would fold over on herself. "Of course you still feel ill," her mother said. "You should be back in bed."

Gladys took her elbow and grunted in surprise when Bev leaned all her weight against her. She should have told her mother about the pregnancy before now. This didn't feel right.

Another cramp seared through her.

"Bev!" Gladys clenched her in alarm. "What's the matter?"

Could this be normal?

Of course not. Nothing about her life would ever be normal again.

Tears filled her eyes. "Oh, Mama? What am I going to do?"

CHAPTER 17

"What do you think?"

Stuart stood in the center of the "stage" he'd set up for a dress rehearsal in his parents' garage to simulate the atmosphere of the high school auditorium on talent show day. Electrical tape marked off the back for the performance area, facing rows of Mrs. Looney's empty folding card table chairs. A few seats were occupied by brooms and mops wearing hats, a punching bag topped with a baseball cap, and a giant plush panda. Their audience.

"I should have brought Rhoda Morgenstern," Alabama said. "She'd have fit right in."

"I wish you had," Stuart replied. "We need all the fake people we can get." Dressed in his new tunic over jeans, he crackled with nervous energy. "Of course, this isn't as big as the auditorium at school, but you get the idea."

He'd been pestering her to have a formal rehearsal for two days, but she'd been reluctant. At some point, she would have to confess that she couldn't really dance any better now than she could when she was eight. When she thought of getting on that stage, her heart would start battering her chest until she was dizzy with nerves. It was madness to contemplate, but whenever she saw Stuart, she felt too embarrassed to back out.

She didn't want to confess to him that she'd been a liar, that she wasn't talented. That, in fact, there was nothing special about her at all.

She was also reluctant because she worried that if she saw him do his Shakespeare thing, he would ask her honest opinion and she would either have to lie or lose her one friend.

As it was, the outfit alone convinced her he was doomed. The tunic was royal purple with gold braid. Stuart loved it. And for some reason, he'd moussed his hair into a curly, new-wavy cowlick, like the singer in Tears for Fears.

He caught her staring at the tunic. "The color is really going to pop under lights. I wanted to make a real jacket—something more fitted—but then I worried I'd screw it up. This gold braid isn't cheap."

She drew in a breath, trying to work up the courage to tell him that she was going to back out of the talent show. She knew he would think she was a chicken, but . . . well, maybe she was.

"We need to hurry up and start," he said before she could get a word out. "Dad'll be home in a little bit. Mom's okay with parking her station wagon in the driveway while we're working, but Dad thinks cars belong in a garage. He's . . . you know . . . the Looney car guy." He sighed, as if having a local celebrity dad was his cross to bear. Just as quickly, though, he snapped out of it and grabbed a box off one of the metal chairs. "First, I've got a surprise for you. Close your eyes."

Dutifully, she squeezed them shut. While she stood in darkness, something heavy plopped on her head.

"Okay—open 'em."

She opened her eyes to her own reflection in the hand mirror Stuart was holding up. His surprise was a wedding veil—traditional in appearance until you noticed that some of the netting was thick with fake cobwebs, and that there were little spiders dotting the material. At the crown, a small stuffed mouse perched next to a plastic wedge of cheese.

She laughed. It was his Miss Havisham look—a take on the old jilted bride from *Great Expectations*. "It's perfect!"

He beamed, pleased by her reaction. "Isn't the mouse great? I found it in a box in my brother's closet. I think it's one of the cat's toys."

"You guys don't have a cat," Alabama said.

"We did until about five years ago. Justin *never* cleans his closet. Anyway, the mouse is stapled to the headband, so you don't have to worry about it coming off during your routine." He picked at the material, arranging it to better show off the spiders.

"I can't believe you did all this," she said.

"Oh, it was fun, and it didn't take me long. I did most of the work in your aunt's class this week.

She's been acting spaced out, and didn't even come over to ask why I was working on a wedding veil. Of course, I would never have admitted that it was because you were too chicken to attach spiders to her wedding dress."

Stuart was still clinging to his Bev-as-Bette theory. "It's not *her* dress," Alabama said.

He sent her a pitying look. "Whatever."

She groaned. They'd been circling back to this argument all week—during lunch, after school, on the phone at night. Ever since the night of *The Old Maid*, Stuart had been convinced a genuine Bette Davis movie plot was unfolding under the roof of his best friend, and he would not let it go. It was so frustrating.

She knew what had upset her aunt that night— Derek. She wasn't going to blurt out the fact that her aunt was a battered girlfriend just to refute Stuart's crackpot theory, though. Bev might assume she was a blabbermouth, but she wasn't.

"We still don't know who the wedding dress belonged to," she said.

"Uh-huh," he drawled.

She wanted to scream. "Bev is *not* my mother." Didn't he see how mad this insane conjecture made her? Did he not care? "I hope you haven't told anyone else about this idea of yours."

"Of course I haven't. Who would I tell?"

"Your parents?"

"No."

"Bev thinks you told Mr. Hill about her broken nose."

"What about it?" Stuart asked, interested.

She bit her lip. *Oh great.* She was practically accusing him of being a gossip and now she'd almost spit out the secret. Even though she was pretty sure Stuart must have pieced it together anyway. "Never mind. It was just my aunt being paranoid as usual."

"I thought of something that could prove my theory about your real mother," he said. "Have you ever seen your birth certificate?"

Alabama frowned. "I don't think so. I'm not even sure I have one."

"Everybody has one. Not having one is, like, illegal."

"Really?"

"Absolutely," Stuart said. "I'm pretty sure."

She bit her lip. Last week when they'd studied vocabulary together, he'd been pretty sure *myopia* was a country next to Thailand. "And my birth certificate would show who my mom is?"

"It's supposed to. Mine does."

"I have no idea where mine is. I never thought to ask. It might be lost."

"You could send off for a copy, I bet. Where were you born?"

"In San Francisco."

Stuart's eyes bugged. "California? You didn't tell me you lived there!"

"Only till I was a year old. Then my mom met some guy and they went to Ashland, Oregon. After that, she thought finding a place for a single person with a baby would be too difficult in San Francisco. We moved around a lot."

"And after your mom—" Stuart swallowed and started over. "Last summer, before you left St. Louis, you didn't see the birth certificate then?"

"I packed up a lot of stuff. . . ." She squinted at the oil-stained cement floor, dredging up those awful days. She could see Bev hunched on her knees in her mom's room, going through the shoe boxes where all the important stuff like the lease was kept. Bev had boxed up those things. At the time, Alabama had been more concerned with preserving sentimental items—clothes, pictures, her mom's costume jewelry.

Funny how Bev had gone straight for the vital records. . . .

"My aunt might have packed it," she said.

"But she didn't show it to you?"

"No," Alabama said, her voice defensive. "Why would she?"

He folded his arms. "The question is, why would she *not* want to show it to you?"

For the first time, Alabama was almost willing to allow a suspicion that he could be right, but that didn't make her like the idea—or his mad embrace of it—any better. In fact, the possibility of its being true made her angrier. "It doesn't matter if

Bev is my mother, because even if she is, she's not. Mom was my mother, and she was beautiful, and funny, and even if she wasn't exactly normal she at least wasn't boring. And even when we had to live on saltines and government cheese, I knew she'd do anything for me. Anything. She would have died for me—"

Her throat clogged, and she was mortified to feel tears in her eyes. She couldn't have a bawling fit at the Looneys'. Probably no one ever cried in this house, except maybe during the Olympics and *Little House on the Prairie* reruns.

"God, Alabama." Stuart stepped forward, apologetic. "I didn't mean to freak you out."

She flicked a tear away from her eyes with the back of her hand. "Then why don't you just drop it?"

"I thought you'd want to know the truth."

"The truth? You think the truth is something you can invent if reality's too dull for you. If you want to face uncomfortable truths, start with yourself."

He drew back. "What's that supposed to mean?"

"It means the first time I ever saw you, you were being bullied by people because of some stupid lip-synching routine you did in middle school. And now you're setting yourself up to be a laughingstock again. Look at yourself."

He glanced down at his outfit, confused. "I think this turned out great."

"Yes—if you were going to join the Ice

Capades. But at New Sparta High School you're going to be the butt of jokes for months."

"By doing Shakespeare, in a real costume?" he asked. "Is that how you think?"

"No, it's how *they* think."

"Well, they're wrong. And they'll all see they're wrong when I'm a big success."

"Oh right," Alabama said. "When you win your Oscar. Academy Award night, 2002. *Then* everybody'll be sorry."

His cheeks flushed red. "Wow—I never suspected you were one of the mean kids."

"I'm not."

"You sure know how they think."

"Because I'm worried about you."

"That's dumb. This"—he gestured around the garage, ending on the stuffed panda—"this is what I'm interested in. If life was all algebra class and vocabulary lists, I wouldn't want to get up in the morning. But it's not. The stuff I love makes all the other crap I have to put up with worth it. If you're going to succeed at what means something to you, you have to have a little courage. I thought you did. But you don't even seem to have the courage to be my friend."

Heat stung her cheeks. "That's unfair. I am your friend."

"Until something better comes along, right? Or until you get whisked away by your rich benefactress in Houston." He snorted. "Good

313

thing *you* don't have your head in the clouds. You're patterning your life after a book, but you don't even have the story straight. At the end of the book, it's not the old lady who's the benefactress, is it? It's the convict, the guy Pip is ashamed of."

She scowled at him. "The book gave me the idea. I didn't say my whole life was going to follow a book plot—unlike *some people* who seem to think life follows bad movie scripts!"

Not long after that, she stomped away. Halfway home, she realized that she was still wearing the spidery veil. She ripped it off her head, then stared down at it, feeling guilty. Stuart was right—the mouse was stapled on really well. It hadn't budged when she'd yanked the thing off. He'd put so much work into it.

And she hadn't even stayed to watch his monologue.

She *was* a bad friend. But the memory of how stubborn he'd been about the Bev question kept her huffing toward her own house instead of turning back to apologize.

She wasn't a coward. But how could she ask Bev "Are you my mother?" without seeming like a doofus?

And what if she didn't like the answer?

Okay, maybe she was a coward.

When she dragged up to the front door, she gave the mailbox a desultory glance. She'd lost hope of receiving another letter from Houston. But today, there it was—the cream-colored envelope, the same compact, spidery writing.

She snatched it up excitedly.

Maybe having your head in the clouds wasn't such a bad thing. Right now, rescue by her long-lost relatives was just what she needed.

CHAPTER 18

"Why don't we go out for dinner?" Alabama said.

Bev was tempted. The week had been exhausting. She'd never realized how much in life hinged on having a nose in good working order. Noses were essential not just for breathing, but for pretty much holding the entire face together. Even sleeping with her nose swollen required effort—pillows propped at precisely the right angle, ice cubes at the ready for the inevitable two a.m. nasal blockage. Talking to people and teaching became a chore. By the end of the week she could pinpoint the exact moment when a student's attention to her words fizzled and he or she began to focus solely on the nose.

But she hadn't taken time off. Today she'd dutifully done her shift overseeing the after-school detention crew, whose job it was to clean the bleachers at Jackrabbit Field. The weather had been unseasonably warm and humid, and what they'd found under those bleachers was enough to put a person off her dinner altogether. Even the idea of sliding a casserole into a hot oven didn't appeal to her. Given her druthers, she would have stayed collapsed on the couch, and maybe gotten up later to make a sandwich. But she had Alabama now.

"We could get hamburgers at Lewanne's," Alabama suggested.

That decided it. Lewanne's Dinner Bell on the highway was her favorite eatery in New Sparta, and she and Alabama hadn't been there since the summer. Going out would make a nice change. "All right."

Getting back in the car, she felt a little jauntier. Maybe this was what she needed. And it seemed a good sign that Alabama had suggested going out together.

After they'd seated themselves at the restaurant, the waitress sped by and slapped two menus on the table. A gasp jerked Bev's attention up to the young woman's face. "Hey, Miss Putterman!"

Bev didn't recognize Mandy Newman at first. "Well, hi. I didn't know you worked here." She introduced Alabama. "Mandy took my class . . . was it five years ago?"

"Five years, a lifetime, something like that." The young woman twisted her lip self-deprecatingly. "This isn't exactly the future I imagined back then."

"A good waitress can always find a job," Bev said. "But no one says you have to stay in this job forever. It's never too late to become what you might have been, you know."

"Oh . . ." Mandy shrugged and, taking out her pad, forced a smile. "But guess what? I still wear that kimono I sewed in Home Ec Two. Remember that?"

Bev couldn't recall the specific result—only the

assignment—but she was tickled all the same. "That's terrific." If only she had a tape recorder so she could play this conversation back to Lon Kirby.

Alabama ordered a cheeseburger, which Bev usually loved but couldn't manage herself today. Her health class had just finished the "trace a cheeseburger" unit, and the very thought of hamburgers called to mind enzymes and digestive track diagrams. She asked Mandy—who seemed to be trying hard not to stare at the nose, which was still yellowish and veiny—for the large chef salad and a Tab.

When Mandy was gone, Bev cast about for a topic of conversation and asked Alabama, "Did you go to Stuart's house this afternoon?"

"Yeah . . ." Alabama's lips turned down. "What was that you said to her? 'It's never too late to . . . something'?"

"To become what you might have been. It's a quote from a writer, I think." For the first time, Bev noticed that Alabama looked troubled. "Is something wrong?"

Alabama shrugged.

Mandy whisked back with their drinks.

When the waitress was gone again, Alabama took a sip of the soda she'd ordered, and then cleared her throat. She pulled a letter out of her pocket and slid it across the table toward Bev. "This came today."

Warily, Bev picked up the note and read it.

Dear Alabama,

Thank you for your prompt and courteous reply to my last letter. I admit that at first I was dubious concerning your intentions. You might believe that makes me a suspicious old lady. So be it. I can't pretend that having a granddaughter appear like a bolt from the blue in my mailbox didn't shake me up a bit. It would have been a shock to anyone with sense.

My daughter, Dot, still feels we need to think through this whole matter more thoroughly. She is a very serious-minded person and worries about the implications of accepting new people into the family.

I am glad you included a picture with your note. It dislodged the image of your mother from my mind, thank heavens. And, despite my firm belief that hair should not be striped like a barber pole, I was struck by your photo. You have a very sweet face.

I should be glad to see that sweet face on Thanksgiving, if you would do me the honor of coming here for luncheon. Bev is certainly welcome to accompany you. Indeed, I hope she will. There are important matters to be discussed.

I will await your RSVP. If you don't know what that means yet, consult Emily Post, or Webster's.
Yours truly,
Dorothy Mabry Jackson

"You sent her a picture?" Bev asked as she scanned the note again.

"A couple of weeks ago. After we got our school pictures back."

Dot probably loved that.

Thanksgiving in Houston. Bev had plans to bring her mom and Wink down for a day in New Sparta. Spending the holiday with the Jacksons didn't appeal to her at all. It would be awkward, and the company would be bad, and the whole experience was bound to churn up memories that had already bubbled to the surface too often lately.

"Can I go?" Alabama asked.

"Do you want to go? I'd planned on asking Mama and Wink to spend Thanksgiving with us."

Alabama's forehead scrunched. "Instead of Las Vegas, you mean?"

Bev was lost. "Who's going to Las Vegas?"

"Gladdie and Wink. Over Thanksgiving."

At first Bev thought Alabama was kidding. But her expression remained matter-of-fact.

"How did you find this out?"

"Gladdie told me when I spoke to her on the phone the other night. Remember? You said you didn't feel like talking."

Because she didn't think there had been anything to talk about—except her nose, which was a subject she'd wanted to avoid. "I didn't know she had news!"

Alabama shrugged as if it was no big deal. "Now you do. It's nothing to flip your lid over."

"I'm just upset because no one tells me things anymore."

Alabama sucked on her drink. "The deal is, Wink won the trip from an easy listening radio station in a quiz contest. Kind of like *Name That Tune*. For the final question, he guessed 'Can't Smile Without You' by Barry Manilow from *two* notes."

"That's incredible."

"Gladdie's real excited. She wants to see Liberace."

It sounded like fun . . . as long as it didn't end with her new husband—still a relatively unknown quantity—losing all their money at the gambling tables. Or running off with a showgirl. Suddenly, so many disastrous "lady beware" scenarios presented themselves that Bev looked out the window to distract herself.

"Gladdie was saying that they should've waited to get married," Alabama continued. "That they could have had the ceremony in Vegas. And you know what Wink said? He said it couldn't have happened that way, because marrying Gladdie was what brought him luck."

The words barely penetrated. Bev's gaze was riveted on two people getting out of a truck in the restaurant's parking lot. It was Derek . . . and some woman. A very young woman. They walked arm in arm toward the entrance. Bev flinched as they passed right by her window, inches from her but not seeing her. In the second or two between when they disappeared from sight and the cheery ring of the bell over the door that announced new customers, Bev's mind raced. Was it too late to escape? The restaurant's back exit was through the kitchen, but she couldn't get there without being seen. And she couldn't very well hole up in the bathroom for an entire meal.

And then Derek and his date were inside, chatting with Lewanne behind the register. The owner gestured for them to take stools at the counter.

Alabama, who was facing away from Derek and the woman, fixed a worried gaze on her. "Aunt Bev?"

Derek hadn't spotted her yet. Thank God. But of course, he was so wrapped up in his date that he probably didn't have eyes for anyone else. Even someone glaring daggers at him from across a restaurant.

When their food came, Bev leaned toward

Mandy. "The couple who just came in—who's that girl with Derek?"

Mandy looked over. "Oh, that's Dee Flowers. She graduated a few years ahead of me. Those two have been coming in for takeout for the past few weeks. Evidently, Dee's condition"—Mandy arched a brow significantly—"makes her crave Lewanne's chicken-fried steak."

Bev's gaze lowered, and for the first time she noticed the telltale bump. *Weeks,* Mandy had said. They'd been coming here for weeks. All those weeks Derek had been "working in Waxahachie."

And a person didn't become visibly pregnant in under a few months. . . .

Alabama twisted and saw them. "What's *he* doing here?"

Bev ripped into a packet of saltines. "It's a free country."

"Yeah, but that girl he's with is practically my age."

"Hardly."

"Closer to my age than yours," Alabama said. "Yuck."

"Shh." Bev looked down at her salad, but her appetite was completely gone. Now that the shock was lifting, anger rose in her throat, choking her. Why had he strung her along? This affair with Dee Flowers had obviously been going on for months and months. For all she knew, it had started before they were together. Maybe she herself had unwittingly been the other woman.

Although looking at Dee, she doubted it. Men didn't risk a relationship with a nubile twenty-something to have a fling with an almost-middle-aged schoolteacher.

But why hadn't he broken up with her? Did he just want someone in reserve for when Dee wasn't available?

Her stomach churned.

At the register, Lewanne was handing over two large takeout bags. Bev stared down at her plate, heart drumming as she listened to the familiar dings of the cash register, the cheery thank-yous and good-byes, and the tinkle of the bell over the door as the couple exited.

Her gorge rose, and she leaped to her feet, half intending to dash to the restroom. Instead, her feet carried her toward the front of the restaurant.

"Aunt Bev?" Alabama called after her.

Bev didn't stop, and was almost running when she hit the door, heedless of the other diners.

She caught up with them at the truck, as Derek was handing Dee into the passenger side. Like someone in the "polite behavior" illustrations from an antiquated homemaking text. *A gentleman always opens the door for a lady and helps her in and out of automobiles.*

A gentleman. That was a laugh.

"Hey!" she called after them.

The two looked up, and for a moment a comical mix of guilt and surprise flashed across both their faces. So Dee had known about her—at least enough to feel shamed when confronted.

"What do you want?" Derek asked her.

"From you? Nothing." She focused all her anger on Dee, intending to uncork the vitriol inside her at her erstwhile rival. But when she looked into Dee's eyes, all the ire burbling inside her shifted. Alabama was right—Dee was so young. Only a little older than most of Bev's students, who she considered babes when it came to the realities of life. A swell of protectiveness rose in her chest.

She pointed to her nose, purposefully drawing attention to what she'd been desperate to hide all week, hoping that Dee would be repulsed by the hideous glob on her face. "*He* gave me this." She indicated Derek with a curt, accusatory nod.

Dee's brows drew together, taking in the nose . . . and what the bruised, nasty state of it implied. Alarm showed in her eyes for a split second and then flickered out. Her lips pulled into a smile. "Really?" She cupped her bulging abdomen. "He gave me *this.*"

Circling around to the driver's side, Derek smirked at Bev. He got in, slammed the door, and revved the engines with a roar. Then he squealed out of the parking lot, leaving her in a cloud of exhaust.

Alabama ran up behind her, stopping at her elbow. "Are you okay?"

Are you insane? she might very well have asked.

And Bev wouldn't have been sure what to answer. All through the years, she'd worked hard to rise above life's indignities. Teasing in school, a boyfriend drought that had lasted from third grade till Tom, always working hard and yet feeling second best. And yet, by and large, until recently, she'd managed to keep herself on an even keel. All that effort—tossed away in the parking lot of Lewanne's Dinner Bell.

Or maybe not. Maybe no one had actually noticed. She straightened her shoulders and peered off into the distance, where Derek's truck had disappeared. Hopefully that was good-bye, Derek. Forever. And good riddance. A banged-up nose and a little embarrassment were a small price to pay to own up to such a huge mistake.

"I'm perfectly okay," she answered, and then turned.

All at once, she was reminded that she lived in a small town. In the windows of the diner, faces turned toward her, hamburgers forgotten, ogling to see what she would do next. The sight should have sobered her, but the seated chorus line of goggle-eyed curiosity made her toss back her head and laugh.

Alabama studied her, worried. "Maybe we should ask for to-go boxes."

CHAPTER 19

The morning of the talent show, Alabama awoke to her aunt's cry of panic. "You're not even up yet!"

Bev, on the other hand, loomed over her, out-the-door ready. Her cavernous purse was slung over her shoulder, and she also carried her usual tote bag of extras taken from the piles of craft supplies tucked all around the house. A few sheets of rolled-up poster board were wedged under one arm.

Alabama shot to sitting and gaped at the flip numbers on her alarm clock. *7:28.* She flopped back down. She'd never make it to school in time.

"Are you sick?"

"No, I just couldn't sleep."

The explanation came out automatically, and there was no retracting it, unfortunately. Being sick would have been an excuse to stay home and miss the talent show. Now she'd tossed away a legitimate reason to skip school.

Nerves had kept her awake almost till dawn. Out of panic, she'd practiced her dance routine the night before—once even getting up and going through it in her pajamas—but she couldn't see herself performing it before an auditorium full of people. She would have to be nuts. She would have to be Stuart.

The only question now was, would it take more courage to go ahead and perform in the talent show, or to confess to Stuart that she was chickening out? Even though they'd been mad at each other lately, he'd done so much to get her ready.

"I'd have thought you'd be up with the birds this morning," Bev said. "You and Stuart have been planning for today practically since school started."

Alabama groaned. If only Halloween had fallen on a Friday. It was so much easier to make an idiot of yourself when you had the entire weekend to recover your dignity. But this was Thursday, which meant she would have to go back tomorrow and live through the consequences of whatever happened today.

"I don't want to go," Alabama said. "I can't do it."

Bev shook her head. "*Can't* never accomplished anything. You've got to step up the stairs, not stare up the stairs."

As the axioms came at her, Alabama took her spare pillow and pretended to smother herself with it.

Bev pulled it away. "Look at me. Did I stay home after the nose incident?"

"No."

Maybe it would have been better if she had. Alabama had heard all sorts of whispers and snarky comments around the school. At first, everybody had been sympathetic about the car accident. Then word about the incident at Lewanne's Dinner Bell must have seeped out, and dots began to be connected.

Not that anyone really cared about Bev's personal life. Alabama wouldn't have been interested if she hadn't been trapped inside it herself.

Bev gave her leg a firm pat of encouragement. "I know it's hard, but some days you have to buck yourself up and do what you planned." She glanced at her watch. "But you'll have to buck yourself up quickly if you're going to ride with me. I needed to leave five minutes ago."

"That's okay," Alabama said. "I'll walk."

Her aunt's brows rose. "You sure?"

She nodded.

"You aren't going to skip, are you? Because that won't solve anything, and you'll end up in detention."

Alabama rolled her eyes. "I'm not going to skip, but I need time to get ready. I might be a little late."

Bev looked at her doubtfully, then stood. "I guess I'll see you at school, then. And if I don't get a chance to say it before assembly, break a leg!"

Alabama could think of worse outcomes. Much worse. In fact, if she could break a leg *before* assembly, that would solve all her problems.

After the front door closed and Bev drove away, Alabama reluctantly crawled out of bed. But as she showered, more positive thoughts came to her—maybe Stuart was rubbing off on her. What was the worst that could happen? If she went through with the dance routine, it would be done and forgotten by lunch. Who cared?

It felt weird to be alone at Bev's house on a weekday morning. In her towel, she padded to the kitchen, slopped some Rice Krispies and milk into a bowl, and settled in front of the television. She stopped the dial at something called *Peppermint Place*—a man in a candy-cane-striped suit was talking to a puppet named Muffin. She sat back to watch, and then mid-bite she boomeranged back in time to when she was a tiny kid in the seventies, watching this same Mr. Peppermint at Gladdie's house. She'd forgotten all about that. That's when her mother had been "in the hospital." Or so she'd been told. The time they'd visited her mom, the facility hadn't seemed like a hospital. More like a country club, from her perspective back then. She remembered she'd felt jealous because they'd had Pong in the recreation room.

Afterward, her mother had only referred to it, rarely, as *that place,* somewhere she didn't want to go back to. How long had her mom stayed there, and how long had Alabama lived with Gladdie? She couldn't remember now. Long enough to have absorbed a knowledge of Mr. Peppermint. Long enough for her mother to spend the rest of her life in dread of *that place.*

Encouraging his audience to face the day with a peppermint smile, Mr. Peppermint signed off, which jogged Alabama out of her thoughts. Oh God. She'd already missed homeroom. No way would she make first period.

She dressed quickly, caking on the makeup Stuart had given her to create an appropriately ghoulish look. Then she put on her costume, which, thanks to her tardiness, she would only have to wear for one period before mid-morning assembly. She stowed her old tap shoes in a shopping bag, along with her change of clothes for after the talent show. The shoes—actually her mom's—were too tight. While she could, she might as well wear the Vans knockoffs she'd bought at Walmart.

Finally came the beehive wig that she and Stuart had bought and spray-painted gray. She tugged it on and topped it off with the veil.

Looking at herself in the mirror, she grinned. Stuart's vision of a mod Miss Havisham stared back at her. He'd really done a fantastic job.

She put on her courage and a peppermint smile and left the house.

When she arrived at school, classes were changing, so she was able to scoot into algebra without much fuss. Most people stared at her, but she was used to that by now. And a few other kids were in Halloween costumes, too. The student council raised money by charging a quarter for not dressing up. The fine resulted in a lot of lame costumes, like kids just wearing a hat. But Jeff Sessions had mummified his head in toilet paper, Mary Margaret Mayer made a passable Princess Leia, and Tommy Clark had a plastic ax buried in his scalp and had gone nuts with some fake blood. Even so, Alabama's costume was the most elaborate.

But where was Stuart? Maybe he'd asked permission to help Mr. Hill set up for the show.

She'd expected him to be there for moral support. Instead, as the minutes of second period ticked by, her courage faltered. While she was at the blackboard solving an equation, her wig went askew. Then, on the way back to her desk, she tripped. Her nerves began to stall out entirely—if she couldn't remain upright walking across a room in sneakers, how could she hope to execute a dance routine in too-tight tap shoes? Also, the wig was hot. Even sitting at her desk, sweat poured off her.

Toward the end of class, she asked permission to go to the restroom. Once outside, she sprinted to the auditorium and scratched her name off the list. After that, she hid out in the girls' bathroom until the last minute, only joining the assembly when there were no seats left except in the back of the section where the freshmen sat.

Mr. Hill was standing outside the little room where the light panel for the stage was run, cuing a kid named Jason to run the lights. First up was Tanya Waters doing an interpretive twirling routine to Kenny Rogers and Dolly Parton. Alabama frowned. Stuart should have been the first. She looked around, but didn't see him in the audience, which meant that he had to be backstage. Was he wondering where she was, or would he just assume she'd bugged out?

"I'm not going on," she whispered to Mr. Hill.

She must have looked frantic, because he put a calming hand on her shoulder. "Are you sure? Everybody gets a little stage fright, you know."

"Oh, I'm sure."

"Did you scratch your name off so Mr. Kirby won't call your name?"

She nodded.

"Then it's okay. Relax."

If only she could. But there was still Stuart to worry about.

Next, a kid from the sophomore class played "Time in a Bottle" on guitar. He wasn't bad, although a certain element of the audience was starting to get restless. Heads bent together in whispered conversations, and at one point, laughter could actually be heard over the song.

The laughter made her glad she'd chickened out—but it also made her more nervous for Stuart.

The principal announced Dawn Halsey, who came out to dutiful applause and started to play some classical piece. Halfway through, she switched tempo to a boogie-woogie beat. If this had been The Villas, she'd have won first prize on the spot. But even for a tough audience like this one, the number was a crowd-pleaser. By the end, people were stomping and clapping.

Alabama turned back to the lighting booth. "Why hasn't Stuart gone yet?" she asked Mr. Hill.

"We decided to go backward up the list. He was the first to sign up, so he'll be the last to go."

Dead last. Poor Stuart. He would be a nervous wreck.

Next up, a freshman named Marty got up in a cape and a construction paper top hat to perform tricks. Everyone knew Marty had asked permission to use the school mascot in his magic act, but the principal had turned him down, because having Bugs would prejudice the audience in his favor. Watching, it was obvious that he needed *something* going for him. Instead of pulling a rabbit out of his hat, he was attempting to do card tricks with a regular playing deck. Sadly, no one beyond the second row could make out the tiny cards, so there was lots of heckling. Mr. Kirby was forced to intervene and quiet everybody down.

"Now, we've got just a few more contestants, and I want you to give them the respect and attention you'd expect if it was you up here," the principal lectured them.

The auditorium of restless teenagers sat stony-faced through a girl playing something classical on the flute, and then woke up when two of the varsity cheerleaders did a dance routine to "Girls Just Want to Have Fun." By the end, kids were whooping so hard, there was no question who would come in first place.

And then it was Stuart's turn.

Alabama felt sick. She caught glimpses of his purple tunic in the wings as he waited for the Cyndi Lauper music to end and then for the clapping to die down. When it did, the principal announced him, and then he came out to silence, standing center stage in his purple-and-gold outfit, his skinny legs encased in black tights. Titters rippled through the student body. As the lights dimmed, leaving Stuart in a spotlight, someone in the back wolf whistled. Stuart kept his head bent in concentration.

Her insides felt as if they were folding in on themselves. Poor Stuart. Would Mr. Kirby have to intervene on his behalf, too?

Finally, he began to speak—in a surprisingly strong-sounding voice. "To be or not to be . . ."

Alabama squeezed her eyes closed.

After a moment, she realized that she couldn't hear anything but Stuart—no rustling, no laughter. When she'd helped him run his lines once, they had made fun of the speech, remembering the episode on *Gilligan's Island* where Gilligan sang it. But the strange thing was, until now, she had never really listened to the words before, or absorbed them. *To be or not to be* . . . The character was talking about killing himself, wasn't he? He was debating life and death, envisioning a never-ending sleep. Now, phrases stuck with her, and the beautiful words caused a painful wrench in her chest.

And by a sleep, to say we end the heartache . . .

She opened her eyes. In his costume, with the spotlight on him, Stuart seemed to take up more space than he did when you were talking to him face-to-face. No, he seemed to *command* more space. She forgot to be nervous for him, and just watched, and listened. Not all of the words made sense by themselves, but she managed to understand, and she guessed from the attention they were paying that a lot of the other kids did, too.

When he finished, she was stunned to hear a big hand of applause for him, and even a boy in the back hollering, "Way to go, Stu-loo!"

She turned to Mr. Hill. "He's good, isn't he?"

He was clapping, too. "He did a great job."

Excited, she didn't even wait to write down her vote and slip it into the box. She hurried to the back of the auditorium so she could exit, circle around the outside of the building, and meet Stuart as he was coming out the back way—the stage door.

Unfortunately, she ran into Bev first.

Angry Bev.

They both stopped in the empty corridor. Alabama had assumed her aunt was inside the auditorium with all the other teachers. Where else would she be?

Patrolling the hallways, evidently.

Bev's gaze traveled up Alabama, from the tips of her sneakers to the rat at the crown of her veil, and Alabama knew she was in trouble. *Crap.* Why hadn't she changed back into her regular clothes?

She decided to brazen her way through. "Hey! Did you miss the show?" Bev didn't say anything for a moment, and Alabama's face started to burn. "Stuart did great."

"What are you wearing?"

Alabama looked down at herself, as if she needed a reminder. "I'm supposed to be like Miss Havisham . . . you know, the old jilted bride in the Dickens book . . . ?"

The words *jilted bride* acted on her aunt like a poker.

"I read *Great Expectations*," Bev said, her chest rising and falling heavily. "Nowhere in that book was that crazy lady wearing *my wedding dress*."

Alabama gulped. It was on the tip of her tongue to say "It was all Stuart's idea," but that would have really been cowardly. Her other instinct was simply to turn and run. Bev's bulgy-eyed expression scared her. Unfortunately, at that moment, the auditorium door behind her opened and a wave of students came pouring out.

Bev closed in on her. "And besides that, I've been looking all over for you. Your name showed up on the absentee list this morning."

"Yeah, I ended up missing homeroom," Alabama said.

"I went all the way home to find you. I was worried. I didn't know you were gallivanting around school in my dress, making fun of me."

Alabama frowned. "Of *you?*"

Bev reached forward and grabbed a fake cobweb. "What have you done to it?"

"Nothing—we were really careful not to hurt it. Stuart even made a whole new veil so we wouldn't mess up the old one. He made it in *your* class. You helped him."

The wrong thing to say. Bev's cheeks flushed a dark pink. If a crowd of students hadn't circled them—their mid-corridor standoff created a bottleneck—who knows what Bev would have done. She looked as if she wanted to rip the dress off Alabama's back right there in front of everybody.

"Take it off," Bev told her.

A few kids laughed, and someone in the back of the crowd seconded it. "Take it off!" As if this were a striptease.

Alabama's cheeks burned even more. "I was going to—"

"Now."

Was she crazy?

"You had no right to wear it!" Bev said. "You knew I didn't want you to, but you had to anyway. Well, you can consider yourself grounded. Forever."

Whoas and murmurs of sympathy rippled behind her.

It should have made her feel better to know that everyone thought Bev was being a jerk, but she just felt conspicuous, and embarrassed—the very thing she'd hoped to avoid when she dropped out of the talent show. She glanced around and caught the eye of Kevin Kerrigan. One of his brows quirked up in commiseration, but for some reason his sympathy only mortified her all the more.

She turned and fled. The crowd parted for her, and as she ran through them their faces were a blur until a hand darted out and hooked her arm, stopping her. It was Stuart.

"What's going on?" he asked. "Where were you?"

She didn't know why she felt like she was about to cry. All her aunt had done was tell her she was grounded. But in front of the whole school. And all over this stupid dress. She wished she'd never laid eyes on it. And if Stuart hadn't pestered her about it . . .

"Thanks a whole lot." She jerked her arm away. "I'm grounded for life, thanks to you."

She hated herself for blaming him, but she couldn't help it. She felt like an idiot. How did she let herself get into this ridiculous position? She didn't belong in this school, in this town, or with her aunt. If only she were back with her mom. If only her mom—

A sob burst in her throat, and she turned and she started running toward her locker. But she didn't stop there. Instead, she ran right out of the building, off the campus, and back to Bev's house. She refused to call it home. It wasn't her home. If she was going to be grounded for the rest of her life, she might as well think of it as what it was. Jail.

She would go live with Gladdie and Wink. Or maybe during the visit with Granny Jackson, she could convince her to take her in starting immediately. If only she could never see Bev again. Ever.

God only knows what people driving down the street thought of a girl running down the sidewalk in a spider-infested wedding veil. She probably looked crazy. But that's how she felt—like another crazy Putterman female. Any minute now, she would probably start ranting about how this was *her* wedding dress.

Wait.

She slowed, then stopped. That's what Bev had

said—that this was her wedding dress. She looked down at herself, confused. *My wedding dress,* she'd said, plain as day. What did that mean? There had never been a wedding. Bev had never been married.

The rest of the way home, she couldn't banish Stuart's crazy Bette Davis movie theory from her mind. It was so preposterous . . . but what if it was actually true? Was this The Really Bad Thing that had made her mother not want to talk to Bev?

But that didn't make sense, either. If Bev was her mother, why wouldn't Bev had gone ahead and raised her?

But if Bev wasn't her mother, why all the secrecy?

Why all the secrecy, period?

Once inside the house, she went straight to the area of the living-dining room where Bev kept a little desk and file cabinet that she called her office. Once a month she sat herself down at the desk and paid bills, but during the intervening time, crap piled up on it. Right now there were Butterick patterns, an antique spice drawer that held a fraction of Bev's button collection, and several rolls of crepe paper in autumn colors of gold, orange, and brown. Alabama pushed all that aside and rifled through the drawers in search of the key to the top drawer of the file cabinet, which was kept locked.

She found it in one of the cubbyholes in the back

of the desk. This seemed almost too easy, but when she inserted the key in the drawer and turned it, it worked. She slid the file drawer open and fingered through the hanging folders. They were all neatly labeled in colored tabs, alphabetized in backward order—*School, Mama, House, FHA, Electric, Alabama . . .*

At least she rated her own folder.

She plucked it out. This was the moment of truth. Why would Bev have started the file unless she had something important to put in it . . . and what could be more important than a birth certificate?

Something else caught her eye. An envelope at the bottom of the drawer, beneath all the other hanging files. She put the hanging folder aside and picked up the letter. Had it slipped out of a folder, or had Bev put it there on purpose to hide it? She frowned at the envelope—a basic white business kind, with writing scrawled over the front. In the center of many cross-outs and additions was her mom's writing. The letter had been sent to Bev, although her mom had screwed up the address. She squinted at the postmark. June—of this year. And the date.

The date of the postmark was the day her mother died.

Her heart hammered. Why would her mother have written to Bev? Especially on that day.

Maybe she wanted to borrow money. They were

always broke. But wouldn't she have asked Gladdie?

She drew the sheet of paper out with cold fingers. Even though Alabama knew it was a letter written by her mother, seeing those loopy letters sloping down the page struck her forcefully, unexpectedly, almost like hearing her mom's voice calling her name would have.

Dear Bev,
   You'll probably think I'm crazy, writing to you after all these years. Swear to God, I'm not. You won't believe that.
   Maybe you won't even open this letter. You'll see it's from me and toss it. Please don't do that. . . .

As she read on, her hands began to shake. The words scrolled past, but it took a minute to wrap her mind around them. Her mother was apologizing to Bev. She was telling her aunt to take care of her. She was saying good-bye.

This was obviously the last thing her mother had ever written. Maybe the last thing she'd ever thought about. She'd sat in their apartment writing it. To Bev. *Not to me.* No letter had ever reached her. There had been no note in the house. That's how Alabama had known her mother's being run over was an accident.

But this was a suicide note. Her mom didn't say

so in so many words . . . but she didn't have to.

As she finished, tears flowed down her cheeks, and she needed to blow her nose. But she couldn't get up to find a tissue, or even go to the kitchen for a paper towel. She couldn't move. Her mother had known she was leaving her forever. Planned it. That last horrible morning, walking to the bus— had she known it then? Had she shoved Alabama on the bus, barely even bothering to say good-bye, knowing that it was good-bye forever?

She read the letter again, greedily, almost angry, her tearful vision blurring the page. And then other details began to sink in. *I started to write this so I could ask you to take care of Alabama. But maybe that's not right. Maybe I should ask you to take her back. Take back what I stole from you. . . .*

What did that mean? *How could Mom have stolen me from Bev, unless . . . ?*

Unless Stuart was right. The letter slipped from her trembling fingertips.

Gulping in several breaths, she bent and picked it up again, folded the paper in the worn creases, and then inserted it back into the envelope. She dropped it back into the bottom of the cabinet, turned the key, and replaced the key in its cubby.

She ran to her room, tossed herself on the bed, and suddenly realized she was still wearing the stupid dress and veil. She yanked off the latter and then unfastened the dress and stepped out of it.

Bev's wedding dress. She shuddered, then started laughing and crying at once, like a loon. She had wanted to discover the truth, but she'd ended up with more truth than she'd dreamed of. More sad truth.

How could her mother have done it? The horrible mental images that she'd tried to keep out of her mind kept replaying now. *I didn't even have time to brake,* the trucker had said. That's how fast it had happened. Why hadn't her mom been more careful? Alabama had wondered.

Turned out, she *had* been careful. She'd probably picked out the intersection weeks before, the moment, maybe even the truck. . . .

She squeezed her eyes shut and rolled over, clutching a piece of her old sloppy quilt—an old peasant shirt of her mother's. She balled her fist and struck the material, crying out. "Why? Why would you leave me? How could you?"

Nothing made sense. It was bad enough to have her worst fear about her mom confirmed . . . but what did the letter mean? All those things about giving Alabama back to Bev. The idea incensed her. As if she were a shirt her mom had borrowed and forgotten to return.

She closed her eyes, but tears spilled out of them anyway. Not just tears of self-pity, but tears of remorse. *How could I have left her all alone like that?* And for what? Swimming at Camp Quapaw. Riding horses. Making lanyards.

And all the while, her mother had been at home, worrying, depressed. Alone.

She didn't care about the truth, or who Bev was. All finding this letter did was make her hate Bev more. She'd known—known all along—and she'd said *nothing.* Who had more of a right to this letter than Alabama did? No one. They'd been living a lie. Bev was always telling her she needed to talk to someone, to open up and share. What a hypocrite! She hadn't even shared this letter—this last communication from her mother.

She vowed then and there never to talk to Bev about this. Never. She didn't want to open up to her aunt, and she especially didn't want confirmation that Bev was anything other than her annoying aunt. She didn't even give a care about the birth certificate anymore.

Diana Putterman was her mother, and always would be. If only she could see her one more time, and tell her that. If only . . .

She cried until she felt wrung out and headachy, and then she dozed off into a jittery, restless sleep.

And by a sleep, to say we end the heartache, she thought, nodding off.

CHAPTER 20

The clock read *3:20*. Something had jarred Alabama awake—had it been the phone? The doorbell? She got up and peeked out the window to see if there was a car there.

No car was visible in the driveway. She pulled on jeans and a T-shirt and went to the door in her bare feet. Standing amid Bev's army of expertly carved jack-o'-lanterns was Stuart, his expression anxious. The anxiety didn't let up when he saw her face.

"What happened to you today?" he asked. "You disappeared. I looked all over for you."

"I skipped out."

His eyes widened. "The whole day?"

She leaned against the door frame. For once, she didn't want to invite him in. Things were already tense between them, but if he came in, he might wheedle her into talking more than she wanted to. She could imagine what a field day he'd have over her mother's letter—final proof that his crackpot theory wasn't so nutty after all.

"Bev got mad about the dress."

"Yeah, I heard that," he said. "I couldn't believe it. You looked great!"

She shoved her hands in her pockets. "I'm sorry I couldn't go through with it. I never really wanted to do the talent show—that was your thing, not mine. I was too embarrassed to admit it."

"Maybe I was a little pushy," Stuart said.

A little. "So . . . people were talking about me?"

"Just in the cafeteria." He shrugged. "And between classes . . ."

So, all the time, basically. *Thanks, Bev.*

She still felt some lingering resentment toward Stuart, for being so obsessed with the stupid talent show to begin with. That's what had started all the problems.

No, what had started all the problems was her moving here. Or maybe Gladdie's gallbladder. Or her mom's accident . . .

Only she couldn't call it an accident anymore. But she couldn't bring herself to accept it as the other thing, either.

She wanted to crawl into a hole.

Stuart shifted his feet. That he wasn't going to be asked in was beginning to sink in.

"It's weird that she would be so mad," he said. "Since you didn't even perform."

"I told you she would be."

"Yeah, you did." He looked down at his feet, then glanced up at her again. "Is something else wrong? I know having your aunt pissed off is no fun, but . . . you look real upset."

"I'm okay."

The silence between them was broken by a dog barking somewhere down the empty street. Stuart backed down a step. "Do you want to come over tonight?" he asked. "We aren't going trick-or-treating, but my mom usually makes caramel apples."

She would, Alabama wanted to sneer. Stuart knew nothing of her life, of what she was going through. He lived in his own perfect Looney bubble.

"I can't," she said. "I'm grounded till I'm eighty."

"Oh, right." He descended another step. "I guess I'll see you tomorrow, then."

She nodded, and he turned to leave. Watching him go, she hated herself for being mad at him. Everything was so mixed up, and it wasn't really his fault. When he was halfway down the walkway, she called out, "Your monologue was fantastic."

He whirled, surprised. "Did you think so?"

She nodded. "Really good. Mr. Hill thought so, too—you were the only one he clapped for. Maybe you'll get a part in the spring play."

He lifted his arms and shoulders in a full-body shrug. "I came in third. They announced it at lunch. The cheerleaders won. I got a ribbon, though."

Something to go on the Looney shelf of honor. "It'll look good next to your Oscar."

He seemed pleased, but then he waved good-bye and kept going. And she felt a lot lonelier than she had before.

Restless, she went back inside. She itched to pull out the letter and read it again, to go over and over the puzzling things her mother had written. When had her mom written it? And what about Gladdie—had she read it? Had she and Bev conferred and decided to keep its contents from Alabama because they worried she would fall apart?

Of course, she *had* fallen apart, sort of. But it was such a shock. It wouldn't have been such a shock if they had told her the truth from the beginning.

Bev would be coming home any minute now. What would she say to her? Would Bev want to sit down and have a talk about what had happened at school, or would she breeze in and pretend nothing happened? Both possibilities turned her stomach.

She went into the bathroom and looked in the mirror. Speaking of Halloween. A seriously depressed ghoul stared back at her. Her face was a horror show of tear-smudged mascara in thick white pancake makeup. She slathered Noxzema over her face, trying to undo the damage. She couldn't believe that Stuart hadn't told her that she looked like a train wreck. It showed that he must have really been worried about her.

And she'd sent him away. That wasn't very nice.

Maybe she should apologize. Going over to Stuart's house would give her a good excuse to avoid Bev for a little while. Of course, she was supposed to be grounded, and she would be in a lot more trouble when Bev figured out that she'd skipped almost an entire day of classes. But if she was grounded for the rest of her life, what else could Bev do to her?

She patted her face dry, shoved her keys into her pocket, and headed out the door. Paranoid about running into Bev, she darted down a side street that she knew Bev didn't use much. It ran close to Sparta Creek, which right now was almost a dry gulch with a trickle of water running down the center. She could hop over and it and be at Stuart's faster that way.

She scooted quickly down the street, but not quickly enough. Behind her, a car honked. She turned, expecting to face the wrath of Bev. Instead, Kevin Kerrigan was hanging out the open window of his old red Mustang. "Want a lift?"

The question surprised her so much, she was tongue-tied. He waved her over, and she backtracked, sidling uncertainly toward the car. Since the day he'd picked up her books, he'd smiled at her in the hallway a few times, but he'd never gone out of his way to talk to her.

"Where are you headed?"

"Nowhere." She gestured aimlessly toward the creek.

"Sparta Creek? That really is nowhere. Unless you're a cottonmouth, and then it's home."

She bit her lip. "I was going to see Stuart. You know Stuart Looney? He's a freshman, too."

Kevin snorted. "Stu-loo? Everybody knows him now. Tights Boy."

Poor Stuart. He'd feel awful to hear his idol dismiss him that way. But of course, it was hard to think too much about Stuart's feelings when Kevin was looking at her with a sparkle in his blue eyes.

"Wouldn't you rather get a Frosty?" he asked.

"Seriously?" The nearest Wendy's was twenty miles away.

"Sure." He leaned over and opened the passenger door. "Hop in."

She hesitated. Kevin Kerrigan was a junior—sixteen or seventeen. She didn't have permission to go riding—especially not to another town. Bev would have a fit . . . if Bev ever found out.

If she was going to be grounded for the rest of her life, this might be her last chance to go for a ride.

She got in the car.

Kevin drove to the end of the block and hooked a right, then headed straight for the highway. "Wake Me Up Before You Go-Go" blared on the radio. "Do you like this song?" he asked.

She wrinkled her nose. "Honestly? It feels like we've been stuck in a whole year of Wham!"

"Whammed!" He laughed and turned the dial, stopping when he heard Huey Lewis and the

352

News singing "The Power of Love." For a foolish moment, she wondered if it could be an omen. He cranked it, and then accelerated.

They talked about stupid stuff all the way to Athens. Bands. People at school she only knew from hearing their names. Trivial things. It wasn't until they were in the drive-through line that she stopped to wonder why Kevin had picked her up. Maybe he liked her. Or maybe he was just bored.

Disappointment needled her as he headed straight back to the highway right after they got their drinks. It would have been fun to go in and sit someplace for a while . . . and not to have to go home. Then, a few miles out of town, he pulled off onto a side road.

"Where are we going?" she asked.

"Detour," he said. "I know a great place."

The place was a boat dock to a lake. The weather was cool enough now that boaters weren't tempted to come out during the week, and the parking lot was deserted. They got out of the car and strolled to the water's edge.

"That sure was weird with your aunt today," he said.

"I felt like an idiot."

"Why? She was the one who came off as a kook."

Satisfaction rippled through her. He understood. As they stood by the water, he took her hand. "You know who you remind me of?"

She shook her head.

"That girl in *The Breakfast Club*—the one with the dark hair. The one who says 'When you grow up, your heart dies.'"

She smiled, amazed that he had given her enough thought to compare her to anyone, much less Ally Sheedy, her favorite character in the whole movie.

"You ought to smile more," he said.

Strangely, his saying that melted her smile right away. How could she possibly be smiling, after what she'd found out? Mere hours ago. It seemed wrong. "There hasn't been much to be happy about this year."

"What—nothing to smile about in the year of Wham!?" When she didn't respond, he squeezed her hand. "I'm sorry. I heard about your mom. I need to learn to keep my mouth shut."

"No you don't," she blurted out. "I mean . . ."

He grinned. "Anyway, when you're with a pretty girl, there are better things to do than yack."

She was tempted to swivel around to see who he was talking about. She didn't think of herself as pretty. Most days she barely thought of herself as a girl. Since summer, her body had felt like a cumbersome shell she was hauling around, as if she were a turtle or a snail.

Kevin pulled her into his arms, wrapping them around her, enfolding her, and pressed his mouth to hers, pushing against hers until she could taste the sweet, milky aftertaste of the Frosty on his cold lips. She sucked in a breath, shocked. *He's kissing me.* This was a real kiss, not a peck like at junior high school parties. This was a boy with muscles hard from years of swinging a tennis racket. This was tongue.

Her stomached fluttered, but she didn't pull away. Not at first.

When she did step back—right after his hands started to roam up her shirt—Kevin grinned at her a little sheepishly. "I figured a girl with red-striped hair would have a wild streak in her. Was I wrong?"

She might have laughed if she hadn't been so flustered. "Yeah, maybe. I didn't expect you to do that."

He shook his head. "Then you've been hanging around Tights Boy too long."

She kept her face trained on the ground as they headed back to the car. He was making fun of Stuart, and she should call him on it, but the words wouldn't form. Oddly enough, Stuart was the person she wanted most to talk to right now. She could hardly wait to get home and call him.

On the other hand, she'd told him that she couldn't go to his house and then went out joyriding. Never mind that she'd been picked up by Kevin on the way to see him—that probably wouldn't make Stuart feel much better. Especially when she told him that she had actually made out with Kevin Kerrigan.

She kept rolling the thought over in her mind. She had made out with Kevin. That she had made out with anyone was a miracle. But being picked by the out-of-her-reach older boy of her dreams? Unbelievable. Stuart would probably accuse her of making the whole thing up.

She hardly knew what they talked about on the drive home. Tennis . . . school . . . Halloween . . .

Boring stuff. Phil Collins bellowed from the Mustang's speakers. She'd parachuted into someone else's life—that had to be the answer. This moment didn't resemble her life at all. Especially not her life of two hours ago. How had this happened?

Bev's Toyota was parked in front of the house when they got back. The sight of it smothered all the joy and wonder out of her drive with Kevin. Eating dirt seemed more enticing to her than walking through her front door and having to deal with . . . with everything.

"You want to go somewhere again sometime?" Kevin asked her.

He was asking her on a date? Her? "I don't know. . . ." She sighed. "I'm grounded."

"Your aunt would let you go out with me, though."

He said it as though it was a sure thing. How could anyone not make an exception for him?

"She's so crazy."

"Okay, maybe I'll talk to you at school sometime," he said, as if it might be difficult to manage. As if they didn't attend a school with fewer than four hundred people in it. This puzzled her. He knew she ate in the cafeteria every day—he could always find her there.

She climbed out of the car and hurried inside. Kevin didn't wait for her to go in—the Mustang was already disappearing around the corner before she got to the door. Good thing, too. As Alabama reached for the knob, Bev yanked the door open.

"Who was that? Where have you been?"

"That was Kevin," Alabama said.

Bev craned her neck out the door, as if looking at the air where his car had been would give her a clue. "Kevin . . . Kerrigan? The mayor's son?"

"Yup."

"You weren't here—you didn't leave a note." Almost without stopping, Bev added, "Kevin Kerrigan's a junior."

"So?"

"You can't just jump into cars with older boys like that."

"I didn't. I jumped into a car with *one* boy like that."

Her aunt crossed her arms. "Where did you go?"

Alabama shrugged. It was hard to keep disguising how much she loved watching her aunt get wound up. "For a drive."

"For a—" Bev sputtered. "You did not have permission to do that. What's more, you're grounded. Which you knew darn well."

"I figured I deserved one last wingding before you locked me in my room, or whatever you intended, Aunt Bev."

"I came home with every intention of trying to rationally discuss what happened today, and why I got so angry."

Alabama sputtered out a laugh. "Really, Aunt Bev? You were angry?"

Bev tilted her head, suspicious. "Why do you keep doing that?"

"What?"

"Calling me Aunt Bev."

"Isn't that what you are, Aunt Bev?"

"Of course, but . . . ." Her aunt's brow furrowed. "Look, I know I seemed a little irritated today—"

Alabama snorted.

"But I don't want to be unreasonable. You have to agree that taking my dress after I specifically asked you not to mess with my things was wrong . . . and you'd obviously been planning it for a long time. And then I come home and you've disappeared, and with a boy I barely know. Who's too old for you."

"He's only two years older."

"But you're still fourteen. That's too young to date. Especially a boy like that."

"You keep acting like he's some kind of demon.

His father's even on the school board, isn't he?"

"Yes, but Kevin's a junior, and he's . . . well, boys like that are used to getting their own way. And you're just fourteen."

"So? You're almost forty, and you went out with a scuzzball."

Bev's eyes bugged in anger, and then she took a deep breath. "The point is—I don't know how we can go on this way with you being so secretive."

Alabama nearly howled. The anger that had been building back up while Bev lectured her suddenly surged. "*I'm* secretive? *Me?*"

Bev paled. "What does that mean?"

Guilty.

"You know."

Bev actually looked as if she had to think about it. "I'm not sure. . . . Is there something you'd like to discuss?"

Alabama's lip curled. The last thing she wanted was Bev to sit her down for a heart-to-heart. Right now, she knew something that Bev didn't—and Bev knew that she knew something, but didn't know what it was. For once, she had the upper hand, and it felt good.

"I guess I don't know what I'm talking about." She turned and strolled back to her room.

"Wait," Bev called after her. "I think we should discuss—"

"Never mind," Alabama said.

"But you wouldn't want to—"

Alabama reached her room and shut the door a split second before her aunt could follow her into it. She flipped the hook-and-eye latch she'd installed. The snub wasn't the classiest of victories, but it was the best she could manage at the moment.

CHAPTER 21

Human childhood lasted so long for a good reason, Bev realized. Those years of loving a cute baby and then an adorable child gave parents time to prepare for the jolt of cohabitating with a teenager. Under normal circumstances, the troubles of childhood would have been ramping up slowly all those years, so that by the time the kid hit thirteen, the parents would be like the proverbial frog in the boiling water. They wouldn't notice that all of the sudden the pleasant little parenthood pool they'd been dropped into over a decade before had turned into a chaotic bubbling kettle of adolescent angst.

Plopped directly into the pot, Bev just felt scalded and bewildered. She had no endless reservoir of love and experience to draw from. She thought she had, but now that she was being tested, her reservoir felt like a puddle. She'd been around teenagers all her adult life, but they were the kind that she could leave at three in the afternoon. And they didn't seem to make a vocation out of hating her.

Maybe this was what her mother had been warning her about last summer when Bev had been trying to tell *her* that she didn't know anything about teenagers. Her own arrogance stupefied her now. How could she have thought she could take on a troubled girl like Alabama all by herself?

Impulsively, she picked up her phone and called her mother. She never would have guessed that Gladys Putterman would seem like a lifeline, but that's how desperate the situation had become.

Wink picked up and was his usual ebullient self. "Hey there, stepchild! How's every little thing?"

"Oh . . . fine," Bev managed. "May I speak to Mama, please?" The fact that she had to ask to speak to her mother now when she called the apartment was galling.

And being someone's stepchild. Ugh.

"Sorry, you just missed her. We're having a big Halloween do in the activity room. I came back up to grab my uke."

Halloween. That's how all the problems had started. The talent show . . . the dress . . . the blow-up.

"I guess y'all are expecting a stampede of trick-or-treaters," Wink said when she didn't answer.

As his comment penetrated her thoughts, a cry of surprise rent the air, and the most astonishing thing to Bev was that it had come from her own mouth. Trick-or-treaters! "I forgot to buy candy!"

She never forgot things like that. Holidays were her time—days when she really shone. But then last week at the store she'd been worried that she or Alabama might tear into the bags ahead of time.

"You'd better remedy that situation," Wink said, chuckling, "or your house is likely to get egged."

Or toilet papered, which was worse, in Bev's opinion. Egg could be cleaned off with a hose, while those little bits of toilet paper lingered for weeks.

"Of course, back in my day, trick-or-treating really meant something," Wink said. "We had candy apples, delicious cookies, and popcorn balls. And real fudge. Remember how that used to taste?"

"I'm sorry," she said, interrupting him. "I should get to the store."

"Fudge that melted on your tongue," Wink continued. "You can't find that now."

"They're waiting on you and your uke downstairs, aren't they?" she prompted.

"Oh, right." Nothing got an extrovert's attention like yelling "Showtime!" "Was there something you wanted me to tell Gladdie for you?"

"No . . . I was just calling to say . . ." What had she meant to say? *You were right and I was wrong. . . . I'm in over my head. . . . Help?*

"Happy Halloween?" he guessed.

Bev didn't feel like confessing to Wink that she'd wanted to talk to her mother because she was in despair over Alabama. "Yes, just tell her that for me. And have fun."

"We always do!"

She hung up, sad that her attempt to reach out to

her mother had been thwarted, but at least she now had something better than sympathy—she had a task to get her mind off her troubles. She went and knocked on Alabama's door.

"I need to go to the store," she called through the wood. "Would you like to come?"

"No." A short pause followed the answer. "What store?"

"The grocery store. I forgot to buy Halloween candy."

"No thanks," Alabama said.

"Is there somewhere you do need to go, then?"

"No."

"Okay," Bev said. "You'll be all right while I'm gone, won't you?"

"What do you think I'm going to do? Kill myself?"

Bev drew back. "No, of course not. . . ." A shiver snaked through her, and she frowned. "I . . . I shouldn't be gone long."

No reply.

Bev sifted through this exchange as she drove the few blocks to the grocery store. Was Alabama just sniping or had she detected something new and bitter in her tone?

She shouldn't have lost her temper this morning outside the assembly. In retrospect, she could have simply asked Alabama to change into normal clothes for the rest of the day and then had a talk about respecting her things when they got home.

But the shock of seeing her dress there, at school, and treated again in such a mocking way had made the incident feel personal.

And now Alabama had snapped. Before today, the only boy Alabama had been interested in was Stuart, and they seemed more friend-friends than boyfriend-girlfriend. But now . . . Kevin Kerrigan? She remembered him sitting at the table with Marvin, when the boys had been chucking sunflower seeds at her. Of course, Kevin's father was the mayor, and the grand mucketymuck of the school board, which practically made the Kerrigans New Sparta royalty. But there was something in the boy's eyes that had always made her uneasy.

Alabama was too young and too emotionally vulnerable to be going out with a boy like Kevin. Or any boy.

Of course, Diana had boyfriends at that age. . . .

Another worry reared in her mind.

What do you think I'm going to do? Kill myself?

Why would she have said that?

She's just trying to scare me.

Bev thought she had detected a deeper meaning behind the words, but Alabama didn't know that Diana had committed suicide. She couldn't know. The letter was at the bottom of a locked drawer.

Unless she'd found it. The possibility had caused a flush of fear, until Bev had checked the file cabinet. The cabinet was locked, and the letter was right where she'd left it.

Maybe she was reading more into Alabama's words than there had actually been. People used phrases like that all the time. It didn't mean anything.

Dark was descending as she parked outside the grocery, and she spied her first flock of costumed kids parading down the sidewalk. She needed to get her brain and her rear in gear. She hurried inside and went directly toward the aisle where the candy was—what little was left of it. The shelves had already been picked clean of the good stuff—the Reese's, the Hershey's miniatures, the one-nut Almond Joys. Sighing, she settled for bags of Smarties, peanut butter logs, and off-brand bubblegum.

Her house might get toilet papered anyway.

"Bev."

She turned. It took her a moment to believe what she was seeing. Glen stood in front of her in a top hat, red coat, jodhpurs, and knee-high boots. One hand clutched a shopping basket full of chips.

"What are you doing here?" she asked. Stupid question. What anyone was doing here was obvious.

From his reaction, though, she began to wonder. He shuffled the basket to his other hand, as if wishing to hide his chip habit from her. "Oh, I . . ."

"Have you taken up fox hunting?" She reached out and tugged his lapel. "Tally-ho!"

He blushed. "I'm supposed to be a . . . a . . . kind of circus character, I guess."

He guessed? "Are you having a party at school for the cast of your play?"

"Not exactly." He took a few steps toward her and changed the subject. "I've been wanting to talk to you, but I wasn't sure if I should call you at home."

"You can talk to me anytime at school," she pointed out. "But I hardly see you . . . except for the rare appearance in my room."

At her allusion to the kiss, he shifted his weight and red climbed up his neck. "Things are so odd this year. And you've seemed . . ." He stopped, then backtracked. "I heard there was an argument after the talent show today?"

Tensing, she turned and reached for a bag of caramels. "Oh, that was just a little dust-up between Alabama and me." No. She should face up to her flubs. "To be honest, I flew off the handle."

He said nothing, but his nod amounted to an unspoken *So I heard.*

"This hasn't been the easiest year," she confessed.

He stepped closer. "That's what I wanted to talk to you about. First your nose, then the parking lot incident."

"You heard about that, too?"

"Bev, I know you're going through a hard time. . . ."

Maybe he meant well, but his sudden concern had the earmarks of swooping back into her life when she was vulnerable, when her resistance was low. Not the best time to forge or repair a relationship.

"I'm doing fine," she said. "I'm managing." *Managing to screw up everything.*

He lowered his voice. "I know you're doing your best, but from what I've heard—"

"You never used to pay so much attention to gossip, Glen." She didn't want him to think she'd lost all sense of dignity. "I'd go crazy if I started listening to all the chatter in this town."

"But this was—"

"Why, hello there!"

Winging around the corner came Jackie Kirby, who would have been an unwelcome sight at any time. But she was interrupting an interesting conversation, and this was Jackie Kirby in a leopard-print catsuit, complete with a headband with perky ears. The rest of her looked perky, too. Slender and perky.

Bev was about to make a joke about how the Food-Save was beginning to feel a lot like the faculty lounge when Jackie dropped a tub of sour cream into Glen's basket. Almost as if it was her own basket.

And then it sank in. They were together. Ringmaster. Circus. Big cats.

Struck dumb, she looked at Glen. He hitched his throat, and his gaze skittered to the nearest shelf.

Jackie laughed softly . . . almost purred, actually. "I know it's ridiculous. When we planned this, Glen and I thought I'd be a lion and he'd be a lion tamer. But all the lion outfits I found made me look like a big tan blob, like Winnie-the-Pooh. This is much better, don't you think?"

Hating her, Bev made a mental note to buy a Jane Fonda workout video. She pasted on a smile and looked from one to the other. "Are you two headed to a big party?"

Jackie put her arm through Glen's. "Just a thing at my brother's."

"How nice." Bev leveled a pointed glare at Glen. "What were we talking about before?" She feigned forgetfulness, then remembered. "Oh, yes—of course I wouldn't mind if you called me at home, Glen. I'm sure you've still got my number memorized."

He looked flustered, as if he didn't know whether she was being sincere, or if she was throwing a wrench into his evening with the leopardess.

"Y'all have fun at the thing." Bev trilled a parting wave to him.

She paid for her candy and fled the store. Driving home, she ripped open a bag and gulped down several caramels. She shouldn't have let Jackie jump on her nerves like that. She prayed she hadn't looked as burned as she felt. Evidently, this was her day for making an idiot of herself.

And she was even more of an idiot for the perverse jealousy coursing through her veins. *She'd* thrown Glen over. She'd broken his heart last year. And for what? A two-timing loser who'd knocked up another woman and then slammed a door on her nose. She'd transformed her life into a county-western song—never a good move.

How awful to realize that she had dismal judgment when it came to men. Add that to the stack of life lessons learned too late that she was piling up this year.

Although . . . Glen was hardly distinguishing himself, coming on to her while Jackie was prowling in the dairy aisle in her catsuit. And he had been so passive while Jackie pranced around, practically taunting her. That was always Glen's trouble. He'd never stood up for her. The only time she'd ever seen him show real backbone was when he'd played Juror Number 8 in *Twelve Angry Men* in a little theater production.

Back at the house, nothing had changed. Alabama was still in her room, although now she was listening to Diana's records. Bob Dylan this time—"Like a Rolling Stone." That snarly yowl had always jumped up and down on Bev's nerves.

As darkness fell, she went out and lit the

pumpkins, then put the porch light on. After that, she retrieved her special little bucket in the shape of a cauldron and emptied all the candy bags into it.

She thought about putting on her witch hat, and maybe adding a mole and a blacked-out tooth. Then she remembered Jackie's catsuit, and Alabama's cobwebby jilted bride, and gave up the idea of a costume. Her heart just wasn't in dressing up this year.

She felt antsy, and one thing especially puzzled her. Before they were interrupted, Glen had said he wanted to talk to her about something. She'd assumed it was going to be a bid to resume their relationship. But he was with Jackie, obviously, and Glen wasn't the two-timing sort. Not like Derek.

So what had he wanted to say to her?

The theme of the Thanksgiving project was A Cornucopia of Thanks. The class was coming off of their household finance block, during which Bev had been dismayed by how flippant the kids had seemed about money. A lot of them didn't even see the point of knowing exactly how much it would take them to live.

"You'll care the first time it's Saturday night and you run out of money," Bev warned them.

One girl had piped up, "My mom's bank has a machine now that gives out cash whenever. She has a little card, like a credit card, only the money's from her checking account. She can get money any time she wants it."

Money any time you wanted it. From machines. Honestly, what message was that sending?

It was good to be doing something creative again, and this project gave the students a lot of artistic leeway. From a magazine, she'd found a model of a cornucopia in the shape of a turkey. "A turkey pooping fruit," is how one of the students described it. Unfortunately, there was a little truth in that, but it was still a cute idea, and the kids would have something fun to take home to their parents or grandparents at the holiday, which never hurt.

She was lining up an entire counter with inexpensive materials she'd saved so that the girls and Stuart could construct their own turkey cornucopia from everyday objects. She had boxes—both wood and cardboard—egg cartons, pinecones, Popsicle sticks, pipe cleaners, feathers . . .

This was going to be a blast.

At the last minute, she'd decided that the Popsicle sticks she'd been gathering and disinfecting all year could use a boost. She'd bought varnish at the hardware store during lunch and now used her free period in the classroom to lay the sticks on newspaper on the floor and stain them. They'd look more autumnal this way, and if she worked fast, the class could hit the ground running first period tomorrow.

She freed Bugs to hop around and opened the window to keep the room aired. It was November, but the afternoons still sometimes spiked into the upper sixties, and this was a perfect, clear day. A regimental march version of "What a Feeling" wafted over from the football field where the marching band was practicing. *Flashdance* with snare drums and sousaphones. She loved fall.

As she was halfway through varnishing, a light knock sounded at the door and Jackie popped her head in. It took her a moment to spot Bev on the floor, and then she noted all the Popsicle sticks with a smirk. "Looks like a summer camp project," Jackie said.

Bev stood. She wouldn't stoop to explaining her work to this woman.

"Lon needs to see you in his office." Jackie's perfectly plucked eyebrows arched sarcastically. "If you can spare the time."

The summons shook Bev to the marrow of her bones. A personal summons . . . not just a message over the school intercom. Lon wanted to see her, and it was the end of the day. . . .

She tried to smile and appear unflustered, though she doubted she fooled Jackie. "All right." She dusted her hands together as nonchalantly as she could, but her mind was in a frenzy.

They left the room and fell into step side by side. Occasionally, she could feel Jackie looking over at her. Was she sizing her up as competition? Watching for signs of nerves?

Bev *was* nervous. One comforting thought occurred to her: This was Tuesday. Most firings happened on Friday. Also, if Lon did fire her today, who would he get to replace her? Firing her would cause a disruption in the middle of the semester. It wouldn't make sense.

But if she was wrong . . . how would she live? There was the mortgage on her house, and now she had Alabama to take care of.

As they approached the office, she clung to the not-Friday theory like a person treed by a bear would hug a precariously thin tree limb.

She was escorted right in and sat down in the chair opposite Lon. The naughty chair.

"Well, Bev," Lon said. "I thought we were overdue for a little chat. That's why I asked you here."

She smiled. *Asked her?* She'd practically been frog-marched here by his sister. "What did you want to talk about?"

Assuming a pensive expression, he regarded her over steepled fingers. "The question is, Bev, what you need to talk about, and to whom."

"I'm not sure I understand."

He leaned forward. "Of course, I don't delve into the personal lives of my faculty. Your life is your business . . . except when it has a detrimental effect on the community here at New Sparta High School."

Or on your sister's love life? Bev tried to keep a neutral expression.

"In that event," Lon continued, "I feel it's necessary to step in."

"Have I had a detrimental effect on anyone?" she asked.

His lips flattened, as if this conversation was becoming more distasteful to him. In reality, she sensed that he was loving every second. "Your behavior this year has been . . . erratic. I understand that your personal situation has changed—your niece is living with you, and . . . well, excuse me, but we've all heard about the incident at Lewanne's. Even the students know about it. You can't feel good about that."

"I'm not sure a conversation I had with a . . . friend . . . is anyone's business but my own."

"Of course. Normally, I pay no mind to gossip—except I did note that the real story of your nose, which I pieced together through the grapevine, turned out to be a little different from the tale you told me."

She blushed. She couldn't deny she'd misled him there. Well, lied.

"But even leaving those things aside," he said, moving on, "there's the matter of having shouting arguments with your niece in the hallway. That's not a good example of how to comport oneself in public, is it?"

"It was just once. I was so surprised by—"

He waved away her excuses. "We all know that teens can try our patience. And everyone is aware that your home situation changed abruptly this year. That's why I'm giving you this friendly warning and offering you the advice to see someone. Jackie would be happy to contact Dr. Land for you."

She shrank back, her cheeks flaming. He wanted *her* to talk to a psychiatrist? The same one she'd sent Alabama to?

"I see," she said. "Is that a requirement?"

"Oh no. Simply a friendly nudge. We all need help sometimes, Bev." He smiled. "Meanwhile, I'll mark in your employment file that we had this little chat."

All the way back to her classroom, her emotions careened between relief that she hadn't been fired, humiliation that everyone thought she was crazy, and panic about her file. Oh, Lon could soft-pedal the matter all he wanted, but there was no doubting his meaning. She'd come unhinged once too often, too publicly. She'd lied. And no telling what Jackie was saying about her.

Hearing an account of her actions in their most unflattering light did make her feel ashamed. Especially lying about her nose. And now it was all being noted in her file. Lon was laying the paper trail so he could let her go at some point in the not-too-distant future.

Her footsteps slowed. She wouldn't have been surprised if Jackie wasn't actually at the bottom of all of this. It would be so handy for her if Bev was out of the way altogether. Then she could have Glen free and clear, and someone else—maybe even Leah—could take over the homemaking classes. And with cousin Larry stepping in to teach health, the Kirby stranglehold on New Sparta High would be a little bit stronger.

It was like the royal court intrigues of the romance novels she sometimes dipped into, only instead of dukes and countesses, the players here were administrators and teachers. Her head wasn't on the chopping block yet, but she felt as if she was headed in that direction. And it was impossible to know who she could trust. Did other members of the faculty think she was losing it, too? Could she talk to Glen?

Glen. She remembered now. On Halloween at the grocery store, he'd said he wanted to talk to her about something he'd heard. Maybe this was it. Maybe he was her ally after all.

And she'd been so snippy and snide with him.

When she approached her classroom, the door was slightly ajar. She sped up, worried. She'd rushed out so quickly she hadn't even remembered to take her purse with her. The school didn't have a lot of trouble with theft, but leaving something out like that was asking for trouble. She pushed into the room, and bit back a shout when she saw someone there.

Then she let out a sigh. It was Oren. It wasn't O time, but maybe he'd forgotten something. *She* wasn't going to be anal about his not keeping to the schedule.

Oren barely glanced at her after she entered. Instead, he remained hovered where the newspapers were strewn across the floor and covered with the varnished Popsicle sticks. An ominous frown was etched across his jowly face.

"What have you done?" he thundered at her.

She rushed forward. Had the varnish spilled? It did smell strongly, even though she'd closed the lid. She was sure she'd—

Looking down, she gasped. Bugs was lying stretched out on his side, his furry little body arched and rigid. In her hurry to follow Jackie, she'd forgotten him as completely as she'd forgotten her purse. And now a half-gnawed, newly varnished Popsicle stick protruded from his triangle of a mouth.

"He's dead," Oren said.

His meaning—and the evidence—couldn't have been clearer.

The school mascot, the very symbol of New Sparta High, had met its death gnawing on her home ec project.

She'd killed Bugs.

CHAPTER 22

"Are you in love with Kevin Kerrigan?"

"What?" Alabama nearly spat up her Mr. Pibb. "No!"

She'd been reluctant to tell Stuart about Kevin at all, but after he saw Kevin pass her a note in the cafeteria, she'd had to confess. He'd been interrogating her for details ever since. It was like walking home with a member of the KGB.

"How many times have you gone out with him?"

"Twice. It's sort of been by accident. He picks me up to go driving . . . and stuff."

"Are you going steady?"

"Going steady? This isn't *Happy Days*. Anyway, does it sound like we're going steady?"

"No. You make it sound more like occasional kidnapping."

She scowled at him. "It has to be that way because I'm grounded. And Aunt Bev thinks he's too old. Or I'm too young."

"So all you can do is sneak around when your aunt's busy. I get that. But would you consider yourself his girlfriend? Has he kissed you?"

"Yes—I mean, yes, he's kissed me." She was doubtful about the girlfriend part.

"Has he done more?"

She had no intention of answering that, but her blush probably gave her away. The second time

379

she'd driven with Kevin, he'd been just as nice during the drive but a lot pushier when they were parked. Not that she didn't enjoy a lot of what he was doing. Remembering where he'd put her hands turned her insides to lava. But she certainly hadn't let him take her clothes off or anything like that.

"I'm not sure I trust that guy," Stuart said. "You should watch out."

"*You* were panting after him for months! Why else were we hanging out by the tennis courts in the heat of August? And now you're telling me I should stay away?"

"I was panting after him because it seemed hopeless, and because he's cute. Unrequited lust is romantic. It's different if he actually notices you. And it's really different if he treats you like a PG-rated streetwalker."

"You're just jealous," she said.

"No, I'm not. *You're* just touchy because you don't want to admit he's using you." They walked in tense silence for a while. Then he asked, "What do y'all talk about?"

"Nothing." Her tone was curt. "Just stuff. The usual."

"Does he like music, like you do?"

"Of course. Everybody likes music."

"I mean, those old rock albums," he said. "Which isn't really old music. Really old recorded music started—"

She interrupted, not feeling like listening to a history of the music industry going all the way back to Edison wax cylinders. "I don't know. I never talk about it with him."

"You said that's what y'all talk about."

"It's *some* of what we talk about. You know. Small talk."

His eyebrows drew together, puzzled. "So he's not very interesting?"

She bit back a yowl of frustration.

But at the same time . . .

She was coming to the same conclusion. Kevin was popular with a certain crowd and good at sports—tennis, at least—and he made decent grades, but he didn't seem all that intelligent. Or original. It was fun having a guy like him interested in her, even if it was only in secret. But the second time he'd picked her up, once she'd forgotten how nervous she was she actually felt . . . bored. She'd tried to talk to him about *Great Expectations* once, and he'd told her that when he was a freshman he hadn't bothered reading it.

"Maybe I could hang out with you guys sometime," Stuart said. "You know—if you go somewhere."

"Where would we go?"

"A movie, maybe?"

She shook her head. "My aunt would flip."

"Not being able to go out and do stuff puts a big damper on a relationship, doesn't it?" Stuart asked. "I mean, you and Kevin don't really strike me as Romeo and Juliet material."

"I never said we were. I just don't want my aunt to wig out. Is that so hard to understand?"

Stuart didn't reply. He didn't have to. It was common knowledge that her aunt had flipped already. The death of Bugs the day before had spread through the school after homeroom—it had almost been a day of mourning. Last night, Bev had moped all evening as she made lemon bars for the big Future Homemakers of America bake sale, but, typically, she hadn't told Alabama *why* she was so depressed. Alabama was as shocked as all the other students when she'd heard the story that morning.

"Well, if you don't want to hang out with just me anymore," Stuart said, "and you don't want to invite me along . . ."

Honestly. It was like having a little brother. "It's not that I don't want to invite you. I told you—it's not something I can ever plan."

"And Kevin thinks I'm a freak, right?"

"No." A lie. Kevin sometimes sneered a little about Stuart. She felt uneasy about that—and disloyal for not making Kevin see what a good friend Stuart was. Sure, she'd told him that she hung out with Stuart, but he didn't seem to care.

Anyway, why should she feel guilty about all this? Was she really supposed to share her sort-of boyfriend with her friend?

"Or he thinks I'm a dork," he said. "All those guys do."

"Why do you say that?"

"It doesn't matter." He stopped at his street. She still had several blocks to go. She would have invited him back to the house . . . except that she never knew when Bev would be in one of her manic phases. Which, in a strange way, felt more like life used to be, with her mom.

Maybe crazy is really all I know.

But also . . . she didn't want to go with Stuart because she was secretly hoping she'd run into Kevin.

"Are you avoiding me because I think Ms. Putterman is really your mother?"

"No." That was partly the reason, but telling him that would just start another argument.

He didn't look satisfied with her answer. "Well, I guess I'll see you at school tomorrow," he said, resentment coming through in his voice and from the slump of his shoulders. "Since you're not interested in doing anything anymore."

He pivoted and headed for home.

She called after him, "Stuart, c'mon. Don't act like a baby."

He didn't turn around.

What was the matter with him?

Why couldn't life be simpler?

As luck would have it, Kevin did drive by, seconds later. She smiled at him when he leaned over and opened the car door for her. "It looked like you were going to Stu-loo's house," he said, grinning.

She frowned. She hated when people called him Stu-loo. "You were stalking us?"

"Nah—just seeing what you were up to."

She got in the car. "We could have included him."

He wrinkled his nose. "No thanks," and then he accelerated.

She grabbed the dashboard. "Where are we going?"

"How about your place?"

"Are you kidding? My aunt might come home."

"No, she won't. I just saw her outside the grocery store, doing a bake sale thing."

That was right. She'd forgotten about the FHA bake sale.

"That business with your aunt and Bugs is unbelievable," Kevin said. "Do you know what Marvin was calling it at lunch?"

Marvin was his friend, another junior, who she knew by sight but had never talked to. She shook her head.

"Murder by homemaking."

She laughed, then stopped herself. It really wasn't funny. That poor rabbit. "I kept looking at all those Bugs Bunny posters they put up for this week's pep rally and thinking about Bugs choking."

"You know what? I have the most awesome idea for those posters."

He told her, and it did seem like an awesome idea. So awesome that, for the first time, they didn't go driving around. They stole some old craft supplies from Bev's garage—water-damaged poster board, tempera paint, and glue—went back to the school, and got to work. They had to sneak around and break into a few rooms, but with Gerald the old security guy on duty, it wasn't that difficult. Gerald was practically deaf.

She returned to the house that night around seven thirty. Bev had only been home for a few minutes, but she was livid.

"Where have you been?"

Alabama took a chance that Bev hadn't been on the horn yet. "Stuart's."

"You could have called. And you're supposed to be grounded. That means no running around after school."

"Sorry—guess I forgot."

Bev pursed her lips in disbelief. "Also, you said you'd empty the dishwasher, remember? If you don't start being more responsible, I'm going to have to dock your allowance."

As Alabama slunk off to her room, it was hard to bite back a smile. Let Bev screech and nag all she wanted. Revenge was nigh.

Tomorrow was going to be incredible.

The next morning, everyone was buzzing about the posters. At first glance, they looked just like the pep rally posters carefully crafted by the cheerleaders and pep squad, with Looney Tunes figures drawn on them. But Alabama and Kevin had retouched them, occasionally gluing the old cartoon figures onto the poster board they'd taken from Bev's to make room for the new slogans. Several of the posters were of Bugs Bunny. Over Bugs's ears, they'd printed WHAT'S UP, MISS PUTTERMAN?

Another poster had featured Elmer Fudd in hunting gear. She and Kevin had broken into the faculty lounge and Xeroxed Bev's faculty photo, and then replaced Elmer's face with Bev's. Instead of Elmer Fudd saying *"Kill the Eagles!"* Bev was now saying *"Kill the Wabbit!"*

The prank was an even bigger hit than Alabama had ever dreamed it would be. Students found the signs hysterical. At first she was dying to blurt out the fact that she was the mastermind behind the posters . . . or at least the assistant to the mastermind . . . but she and Kevin had sworn themselves to secrecy. Breaking into the faculty lounge could bring a load of trouble down on them.

Some kids in her algebra class discovered Bev was the second-period hall monitor, and they took turns going to the bathroom so they could ask, "What's up, Miss Putterman?" Apparently, the trend spread. At midmorning assembly, Lon Kirby announced that frivolous trips to the bathroom would not be tolerated. To which one wiseacre senior called out, "What's up with that?" Within seconds, a chorus of "What's up?" rippled through the auditorium.

Mr. Kirby went beet red. When one of the more serious-minded students bravely stood and asked what constituted a frivolous trip to the bathroom, and how the principal would be able to verify that it was frivolous, laughter broke out. Mr. Kirby shushed them all and changed the subject. They were warned that any defacement of school property—including pep-rally posters—would be considered theft and vandalism and subject to a three-day suspension. What's more, his office was working diligently to discover the identity of the culprit behind today's prank.

The dead serious tone in his voice sent a chill through Alabama. Then, from across the auditorium, Kevin winked at her. She smiled, but not too much.

By lunch, all of the posters save a few outliers had been found and removed—presumably to be studied for clues. Alabama made a mental note to replace the missing poster board in Bev's garage. Now that the first rush of excitement was over, paranoia set in. She kept imagining Mr. Kirby and Gerald battering down her door some night and dragging her in front of the school board in her pajamas.

She hadn't told anyone, not even Stuart, but what if Kevin boasted to his friends? Could they be trusted? Some of those boys seemed like big mouths.

At lunch, Stuart was later than usual getting to their table. "Somebody wrote 'What's Up, Miss Putterman?' in Magic Marker on the boys' bathroom mirror," he explained as he unloaded his lunchbox. "It took me forever to clean it off. I had to ask the janitor for some cleanser."

"Why'd you wash it off?" she asked.

He stared at her in confusion. "Because it's so mean. I know she grounded you and all, but I felt so bad for Ms. Putterman in class this morning. She seemed seriously shaken up."

"Really?" It took effort not to sound too gleeful. The bomb had hit its target. Eureka!

He poked the straw into his juice pouch and took a sip. "At one point, I could swear she was crying. The whole class got real quiet. It's awkward in there anyway, what with the sad empty cage and everything." He shook his head. "Who would be that vicious?"

Alabama nibbled a chicken nugget. "It was just a joke." Maybe it *was* a little mean, but she wasn't vicious.

Was she?

"Some of the kids are being so nasty," Stuart said. "I won't tell you about the drawing that was also on that bathroom mirror."

She sat back, frowning. She'd assumed people would laugh at the joke and move on. And they probably would. Stuart was just in his moralizing mode. A few days earlier he'd held forth for the entire lunch period about the hole in the ozone layer. No wonder they usually ate by themselves.

Glancing over at the faculty table, she noted that Bev hadn't shown up for lunch.

"People don't know what it's like to have something like that happen to them," Stuart said.

He spoke as if *he'd* had personal experience. Or maybe he just meant people calling him Stu-loo and tripping him in libraries. That was probably bad enough.

Between classes that afternoon, Bev stopped Alabama in the hallway.

Alabama's heart was in her throat. Their public encounters didn't always go well, and there was the very real fear that Bev had connected her brief disappearance last evening with the appearance of the posters this morning.

Would her own aunt turn her over to the school authorities?

Bev frowned. "Is something wrong?"

"No," she said quickly.

"I can give you a ride home this afternoon," Bev said. "I don't have any afterschool goings-on today." Under her breath, she added, "Thank heavens."

A group of sophomores passed them, and someone called out, "What's up, Miss Putterman!"

Bev followed the kids with her eyes, as if trying to ferret out the guilty party. But what could she do? The school couldn't expunge the words *What's up?* from everyone's vocabulary.

She returned her gaze to Alabama, who noted that her aunt's eyes were bloodshot. She remembered Stuart saying that Bev had seemed shaken. Yeah, that's how she looked.

"Actually, I thought we could go shopping," Bev said. "You'll need some nice new clothes for Thanksgiving if you're going to meet your Jackson relations. You want to make a good impression."

Bev was offering to buy her clothes? Actually *buy* them, at a department store? Suspicious, Alabama opened her mouth to question her. Unfortunately, the only words that came to mind were *What's up?*

"I've got clothes," she finally managed.

Bev shook her head. "Not River Oaks clothes. Believe me, you'll thank me later."

Alabama shifted her books. "Sounds like you want my trip to be successful. Are you trying to get rid of me?"

"Let's just say, with my reputation as a notorious mascot murderer, my job security has fallen a few notches. There's never been a better time to cultivate your rich relations."

That sounded terrible. "You're going to lose your job, just because of Bugs?"

Bev laughed humorlessly. "Well, not today. I hope. It might help if people could forget . . ."

Alabama remembered the principal getting heckled in assembly. And then, from farther back, she recalled Bev saying Mr. Kirby had it in for her. Today's incident probably made him hate her more.

Strange how a few nights ago—just this morning, even—this would have seemed like a triumph. Now all the trouble just made her stomach queasy. What if her and Kevin's posters ended up getting Bev fired? "I'm really sorry about what happened."

"Why? It wasn't your fault." Bev reached out and squeezed her upper arm. "Meet me out front after the last bell." She turned and walked away.

Alabama marveled as she shuffled toward her next class. Bev was eager for her to make a good impression at Thanksgiving. As if she wanted the Jacksons to take her in.

If Bev wanted to get rid of her, she should be happy. That was what she wanted.

But what if Stuart's Bette Davis theory was correct? If Bev really was her biological mother and still wanted to pawn her off on the Jacksons, what did that say about Alabama? She'd be losing two mothers in the space of six months.

Behind her, she heard someone calling out, "What's up, Miss Putterman!"

The phrase worked on her conscience like a

rebuke. Stuart saying the word *vicious* echoed in her mind.

I'm not vicious. It was a joke. She hadn't known people would get so carried away, or that Bev would take it so hard.

Except a memory of Bev looking so depressed as she made those lemon bars the other night pushed its way into her mind. If Alabama had given the matter serious consideration, she would have known Bev would feel mortified and hurt when she saw the signs.

But that was the problem. She hadn't given serious consideration to anything. She'd just drifted along with the joke. In fact, she'd relished zinging Bev.

She scooted into history class a hair before the bell. As she plopped her books down on the desk, a kid sitting next to her asked, "Hey—what's up?"

She sank into her seat without a word. The joke had seemed so funny last night, so clever, with Kevin. Now, it just . . . wasn't.

CHAPTER 23

"Maybe the next time we have a long drive somewhere, I'll be able to help more," Alabama said when they were halfway to Houston. She leaned against the passenger window. "I'll get to take driver's ed soon."

"Not too soon."

"I'll be fifteen in February."

"But by . . ."

Bev stopped herself from saying *By then there won't be any more road trips.*

"Soon I'll be able to get a real job and help pay my own way," Alabama said. "To help you out."

It was nerves causing Alabama to start babbling about helping, about the future. Maybe she also was afraid that the Jacksons wouldn't like her—that she would be sent back to New Sparta unwanted and have to make the best of things.

Bev was glad now that she hadn't told Alabama more about this long-lost family she was so eager to know. If she had, Alabama might have been even more nervous.

God knows her own nerves felt rattled. If she knew one thing about the Jacksons, it was that they didn't welcome newcomers with open arms. Her feelings were so conflicted. She didn't want to lose Alabama, but she didn't want to stand between her and her birthright, and she certainly didn't want to see her rejected.

The Jacksons seemed to have the knack of throwing her emotions into disarray. The last time she'd made this trip, with her mother in the summer of 1970, she'd been just as upset, although for completely different reasons. And her visit had had a very different motive behind it.

It had started with the phone ringing. Bev had been in the bathtub, or she would have picked up. Ever since Tom and Diana had disappeared, she'd never been more than a few feet away from the telephone if she could help it. During the first days, she'd kept a nearly sleepless vigil, awaiting what she feared would be horrible news. Then, the postman had delivered a postcard from New Orleans scribbled in haste by Diana. *Everything's fine! Sorry if we worried you. Hope y'all are having fun, too!!*

Having *fun?*

"At least we know she's okay," Gladys had said after reading it.

Bev was incensed. "Yes, we know that Diana's back to normal, having fun and not giving a fig about anybody else—probably not even about Tom. What is he doing in New Orleans? He's supposed to be going to Officer Candidate School."

"That's his business," her mother said. "Maybe you're well out of it."

She didn't feel out of it. Her heart was still involved, not to mention her stinging pride. She'd recovered from the mumps—and worse—and now she had the summer off. A whole summer to stew over Tom and Diana's betrayal.

Tom never called to explain or apologize. She hadn't received so much as a postcard from him. This stung her more than Diana's behavior. Tom had been more than a would-be fiancé. He'd been her friend. With his defection, the world as she'd known it evaporated.

Every day, she expected to hear that the relationship between those two had hit the skids. The bust up had to be coming. Had to be. Diana never held onto boyfriends for longer than six dates. And she and Tom had nothing in common. Bev gave them two months.

And then two months went by.

Diana's absence wore on Gladys, too. Bev could tell her mother was worried about Diana's well being, in addition to the fact that Diana was living in sin with a man. Not that Gladys concerned herself with what the neighbors would say. It was Diana she feared for. "Without marriage, he could just abandon her," her mother said.

"No kidding," Bev shot back.

Later, Gladys received another picture postcard, this time from Oklahoma, with prairie dogs on it.

I'm here till Tom's done at Fort Sill. It's so boring! I don't know what I'll do when they send him overseas.

"If only they would send Diana instead," Bev grumbled. "She's the perfect toxic weapon. More potent than Agent Orange."

When the phone call came, Bev heard her mother pick up in the next room. She sat still in the bathtub, straining to listen, but all she caught were her mother's murmurs in answer to whatever was being said. Moments later, Gladys barged right through the bathroom door, so upset that she was speechless as she sank down on the closed toilet seat next to the tub.

Even submerged in hot water, Bev's body went cold.

"That was Dorothy Jackson," Gladys informed her. "I have . . . news."

"Oh God." Something terrible had happened to Tom. Horrors paraded through her mind. *Killed in a training exercise . . . helicopter crash during maneuvers . . . jeep overturned . . . food poisoning . . .*

"We've been invited to a wedding," Gladys said. "Diana and Tom's wedding."

Bev sat up so abruptly, sudsy water sloshed over the side of the tub. "Diana doesn't believe in marriage—she says it's barbaric. How can they get married?"

Why would they? She'd gone out with Tom for

years—*years*—and they'd never even discussed marriage seriously.

"Tomorrow at noon, at some church in Houston," Gladys said.

At first, Bev argued for a total Putterman boycott of this sickening event. Barring that, her mother was of course free to go, but she herself would be staying home.

Diana had been a thorn in her side her whole life—always insisting on attention, or getting into embarrassing situations. Like the time she'd showed up at school with no underpants. (*Fourth* grade! Way too old for a stunt like that.) The principal had sent Bev home with her, as if it was Bev's fault or something. And all through their childhoods, Diana had tormented her, tattled, tried to outshine her in every way that didn't require application or brainpower. Diana wasn't capable of making good grades, so she opted for making a nuisance of herself. And no matter how tight money was at home, she got things. The attic was littered with the detritus of her castoff manias—a clarinet and guitar took their places next to tutus and tap shoes, the ventriloquist dummy and the little equestrian outfit she'd *had* to have for the lessons she'd begged to take . . . before realizing that she was terrified of horses. Not to mention all the discarded toys that were up there.

Tom would be discarded soon, too. She was sure of it. Marriage or no marriage.

Despite Bev's boycott threats, the next morning at first light she helped her mother load the car and then seated herself on the passenger side.

Gladys made no comment about her change of heart until they were out of town. "I appreciate your coming with me."

Bev drummed her fingers on the door's armrest.

"I understand that from your perspective this marriage is a—"

"An abomination," Bev said.

"It's not ideal," Gladys agreed. "But Diana isn't like you. She's not like me. She doesn't have much to fall back on. Anything could happen to her."

"So it's okay if she falls back on my boyfriend?" Bev almost said *my fiancé,* which wasn't accurate. Technically. Especially now. But Diana had known what Tom meant to her. She'd seen the wedding dress, and worse, she'd overheard her telling Dr. Gary about the baby. She knew everything—and still she'd stolen him.

"She's made some foolish mistakes," Gladys said. "Who hasn't?"

Bev's cheeks burned. She knew what her mother meant. Her generation would never condone making love to a boy without getting a ring on your finger first, even if you'd been going out with the boy—man—for four years and he was about to go to war. To her, that poor lost child would always be Bev's "mistake."

"Maybe this is what she needs," her mother continued. "They must be in love to have run away together like they did."

Ha. "She lured him."

"I just want to be there and make certain the marriage takes place," Gladys said.

Interesting. Because Bev wanted to be there to see that it didn't.

They arrived in Houston an hour ahead of time and drove straight to the Jackson house. The driveway and surrounding street looked deserted, which threw Bev. She'd expected more activity. She also expected a maid to answer the door. Instead, she came face-to-face with Dot, now eighteen, who was wearing a simple navy-blue dress and white gloves. She took in Bev and her mother with a tight smile that held what Bev could have sworn was a hint of derision, and called out behind her, "The Puttermans are here!"

After Bev introduced Gladys, Dot escorted them back to the walnut-paneled library. Far from festive, the house was as quiet as a tomb, and as they walked along the impressive hallway, Gladys shrank a little, gaping at the enormous chandelier above as if it might come crashing down on her head.

Tom and his parents were assembled in the library, huddled in a tight knot in their Sunday best. There were no guests. Right away, Bev understood. No Jackson considered this a happy occasion. No one at all did, except maybe Diana. The bride was probably her usual heedless, ecstatic self.

When Tom caught sight of Bev, he seemed to snap awake. "No one told me *you* were coming."

For over two months she'd yearned to talk to him, to find out what had happened. Why he'd abandoned her. But now that they were suddenly face-to-face, she didn't have to wonder. She knew. He was the boy his sister had described to her—the weak-willed one who fell for flaky girls. He'd found himself a doozy.

Bev couldn't think of any response that didn't involve slapping his face. Instead, she forced a smile and spun on her heel back toward Dot. "Is Diana here? I'd like to see her."

"Sure," Dot said, grinning.

She led Bev upstairs, but not to the room they'd shared when Bev had stayed before. Diana evidently rated the guest room.

The bedroom—which, with fresh paint and bright floral curtains did show signs of having been recently renovated—already looked as if Diana lived in it. Rumpled bedcovers were strewn across the mattress of the four-poster, and discarded clothes were scattered everywhere. Diana, in a long white dress with flowing sleeves, sat slumped in front of a massive, elaborately carved vanity. Her face was glum and pale, and seeing Bev didn't cheer her up. "Oh God. It's you."

Bev turned to Dot. "You don't have to stay. Diana and I are going to have a chat. You know—sister talk?"

Dot's reluctance to miss the show couldn't have been more obvious. The girl finally backed out of the room, however, and shut the heavy door behind her.

Diana exhaled. "That one's a real pain in the ass."

On that, at least, they were in total agreement. For a moment, Bev weighed whether Diana's getting stuck with Dot for a sister-in-law counted as just desserts. But no, that wasn't punishment enough. Nothing would be punishment enough until Diana was banished from Tom's life forever.

"Welcome to the world of little sisters," Bev said.

Diana buried her head in her hands and groaned. "Give me a break, Bev. Please." A split second later, she rebounded slightly as a possibility occurred to her. "You didn't happen to bring anything to drink, did you?"

"No."

"Smoke?" She saw Bev's unspoken answer—a glare—and sagged again. "I should have known. Are the Jackasses getting impatient down there?"

Bev was stunned. Outraged, even—and she didn't like the Jacksons all that much, either. "Diana, they're supposed to be your new family!"

"So? They've been treating me like I'm a disease."

"That's just the way they are."

"Not to you, I bet. They *love* you."

"No, they don't."

"Well, they don't even *like* me. After Tom told them he wanted to get married, the four of them spent half the night in conference, and then yesterday Mrs. Jackson hauled me off to Neiman's to buy this getup." She flapped her arms, showing off the sheer, fluttery sleeves. "Isn't it awful? It's like a diaphanous muumuu. I'm not sure even Phyllis Diller would wear it."

Bev lowered herself onto the bed. "What's wrong with you? You're supposed to be getting married in an hour. Can't you think of better things to be doing now than bad-mouthing your in-laws for their generosity? And that's leaving aside the fact that you could watch me walk in here without showing a hint of shame. Not a hint! Tom at least winced a little when he saw me."

"Oh, I bet he did," Diana said. "Mr. Worrywart." In imitation of her fiancé, her voice tightened into a squeaky whine. *" 'What have we done? What about Bev?' "*

If Diana hadn't been so irritating, Bev might have been gratified at this hint that Tom had at least spared her a thought. But how could she be so sarcastic about the man she was about to marry? About Tom.

Yes, he'd behaved like a jerk, but even a jerk was too good for Diana.

"What are you saying?" Bev feared she was yelling, but she couldn't help it. "You don't like Tom's family or Tom, either?"

"Shut up, Bev. You don't understand how much pressure I've been under."

"You have no right to tell me to shut up!" Bev said, exploding. "You have been a menace to me since you were born—a menace to everyone. Including Mama, who you never seem to think about. Even if you didn't give a damn about crushing me when you ran off with Tom, you might have at least spared a thought for her. There Mama was, dealing with one sick daughter, and the other one disappeared. For all we knew, you were dead!"

"I wish I was."

"No, you don't," Bev said in disgust. "You live to create drama. You're never happier than when you've screwed up and you're watching the rest of us try to figure out how to straighten everything out again. But there's no straightening this out. If you marry Tom today, mark my words, your life will be cursed!"

Diana sputtered out a cackle of surprise. "Cursed? Are you God now? Are you casting some horrible spell on me?"

"I wish I could. I wish I could banish you from my sight, from Mama's, from everybody's. All you do, all you've ever done, is bring people misery. You failed at life and resented me because I didn't, and so all you could think to do was run off with the only person I've ever cared about."

"Oh, right. I'm always to blame for everything." Diana fitfully opened a lipstick, slapped the cap back on, then tossed it back into her cosmetic bag. "I'm sick of it." She twisted back to Bev. "Okay—you want to know the truth about what happened?"

"I can't wait to hear this," Bev drawled.

"The truth is, it was all your fault."

Bev rarely expected her sister to make sense, but even coming from Diana, this took monumental gall. "*My* fault? All I did was come down with the mumps."

"Before that," Diana said. "You're always so . . . so you. Solid Bev. Practical Bev. Hard-working Bev. Who does Mama always turn to? Bev. It's like having Walter Cronkite for a sister."

"Are you out of your mind? You're talking like a child."

"See? You're so condescending. Always. So, okay, maybe I expected to have a little fun with Tom at your expense. I thought he'd be like you, with pants. I expected to laugh at him. But then he showed up, and we went out, and I actually had fun. Real fun. He was cute and funny and smart. Only he didn't treat me like an idiot, like you do. And I could tell he was attracted to me, and that was such a turn-on, because he wasn't like most of the meatballs I've gone out with. You can see how I fell for him, can't you?"

Bev's anger rose. "Of course. Especially when it provided you with an opportunity to ruin my life."

"That's not how it was. When Tom and I are together—"

"I don't want to hear any more!" If Diana had gone on for another second, Bev would have had to cover her ears. "You are an affliction. Tom might not know it yet, but you're going to make him miserable. I thought he was supposed to be at Fort Sill right now anyway."

Diana slumped. "He washed out of officer training."

"Washed out?"

"We had a spat. I ran away and he . . . well, he kind of went AWOL. It didn't go down so good with the top brass."

"Oh God," Bev said.

"It's okay now. He's not going to be court-martialed. Only, his parents threw a fit. I think they had to pull strings to keep him from getting tossed into the brig, or whatever they call it. And so he insisted we come back here and get married. I said I'd be happy to go to a justice of the peace. Or Vegas—that would have been fun. But Tom seemed to feel that since we'd made so much trouble, we could at least please his parents by doing the traditional thing and getting married at home. But of course, the first thing they tried to do was talk him out of it. I guess he convinced them. It seemed like something he was just doing out of principle by the end, though. I don't believe he's thinking of me at all."

Bev barely listened to the last part, about the wedding. She was too shocked. Tom hadn't finished his training—had gone AWOL. He could have been tossed in jail, or court-martialed. It was lucky that he hadn't been. But now he was probably going to be assigned to a unit and shipped out soon.

"The weird thing is," Diana continued, "I was actually beginning to believe in fairy tales and happy ever after and all that crap. And then we got here, and his parents were so cold and snooty, and they called Mama, and stuffed me in this dress, and here I am. The lamb to the slaughter."

"Oh, who cares?" Bev cried. "Would you for once look at someone besides yourself? What's going to happen to Tom?"

"I don't know." Diana looked as if she might cry. "There's all this pressure now, and we only have another day before he has to go back. I feel sick. I don't know about anything anymore."

"Are you saying you don't want to get married?"

"I don't . . ." Diana shook her head. ". . . know."

Or maybe she meant *no*. Bev couldn't tell. Either answer should have filled her with glee. But this was so messed up and confusing. She didn't want Tom and Diana to get married, but a part of her didn't want Tom to be jilted, either. Especially after Diana had already disrupted his life.

"Maybe I should go someplace and hide away," Diana said. "California or somewhere like that."

"Diana, that's insanity." Maybe Diana was rubbing off on her, though. She'd marched in bursting with righteous anger. Now it looked as if the marriage she'd been hell-bent on scuppering might not even take place. Even that thought gave her no satisfaction.

"Well, what else am I going to do?" Diana gazed at her with desperation. She looked terrible. Her mascara was smudged even more now, its dark rings shadowing her eyes.

"Why ask me?" Bev said. "You never take my advice."

"I would now."

Fuming again, Bev stood. "You sit there saying you're so miserable, but do you have any idea what you've done? You stole my life, my happiness. Even when you knew it would ruin me, ruin my child's life. You didn't care! You did it anyway, when you weren't even sure whether Tom was someone you really loved. You still don't know! And now you've got the gall to say you want my advice. I'd like to wring your neck."

Diana gaped at her through the whole outburst. "Wait—back up. *Child?*"

407

Bev tossed her head. "Don't act dumb. You knew. You heard Dr. Gary."

"What did Dr. Gary say? When?"

"When I told him I was pregnant."

"You're *pregnant?*"

"You were hanging out right outside the door."

"No, I wasn't." Diana shook her head frantically. "I didn't know . . ."

"You acted like you knew." A little of Bev's certainty slipped away. "When Mama came back from work that afternoon—you made innuendo."

Diana covered her mouth and turned away, clearly letting Bev's words sink in. Then, as if gravity was suddenly too much for her, she slipped off the seat and sank to the floor.

"Oh God. Oh God."

Diana's reactions were always over the top, so it was hard to tell what was real and what was theatrics. She looked distressed, but Bev had seen her react the same way when NBC canceled *The Monkees*.

"You don't have to overdo the Sarah Bernhardt routine," Bev told her. "There's no baby now."

"You had an abortion?"

Bev gritted her teeth. "A miscarriage."

Her sister's face was a mask of shock.

"Is it such a surprise?" Bev asked her. "I was under stress. My own sister ran off with my baby's father. As far as I'm concerned, you killed that child."

Diana recoiled.

Actually, the doctor had said there was a correlation between the mumps and an elevated risk of miscarriage. But Bev hadn't wanted to believe that anything but her sister's treachery had caused her misfortune.

"Oh God. I *am* cursed!" Diana lurched to her feet and started tossing clothes into her overnight case without even bothering to fold them. She slammed the case closed. "I had no idea, Bev. None. I never . . ." Then she shoved her feet into sandals and slammed her bag shut. Before reaching the door, she swung back. "This is all your fault! Why didn't you tell me?"

And then she ran out.

"Diana!" Bev tore after her.

Her sister didn't stop. Diana took the stairs so fast, Bev worried she was going to trip over the flowing skirt of her wedding muumuu.

Diana reached the first floor and streaked across the marble foyer. Tom glimpsed her from the library and ran out as Diana was throwing open the front door. "Diana! What's the matter? Where are you going?"

Bev arrived at the bottom step.

"Where is she going?" he asked her.

"I think she's having second thoughts," Bev told him.

His face screwed up, perplexed, and then he dashed after her.

The Jacksons and Gladys appeared in the hallway—just in time to see Tom's back as he slammed out the door after Diana, calling her name.

It was the last time Bev saw him.

"What's happened?" Dot asked, running to peek out the front window. "Why is Diana stealing Tom's car?"

"She's got the jitters," Bev explained.

"Jitters!" Mrs. Jackson scoffed. "What does *she* have to be jittery about?"

"Your son, for starters," Gladys said.

They all gaped at Gladys, none more shocked than Bev.

"Our son?" Dorothy Jackson drew up to her full height. "Our son has sacrificed the position of an officer to chase after your girl."

"Now he's chasing after her in Daddy's Cadillac," Dot informed them.

"Your son was flaking out before he ever met Diana," Gladys said, and Bev wasn't sure which was more surprising—to hear her mother speak sharply to their hosts, or that she used the phrase *flaking out*. "He behaved abominably to Bev, making all sorts of promises and then up and deserting her when she was in a delicate condition."

The three Jacksons pivoted toward Bev. Her heartbeat raced, and she had to fight the urge to flee like Diana had. She shook her head. "She means I had the mumps."

Dorothy Jackson looked relieved to hear it, until Gladys piped up, "And it might be those mumps that got your son out of a paternity suit."

"Mama!"

Turning away from the window, Tom's sister squeaked in surprise. Bev had never seen anything rounder or brighter than Dot Jackson's eyes at that moment. "You mean you were pregnant? By *Tom?*"

"Dot, go upstairs," Dorothy ordered.

Dot wasn't budging. "Is there going to be a lawsuit?"

"No, there definitely is not," Dorothy Jackson said.

Gladys lifted her chin. "Oh no—you dodged that bullet."

Dorothy rounded on Gladys. In their summer church outfits and helmets of hair sprayed into place with Aqua Net, they looked like two pastel prizefighters facing off. "I don't believe we've dodged a bullet." Dorothy Jackson's voice was ice. "We've exchanged one bad alliance for an even more unfortunate one."

"Unfortunate!" Gladys exclaimed.

"Your daughter—Diana—snatched our son out from under Bev's nose, then ran off with him like a hoyden, luring him away from his training and ruining his chances at a career. And then, ever since our son brought her here to us, she's been nothing but unpleasant. Why, even though we were against his marrying a waitress, we went out and bought her a nice dress and some things for her trousseau. And all because she told Tom that she was"—Dorothy shot a sidewise glance at Dot—"you know."

Bev was struck dumb. Diana, pregnant? Why hadn't she said?

Dot crossed her arms. "Wait—*Diana's* knocked up, too?"

"Dot, hush. That's vulgar."

The girl practically crowed. "No kidding! Tom seems to be batting a thousand for once."

"Dot—enough!" Dorothy said. "We don't even know if this is true."

Bev looked over at her mother, who was pale as the marble under her feet. "Why would you doubt it?" Gladys asked.

"Now, now," Thomas Sr. said. "We needn't discuss this right here, right now. The important thing should be—"

"Why *should* we believe her?" Dorothy said, interrupting him. "She just dropped from the sky, and then led poor Tom on a chase that very nearly cost him his honor. That speaks very poorly for her. And then the tales of pregnancy—of *two* pregnancies—and now she's run off. Well, forgive me if I'm skeptical of her ever fitting in with our family. Jacksons simply don't behave this way."

"Diana is not part of this family," Gladys

declared, "and if she takes my advice, she never will be. I came here hoping to see my daughter married, but after half an hour in this house, I'm glad she's run away. Better she be on her own than beholden to your grudging charity for the rest of her life."

"There was nothing grudging about it. We even offered to let her stay here in the house with us while Tom is overseas."

"Two days in this mausoleum would kill Diana," Gladys said.

"Well!" Dorothy said. "I can see the apple didn't fall far from the tree."

"The *rotten* apple," Dot chimed in, using her tattling voice. "Diana called us jackasses, Mother. I heard her say it through the door."

The Jacksons stiffened in outrage, but Gladys let out a full-throated cackle. "Come on, Bev. We're leaving."

Bev was stunned. "But, Mama . . . if it's true about Diana . . ."

Mr. Jackson stepped forward. "That's right. Let's not be rash—"

"I'll handle this, Thomas," Dorothy snapped at him. "Lord knows, I'm not a woman who believes in burning bridges, but I have to speak my mind. Our son must be crazy to have gotten involved with any of you people, much less two of you."

"I'll agree that your son's crazy," Gladys said, "and I can see where he gets it."

• • •

In the car afterward, Bev sank down into the seat. She'd taken the driver's side, since her mother didn't appear in any shape to be behind the wheel. She wasn't sure she was any better off. Her whole body felt boneless and trembly.

Gladys let out a long, slow breath. "That didn't go as I expected. What is the matter with you, getting us involved with people like that?"

"Tom's different." Weak and foolish, he might be. But he wasn't cold-blooded.

"So you say. But while you were upstairs, he let that mother of his go on and on. And then that daughter—she's a real chip off the old ice cube, that one." Her mother turned and pinned her with her gaze. "Where did Diana say she was going?"

"I don't know . . . I think maybe she mentioned California?"

"What!"

"She was upset. We had a little argument."

"I never should have let you go up there. *I* should have seen to Diana and left you in the library. If I'd known of her condition . . ."

"I'm sure she'll be back," Bev said. "Tom went after her."

"What did you say to her?"

"Just . . ." Bev remembered some terrible things. Calling her a menace. Saying she would be cursed, and that she never wanted to see her again. . . . But what had she said that Diana didn't deserve?

As far as I'm concerned, you killed that child.

She hunched over the wheel, head aching. "I'm sure she'll come back," she repeated. "Or Tom will bring her back. She'll never be able to manage on her own. Especially not with a baby."

"That's what I'm afraid of," Gladys said.

"Aunt Bev?"

Bev looked over at Alabama. She'd been so lost in memory she wasn't even sure how far they'd driven.

Alabama looked as if she'd been thinking, too. The earphones from the Walkman she'd retrieved from Gladys were dangling around her neck. "What if the Jacksons don't like me?" she asked.

She sounded so desperate to be accepted, to be loved, Bev felt her heart might shatter into pieces. Alabama was dressed in her new clothes and wasn't at all scruffy looking for once, if you didn't count the laddered stockings from where she'd scratched at her leg nervously, or the striped hair, or her earrings, which at first glance seemed to match her new tomato-red jacket but upon closer inspection revealed themselves to be miniature chattering teeth.

"Of course they'll like you. Why shouldn't they?"

Alabama mulled the question over and seemed calmer. She sank back against the seat rest.

They won't like her, Bev thought.

She felt that certainty in her bones. That cold old lady and her daughter would chew up Alabama's hopes and spit them out like an olive pit.

And then what would happen?

CHAPTER 24

Her aunt was lying through her teeth about the chances of the Jacksons liking her. Alabama could tell. Why else would she keep repeating the advice to "hold your head high and remember you're as good as anyone else" as they finally came to the outskirts of Houston?

Driving through her new grandmother's neighborhood, she began to understand. The houses were enormous—hulking, swank edifices like nothing she'd ever seen, except on television. All had perfectly clipped lawns, some of them green as golf courses even in November. They reminded her of the big house in the opening credits of *Dynasty*, except there were scores of them all packed into one neighborhood. She was stepping into a new world.

It didn't occur to her until later, much later, that Bev never consulted a map to navigate her way through the neighborhood.

"Granny Jackson lives in one of these?" she couldn't help asking. "All by herself?"

"She probably has help," Bev said.

Of course. Maids and gardeners, a cook, and maybe even a chauffeur. Or a butler. Did people still have butlers, or was that only in the movies?

During all these weeks, she hadn't imagined her grandmother as a physical person. So far, Dorothy

Mabry Jackson had existed as slanted writing on a page, and spiky opinions, and a dream of something different, something better. But now, in this setting, Alabama feared she was out of her league. A person in a house like one of these would be used to pulling strings and getting her way, like Phoebe Wallingford from *All My Children*. That character never liked anybody.

She chewed down an entire thumbnail in the last three blocks before Bev stopped in the driveway of a two-story brick house. It seemed older and not quite as huge as some of the ones around it. Still, its elegance intimidated her. A long flat lawn led up to a raised porch with several columns shooting up to an overhanging balcony. The house and grounds were shaded by extravagantly large trees, including a magnolia that looked as if it was going to devour the side porch.

"Don't worry. She really is just a person," Bev said. "Also, don't forget we have a car. Give me the signal, and we can always make a quick getaway."

They got out and approached the imposing front door, which was painted a thick glossy black. In the center of it, a brass lion head knocker peered at them from eye level. Bev lifted the lion and let it drop, and the resulting sound was so loud that Alabama imagined neighbors sending their maids to peer out the window and report back.

She didn't know what to expect next—a tuxedoed butler, maybe. Not the person who opened the door. The woman, around Bev's age, was tall and made no attempt to disguise it. She even wore chunky high heels with her pantsuit. Her hair was dark, almost black, and cut short, although she wore enough gold and sparkly jewelry to counteract the mannish hairdo. Her dark eyes, shadowed with shades of brown, zeroed in on Alabama, inspecting her, before they spared Bev a glance.

"Hello, Bev," the woman drawled. "You haven't changed a bit. Glad you could make it."

Bev's tight, superficial smile mirrored the other woman's. "I couldn't let Alabama make the trip alone. She's only fourteen, you know."

The woman's gaze snapped back to Alabama. "She looks older than that."

"I'm almost fifteen," Alabama said.

"Dot, let me introduce my niece, Alabama." Bev laughed dryly. "Well, *our* niece, we could say."

Dot's glassy smile turned on her again. "We could, but why don't we wait?"

"Alabama, this is Dot Jackson," Bev said. "Tom's sister."

The sensible judge. *My aunt.* She didn't look like any woman Alabama had ever expected to be related to, and those sharp dark eyes told her that Dot wasn't relishing the idea of kinship. "Hi," was the most that Alabama could choke out.

Unimpressed, the woman motioned them inside. "Mother is waiting for us in the library."

She ushered them into a hallway that made Alabama's mouth gape. The black-and-white marble floor and high ceilings were polished to a high gloss, and a huge chandelier hung from the ceiling, near a wide staircase that twisted up to a second floor. It felt as if she was in a museum, or on *The Beverly Hillbillies* set. She made mental notes so she could tell Stuart all about it.

Dot Jackson's heels clacked behind her. Alabama felt as if she was being herded.

"You remember the way, don't you, Bev?" Dot asked.

"How could I forget," Bev said.

The frosty exchanges between those two intensified Alabama's nervousness. It sounded like they hated each other. And obviously Bev had been here before. In this house. That thought confused her. Why hadn't she said so?

As they approached a large carved door, Dot accelerated so she could reach it first and announce them. "Mother, they're here."

At the threshold, Alabama felt Bev's hand on her arm for an instant. The light squeeze reminded her of Bev's words. *Stand up straight. . . . You're as good as anyone else. . . . The car's outside and we can always flee.*

The room seemed designed to make people feel small. Floor-to-ceiling bookcases in dark wood lined the walls and were packed with expensive-looking volumes in cloth and leather bindings with gold lettering. Overhead, two heavy iron fixtures hung down, their amber shades casting a twilight glow even though it wasn't even noon yet. A real statue of a mostly undressed woman holding grapes stood against one wall, but littler treasures—knickknacks and clocks and framed photographs—resided on every table or shelf. Alabama wondered if she could go through an entire day without touching anything.

At the opposite end of the room from the statue, next to a set of double doors whose curtains had been drawn back to give a view of the outdoor patio, sat an old lady. She wore a burgundy jacket in raw silk over a matching dress, and her hair was impressive and upswept, like Margaret Thatcher's. She was obviously a tall woman, like her daughter, although it was a little hard to tell because she was leaning forward with interest, and the chair she sat in was a wheelchair.

As Alabama drew closer, the woman's head jutted forward, and she regarded her with bright, birdlike eyes.

"This is the girl, Mother," Dot said.

Bev bristled. "Her name is Alabama."

The older woman's gaze flicked over to Bev. "You're looking well, Bev. You certainly haven't changed much."

"Thank you. Neither have you."

"Nonsense," the woman snapped. "I've got arthritis and a bad hip. Can't even golf anymore.

I'm fifteen years older, and I wasn't a spring chicken when you knew me. But you always seemed older than you were, so naturally you seem the same."

Bev didn't answer, but a response didn't seem necessary, since the older woman had gone back to inspecting Alabama. Alabama tried hard not to flinch under that keen, unwavering gaze. Dot's attitude must have been wearing off on her, because she felt like a fraud. After all, only her mother's say-so connected her to these people . . . and had her mother been the most reliable source? Obviously not. Recently, she'd even begun to doubt that her mother was actually her mother, so how could she possibly trust her mother's word on who her dad had been?

"Alabama Putterman!"

She gulped. The way Dorothy Mabry Jackson intoned her name was like a judge about to pronounce sentence on the condemned. *She thinks I'm a fraud, too.*

"Look at her, Dot," Dorothy said.

"I did." With those two short words, Dot conveyed how unmoved she was by what she'd seen.

"Come closer," Dorothy Jackson commanded.

Alabama took two tentative steps.

In the wheelchair, her gaze razor sharp on Alabama, the woman began to tremble. It was a little bobbing of her head at first, but then grew so pronounced that Alabama worried she was having some kind of seizure. The woman's shaking hands grabbed the arms of her chair and she pushed herself up onto legs that wobbled like a newborn colt's.

Dot bolted forward. "Mother, wait!"

But Dorothy took an unsteady step toward Alabama, almost stumbling into her.

Alabama reflexively reached out to grab the woman's arms, thin as twigs. They ended up clutching each other by the forearms. This woman, she realized, wasn't really that much taller than herself—she just projected big.

She wasn't sure she should go on holding the arms, which felt as if a little too much pressure could snap them, but when she tried to let go, Dorothy Jackson clung that much tighter, her manicured nails digging into Alabama's forearms like needles. The woman's glassy eyes frightened but also mesmerized her. Ferociously they drank in all her features, and Alabama fought the urge to break eye contact.

It seemed as if they stood locked together for an eternity. Then, slowly, she realized that what she'd perceived at first as fierce was really frantic, raw emotion. Tears stood in Dorothy Jackson's eyes.

"You're my Tom all over again." Her voice cracked, and as she lifted one hand to Alabama's face, the tears spilled over. "You've got his eyes, exactly. I didn't see it at first, but when you stepped into the light of the window, it was as if Tom was standing in front of me, after all these years. As if he never went away . . . never died so far away."

Alabama swallowed. "Nobody told me that."

"Oh yes—look at a picture." Dorothy turned, took a painful step, and then pointed to a shelf nearby. "Dot, bring me that picture of Tom."

Her daughter reached over and then handed the silver-framed picture to her. Dorothy showed it to Alabama.

"You see?"

The black-and-white photo was of her father, who was sitting on a bench outside with a woman who was only visible in profile—Bev, she noticed when she looked closer. In the background she could make out the side of a house that appeared to be this one. It reminded her of the pictures she'd seen in Bev's attic. Maybe it was from the same batch.

"Who took this?" Alabama asked.

"I did," Dot said.

No one seemed to think it was necessary to explain the reason why Bev was in a picture that Dot had taken of Tom. Her grandmother reached for another picture. "And here's one of Tom when he was a teenager, closer to your age now."

It was a school photo. Although she was distracted by his hair, which was parted severely on one side with a wavy curtain of bangs across his forehead in a style she thought of as early Greg Brady, Alabama could see that the shape and color of their eyes were similar. She hadn't noticed that when she'd looked at pictures of Tom Jackson before. Maybe it was a thing only a mother would notice.

"I've always thought Alabama favored him," Bev said.

Alabama flinched. Even now, she couldn't forget Stuart's theory, or her mother's—Diana's—letter.

From that moment on, Dorothy Mabry Jackson appeared to embrace her wholeheartedly as a member of the family. Her grandmother instructed her to walk beside her chair—Dot was relegated to pushing—and gave her the grand tour of the house, or at least the first floor of it. The old woman would direct Dot to stop at points of interest—Thomas Sr.'s portrait, for instance, or the cabinet that she'd found in England during her wedding trip, which had cost more to ship, even back in those days, than the antique dealer had charged.

Strolling dutifully alongside the chair, Alabama felt as if she were in a dream. Her new clothes, which Bev had let her pick out and buy even though they weren't even on sale, made her stand straighter, like a different person. A Jackson? And yet, she couldn't help wondering . . . what if her eyes had been a different color? Would her

425

grandmother have rejected her, banished her from her sight?

Thanksgiving dinner marked the first time she'd eaten a meal served by a maid, although Alicia didn't *look* like a maid. She wasn't wearing a uniform or anything. It felt weird. They sat around the dining table, in a room decorated with gold-flocked wallpaper and a huge painting of a windmill, waiting for Alicia to come in and put dishes down for them to hand around, including a turkey big enough to feed fourteen people, not four. Talk was strained, and Alabama couldn't help thinking that they could have started eating a lot quicker if they'd given Alicia a hand.

After she was done, Alicia smiled and withdrew to the kitchen.

"Doesn't Alicia get to have Thanksgiving, too?" Alabama asked, watching the connecting door to the kitchen swing to a standstill.

Dorothy chuckled. "Of course. She's going to eat with her family tonight."

"I told her she could bake something for her family while she's waiting to clean up today." Clearly, Dot thought she'd made a queenly concession. "And she's always welcome to leftovers."

It seemed weird to be pigging out on turkey while somebody else sat in the next room waiting for them to finish.

"It all tastes wonderful, doesn't it, Alabama?"

Bev asked her—pointedly—drawing Alabama's gaze away from the kitchen door.

Even though she hadn't taken a bite yet, Alabama murmured her agreement and focused on her food. Unbidden, a memory of last Thanksgiving came to her. It was the last happy holiday she and her mom had together, and it had been perfect. Almost perfect. Before, she and her mom had usually ordered Chinese takeout or pizza on Thanksgiving, but last year, because of Charlie, her mother wanted to do a turkey and all the trimmings. The holiday began with staying up late so Diana could put the bird in the oven in the middle of the night. That's what Gladdie had always done, she said.

"At two in the morning?" Alabama asked.

"Or thereabouts."

"Couldn't we check the time in a cookbook?" Alabama was pretty sure there was a battered, stained *Joy of Cooking* somewhere. For years it had been used to prop up a couch with a broken foot. Then they'd moved, and abandoned the couch. She began opening and closing cabinets. Where was it?

"Silly, these things are tradition," her mother said, cutting off her search. "You don't have to look them up."

You do if your regular tradition is Domino's. But Alabama didn't want to spoil her mom's mood with an argument, so their bird, which for budgetary reasons was actually the size of a plumper-than-average chicken, was stuffed with sausage and bread crumbs and stuck into a hot oven at two in the morning.

When they woke up, the house smelled wonderful.

"We should just have Thanksgiving breakfast," Alabama said.

Her mother had laughed, showing rare Julia Child–like kitchen confidence. "You'd die if you ate that turkey now. You've got to cook it thoroughly, or it's deadly. You could end up with tularemia, or botulism, or something."

So the bird roasted another four hours. By the time they sat down at the table, it was turkey jerky. Charlie said chewing it made his jaw hurt, but he'd had two helpings. Alabama never saw her mother so happy again.

Her grandmother's turkey—Alicia's turkey—was perfect, of course. But as Alabama thought about her mother, everything on her plate might as well have been made of cardboard. The whole horrible year passed before her eyes, killing her appetite.

She looked around at the gleaming table and linen napkins and silver service with more forks and spoons than she knew what to do with, and then remembered all the places she and her mom had lived. What a contrast. *What am I doing here?*

"My heavens, Alabama," her grandmother drawled. "You look lost in a fog."

"I was thinking about Mom."

That simple statement plunged the table into an uncomfortable silence. Dorothy Jackson finally said, "I don't think we need to bring up unpleasant topics at the dinner table right now, do you?"

Alabama's face burned, and across the table her aunt's eyes widened. Alabama guessed Bev was trying to warn her to be quiet, but she felt she would explode if she didn't say something. "She wasn't a topic. She was my mother."

"And I'm very sorry about her," her grandmother said evenly. "But this is a moment for giving thanks, not mourning."

"I can't help thinking about her."

"No more than I can help thinking of my Thomas and, even after all these years, poor Tom," Dorothy said. "But you have to discipline your mind not to speak every time you feel sad. Talking about it does no one any good."

Dorothy Mabry Jackson's tone was so matter-of-fact, she made forgetting sound simple, as if memory came with an off/on switch. And she had lost her son, and then her husband, which couldn't have been easy. Looking at her grandmother, who seemed so sensible and composed, and knowing that there was even more sadness sloshing around in that head than in her own, made Alabama feel almost ashamed for sounding so whiny. Discipline. Mind over misfortune. That's all it took.

So it was all the more surprising when Bev, her face crimson, slammed her utensils down on her plate. The rest of them hopped in their seats.

"That's the most heartless thing I've ever heard." Bev's voice crackled with tension.

"Not heartless," Dorothy Jackson said. "Practical."

"Heartless," Bev repeated.

Oh God. Alabama could recognize the warning signs too well now. Her aunt was revving up to another Lewanne's Dinner Bell-parking-lot-style scene.

"Diana's only been gone six months," Bev continued. *"Six months.* Can you imagine how that feels for Alabama?"

"Of course I can," Dorothy said. "My mother is no longer alive. I went through the same thing."

"Not at fourteen."

"That's why Mother invited the girl here," Dot said. "We couldn't help pitying her."

Pity! Alabama's head whipped toward Dot.

"The girl is sitting right across the table from you," Bev pointed out, "and believe me, she knew how much you wanted her here when you took weeks to answer her letter. And then wrote about consulting lawyers!"

"You can hardly blame us for that," Dot said. "Mother didn't want to be imprudent. And Alabama *was* invited. She has no cause to complain."

430

"Oh no," Bev said. "Certainly not. Who could complain after being snubbed for nearly fifteen years? And after her mother was *never* invited."

"Diana wanted nothing to do with us," Dot said. "She ran away and never came back."

Bev stood so abruptly she bumped the table. Water glasses trembled on their graceful stems. "Diana left because of me. We had a fight—it had nothing to do with you. But you wouldn't know that"—she pierced both Jackson ladies with her eyes—"because you were so happy to see the back of her. You were probably too busy counting your blessings to care what she was going through."

"She tore Tom away from us—that was enough."

"*War* tore Tom away from you. The war you were so eager for him to participate in," Bev said. "And how do you think Tom would feel about the way you treated Diana? And his daughter?"

"We had no obligation to your sister," Dot said. "And we had no way of knowing if Alabama was really—"

A muffled shriek tore from Bev's throat before Dot could finish. "Don't you dare say that." She jutted a finger at Dorothy. "Your mother knew just by looking at her. *One look.* What would have happened if she'd bothered to look fourteen years ago, or even ten? If there had been someone to reach out to Diana, to help her, to save her—"

431

Bev's voice broke, and she dissolved into tears. A split second later, she fled the room at a sprint.

The front door slammed.

Alabama sat frozen. Staggered. What the heck had just happened?

"Like history repeating itself," Dot grumbled under her breath. "All Puttermans are crazy."

Silence stretched on for another uncomfortable minute, and then Dorothy reached forward, picked up a small silver bell, and rang it.

What next? Would her grandmother cancel Thanksgiving now and send her home? Have her escorted out?

The maid appeared at the door.

"More bread, please, Alicia," Dorothy said, unruffled. "And you can take away the fourth plate. Perhaps Bev will join us again for dessert."

Or maybe Bev had gotten in the car and was already heading back to New Sparta. Alabama still felt stunned. What was she supposed to do? Should she walk out, too? Part of her wanted to, but she could see the Jackson point of view, as well. A little. Dot's saying that she'd been invited out of pity had made her furious at first . . . until she realized that she had *wanted* them to feel that way. Her letters had shamelessly played the pity card. She wanted to stand by her mother—and, she guessed, her aunt—but she didn't doubt that her mother had made a bad impression on the Jacksons.

"Have some more mashed potatoes," Dorothy urged her.

Alabama reached for the gold-rimmed bowl, feeling guilty for not showing solidarity with Bev. But it would seem a little stupid to get up and stomp out now, after she'd hesitated. War raged in her conscience as she dutifully scooped potatoes onto her plate. Bev was so crazy, and irritating . . . and she'd kept important things secret, things that still didn't make sense. . . .

She'd admitted that *she* was the reason Diana had run out all those years ago. Over some argument. About what? So they'd all been here together, and fought. But today Bev had stuck up for Diana. Why?

She put the serving spoon down. She didn't want another helping of potatoes, or to leave in a righteous huff. She wanted to know the truth. And she might as well start now.

She turned to Dot. "How did you end up taking so many pictures of Aunt Bev with my father?"

CHAPTER 25

"I'm so sorry."

Bev's words were the first either of them had spoken since leaving the Jackson house fifteen minutes before. After a long walk to blow off steam, Bev had slunk back inside in time for the after-dinner coffee, uttering a non-heartfelt apology for disrupting the meal. She hoped her niece would realize that her apology now was sincere. She'd never meant to cause a scene, or abandon her.

"I had to get out of there for a while," she confessed to Alabama. "I was suffocating." Her voice lowered to a growl. "All that talk from Dot about being prudent made my blood boil."

"Dot did a lot of talking after you left," Alabama said.

"I'll bet."

"All about you and her brother. My dad."

Bev should have been used to Alabama's simmering glare from that side of the car by now. Their relationship had begun with a long, silent ride. But this felt different.

"I've been confused for so long," Alabama said. "Mom would never tell me about why you two never spoke to each other. And she never talked about my dad much, either. Basically, nobody told me *anything*. I guessed Mom avoided Texas, and you, all those years because you were so mean to her. I had to fill in a lot of blanks, and I made you the villain, because Mom didn't want to be near you. And then when I moved to New Sparta, I kept finding weird stuff, like the dress and the pictures."

"What pictures?" Bev asked.

"Your photograph album in the attic. I assumed it had to be Mom's, because there were pictures of Dad in it. But it's yours, isn't it? And the dress was really yours, too. When you said that, I thought you were ranting, but you probably made it because you thought you were going to marry Tom Jackson. That's what Dot said."

Bev kept her gaze trained on the road. She felt exposed, but there was no way to shield herself from the bare truth now. "He never asked me," she told Alabama. "We went together for years—almost all through college—but he never proposed."

"But he was going to, wasn't he? Dot said they all expected him to ask you—that he'd even hinted he might when he drove up to Dallas after basic training. They said they were afraid you two would elope, but the next thing they knew, Tom had disappeared with Mom instead, and then even went AWOL. What happened?"

Bev frowned. She'd known that going to the Jackson house would be awful, but she hadn't expected Dot to be such a Chatty Cathy. No telling what she'd told Alabama. "I had the mumps."

Alabama blinked at her. "The mumps? What does that have to do with anything?"

"The day of Tom's visit, I came down with the mumps." She explained the bare time line to the best of her ability, from the mumps until two months later, when Gladys stormed out of the Jackson house in a fury, after Diana had fled. She only left out one detail.

"So that's what Dot meant about history repeating itself," Alabama said. "But where did Mom and Tom go?"

"Diana ran off to California, where she had you. Tom's parents had pulled strings to keep him from getting disciplined for disappearing and washing out of Officer Candidate School, and he was sent to Fort Hood almost immediately. I believe he traced Diana, but they never had any more time together. He was shipped out a few weeks later, and of course he died before you were born. The Jacksons were very bitter and held Diana responsible for . . . well, for everything."

Alabama stared at the road. "So why didn't they get married?"

Bev felt stricken, remembering that horrible confrontation in the guest bedroom, and all the awful things she'd said.

"A little while ago, you said you always thought of me as the villain. Well, you weren't wrong.

Diana felt responsible for . . . well, for what happened between Tom and me . . . and that was my fault. I said some things to her, things I regret now. Bitterly."

Alabama frowned. "In the letter, *she* came off as feeling guilty. And she also seemed to think that I—"

Her words cut off.

Bev tensed. "What letter?"

Alabama glared at her. "The one you kept from me. In your file cabinet."

"You broke into my file cabinet?"

"I had a good reason. Stuart had this weird theory that you were actually my mother—"

"What?"

"—and I told him he was crazy, but he said I should find my birth certificate, so I went looking for it, but instead of my birth certificate, I found the letter Mom sent you."

"Oh God." The blood drained from her face. She couldn't imagine Alabama stumbling across that letter, reading those words, and mulling them over all alone. "When?"

"Weeks and weeks ago." Alabama shrugged. "Halloween."

And she'd been keeping that knowledge a secret all this time. Regret overwhelmed her. *She's right. I should have showed her the letter, talked to her about it.* Alabama should have been told all this, long ago.

"Why did you keep it from me?" Alabama asked.

"It was so upsetting—"

"You had no right! You let me go on thinking that it was an accident, when really she wanted to die. She didn't want to take care of me anymore."

"That's not true. If I gleaned one thing from that letter, it was that she loved you more than anything. She would have done anything for you, but she . . . well, I don't know what happened."

"She killed herself."

Alabama's tone was so certain, so even, it chilled Bev to the bone. A fourteen-year-old shouldn't have to had to deal with so much. She pulled the car over to the shoulder and braked. "Listen to me."

Alabama groaned. "Not again. Can't we just keep going?"

"No. I want to make sure you understand. Diana died in an accident," Bev said. "Because she'd been drinking. And was depressed, obviously. But her death was ruled an accident."

"Only because the police never saw that letter." Alabama shook her head. "I thought it was an accident when she didn't leave me a note. But that letter was a suicide note. And she wrote it to you."

"She'd probably been drinking when she wrote that letter," Bev said. "A person who's drunk too much isn't really in her right mind."

Alabama seemed to be considering whether this

438

was true or not. "She wasn't in her right mind for a lot of her life. When I was little, she went to that place, remember?"

"It was a drug rehab center. Mama paid for it and took care of you until Diana quit using hard drugs. Neighbors had called Child Protective Services on Diana, and she was so worried about losing you that she would have done anything. Anything."

"I thought she was at a country club," Alabama said. "Because the place had a Pong game and a pool."

They remained silent for a moment, each lost in her own thoughts.

"I'm sorry you saw the letter," Bev said. "I'm sorry I didn't show it to you sooner. That was wrong of me. But I didn't want you getting upset again."

"I got upset anyway," Alabama said. "And it was so confusing, because she made it sound as if I *was* your kid. I started to wonder if Stuart was right after all."

"He most certainly was not right."

"Then why did Mom say she was giving me back to you? Why would she have used those words?"

Bev's mind raced. That was the detail she had left out of the story—the pregnancy. She'd never told a soul about that, except for Dr. Gary, her mother, and Diana. The Jacksons also knew, but it seemed they'd been tactful for once and not told Alabama.

"I wondered if maybe something weird had happened, like you had me and gave me to my mom," Alabama said. "But why would you have done that? You were Miss Homemaking and Mom was . . . well, kind of screwed up. And she wasn't even married, so it wouldn't have been like *The Old Maid*."

"The what?"

"That Bette Davis movie. That's when Stuart came up with his theory. Because you got so upset about the wedding dress, and then you thought that movie was so sad—"

"It *was* sad."

"—but I figured out that you were really upset about Derek that night. Then, later, when I saw the letter, I wondered again if maybe Stuart was right. Why would Mom have said she was giving me *back* to you? What did that mean?"

"I . . . I don't know."

"Yes, you do. But you think I shouldn't be able to hear it, or something. What did she mean?"

Bev took a deep breath. "I was pregnant when Diana and Tom ran off together."

Alabama went rigid. "You had a baby?"

Bev shook her head. "I lost it early on."

Alabama swallowed. "You mean it was Dad's. It would have been, like, my half brother or sister."

Or simultaneously, her cousin . . . but Bev didn't want to disturb her any more than she probably already was.

"That's awful," Alabama said.

"It was awful, but Mama was the only one who knew until I blurted out the truth to Diana when we were all at the Jacksons'. Diana got upset. I said some hateful things to her, things that were never forgotten. Diana always felt bad about how it all happened. I think—I know—she held herself responsible, because I lost the baby after Tom and Diana had run off together. I was angry with her for a long time."

"So you *were* in love with my dad," Alabama said.

"Yes."

Alabama pondered this for a moment. "You must have hated her."

"I felt like she'd stolen my life. But then Tom died, and Diana was gone, and she had you. We didn't speak." Tears welled up, and she had to gulp back a keening tension in her throat. "I suppose I did hate her sometimes. I've been a small person, in a lot of ways. I can't tell you how differently I wish I'd acted now. These past months, and weeks, it's all been bubbling up, haunting me. She was my little sister, and I cursed her. I let her down because I was so full of resentment I couldn't see how much help she needed, how much I . . ."

Her words broke off.

"She wouldn't have accepted help even if you'd offered it," Alabama said.

"I'll never know for sure, will I?"

Bev blew her nose, checked the rearview mirror, and then pulled back onto the road.

Alabama didn't say anything for a few miles. "But you took me in. After all that. You wanted to offer me a home even before you'd seen the letter."

"Of course."

"Even when I didn't want to go to New Sparta."

"Well, why would you? It probably seemed pokey, after living in cities all your life."

She scowled at the passing landscape. "I wasn't very nice."

"You were still reacting to terrible things that had happened," Bev said. "I couldn't imagine enduring what you went through."

Alabama bit her lip. "I always wondered why Mom never talked about my dad. I guessed it was because she loved him so much that thinking about losing him made her too sad."

"It probably did. Don't forget, you're only hearing the worst about Tom—the mistakes he made. They were huge, I know, but he was actually a sweet, funny person. A mixed-up person. But he was also young. We all were."

"But the point is," Alabama said, "Mom didn't

know him all that well, did she? Not as well as you knew him."

"I'm not sure. Maybe not." Bev frowned. "Although maybe their time together was more . . . intense. If you ever do want to talk about Tom, I'd be glad to share some happier memories."

"Maybe someday," Alabama said, scooching down in her seat. She thought for a moment and then said, "You see things from both sides, don't you? Like that corny Judy Collins clouds song. I don't think my mom did that very well. She was always so focused on what was directly in front of her. Usually bad things. It was like she had no defenses—she was all exposed nerve. I'm a little like that, too, I guess."

"Everyone is. It's natural to focus on your own problems. You have to."

"But not to see other people's?" Alabama shook her head. "I don't want to be like that. What did you say that one time, about becoming something different before it's too late . . . ?"

"It's never too late to become what you might have been," Bev said.

Alabama repeated it in a low voice, quickly, as if memorizing it for a test.

"I'm sorry I ruined your trip," Bev told her.

"You didn't," Alabama said. "I mean, it wasn't all your fault."

"I've been losing my temper a lot recently. I'm

443

not usually like this. It's no wonder you wanted to find a . . . what did you call it?"

"A benefactress."

"And now I've sabotaged that. It wasn't on purpose."

Alabama folded her arms. "It's okay."

Resignation wasn't her niece's style. It made Bev nervous.

They lapsed into a thoughtful silence for several miles.

Bev was expecting more discussion of Diana. She didn't know whether to be disappointed or relieved when Alabama changed the subject.

"Would you mind if I listened to some music?"

"Of course not." Her gloomy thoughts weren't conducive to conversation anyway, and she'd be just as happy to stew in them in silence.

But instead of putting on her earphones as Bev expected, Alabama turned on the radio and searched the dial until she found a station that came in clearly. "Take on Me" blared from the speakers, and Bev sat up straighter. It was so rare that Alabama wanted to listen to the radio when they were together, and the upbeat rhythm made it hard to sag in her seat.

"This song is on all the time," Alabama complained.

Bev had heard it on several occasions, but never paid attention to the lyrics. Listening to them now, the words didn't seem to add up to anything that made sense. "What are they talking about?"

"I'm not sure, exactly. A-ha is a Norwegian group. I think it's all less confusing if you don't think about it too hard."

Which summed up a lot of things in life.

"Actually, I sort of like it," Alabama admitted, leaning forward to turn up the volume.

CHAPTER 26

Alabama called Stuart's house several times over the weekend, but he never called back. Which was odd, for Stuart. On Monday, she saw him briefly as he skittered in late to algebra, but she didn't want to talk about personal matters when there were a lot of people around. She dreaded telling him that the meeting with her grandmother hadn't been all that she'd hoped for. That it had in fact been, with the exception of her grandmother's acknowledgment that Alabama *was* her granddaughter, a humongous letdown.

But she did look forward to telling Stuart he'd been wrong about Bev. She wasn't her mother.

In a lot of ways, the trip to Houston hadn't been a complete waste of time. It had opened her eyes. All her life, she'd been looking at things so narrowly. It was as if she'd only seen a tiny bit of a picture, and suddenly the scope had zoomed out and she was viewing everything all at once for the first time. She knew The Really Bad Thing that had happened between her mom and Aunt Bev. Finally. She knew Bev wasn't a monster, wasn't a terrible and coldhearted sister hater. Bev was even willing to admit her own mistakes.

Ambling down the hall on the way to lunch, she found a picture of Bugs Bunny with the words *What's Up, Miss Putterman?* written over it and taped to the bathroom door. She tore it down, crumpled the paper, and tossed it away. People were still saying "What's up?" to her aunt. It was not funny anymore.

It hadn't been all that funny to begin with. It had just seemed like it when she was with Kevin. Now she shuddered to think about her part in that escapade. It felt like something that had happened in another lifetime.

Stuart wasn't in the cafeteria. She gulped down a disgusting chili dog and went to see if he was holed up in the library. Still no Stuart. She ran into him just before the next class, edging along the lockers like a kid trying to make himself invisible. His expression when he saw her seemed wary.

She captured him by the shirtsleeve, afraid he might actually run away from her. "What's the matter? Why are you acting all weird?"

"What do you care?"

Her breath hitched. She'd come to expect all sorts of odd behavior from Stuart, but hostility took her by surprise. "I'm your friend."

"You've got other friends."

"Since when?"

"Since Kevin Kerrigan," he said, almost bitterly.

"What's the matter with you? Did something happen at Thanksgiving? I leave town one day and you go psycho on me." She laughed. "Are you jealous?"

His cheeks blazed. "No, of course not. Be friends with whoever you want. I don't care."

She put her hands on her hips, feeling almost like Bev in one of her scolding moods. "You're wrong. Crazy wrong. I'm *not* friends with Kevin Kerrigan, really. Maybe I ran around with him a few times, but for your information, I was going to tell him I didn't want to hang out with him anymore. So if you've decided that you want to dump me on account of past association, that leaves me with exactly zero friends."

He angled a glance up at her. "Really?"

"Really. Now, what's going on?"

His gaze scanned the hallway, where clusters of kids were gearing up for the next class. "I can't tell you now. Why don't you come home with me after school? Mom made so many pies, we've still got a whole pecan one left over."

Pie sounded good. She'd been too nervous to eat much dessert on Thanksgiving. But she mostly wanted to talk to Stuart. "Okay, but I don't know why you can't just say what the matter is. I'm worried now."

"I'd just rather not. Not here."

Her anxiety didn't lessen when Stuart insisted on taking the long way home after school, because he preferred sticking to Main Street rather than cutting through the smaller streets that were quicker.

Once there, they loaded pie onto plates and

retreated to his room, where they could gossip about the holiday weekend in private. Nice as Mrs. Looney was, Alabama didn't feel comfortable talking about her messed-up family in front of her. And she had a feeling that whatever was preying on Stuart's mind wasn't the kind of thing a person wanted to spill in front of his parents.

"Tell me what's wrong," she insisted as soon as the door was closed and Stuart had put on his Amy Grant album. He'd decided he really liked Amy Grant after all and had started listening to her songs obsessively.

"You first," he said.

She told him about the trip, and he questioned her in detail. His disappointment that Bev was not her mother was overshadowed by his amazement—and feeling of vindication—upon learning that there had been a baby, even if the poor thing hadn't made it. "I knew there had to be some-thing like that," he said. "That's how it always is on the soaps."

"It felt like a soap opera, for sure." She described the big house, her grandmother who'd seemed so intimidating, and the sniping between Bev and Dot, and Bev storming out. And finally the long drive home.

"The strange part," she said, summing up, "is that after everything, I like everybody more."

"Even Dot? She sounds awful!"

She had to think about that. "I don't much like

Dot, but I can't totally hate her. Mom always called the Jacksons the Jackasses, but to me, they seemed sad . . . and all alone. Even when Dot was acting all snippy and snooty, I kept thinking that she and my grandmother had probably been through so much together, and now they were by themselves, like my mom and I were. I wouldn't have wanted some strange kid showing up on the doorstep, so why should she?" She shook her head. "I thought I would hate her, but I couldn't. I guess it's pretty stupid to hate people before all the information is in. I made that mistake with Bev."

Stuart weighed what she was saying. "Well, your aunt could have told you all this earlier. You might have understood better."

"But she didn't know the things I was thinking. And I didn't give her much of a chance."

"So do you think you're going to live in Houston now?" Stuart asked.

"I doubt it. I don't even care anymore."

"I thought you wanted to live with Granny Jackson."

"I did. But after seeing that place, I don't know if I'd fit in there, either. I don't know where I fit in. I didn't mind Granny Jackson, actually, but Dot was kind of scary. I can't imagine calling her Aunt Dot, or being related to her at all. Anyway, I don't think I made much of an impression. Especially not with Dot. And my grandmother puts a lot of weight on whatever Dot thinks."

"Well, then maybe it's a good thing that you like Bev better now. 'Cause it looks like you're stuck with her."

"Yeah." She blew out a breath. "Now I've got to try to make up for all the bad stuff."

"What bad stuff?" Stuart asked.

She'd been thinking of the Bugs posters, but he didn't know about her involvement in all that. "Just . . . not being nicer to her. You know." She crooked her head and regarded him seriously. "Why were you acting so freaked out this morning? Why didn't you return my calls this weekend?"

He ducked his head and his face took on that dull expression again. That face that said he wanted to disappear.

"For God's sake, what's the matter?" she asked. "I've been so worried, imagining all sorts of awful things."

"Like what?"

"I don't know . . . like you found out you're dying or something."

"That's not far from the truth. Or at least—"

"What?" Panic swelled in her. "Are you sick?"

"No—not that way. But I feel like I'm . . . well, like I can't ever be me anymore."

She could feel her brows drawing together. "Why not?"

"Because . . ." He inhaled deeply. "Maybe it

won't seem like that big a deal. You've probably been at city schools where there were guns, and switchblade fights in the halls."

"No, I haven't—that stuff's mostly on the news, not in real life."

He twisted his lips. "Well, what happened to me's not that bad."

She sat up straighter, losing patience. "Then . . . *what?*"

He shrugged again. "Someone's been leaving notes on my locker. Stupid stuff, but mean. Calling me names."

"Like what?"

"Just . . . you know. Stuff they consider mean."

"What, exactly?"

"What does it matter?" His voice rose, as if *she* was attacking him. She supposed he was right. It didn't matter—whatever it was, it was obviously meant to scare him.

What alarmed her most was his reaction. He was always catching crap from other kids. Whatever had been happening lately must have been way more threatening, more personal, to have him so worried and depressed. "Who's doing it?"

"I don't know," he said. "I sort of had an idea, from the guys who tease and hassle me in the halls between classes."

Her chest was heaving with anger. "Who?"

"Just guys. Older guys, mostly. What does it matter?"

"It matters," she insisted. "They should get in trouble."

"For what?"

"For bullying you."

"It's just names, though. We're not supposed to let that kind of thing get to us."

She shook her head. "This isn't third grade and some guy saying you have cooties. You know it's not—you don't even feel comfortable walking down the side streets of New Sparta."

He bit his lip. "I don't really know for sure who did the signs, and even if I did, telling on them would only make them bug me more, probably."

"But they can't get away with it."

He was silent for a moment, then asked quietly, "So you'd never heard anything about this?"

"No!" She shook her head, then backed up. "Wait—how long has this been going on?"

"For a couple of weeks? It didn't seem like that big a deal at first. When I show up to school before homeroom, there's sometimes a sign on my locker. But they've been getting meaner, and creepier. I've been trying to get there earlier to tear it off before anyone can see."

"What jerks! We've got to find out who they are. Why didn't you tell me this was going on?"

"Well, I've been busy with tech rehearsals for the school play. And also, things have been weird between us. Ever since the talent show."

That stupid talent show. "Not so weird that I

wouldn't want to know when something bad was happening to you. I'm your friend."

"I sort of thought . . . after you said all that about my costume, about how people would make fun of me . . ."

She flinched, remembering. "I didn't mean you'd deserve it. Or that jerks would be justified in bullying you."

"Yeah, but . . ."

Her breath caught. "You didn't think *I* put signs on your locker, did you? Is that who you think I am?"

He looked doubtful, and she realized that the thought—or something close to it—had crossed his mind. How could he think she would do something like that? *Why?*

She was outraged, until she recalled that she *had* made mean signs . . . about Bev.

She remembered Stuart's sympathy for Bev when the signs appeared, and his saying the people who made them were vicious. She understood now. Anybody who would bully Stuart was lower than low.

"I wouldn't do that to you," she said. "Ever."

"I know."

She fumed. "I still can't believe this." And a horrible suspicion took root in her mind. If Stuart could even dream she would do something like that, there had to be a real reason. Like who she'd been hanging out with.

Kevin's calling him Tights Boy jumped to mind. But Stuart wouldn't bug out over something mild like that.

"Please don't tell anyone," he begged. "I only told you because it felt good to talk to somebody. Maybe it will go away. Jokes get old, even to bullies."

"Jokes?" she exclaimed. "This isn't funny."

He tried again. "Maybe, with Christmas coming up, people will be nicer. Or at least have better things to think about."

She rejected the idea that the Christmas spirit would give these bullies a change of heart. They argued back and forth, but in the end she had to agree to Stuart's request for her to keep her mouth shut. It was his problem, he kept saying. And he was afraid creating a federal case out of a few signs would make things worse for him in the long run. Besides, they didn't know who was doing it, so what good would it do to tell Mr. Kirby?

On the way home, she wasn't surprised to hear the familiar sputter of the Mustang's motor behind her. She'd sensed all day that she'd run into Kevin sooner rather than later.

He leaned over and opened the passenger door. "Hop in."

"No thanks," she said.

"Don't you want to go somewhere?" He waggled his brows at her.

"I'm grounded, remember?" Although she wasn't

even sure this was true anymore. Bev had seemed ready to withdraw that punishment. But it still made a good excuse to avoid Kevin. "Besides, I've got a lot of homework."

"Give you a ride home?" he asked.

"I think Aunt Bev is waiting for me at the house. She'd be mad."

"She's not mad that you hang out with that little—" His words bit off.

She lifted her chin. "That little what?"

"Never mind."

"No," Alabama said, not willing to drop it. "I do mind. What were you going to say?"

For a moment, his jaw appeared clenched tight enough to crack Brazil nuts. He eyed her coldly. "You aren't so grounded that you couldn't hang out with your little friend. You don't have too much homework for that."

"Stuart helped me with my homework," she lied. "We have classes together, and things in common. You and I don't."

He drew back, blinking. "So what is this, the brush-off?"

"It's not like we were going together," she reminded him. "I'm just some freshman you were messing around with."

"Yeah, right." He sneered. "It was loads of fun, too. Frigid little—"

He slammed the door shut on his final insult, which she was happy not to hear. Then he threw the car into gear and tore off down the street. In a daze, she watched him go. How could she have made him so mad? He never even seemed to like her all that much.

Boys like that are used to getting their way, Bev had said to her once.

Maybe that was it. He wasn't getting his way. Spoiled rich boy.

She hurried home, steaming from the encounter with Kevin, but relieved at the same time. From afar—or at least from the bleachers near the tennis courts—he'd seemed like a Greek god. Perfect, gorgeous, out of reach. If only he had stayed out of reach. She wouldn't have had to come face-to-face with the fact that he was bad tempered, pushy, and immature.

At least she could put it all behind her and start fresh now. *It's never too late to become what you might have been.*

At the house, Bev was talking on the phone. Alabama scurried to the kitchen, poured some tea to take back to her room, and spent the time until dinner writing a list of resolutions.

1. I will not be a jerk. Except to people who deserve it. Ever.
2. I will not go out with a boy just because he's good looking and asks me. Or I'll go out once, maybe, but not twice. And only if he officially asks me out—not

because he happens to drive by and I seem better than nothing. I'm a lot better than nothing, and a whole lot better than Kevin Kerrigan.

3. I will make better grades!!!
4. I will cancel Columbia House and learn to resist mail order anything.
5. I will save money to pay Columbia House before they come and arrest me.
6. I will be a better friend to Stuart.
7. I will find a way to buy nice Christmas gifts for Gladdie, Bev, Stuart, and Wink. Or I might have to make them. (On account of #5)
8. I will learn some useful craft that will enable me to make gifts that won't cause people to gag when they open them.
9. For the rest of my life, I will not do anything dumb, cowardly, mean, or too expensive.

Bev knocked on the door and then poked her head in. "Supper?"

Alabama slammed her notebook shut and joined Bev in the kitchen, where preparations for broiled mustard chicken were well underway. Alabama hated mustard chicken nights. She almost complained, but then she remembered she'd been lucky to have a hunk of Mrs. Looney's pecan pie and wasn't even that hungry anyway. While Bev extracted wedges from a head of lettuce, Alabama thumped two place settings onto the table, grabbed napkins from Bev's hand-painted rooster napkin holder, and sat down.

When the chicken breasts came out of the oven, perfectly charred, and joined on the plate by boiled new potatoes, she wondered if this was really how her life was going to be for the next four years. For the first time, she wasn't filled with dread at the thought. Really, given all that had happened, things could have turned out a whole lot worse. What if there had been no Bev at all?

There. She'd adopted an attitude of gratitude—one of Bev's sayings—and it didn't even make her want to vomit.

Maybe this was progress.

She looked at her aunt, who was unusually silent. Her face crinkled with tension, and worry.

"Is something wrong?" Alabama asked her.

"No." Bev straightened and brightened. "Do you have a lot of homework tonight?"

She shrugged. "The usual. Why?"

"You looked busy when I popped into your room earlier. Now, I wasn't meaning to snoop, so don't—"

"I was making a list of resolutions."

Bev's fork halted in midair. "What a terrific

thing to do—prepping yourself for New Year's."

"Actually, I thought I might as well consider this a new year right now. January first is an artificial marker, isn't it? I mean, every day's the start of a new year, when you think about it. So why not start my new year now?"

Bev's mouth dropped. "Oh my word, I'm so impressed! That's profound—almost worthy of a poster."

Alabama shuddered at the reminder of poster making. "Cue the glue and glitter," she muttered.

"Don't be self-deprecating," Bev said. "There are plenty of people in the world who will want to put you down. Don't do their work for them."

"Wow. It's like we're sitting at the table of wisdom."

"Well, *I* thought it was clever." Bev took a bite of chicken and while she chewed, her face lapsed back into worry.

What was it with people and suffering in silence today? "There must be something wrong," Alabama said. "You only get that look when something's really bothering you. Is it school?"

"No." Bev wiped her mouth. "Well, yes. I do worry if my job's going to disappear someday, but my biggest concern right now is Mama. She hasn't called, and when I ring the apartment, no one answers."

"Maybe we should get her an answering machine."

"Lord, I tried that. She won't have one of the things. She thinks it's rude to have a machine answer the phone for you. But evidently it's perfectly polite to take off to Las Vegas with a man you barely know and never get in touch with your daughter to let her know whether you're dead or alive."

Alabama laughed. "Wink's not a stranger."

Bev's voice held a note of hysteria. "They were supposed to be back last night. I even resorted to calling Brenda Boyer this afternoon to see if she'd heard anything. Of course she hadn't."

"Maybe they missed their flight."

"Maybe," Bev said, sighing. "One thing's clear. No hospital in Las Vegas has seen either one of them."

Alabama gulped. "You *are* worried."

"At their age, anything can happen."

"Anything can happen anytime," Alabama said.

For instance, your whole world could come crashing down while you're off canoeing. And someone you've hated your whole life could become the person whose worries you share at the dinner table.

The next morning, she awoke before her alarm and left a note for Bev while her aunt was in the shower, saying that she needed to get to school a little early and couldn't wait for a ride. She speed-walked to school, arriving there ten minutes before the first bell. Her first stop was Stuart's locker.

She wasn't sure what she'd expected—maybe nothing—but she felt stunned, then sick. Someone had cut a picture of a shriveled, dying Rock Hudson out of an old *National Enquirer* and taped it to a blue piece of poster board. With red paint, they'd slopped the warning THIS IS WHAT HAPPENS TO HOMOS!!! all across the poster and picture. Beneath, the words YOU WILL DIE!!! had been added, in case the original message hadn't come through loud and clear.

And the worst part? In the lower left-hand corner, the poster board was discolored and water-stained. Just like the poster board she and Kevin had stolen from Bev's garage.

Lunging forward, she pulled the poster down, rolled it up, and then sprinted down the hall to stow it in her own locker. She stayed in the library until class time. Later, when she saw Stuart in algebra, he looked calm. Calmer than she felt, for sure.

"Hey," she said.

"You want to meet in the auditorium during lunch?" he whispered. "I have to practice giving a speech on the history of the United Nations."

"I . . . I don't know if I'll be able to. I've got to do something."

"What?" Stuart asked.

"I'm going—"

Mr. Atkins glared at them, and she shook her head at Stuart and hunched over her textbook. Only to herself did she finish the thought. *I'm going to do something that will make you hate me.* In fact, it might make everyone hate her.

CHAPTER 27

Bev skipped assembly in order to sneak into her classroom and set up a film projector for fourth period. Technically, this was Oren's time to have the classroom, but the anti-drug film she wanted to show was long, and if she didn't set up the projector in advance, she wouldn't have time to finish her lesson plan before the end of class.

She signed the projector out at the library and set off for the biology room as fast as she could, given the wobbly metal stand it came on, with a wheel that kept sticking. She supposed the film projectors didn't rate new carts now that videos were more common. But some of her favorite materials hadn't been transferred to videotape.

As she backed into the classroom, she was greeted by a bellow from Oren at the desk.

"This is O time."

"I know," she said, "and I'm so sorry for the intrusion, but if I don't get the projector set up, then I won't have time to show the film and do our worksheet too, so . . ." Even after the explanation, his nostrils were flaring. "I know it's a huge favor to ask."

"This is not what we agreed. If we don't follow the rules, then what was the point of making them?"

"But if we can't work together and compromise, what example does that set for the students? Plus, I've already checked out the projector, and if I take it back now, I'll have to explain why, and we'd both look a little silly if I did that, wouldn't we?"

He exhaled a gust of exasperation. "Well, all right. But hurry, and please don't make too much noise. I'm trying to concentrate on these papers. I *thought* I'd have a few moments of peace and quiet."

"I'll be quiet as a mouse."

It didn't work out that way. First, she had trouble getting the film canister open, and tugged until the metal top popped off, clattering onto the tile floor. "Sorry," she whispered to the vein throbbing on the dome of Oren's bald head.

A few minutes later, as she was spooling the film into the machine, a loud crackle broke the silence in the room, which was always a precursor to an intercom announcement. Jackie's voice traveled through the speaker box on the wall. "Bev Putterman, please come to the front office. You have an urgent message."

The film slipped out of her cold fingers. "I have to leave this," she told Oren.

"I guess you do," he agreed, sounding almost sympathetic. He was probably glad it would get her out of the classroom. "Hope it's nothing serious."

Her first worry was that something had happened Alabama.

But as she hurried down the hall to the office, another possibility occurred to her. What if this was a pretext for getting her into Lon's lair, so he could fire her? Did he already have enough black marks in her file to justify terminating her?

She rushed into the office and stood at the high counter that separated Jackie's work space from the rest of the world. The woman was at her desk in the far corner, typing, and didn't look up when Bev came in.

"You said you had a message for me?" Bev asked.

Jackie glanced over but kept typing, in no hurry to cough up this urgent message. "I intended to deliver it to you during the assembly, but you weren't there."

"I had something to tend to."

"Lon doesn't like the faculty to skip the assembly."

"I know, I'm sorry."

"It's Lon you should be apologizing to. Assembly is meant for the entire school, to create a together moment. He sees the school as family, you know."

Given the nepotism in his hiring practices, the entire faculty might actually be his family soon.

By force of will, Bev held her tongue. "The message . . . is it about Alabama?"

Issuing a long-suffering sigh, Jackie got up, ambled over to the tray where she kept a pink pad for phone messages, and read it out to Bev. "Your mother. She said to tell you that she will call you when she gets back from New York."

Bev tilted her head. "You mean Las Vegas?"

"She said New York."

"B-but that's impossible."

"I took the message myself."

"She went to Vegas," Bev insisted, but for her own benefit, not to be argumentative. Then she asked, "She didn't say anything else?"

"I wasn't going to demand your mother's life story over the telephone. The office phone isn't supposed to be used for faculty personal business, you know, except in real emergencies. I'm not a switchboard operator."

All the way back to her classroom, Bev tried to puzzle out what could have happened. How did a seventy-seven-year-old woman go to Las Vegas and end up on the East Coast? Was there an emergency? There must have been, or why would she have called the school? Had something happened to Wink? Maybe he'd snapped, and Gladys fled Las Vegas to get away from him?

As she returned to a barely civil Oren and threading the projector, she envisioned Gladys holed up in a fleabag hotel in Hell's Kitchen, cowering in fear for the moment when her crazy, ukulele-wielding, plaid-pantsed geriatric husband would crash down the door.

The door behind her opened suddenly, making her jump, startled. Alabama poked her head in and said, "Oh, sorry! Can I talk to you for a minute?"

Bev didn't know whether the apology was for scaring her half to death, or in response to Oren's exasperated glottal emissions. She said, in a low voice, "Now's not a good time. I need to finish this."

"It's *really* important," Alabama said. "Like, life and death important."

Bev frowned. "All right. If you think it can't wait."

Her niece cut a gaze over to Oren. "But I sort of need to talk to you alone?"

"We can go out in the hallway."

"It needs to be in private," Alabama said.

The scrape of Oren's desk chair screeched through the room. "I'm going to the faculty lounge for coffee," he said. "My concentration's shot here, anyway. You have five minutes."

"Thank you, Oren," Bev said.

Alabama kept her head down until he'd huffed out.

Bev noticed a rolled-up piece of poster board in Alabama's hand. "What's going on?"

"You know how you were telling me that it's never too late to become what you might have been?"

"Yes . . ."

"Then, maybe, is it never too late to do what you should have done in the first place so you wouldn't have become someone besides who you originally wanted to be?"

Bev frowned. "I'm not sure I followed that. I think you'd better back up and tell me what this is about."

Alabama took a long, deep breath. "Someone's threatening Stuart."

For some reason, that was the last thing in the world Bev had expected to hear, especially after that buildup. "Why?"

"Because he's gay."

The statement rattled Bev. Not because it was hard to accept—*of course he is,* she thought immediately. The words took a moment to absorb because in small towns in Texas, being gay wasn't something high school boys advertised. But Stuart wasn't about hiding his light under a bushel. Falseness wasn't in his character.

She hoped strength was.

"I mean, he's never had a boyfriend or anything," Alabama continued, "but he's pretty sure he is, and some of the stuff he does makes all these idiots in school hassle him. But I think they might do that no matter what, because he's different and they aren't nice people. Some of them, at least."

"Has someone beat him up?"

Alabama shook her head. "Not that I know of. . . . It's more psychological than that. It's like they're trying to make him freak out. He's really nervous."

"What have they said to him?"

Alabama held back, rolling the poster board in her hands nervously, until she finally said, "Stuff like this," and unfurled it in one movement.

Bev stared at the macabre, mean-spirited, hateful message. How could someone do something like that at New Sparta High School—and to Stuart, of all people? Who had Stuart ever hurt? Her blood pressure shot through the roof.

"I found it on Stuart's locker this morning. I tore it off before he could see it."

"Does he know who's doing this?" Bev asked.

"No, but I do," Alabama said. "Only, Stuart doesn't know that I know who did it. And he's told me that he doesn't want to tell the principal anyway, because he's afraid it would just make everything worse."

"He's wrong. He should tell—and if he won't, I will. This is awful."

"I should go to Mr. Kirby." Alabama bit her lip. "But the thing is, when I tell, I'm going to be telling on myself. In fact, I might get thrown out of school."

Bev didn't understand, but her niece's tone sounded so deadly serious, she knew something bad was coming. "How could that be?"

"Because I know who this poster board belongs to. It's yours." She pointed to the water-stained corner, which was discolored and warped. "I was there when Kevin Kerrigan took it from our garage. I told him about it, and gave it to him."

How awful. She never had trusted that boy.

"But you didn't know he would do this," Bev said.

Alabama's head drooped. "No, but I helped him do the other posters. The *What's up, Miss Putterman?* ones."

The confession tapped through Bev's mind like words on a teletype—it took her a moment to string them all together and process the meaning. Disappointment knotted her insides. She searched for something to say, but failed.

As if it took her last drop of courage, Alabama looked up at her, lower lip trembling. "I'm so sorry, Aunt Bev. It was me who did those posters—Kevin and me," she confessed. "But that's how I know that it's Kevin doing this now."

"This is a thorny situation." Lon clasped his hands together in front of him, staring at his knuckles with exaggerated gravity. "We've got your niece's word against Kevin's. He says she's lying. For all we know, she might have made those earlier posters all by herself."

Bev pinched her hand to keep her temper at bay.

471

"She had no reason to confess—she could have gotten off scot-free. No one suspected her—least of all me."

"Doesn't exactly make her testimony unimpeachable, though, does it?" he said.

"To my mind, it does. She had no reason to say anything except that she wants Kevin to stop bullying Stuart and she worries he won't unless he's punished. She knew when she told me that there would be consequences for herself, as well, for the other incident."

"You bet your bottom dollar there will be."

Bev flushed. "But whatever happens to Alabama, Kevin should be punished twice over. His acts were threatening. What else could you call writing 'you will die' on a poster and putting it on someone's locker? Stuart Looney's been nervous walking home in broad daylight."

Lon leaned forward. "It's just boys giving each other a hard time. Maybe you wouldn't understand, but this kind of thing is perfectly natural."

"You don't have to explain natural to me," she said. "I've been around teenagers as long as you have, and I've seen all sorts of harassment and teasing. I've seen boys after they've been beaten up. But I haven't seen anything as mean-spirited and premeditated as this. According to Alabama, this is one incident of many. Stuart destroyed the other posters."

"Because he probably didn't think they were

that big a deal until his little friend saw one and he realized he could milk the situation for a little sympathy from a girl."

How many layers of obtuseness could a person have? "Because he was embarrassed, and scared." Bev wanted to reach across the desk and whack him with his stapler. "I can't believe you, Lon. You're always going on about how we need to be modern and forward-thinking. What is this"— she held up the poster again, which he had barely glanced at—"except the worst kind of Neanderthal bullying? Is this what you want in your school? What if the newspaper got hold of this story?"

He straightened, alarmed. "This is school business."

"This school is part of the community."

He narrowed his eyes. "I'm not so sure the community would get behind you on this, Bev."

"I think they would. It seems to me that your hesitation to bring Kevin Kerrigan to account has a lot to do with the fact that Keith Kerrigan is the mayor, a school board member, and an old golf buddy of yours who helped swing the donation of the computer lab. So basically, if you're a bigwig in this town, your kid can terrorize younger kids to his heart's content."

Red in the face, Lon began to sputter out objections so fast his words tripped over themselves. "Terrorize! Who said . . . Yes, Keith Kerrigan is a good friend and solid member of this community. . . . And no matter what you say, it's Kevin's word against Alabama's."

"If nothing's done, I'm going to make a fuss, Lon."

"Oh, something will be done," he said, his lips flattening into an implacable line. "Alabama is suspended for three days. Theft and destruction of school property."

Bev stood up. "I will be at the next school board meeting, and I intend to bring this up with your friend."

"Keith Kerrigan is a pillar of this community, Bev. A pillar."

She stood and rolled up the poster. "Fine. When you tell this pillar that his son is suspended for *six days,* I'll be willing to consider you both pillars. But right now, I think you're being"—*a weasel* was what she nearly said—"weak."

Cheeks flaming, she turned to leave as fast as she could, before she gave him enough ammunition to simply fire her on the spot. She probably already had.

He stopped her before she could reach the door. "Bev."

She pivoted.

He held out his hand. "The poster? I would prefer that you leave it with me."

She cupped both hands around it. She could just imagine the evidence conveniently disappearing before the school board meeting. "I can't do that. It belongs to Stuart Looney. Your friend's son gave it to him."

That night, she and Alabama rented *Splash* and Bev made Hamburger Helper chili mac. They needed comfort food, although Alabama seemed to be taking the situation with more equanimity than Bev was. Bev worried all she'd done was secure Alabama's suspension, guarantee Stuart's being ostracized, and hasten her own unemployment.

When they sat down to eat, Alabama laid down her fork. "I'm really sorry."

"You've apologized, and I've accepted your apology," Bev said. "I wasn't thrilled to know what you did, but you were hurting and confused at the time . . . and part of the reason was that I wasn't truthful with you. Both of us have made mistakes these last months. Anyway, it took courage for you to confess, and I'm glad you decided to stand up for your friend."

Alabama shrugged glumly. "He might not be my friend anymore. He was really mad that I told you."

"He'll get over it."

"I'm not sure. . . ." Alabama twirled a noodle around her plate. "Because now all the kids in school will know what happened, and maybe make fun of him—"

"How will they find out?"

"From Kevin. The minute he left the principal's office—after *lying*—the story started spreading that Stuart was making things up about being bullied. Like he'd ever do that. Poor Stuart—we both used to think Kevin was great. We didn't know him."

Bev shook her head. Now was probably not the time to lecture on judging a book by its cover. Alabama was getting a crash course in that already.

"What am I going to do while I'm suspended?" Alabama asked.

"I'm not sure," Bev said honestly.

"Can I go to Gladdie's? Not forever, but—"

Bev clapped her hands to her cheeks.

Alabama's face screwed up in confusion. "What?"

"Mama! I forgot all about her!" Her imagination had last left her mother cowering in a hotel room like Shelley Duvall at the end of *The Shining*. All the other events of the day had knocked it clear out of her head. "She's in New York."

"Cool!" But, seeing Bev's distress, she asked, "What is she doing there?"

"I don't know. She left me a message at school, but all it said was that she was in New York City."

"Wink's with her though, right?"

"I'm assuming." She didn't mention her fear that Wink had turned into a maniac. Surely he hadn't. Maybe they'd gone east on a whim, or because Wink grew up there. That was entirely possible. Bev really had no idea about Wink's past, or where he was from, or what he'd left behind him before moving to Dallas and . . .

Oh God. Every time she tried to imagine what they were doing, she ended up with a lurid Movie of the Week flickering through her brain.

"Did she leave a number where you could call her?" Alabama asked.

"No."

Now Alabama looked worried, too. "That's bad, isn't it?"

"No, that's Mama. She wouldn't want me to call her back and pay for the long distance."

When the doorbell rang, Alabama jumped up to answer it. "Maybe it's Stuart!"

She returned, disappointed, with Glen trailing behind her.

Startled to see him in the house after so long, Bev stood. "What are you doing here?"

"What do you think?" He stepped forward, grabbing a chair back for physical or moral support. "I had to come."

"I'd better do my homework," Alabama piped up, backing toward her room. "I only have a week now to finish it. . . ."

When they heard Alabama's door click closed, they looked at each other. For some insane reason, Bev felt like hurling herself at his chest and feeling his arms wrap around her as they used to, seeking that comfort of someone to lean on. But she wasn't even sure that was possible anymore. She didn't know what was going through his mind, or if she would lean on him and discover his support was so weak it snapped.

"I had to stay at school for rehearsal, but I came as soon as it was over to see how you were."

"Well, as you can tell, I'm fine." She looked down at the table. "Would you like some chili mac?"

He was obviously about to refuse automatically until his gaze alighted on the food. "Do you have enough?"

"Of course. Neither Alabama nor I was very hungry."

Glad for something to do with herself, she fetched another plate, loaded it, and set it in front of him.

He took a bite. "Mm. I've missed this."

Did he mean the food, or the intimacy of sharing a meal at home together?

Their gazes met and held until she looked away and began folding her napkin into an ever-smaller square. When he'd first walked in, she'd wondered if he had been sent here as an information scout by the Kirbys. But the warmth in those eyes, the concern, let her know he was here for her. "So you heard what happened with me in Lon's office today?" she asked.

"Oh yes. You can't call the principal a bastard without it leaking out."

The word shocked her. "I never did!" She felt stiff with fury. "Who's saying that? I called him weak—which was bad enough."

"They might be starting a whisper campaign against you. The Kirbys are afraid you're going to take a stand against Kevin Kerrigan at the next school board meeting."

"I'm going to make a stand for Stuart Looney and other kids like him, for students to be treated with respect, and for punishment to be doled out fairly."

His eyes narrowed. "Was he really so awful to Stuart? Are you sure?"

She nodded. "Why else would Alabama have confessed when she didn't have to? And her story makes sense."

Glen shook his head. "I'd wondered why Stuart seemed in such low spirits lately. He's assistant stage manager for the fall play, and he hasn't been his usual self in rehearsals. Sort of listless and withdrawn. I thought maybe it was because he wished he had a part instead of having to work backstage. But this explains it." Lowering his voice, he said, "You know, Kevin's saying that he rejected Alabama, so she's made all this stuff up to spite him."

Kevin had been shooting his mouth off a lot today, evidently. "Where did you hear this?"

"You can pick up a lot of scuttlebutt during a high school play rehearsal. And Stuart wasn't there today."

"The gossip is utterly false. But why, even if that bit of slander were actually true, would Alabama seek revenge on Kevin by doing something so hideous to her best friend?"

"But according to Jackie, when he was questioned, Stuart said he never even saw the poster your niece showed you."

"There were others. He told Alabama about them. That's why she went to school early and found it there on his locker—she wanted to see if what he'd told her was true."

He put his fork down and aimed a serious gaze at her. "So you're going to show up at the public school board meeting next Monday."

"I am," she said.

"Are you sure that's a good idea?" he asked.

"Of course! Maybe not for my job . . ."

He tilted a wry smile at her. "And what *are* your professional plans, post–New Sparta High?"

She laughed in spite of herself. "Well, Alabama told me once that with all the stuff in my house, I could open my own craft store."

She expected him to laugh along with her, but he didn't.

"What's the matter?" she asked.

"That's not a bad idea—sell the stuff you've got around here. It's kind of clever."

"Oh, *very* clever. I think they call it a garage sale."

"No, but if you opened a place in one of the empty storefronts downtown—Bev's Craft World, or whatever. That's a great idea."

"At the very least, it would save me some trips to Dallas." She thought about it, seduced by the idea for a moment. She could be her own boss, for once. And she could spend all day in a world of her own creation, instead of the fishbowl world of school. There weren't any stores like it nearby, and what had Cleta told her once? Mail order was the wave of the future. People wouldn't even have to come to New Sparta—she could design a catalog. She might even surprise the world and make a fortune.

That word—*fortune*—brought her crashing back to earth. She would need a small fortune to start such a business. A small fortune she didn't have. It was like being the first teacher in space all over again. "Another impossible dream," she said.

"Not impossible," Glen said, and looking in his eyes, she felt a stirring. It was a glint of sun on a magnifying glass, rekindling feelings she feared had died. "Nothing's impossible."

CHAPTER 28

Within days, the whole town seemed to have chosen sides in the Stuart-Kevin matter and mentally suited up for combat. In a few cases, it was worse than that. The Looney car dealership was vandalized one night, with the showroom windows broken and spray painted.

Stuart wasn't answering Alabama's calls. Bev was actually thankful that her niece wasn't at school, and that she wanted to stay home and read and keep up with her schoolwork rather than run around town. Town wasn't always a good place to be these days. Bev had endured more than one public lecture about making mountains out of molehills, and how boys would be boys.

Leaving for school one morning, Bev nearly stepped on a dead rat on her doorstep. She wanted to believe that this was a coincidence, but her welcome mat was a peculiar place for an animal to go to die.

And yet, she found surprising pockets of support. When the grocery checker handed her change one evening, the woman glanced furtively around and said in a confidential voice, "That Kerrigan boy has always been a bad one. I caught him stealing a candy bar."

"When?" Bev asked.

The checker frowned. "Nineteen seventy-eight, I think."

New Sparta was a town with a long memory, no doubt about it. That fact gave Bev pause. People remembered basketball stats from games played decades ago. They knew who dated whom, and for how long. Something like this—a stink made at a school board meeting—wouldn't be forgotten soon. She felt she was seeking fairness, but if the rest of the town didn't view it that way—if the school board didn't—the result would be hard to live with.

There were moments, like the rat, when she was tempted to let the whole thing go, to believe that she was making a mountain out of a molehill. But then she would remember Alabama telling her about Stuart being afraid to walk on side streets.

Her town was better than that.

Amid all the troubles, she was teaching and trying to feel enthusiasm for the coming holiday season. She wanted to make Christmas nice for Alabama. But maybe, this year, Alabama wouldn't want anything too festive. It was hard to gauge the appropriate level of cheer.

Meanwhile, anxiety over what was going on with her mother kept up a constant backbeat in her mind. Days went by, but Gladys never called again. Who knew where she was, or what was happening? She couldn't help worrying. Last spring her mother had pneumonia, and she was just getting back to 100 percent after her gall-bladder surgery in July. What if something happened while she was traveling?

Every time the phone rang, Bev was disappointed. Sometimes there was nothing but dead air over the line for several seconds before the caller hung up.

Then, one night, Dot phoned.

"Bev, this is Dot Jackson," she announced, as if Bev could ever mistake that authoritative voice.

"What can I do for you?" With everything else going on, Bev had nearly forgotten the Jacksons.

"I wanted to inform you that we are working on a solution regarding Alabama."

She made it sound as if Alabama were a current events topic, like the scourge of homelessness, or crack cocaine. "I wasn't aware our niece was a problem," she said. "But I'm interested in hearing your solution, as you call it."

"I'm not at liberty to tell you what the arrangement will be, but I wanted to warn you that, as of now, Alabama is not a beneficiary in Mother's will."

"No one ever thought—"

"As of now, it's doubtful she ever will be," Dot finished.

How was she expected to respond to that? And how would Dot have phrased this if Alabama had picked up the phone? Bev guessed that she wouldn't have talked to Alabama—that, like the crank caller, she would have hung up. "Why are you telling me this?"

"So you can prepare Alabama. No one wants to crush her hopes."

"Alabama doesn't give a whoop about your mother's will. She never has."

Dot ignored her protest. "Mother still thinks a gesture should be made to the girl, since she's convinced that Alabama is Tom's daughter. Our family attorney is working on it."

"Wonderful." Bev took a deep breath. "So . . . any hints? Or were you just calling to irritate me?"

"We'll be in contact soon. I didn't want you slapping a lawsuit on us in the meantime."

"Lawsuit?" Bev had to laugh at that. As if they didn't have enough problems. "I think you've misjudged Alabama, Dot. Not everyone is like you."

"Really?" Dot sounded unconvinced. "My experience has been that when there's money at stake, most people are unable to resist making a grab for it."

"Alabama isn't most people," Bev said.

A light laugh trilled over the line. "Well, we'll see."

There were so many worries all at once that it felt as if the day should be divided into angst blocks.

In her spare time, Bev attempted to get some momentum for the school board meeting.

485

Appealing to her fellow teachers didn't help. Most were sympathetic, but didn't want to rock the boat. When she raised the issue with Oren, of course, he brushed her off in no uncertain terms. "That's none of my business."

Her friend Cindy told her that Kevin was the rowdiest student in her typing class, yet even she was reluctant to go to the meeting.

"I'm down to one class as it is. If I lose this, I'll have to find another full-time job."

Bev couldn't blame her. They hardly had socialized all semester because Cindy was so busy working weekends and evenings at a clothes store to make ends meet.

Glen said he would be there, on her side, but his recent history with the Kirbys made her wonder, still, to what extent she could count on him.

The most daunting problem she faced was that they couldn't even depend on the Looneys for support. Threats to Stuart were at the heart of the whole matter, yet when she approached Mr. Looney at the dealership one evening, he expressed the wish that it would all blow over. It was striking how much the strain showed in the face that she knew best from his manically goofy "Looney Deals!" commercials. He was protective of Stuart, and fearful that the incident would crush his son's spirit. Most of all, he worried that antagonizing the Kerrigan family would only make things worse.

She sympathized . . . to a point. How could he let this stand? How could he want an injustice like this to "blow over"? She nodded to the dealership's broken windows, still patched with duct tape and cardboard. "Does that seem like something that will blow over?"

"The police are searching for the culprits," he said stoically.

"They might start at the mayor's house," she grumbled.

She was so preoccupied with mulling this over on the way home that she pulled into her drive and nearly rear-ended a car that was already parked there. A yellow Pontiac about twice the length of her Toyota. It took her a moment to realize to whom the boat belonged: Wink. They'd kept his vehicle and sold Gladys's Buick.

She shot out of the car and ran to her front door, not knowing what to expect as she skidded into the living room. Certainly not the sight of her family having tea.

"Mama! Where have you been?"

"I told you," Gladys said. "We were in New York."

Bev ran over and hugged her, and then allowed herself to be enveloped in a warm embrace by Wink. "Your call to the school scared me to death," she said to her mother. "I thought there was some emergency."

"So did we," Gladys said. "When I phoned The

Villas to tell them we'd be coming back later than planned, Brenda Boyer said you'd been trying to reach me."

"Because I wondered where you were," Bev said. "I was frantic."

"I don't see why. We were just in Niagara Falls. At least, that's where we were when we called you."

"Niagara Falls? I thought you were in New York City."

Wink chuckled. "That's what Alabama was telling us. But I heard Gladdie leave the message, plain as day. She said to tell you that we were in New York."

Maybe that's what Jackie had said—Bev couldn't remember anymore. She sagged into a chair. "Well, at least you made it back. What were you doing in Niagara Falls?"

"What does anyone do there?" Wink asked. "Glad-Rags and I hit it big in Vegas, so we decided to shuffle off to Buffalo for an impromptu second honeymoon."

"Gladdie and Wink won sixteen thousand dollars!" Alabama exclaimed.

Her mother smiled. "Well, Wink won it—at craps."

He put his arm around Gladys. "Glad-Rags here was my good luck charm. Couldn't have done it without her. She's made me the luckiest man alive."

Bev couldn't believe it. "I didn't think anyone ever won in Vegas."

"Well of course they do," her mother said. "Why would anyone keep playing if no one ever won?"

Why indeed.

"Look at the souvenirs they brought back for me." Alabama reached into a paper tote bag and brought out a Niagara Falls snow globe and a *Cats* T-shirt. "Aren't they fun? She got you a shirt, too."

"We went to Manhattan for two nights so we could catch a show and say we'd taken a bite out of the Big Apple," Gladys said. "You two should go sometime. You'd have a ball."

She couldn't remember a time in her life when her mother had seemed so happy, so ebullient. When had she ever counseled anyone to take a vacation, or taken a real frivolous vacation herself? Never, that Bev could remember.

Of course, taking a vacation anytime soon would be impossible. But it was fun to see her mother in such a cheery frame of mind.

Alabama stood up. "Is it okay if I go see Stuart?"

Bev almost argued that Gladdie had just gotten here . . . but she realized that *she* was the one who had just arrived. Gladys and Wink might have been here all afternoon, for all she knew. And the fact that Alabama and Stuart were obviously talking again was a hopeful sign.

After Alabama left, Gladys went to the kitchen with Bev to make another pot of tea. "What's going on?" she asked.

"That's a hard question to answer all at once," Bev said.

"We drove in early this afternoon, expecting to have time to leave you a note saying that we'd go for lunch and come back when you all were out of school, but Alabama was here at the house. She said she got kicked out."

Bev shook her head. "Suspended."

She tried to walk her mother through all that had happened, both at school and with the Jacksons, about what was going on now, and the school board meeting that had yet to take place. Through it all, Gladys listened, arms crossed, gaze locked on the linoleum.

When Bev finished, her mother looked her in the eye. "You haven't had an easy time of it, have you?"

For some reason, the simple question made Bev want to cry. For weeks, she'd been holding on to her sanity by the thinnest of threads. This little bit of compassion from her mother nearly tipped her over the edge. "It's been . . . rough."

"Sounds to me like it might get rougher. You could lose your job defending a boy who's nothing to you."

"Not nothing." Bev lifted her chin. "He's my student, and Alabama's friend."

Her mother frowned. "Well, good for you. You can find another teaching position, can't you?"

"Maybe, but I don't want to. I like it here. It's been my home for nearly a decade now. I love my house, and the people." She added, "Most of them. Even if I didn't teach, I'd like to stay and try to figure out something. I might try a new venture anyway. Glen and I were talking—"

"Glen!" Her mother's brows rose. "Is he back in the picture?"

"A little," Bev admitted. "He thinks I should open a craft store. He says I can't be the only person around here who would drive fifty miles to find the right-sized chunk of Styrofoam." She shook her head, daunted as always when she considered the difficulties. "But I'd have to get a bank loan, and I don't know how I'd manage that."

Her mother gaped at her. "You're afraid to apply for a loan? For Pete's sake, I worked in a bank the whole time you were growing up. I'll hold your hand and take you through it step-by-step if need be."

"I don't have any equity."

"If you think you could make something happen here, we will get you through this," her mother said. "Don't forget, you have rich relations."

Bev shook her head. "You and Wink need to hold on to your winnings, Mama. From the looks of you, you might have a third and fourth honeymoon in you yet."

Gladys laughed as they carried the refilled pot of tea back out to the dining room. While they were away, Wink hadn't wasted his time. Rhoda Morgenstern was decked out in an I ♥ NY T-shirt and Gladys's sun hat.

Monday morning after home ec, Stuart approached Bev's desk. She noted that he was wearing a *Cats* T-shirt, which couldn't be a coincidence. "I like the shirt," she said.

"Alabama gave it to me. Isn't it cool? It was really nice of her."

"I'm glad you two are talking. She was depressed all last week because she thought you were mad at her."

"I was, at first. I wish she hadn't said anything. She promised not to."

"Do you feel that way still?"

He nodded. "I wish you wouldn't make a big thing about it at the school board meeting tonight, Ms. Putterman. It won't change anything."

"You don't think so?"

He shook his head. "People are the way they are. I know that. But I've already overheard some things they're going to say at the meeting—my dad got a call from Keith Kerrigan."

She frowned. "It can't be worse than things they've said about you already."

He shook his head. "Not about me. About Alabama."

"I don't care if Kevin said that she's a woman scorned. That's nonsense."

"But he's also going to say that Alabama's crazy. That she's been mentally disturbed since her mother died and has been seeing a shrink because she's unbalanced and promiscuous, and—"

Bev had to stop him. She felt nauseated. "Where did they come up with this? They can't say things like that!"

"Why not? It's true that her mother died, and she's been depressed, and she saw a psychiatrist."

"Twice!"

"But there's enough truth to make it hold up in the minds of a lot of people," Stuart said. "It would make life pretty miserable for her."

Bev slumped in her chair. She'd never thought grown men would stoop to slandering a girl. A girl who'd been through a tough year already. Just the thought of it made her ill.

"Maybe it sounds self-serving," Stuart said, "but I really wish we could drop the whole thing."

For the first time, she felt defeated. And she saw his point—the point Mr. Looney had been trying to make, too, when she'd talked to him. He just wanted to protect his child from more hurt. That's how she felt now. She wanted to protect Alabama.

"All right," she said. "I'll . . . well, I'll think about it."

His lip twisted into a frown. "I'm sorry this all happened. I should have kept it to myself."

She reached out to him. "No. That's the one thing you shouldn't have done."

For the rest of the morning, she dragged from chore to chore—from hall patrol to health class to lunchroom duty—barely able to keep her head up. She was capitulating, and it felt awful.

At the end of lunch, Glen approached her. "Are you okay?"

She brought him up to speed.

"So you're *not* going to the school board meeting tonight?" he asked.

She shook her head. "It irks me to see the Kirbys and Kerrigans of the world win, the bullies, but what can I do?"

His brow clouded with what seemed like disapproval. "I guess I see where you're coming from, but still . . ."

"I know. I'm supposed to fight the good fight. But if doing that hurts the people I want to protect, who will I be fighting for?"

After school, she went home and made vegetable soup and cornbread, the best fall-winter comfort food of all time. Cooking was usually a welcome distraction, her after-school release valve, and she loved chopping up all the winter root vegetables— parsnips, rutabagas, and turnips. Foods so old-world and earthy that they were almost exotic.

But her mind wasn't really on cooking. Her gaze

kept roaming to the sweep of the cat clock's tail. She watched the minutes tick by, creeping ever closer to seven, the time when the school board meeting would start.

At six thirty, Alabama came out of her room. She gave Bev an up-and-down look, showing dismay for her pleated jeans and Keds. "Why are you dressed like that?"

Bev rolled her eyes. "I know you think I'm nerdy, but after all, it's my own house."

Her niece lifted onto the balls of her feet. "I don't care about that. But you're not going to dress like that for the board meeting, are you?"

Bev went back to stirring the soup. "I'm not going."

Alabama gaped at her. "But you have to go. You said you would."

She shrugged. "I changed my mind."

Alabama's eyes widened fretfully. "Why?"

"Because . . ." Bev said, trying to think of something. She should have been prepared for this moment, but she hadn't thought Alabama would care all that much. Given what Stuart had told her today, Bev would have thought a part of her would be relieved. But maybe Stuart hadn't told Alabama what he'd told Bev. Maybe he'd wanted to spare her that.

"I don't think it's worth dragging your and Stuart's names through the muck and creating a big brouhaha, just because some spoiled boy—"

"But the controversy's already been created," Alabama said, interrupting. "You said you'd be at the meeting."

"I changed my mind."

"Well if you won't go, I will!"

Before Bev could stop her, Alabama turned and ran for the front door. She had slammed it behind her before Bev had even turned off the burner under the soup. She hurried to her room and threw her school clothes back on, forcing her feet into pumps without hose.

She didn't see Alabama on the street—she had probably run halfway to downtown by now—so she got in the car and drove to the community center where board meetings were held. To her surprise, as she approached the community center there was a crush of people at the front door. She hunted down a parking spot and hurried up the walkway to the center. The first person she spotted on the outskirts of the crowd waiting for the doors to open was Cindy.

What was she doing here?

"I thought you were afraid of losing your job," Bev said, concerned. She didn't want to be responsible for a friend's diminished income.

Cindy gave her a hug. "Well, Glen told me since it's only one class, I don't really have a whole lot to lose. He's right."

Glen? "What are all these other people doing here?"

She spotted neighbors who'd been avoiding her eye for days, faculty members whose arms she'd twisted to no avail, and even a big group of her students. Maybe some of these people were here to support Kevin . . . although she didn't catch any hostile glances from the crowd. Many gave her bracing touches, as if she were a prizefighter heading to the ring.

"Glen probably convinced them," Cindy said. "He was making phone calls all afternoon."

He must have been. Bev's jaw dropped. Even Oren was here!

"Hey, Bev," he said, a little sheepishly.

All at once, the crowd quieted down and turned in unison toward the parking lot, like a school of fish. Several board members, including stocky Keith Kerrigan and Lon Kirby, were coming up the walkway together. A defensive line of local power. The crowd parted for them, but there was no warmth in any of the few greetings. For the first time ever, Bev saw a look of genuine worry pass across Lon's face.

Glen appeared at her side, and they made their way to the front of the crowd.

Opening the door, Lon tossed her a sour look. "Yes, you might as well come in first, since you're the one who's causing so much trouble," he said.

"The trouble was caused by the bully, Lon," Glen said. "Bev's just here to remind you of that fact."

From the top step of the community center, Lon scanned the crowd, his frown deepening when he saw the Looneys, especially. Bev spotted them at the same time. Mr. Looney wore a grim expression and held a rolled-up piece of blue poster board. Near him was Alabama, standing next to Stuart. Alabama sent a supportive smile Bev's way.

Lon had apparently counted on the Looneys not showing up. His lined brow indicated that he realized his whispers and threats hadn't been enough to keep people away, or to silence the accusers. Sweat beaded on his forehead, and he looked like a man who knew he was about to be soundly beaten.

"What are the rest of you here for, then?" he asked petulantly.

Glen took the last step up and stood eye to eye with Lon on the threshold, as did Bev.

"I imagine they're here because they're against bullying, and they want to stand up for Stuart Looney," she said.

"And Bev," Glen added. "We're here to stand with Bev."

CHAPTER 29

According to Stuart, *Out of Africa* was the best movie ever. Bev and Glen took them the night it opened, and Stuart was practically walking on air as they left the theater.

"I loved that scene in the airplane," he said. "When Robert Redford reaches forward to grab Meryl Streep's hand."

"She reached back, you mean," Alabama said.

His brow crinkled. "He leaned forward."

"It was the other way around. She was in front of him. How could she have known that he was holding out his hand? It was noisy and windy up there. That would have been impossible. She *had* to reach back first."

They were so absorbed in their argument that they outpaced Bev and Glen by a block, and had to backtrack down the sidewalk. Even though they'd gone to the earliest showing of the movie, it was dark now that they were out, and cold. Alabama wore only her red jacket, and her teeth chattered as she approached the empty storefront Bev and Glen had stalled out in front of.

"Glen thinks this is the best spot for Bev's House of Craft," her aunt said.

"The old pharmacy." Stuart cupped his hands around his eyes and leaned against the glass. "The long counter's still in there, and all the

499

shelves. Would you keep the soda fountain?"

"I don't know if ice cream floats and my craft supply inventory would make a good combo," Bev said. "I'd certainly keep that polished oak counter, though. It would be perfect. There's lots of storage room in the back, too."

All month, Bev had been considering the possibility of opening the store. She hadn't lost her job—in fact, the paper had written a glowing feature on her speech at the school board meeting. In the end, Kevin Kerrigan had only been suspended three days—the same as Alabama had been—but the menacing signs had stopped, and the school board was considering a zero tolerance policy for bullies. At least it sent a message to the other kids that they couldn't act that way. Maybe they would anyway, occasionally, but now they'd pay a penalty for being jerks.

Plus, it had just felt good knowing that the whole town wasn't part of the dead rat brigade. That had been a minority. In fact, Alabama suspected that it might have all been Kevin and Marvin.

But even though it looked like Bev was going to keep teaching home ec and health, she was still contemplating starting the craft store. She'd been reading books on opening a small business and had even had an interview at the bank to see about the possibility of a loan. Wink and Gladdie wanted to put money up front to get her started, and Bev even had several people all ready to turn in their applications to work there, including Cindy, and Mandy, the waitress from Lewanne's. Yet Bev remained on the fence.

"I'd be so busy all the time," she said.

"We're still youngsters," Glen said. "And think of it this way—you wouldn't have to worry about what to do with all those boring summers off anymore."

"Right." Bev laughed. "It's always *so awful* being at loose ends for those three months."

Alabama and Stuart exchanged glances. She was pretty sure they were joking. Teacher humor didn't always compute in the brain of a normal person, but Bev and Glen seemed to crack each other up. In fact, ever since the school board meeting, the two had become inseparable. They even held hands in public, like now. They stood close together, and Glen nuzzled Bev's ear—which was nothing Alabama wanted to see.

She and Stuart walked ahead again to give them privacy.

"I bet Mr. Hill asks your aunt to marry him next year."

Alabama's lip twisted. Not that she minded Glen, but . . . more change? And Glen would be like a father. She'd never had one of those.

But he was really nice, and if he made Bev happy . . .

Of course, Stuart thought it would be great.

He'd had even more access to all of Glen's play collection, and the inside scoop on what productions the school would be doing in the future.

They got back to the house way ahead of the lovebirds. Alabama grabbed the mail out of the box and opened the door. The house greeted them with the smell of evergreen from the newly decorated Christmas tree, and when Alabama switched on the lights, the living room seemed to blink to life. Next to the tree, Rhoda Morgenstern stood in a red Santa coat and hat, courtesy of Stuart.

Alabama tossed the mail down on the table and sat down, staring at the tree. Its star tipped the ceiling, and everything about the decorations was gaudy, blinky, and cheerful. Yet the sight of it all lit up never failed to bring a lump to her throat. Last year she never would have guessed this was where she'd be spending Christmas this year. More than any gift in the world, she wished her mother could be here on Christmas day, that they could all be together as a family. Everybody— Bev, Gladdie, Wink, Glen, Stuart . . . all the people she considered her family now. All those years, she'd been part of a duo. She'd lost half of herself this year, but she'd found so many new people, too. She wished her mother could have lived to be part of that, and share it with her. It seemed so unfair that some people, for whatever reasons, never found lasting happiness in life.

"Can I have some eggnog?" Stuart asked.

"Yeah, sure." She got up and went to the kitchen with Stuart.

A few minutes later, Bev and Glen came in, and Bev called to her. "You got a letter, Alabama. Did you see it?"

Alabama peeked her head out the kitchen door. "Who's it from?"

"Houston."

Frowning, she took the familiar cream-colored envelope from her aunt and opened it. "It's from Granny Jackson." Bev and the others were looking at her expectantly, so Alabama read it aloud.

Dear Alabama,

I hope this letter finds you well. It was a treat for me to meet you at Thanksgiving, and I've thought of you often since. I won't say that it was a treat seeing your aunt Bev again, because it wasn't.

Bev laughed.

I never lie about things like that, even when most people would. It's best to be frank.

And yet, seeing your aunt reminded me of how dire your situation is, and made me determined to rescue you from the clutches of Puttermans, if at all possible. I owe my son's memory that much. It's taken me a few weeks of consulting with Dot and our lawyers to hit upon a solution that might benefit us all.

My daughter, Dot, means the world to me, as you can imagine. After graduating from Harvard, she came home to be near me when she had job offers in her choice of cities. All these years, I have told her that she will inherit everything from me, and I am not inclined to disappoint her in that expectation.

And yet, there you are. Tom's girl. It pains me that we've lost so much time we could have spent together. So I've spent the last weeks making inquiries. There are many excellent private schools here in Houston, and surely you're smart enough to get into one of them. In any case, the Jackson name still means something, and we should be able to get you in somewhere. Naturally, I will pay for your tuition, books, and clothes, and give you a sensible allowance. You can live here at the house, in Tom's old room. If you feel the need to visit your Putterman family, I would certainly not object to your seeing them during the summers or for a holiday during the school year.

I've been told that this is a more than

generous offer. The only thing I would ask in return is that you change your family name to Jackson, in honor of Tom. I don't think anyone, least of all you, should object to that.

Please let me know as soon as possible what you think of this proposal. My lawyers will draw up agreements and any legal documents needed. Time is of the essence if we are to try to get you into a new school for the spring semester.

I hope you have a Merry Christmas. I am enclosing a check as a gift. Dot tells me it's too much, but I know you've had a difficult year.

Yours sincerely,
Dorothy Mabry Jackson

P.S. My regards to your aunt and her mother.

When she finished reading, the room was quiet. They all stood around the dining table, staring down, their faces changing color in the reflection of the Christmas tree's blinking lights.

Finally, Stuart broke the silence. "Wow! It actually worked."

"What?" Bev asked.

"Alabama's crazy plan to find a benefactress. You did it."

Alabama's cheeks burned. There was something not quite right about the way she felt. She kept her eyes focused on the letter so she wouldn't have to look at the hurt in Bev's eyes. Because she knew there would be hurt there.

Her gaze fell on the section that troubled her most. *The only thing I would ask in return is that you change your family name to Jackson, in honor of Tom. I don't think anyone, least of all you, should object to that.*

Well, she did object. She didn't think Gladdie or Bev would feel good about it, either. And her mother would definitely have seen it as a betrayal of who she was. In fact, if she went along with Dorothy Jackson's plan, she might as well change her name to Alabama Jackass, because that's how she'd feel.

"It is a generous offer," Glen said. "Except . . ."

Bev shook her head and nodded all at once. "It's very generous. She could offer you so much—great schools, probably any lessons you wanted, clothes . . ."

True. And what was the alternative? Three and a half more years in New Sparta, Texas, with flaky Aunt Bev, going to New Sparta High and cheering on the Fighting Jackrabbits.

And being friends with Stuart, and visiting Gladdie and Wink on weekends. And staying close to the people who knew who she really was, and understood what she'd been through. People who knew why she would want to cling to her odd-sounding name.

Alabama Putterman. For better or worse, that's who she was.

"You know I'll love you, whatever you decide." Bev's eyes shone. "Really, you'd have to be crazy not to take her up on the offer."

Alabama nodded. "Right."

Dot Jackson had said it best: All Puttermans were crazy.

Slowly, Alabama folded the letter again and started shredding it into strips, and then tinier and tinier pieces. "So . . . it's all settled, then."

Maybe I am crazy. God knows, she'd had years of experience, so she should know it when she saw it. But maybe the real insane move would be leaving the people she knew truly loved her. That had been her mother's mistake. She didn't want to make it hers.

She looked into her aunt's eyes and smiled. "I guess you're stuck with me."

She tossed the shredded letter into the air, and the pieces caught the Christmas light and rained down on them like homespun holiday confetti.

Discussion Questions

1. The book features the evolving relationship between a girl, Alabama, and her aunt Bev, who steps in to serve as guardian after Alabama's mother dies. In your own life, has there been someone other than your parents—such as an aunt or uncle, cousin, or teacher—whose guidance made a huge difference to you?

2. Alabama and her best friend, Stuart, both see reflections of real life in fiction—especially *Great Expectations* by Charles Dickens and *The Old Maid*, a Bette Davis movie. Was there ever a work of fiction, a movie, or a song that resonated so strongly with you that you felt it guided you or changed your life?

3. Bev steps into Alabama's life during a difficult time. What mistakes does Bev make? Are they forgivable?

4. Alabama dislikes her aunt at the beginning of the story, but her feelings are based on secondhand prejudices passed to her by her mother. Did you ever misjudge a person based on hearsay and come to like them later?

5. Bev is crushed when she's turned down for NASA's first teacher in space program, and she views this as proof of her bad luck. Has there ever been a disappointment in your life that actually turned out to be a lucky break?

6. Did you take home economics in school? Do you remember any projects you did for class?

7. Alabama gets caught up in a practical joke she soon regrets. Have you ever taken part in a prank that came off well . . . or one that backfired?

8. Alabama has to confess to having done something bad to Bev when she discovers that her partner in crime went on to bully Stuart. Yet Stuart just wants to let the matter drop. In confessing and telling on Kevin, is Alabama doing the right thing? Or should she have honored Stuart's wishes and said nothing?

9. Did you ever take part in a talent show or some other public competition?

10. One challenge Alabama faces in her new life is adjusting to a small town after living in cities all through her childhood. When you

were in school, did you have to switch schools often? Did you ever relocate to a place that seemed foreign to you?

11. Letters play an important role in *The Way Back to Happiness*, which is set in 1985. Obviously, much of this correspondence would be done via e-mail today. Is there anyone you still correspond with by "snail mail"? Do you think anything has been lost by the switch to e-mail?

Center Point Large Print
600 Brooks Road / PO Box 1
Thorndike ME 04986-0001 USA

(207) 568-3717

US & Canada:
1 800 929-9108
www.centerpointlargeprint.com